"Wood strikes on a potent irony in her telling of the Wilson presidency by imagining the immense power wrought by a First Lady in an era where women could neither vote nor hold office. Fans of revisionist historicals with strong female leads should check this out."

—*Publishers Weekly*

"Fascinating… Wood's meticulous research and attention to detail provide the context we need to understand Edith's decisions as she wrestles with an overwhelming workload and her conscience: Is she doing the right thing, or doing more harm than good? A great choice for fans of books by Marie Benedict, Fiona Davis, and Patti Callahan, featuring amazing but often unheralded women."

—*Booklist*

"A stately and dignified account that is beautifully leavened by intimate glimpses of Edith and Woodrow in their happiness, grief, anger, and optimism."

—*Library Journal*

THE ENGINEER'S WIFE

"This important work of historical fiction brings to life the strength and resolve of a nineteenth-century woman overshadowed by men and overlooked by history books."

—*Booklist*

"Well researched with great attention to detail, *The Engineer's Wife* is based on the true story about the exceptional woman who was tasked to build the Brooklyn Bridge. Though the great bridge would connect a city, it would also cause division and great loss for many. Tracey Enerson Wood delivers an absorbing and poignant tale of struggle, self-sacrifice, and the family transformed by the building of the legendary American landmark during the volatile time of women's suffrage, riots, and corruption. A triumphant debut not to be missed!"

—Kim Michele Richardson, *New York Times* bestselling author of *The Book Woman of Troublesome Creek*

"The Engineer's Wife is just the sort of novel I love and—I hope—write. Against all odds, a dynamic, historic woman builds a monument and changes history as she and her surrounding cast leap off the page. What a life, and what a beautifully written and inspiring story!"

—Karen Harper, *New York Times* bestselling author of *The Queen's Secret*

"The Engineer's Wife is historical fiction at its finest. Tracey Enerson Wood crafts the powerful and poignant story of Emily Warren Roebling, the compelling woman who played an instrumental role in the design and construction of the Brooklyn Bridge. This is necessary fiction for our time—paying tribute to women's overlooked contributions and reminding us of the true foundations of American history."

—Andrea Bobotis, author of *The Last List of Miss Judith Kratt*

"Who really built the Brooklyn Bridge? With its spunky, tough-minded heroine and vivid New York setting, *The Engineer's Wife* is a triumphant historical novel sure to please readers of the genre. Like Paula McLain, Tracey Enerson Wood spins a colorful and romantic tale of a storied era."

—Stewart O'Nan, award-winning author of *The Good Wife*

"Wood's satisfying historical feels true to its era yet powerfully relevant to women's lives today."

—*Publishers Weekly*

"Tracey Enerson Wood raises Emily Warren Roebling from the historical depths, bringing to vivid life the story of the woman who saved the Brooklyn Bridge."

—Anne Lipton, MD, PhD, coauthor of *Putting the Science in Fiction* and Harlequin Creator Fund recipient

THE WAR NURSE

"Tracey Enerson Wood achieves two particularly difficult things with this novel: a fictionalization of a real person's life, which is always a challenge, and the feat of writing a character from a century past who is accessible to a modern audience but still entirely of her era. In *The War Nurse*, based on the true story of pioneering WWI nurse Julia Stimson, we are transported to early-twentieth-century France, where a band of medical professionals struggles to meet the ever-changing demands of a war zone. You will smile, shed a few tears, and learn alongside Julia in this impeccably researched, well-drawn, based-on-a-true-story tale, written by a former RN. As our collective interest in WWI is reawakened, *The War Nurse* shines an important light on a woman whose story was, until now, lost to time."

—Kristin Harmel, *New York Times* bestselling author of *The Book of Lost Names*

"*The War Nurse* is a vividly rendered, moving tribute to one woman's determination to make a difference in the world. Tracey Enerson Wood sets us down in war-ravaged France and immerses us in the lives of a band of courageous nurses braving battles both physical and moral. A riveting and surprisingly timely story of courage, sacrifice, and friend-ship forged at the front lines."

—Kelly Mustian, author of *The Girls in the Stilt House*

"An incredibly well-researched historical fiction novel with a sympa-thetic heroine... Any readers who enjoyed the mix of romance, intrigue, and medical accuracy of *Call the Midwife* would love *The War Nurse*."

—*New York Journal of Books*

"*The War Nurse* is a fascinating, intimate look at the true story of Julia Catherine Stimson and the incredible work she and her nurses did to save lives during World War I. Through careful research, this book shows the incredible bravery and compassion of women who find them-selves in extraordinary situations."

—Julia Kelly, international bestselling author of *The Last Garden in England* and *The Light Over London*

"Based on a true story, Wood's latest highlights Julia's quick thinking, organizational skills, and endlessly caring heart, bringing life to a brutal era. Fans of Patricia Harman will love Wood's treatment of medical expertise in a historical setting."

—*Booklist*

"*The War Nurse* is a rich, gripping history of one woman's lifelong battle against systemic prejudice. As Tracey Enerson Wood's heroine says of her-self, 'I wasn't a man, for whom the things I wanted to do would have been easy. I was meant to break down the wall in between.'"

—Stewart O'Nan, award-winning author of *The Good Wife*

"If you've read *The Engineers Wife*, Tracey Enerson Wood's debut, you are already aware of her talent for merging fact and fiction into a story that will make your heart hurt and hold you captive until the very last page. She doesn't disappoint with *The War Nurse*. I LOVED, LOVED, LOVED this book!"

—Barbara Conrey, *USA Today* bestselling author
of *Nowhere Near Goodbye*

"Once again, Tracey Enerson Wood, with her impeccable research and evocative prose, kept me glued to the page. Wood has a talent for bringing strong yet lesser-known women from history to life. Her fictionalization of WWI nurse Julia Stimson, as well as the supporting cast, transported me back in time and had me smiling, crying, and learning. Fantastic!"

—Linda Rosen, author of *The Disharmony of Silence*

"If you, like me, are a voyeur of historical drama that unfolds as if the kitchen window flew open and the characters were caught in action, then *The War Nurse* is for you. Tracey Enerson Wood's storytelling verisimilitude—the detail, persuasive dialogue, and twinning of history with a hidden love story—prove her skill at immersion but also that rarest of traits: a big and generous heart that roots for the unsung heroines and heroes of the time. This author shines a light for us all to see our past anew."

—Diane Dewey, author of *Fixing the Fates*

ALSO BY
TRACEY ENERSON WOOD

The President's Wife

The Engineer's Wife

The War Nurse

Homefront Cooking: Recipes, Wit, and Wisdom from American Veterans
and Their Loved Ones (coauthor)

Life Hacks for Military Spouses (coauthor)

KATHARINE, *the* WRIGHT SISTER

TRACEY ENERSON WOOD

sourcebooks
landmark

Published by Sourcebooks Landmark, an imprint of Sourcebooks
P.O. Box 4410, Naperville, Illinois 60567-4410
(630) 961-3900
sourcebooks.com

Library of Congress Cataloging-in-Publication Data

Names: Wood, Tracey Enerson, author.
Title: Katharine, the Wright sister / Tracey Enerson Wood.
Description: Naperville, Illinois : Sourcebooks Landmark, 2024.
Identifiers: LCCN 2023058092 (print) | LCCN 2023058093 (ebook) | (hardcover) | (e-pub)
Subjects: LCSH: Haskell, Katharine Wright, 1874-1929--Fiction. | Wright, Orville, 1871-1948--Fiction. | Wright, Wilbur, 1867-1912--Fiction. | LCGFT: Biographical fiction. | Novels.
Classification: LCC PS3623.O6455 K38 2024 (print) | LCC PS3623.O6455 (ebook) | DDC 813/.6--dc23/eng/20240112
LC record available at https://lccn.loc.gov/2023058092
LC ebook record available at https://lccn.loc.gov/2023058093

Printed and bound in the United States of America.
VP 10 9 8 7 6 5 4 3 2 1

To my precious grandchildren: Harrison, Eleanor, Rebecca, Theodore, Marilyn, David, Oliver, and James. May you dream big dreams and act on them to make the world a better place.

WILBUR

W ind. We chose a place where it abounded, in order to capture it and soar like the birds. But nature wasn't eager to be tamed, as the howling tempest threatened to pick up me, my tent, and my crated glider, and toss us all into the sea. I had barely survived the gale that hit just as I had begun the last leg of the journey—the overwater portion—in a very unseaworthy boat. And I had failed to acquire the spruce lumber I needed for the glider's eighteen-foot wing spars.

I curled myself up into a shuddering ball as the relentless wind stole every last ounce of my body's heat and my motivation. The whole experiment would likely fail, and we would have to wait another year to test our theories.

My brother Orville had yet to join me in North Carolina, and our bossy, hard-driving sister, Katharine, was safe in her warm bed in Dayton. It was Katharine who had declared Kitty Hawk to be the perfect place to test the flying machine. Steady winds, perfect mounds of earth to take off from, and soft sand to crash upon. It was also Katharine who insisted, against my objections, on packing salt crackers and her homemade jam in my knapsack. I risked chilling myself further as I reached for the bag and rifled through it to find the food. The sweet and sour raspberries tickled my tongue as I relished the only sustenance I'd had for days.

We were on a mission, my brother and I. And I knew in my bones that we wouldn't stop until both of us were either dead or too broken to go on. As for who sent us on this do-or-die mission, once again it was Katharine. Despite urging us to be cautious, it was her dream as much as ours. History will note Orville's and my successes and failures in equal measure. But it is Katharine's inescapable current lifting our earthborn feet and guiding us ever forward that is in danger of fading away unnoticed. So this is her story.

KATHARINE

DAYTON, OHIO

1884–1886

None of us could pinpoint the exact moment we knew what we were destined to do. Will had been reading about flight since I was a little girl on his lap, spreading his arms as great wings, ready to fly us to the moon as he read words beyond my understanding.

We all loved the helicopter toy, with its rubber bands on a thin stick that would spin a little metal propeller. "Higher, higher," I shouted. So Orv used a bigger rubber band and Will fashioned a better propeller. Before she got sick, Mama loved building things. She would dry off her hands after doing the dishes and take a hammer to the metal parts of the helicopter to get them back into place after a crash.

When the boys were at school and I was still too young to go, I played with the models of helicopters and gliders they had made, often earning their wrath when they came home to splinters. But they would build them again, the next time making the nose sturdier or the wings lighter.

"This is for you, Katie girl," Will said to me as I opened presents on my tenth birthday. It was the best glider yet, almost two feet long and made of balsa wood. I just knew it would soar as high as the house. I swung my legs impatiently, wanting to take it out right then. But it was also Orv's birthday, his thirteenth, and Will had hurried off to get his present. He came back, wheeling in a bicycle. It wasn't like the ones I saw in the store window of Rike's Dry Goods. This one seemed built of bits and pieces: a crowbar, crude wheels, and gears and chain from who knows where.

I wasn't sure whether to be proud or embarrassed about the homemade bicycle, but Orv gave Will a great big hug. Together they pushed it out of the house, forgetting about me and my new toy flyer.

❧

On a brisk February morning, Orv chased me round and round the yard in crunchy snow, trying to grab a pink ribbon I had snitched from his room. I suspected it belonged to the cute little blonde girl who lived next door. "Orville's got a girlfriend," I singsonged as I held up the evidence.

"Leave him alone." My brother Wilbur snatched the ribbon from my hand. He was eighteen, seven years older than me and no fun at all. Ice skates hanging from his shoulder by their laces captured my attention.

"Where are you going? Can I come?" I knew he wanted Orville, not me. My three eldest brothers, Reuchlin, Lorin, and Wilbur, used to share all the adventures, but with Reuchlin and Lorin now off starting their own families, Wilbur was the boss and Orville was his favorite accomplice.

"Sorry, Katharine. You can't skate. I'll teach you another day."

Wilbur was a champion skater. And footballer, and any other sport you could dream up. He also made perfect marks in school and barely got into any trouble, unless he fell for one of Orville's pranks. Mama and Pop thought the sun and moon circled around Wilbur. It was hard not to hate him.

"I can so," I insisted, although my wobbly ankles thought otherwise.

"Get your skates, Orv. We're meeting some chums at the pond behind the Soldiers' Home." Will dropped the balled-up ribbon into Orv's hand.

Then Orv surprised me. He handed me the ribbon. "I was saving this for you."

Whether or not he was telling the truth didn't matter. I felt ashamed of taunting him, so I took the ribbon and started walking back to the house, my head bowed in dejection for extra effect. "Have fun, boys," I murmured.

"Wait." Orv called out to me, then asked Wilbur, "Mama told us to look after her. Can't she come?"

Soon we were off, riding the open-air streetcar down Third Street. I turned into the wind and let it smack my face and blow my hair. Hand-me-down skates dangled from my shoulder but that was just for show; I had no intention of putting them on. We arrived at the campus of the Soldiers' Home. First we passed through the cemetery, with its statue of a Civil War soldier high atop a marble column, and rows and rows of white headstones. We paused, and the boys removed their hats to pay our respects before we headed to the pond beyond the brick buildings where the old soldiers lived.

A gang of boys skated on the frozen pond, zigzagging across the ice, pushing a flat puck with hockey sticks. I rewrapped the muffler around my neck and pulled it up to cover my nose, its tip already numb.

"Is that the little Wright girl hiding under all that wool?" It was Oliver Crook Haugh, my brothers' nemesis. Although not even halfway through high school, he was as big as a bear and just as mean. Pop, always looking for the good in people, said it wasn't Crook's fault; it was the toothache drops the druggist gave him that made him that way.

I pretended not to hear Crook over the slap of the sticks and the playful shouts of the boys as I walked toward a park bench to watch.

"Are you deaf? Where you going, little girl?" He chased after me, and I took off, but the ground was treacherously pitted with footprinted snow.

He grabbed my coat, then pulled off my hat along with some of my hair as I tried to escape. Orv stumbled toward me, his skates a hindrance on the jagged ground. I yanked away from Crook and hid behind my brother.

"Leave her alone." Orv could do little but use his words to defend me. "You're nothing but a big bully. Always have been, always will be. Go back to your cave, you Neanderthal."

Crook's eyes blazed with fury. I heard an awful thud as his fist landed in Orv's stomach, sending both of us to the ground.

"Hey, what's going on?" Will hobbled over, one skate on, one skate off, using his hockey stick to steady himself. "Now what have you done, Crook?" Wilbur dropped his hockey stick as he bent to check on us.

Crook picked up the stick. I thought he was feeling bad for hitting Orv. But the bully raised the stick, and just as Wilbur helped me to my feet, Crook swung it full force at Wilbur's head. Wilbur stumbled back and fell into a mound of crusted snow. He didn't make a sound as blood gushed from his nose and mouth. Then his eyes rolled back and he went limp. Terrified, I screamed for help.

A few days after the attack, I heard Will moaning in his bedroom. I tiptoed past his door to my parents' bedroom. My mother was resting, as she often did during the day, being tired from the consumption that had made her so ill. I drew closer and saw she was weeping.

"Mama, what is it?"

"Poor Wilbur, he's in so much pain."

It seemed my mother was hurting just as much. "Why isn't the doctor helping him? Can I do something to make it better?" I pleaded, with little hope of an answer.

Mama reached into a drawer in her nightstand. "I can't take it anymore. Here. The doctor wrote a prescription. Go to the druggist on the corner."

I clasped the paper to my chest, grateful to be able to do something. I knew the druggist, Mr. Harrison, as I'd picked up cough syrup for Mama several times when she was too sick to go out in the cold. I said a little prayer that whatever Will was getting would help more than that syrup ever did.

On the way to the druggist, I peeked at the little slip of paper. It had strange writing and symbols, but I could make out *4 gtts on each tooth*... Oh no. Was this the same stuff that had made Crook so mean?

A wave of heated air hit me as I stepped inside the drugstore, then closed the door behind me, making the bells hanging on it jingle. A dozen or so customers milled about, and it seemed all eyes were on me. I ignored them and marched down the aisle to the high platform in the back where the prescriptions were filled.

"Well, hello there, Miss Wright. Are you here for your mother's syrup?"

"No, Mr. Harrison." I unwrapped the muffler from around my neck. "This is for my brother Wilbur. He got beat up pretty bad."

Mr. Harrison sighed. "Yes, I know. That Haugh boy used to work here, but no more. We can't be having that kind of behavior. Let me see what you've got there."

He held out his hand for the prescription, but I clutched it for a moment more. "My father told me that Crook was taking tooth drops too."

"That's right. A whole set of rotten teeth that boy has. No wonder he's so mean." Mr. Harrison plucked the paper from my hand, then turned to pull a large brown bottle and a smaller one off the shelf.

"Do you think maybe the drops had something to do with it? My father says…"

"Listen here, little girl. Is your father a doctor? A druggist?"

I shook my head and wanted to slip out of there before I really got into trouble.

Mr. Harrison poured a liquid through a funnel into one of the small bottles and screwed on the cap.

"Tell your brother to use this eye dropper and put four drops on each loose tooth, or the hole where a tooth used to be. The cocaine will start working right away."

"Yes, sir."

I walked home, more slowly than usual. I had in my hand something that would finally give poor Wilbur some relief. But what else would it do? I thought of the crazed look in Crook's eyes when he punched Orv and whacked Wilbur with the hockey stick. Would these drops make sweet, gentle Wilbur a monster as well?

Surely Mother knew what the drug was. That was probably why she had waited two days since the doctor came. I should ask her, but remembering her tears, I couldn't bear to. But should I warn Wilbur?

He wouldn't take even a sip of whiskey, believing it led a person down the wrong path. But his pain was so great, and poor Mother was suffering right along with him. It had to be Wilbur's decision, I told myself.

When I returned home, I found Wilbur in the dining room. He was trying to slurp some soup from a spoon into the one corner of his mouth that wasn't raw.

"I've got something for you." I held out the brown bag with the medicine bottle and eye dropper.

His face was so swollen and bruised that I couldn't look at it.

"Thanks, Sterchens." That was my brothers' pet name for me, from the German word for *little sister*. Our mother was of German and Swiss descent and sometimes called me *Schwesterchen*. "I can't eat, but maybe I can get some sleep with a little help."

"It's cocaine. Just like Crook takes."

Will had opened the little bottle and was inserting the eye dropper, but stopped.

"Oh." He stared at the bottle for a long time. I didn't know what to say, so I just chewed on my lip. *I shouldn't have told him*, I berated myself.

"Go on, take it. The doctor says you need it, and the druggist…"

Will put the bottle back in the bag. "Thank you, but no. There are things worse than a little toothache."

None of us was the same after that. Wilbur lost his front teeth, and his face was so painful and unsightly that he barely left his room for months, except to take care of Mama. He often complained that his heart was jumping around in his chest. He had never said that before he got beat up. Pop said it was nerves.

Orville, who had always been shy, no longer spoke to anyone outside of the family. He seemed to blame himself, particularly his words, for what happened. He started struggling in his classes and soon left school to start a business printing newspapers instead. I knew it was so he wouldn't have to talk to anybody.

Wilbur had his pick of Ivy League colleges because he was such a good student. He had chosen Yale, but now refused to go. It took over a year, but he recovered well enough, and with his new false teeth, one could hardly tell he had had his face smashed in. He spent his days reading and taking care of our mother. It became my job to haul home books from the school and city libraries for him, since Orv had to leave early for his printshop. Literature, philosophy, and lots of science. Physics was his favorite, and anything to do with flying, from hot-air balloons to kites to Leonardo da Vinci's drawings of flying machines.

Will read them all, and Orv read most. Then they left them in a neat pile by the side door, ready for me to return. Sometimes I felt like grumbling about the weight as I loaded my knapsack, but then I remembered who my brothers had been defending that day.

Mama fussed at Will for not going to Yale, but at the same time needed him to cook the meals and carry her up and down the stairs, as she was growing too weak from the consumption.

After school, I helped Will in the kitchen, and he taught me lots of things. How to save the carcass of a duck or chicken, then pile it into a pot of water with some root vegetables and simmer to made a rich stock. How to make biscuits with flour and bacon fat and sourdough culture. And some less fun things, like pumping well water in which to scrub the pots and pans and laundry.

If I complained, Pop would go on about strength of will and character and responsibility, as if he were preaching from the pulpit. I learned not to complain. Pop never did, even when something worried him a great deal.

He sat at the desk in the sitting room, paying bills and adding columns of numbers in a ledger. As he raked his fingers through his hair and beard, crossing things off a list and staring at it all as if he could will it to change, I summoned the courage to ask, "Do we have money troubles, Pop? Because maybe I can help somehow…"

He pulled me close, gently scratching his beard against my cheek. He smelled of cedar, from the shaving lotion kept in the container shaped from a slice of a small log. "Nothing for you to worry about, dear girl."

But I did worry. It was pretty clear Mama would not survive, and that Will would have to find work. Which meant I would have to take over his household duties. And with Will's fading prospects of a good salary, I had to think beyond that. I knew by age twelve that I would need to get an education and help support the family.

WILBUR

I t was no sacrifice to attend to Mama. My brothers Reuchlin and Lorin wrote from out west, telling us of the struggle to house and feed themselves, and Reuch to feed a family as well. I felt fortunate indeed to live in a comfortable home, a wooden frame house on the west side of Dayton.

Each of us now had our own upstairs bedroom, and downstairs first from front to back was the Sunday parlor, where the Christmas tree would be set and front-door guests could be met. Next was the sitting room with a fireplace, stairway, and the side door. Here we gathered with family and close friends, sometimes suffering through Orville's practicing on his mandolin. Then came the dining room, just big enough for a table and six chairs, and lastly the kitchen, where Katharine was learning to cook for all of us.

We called Pop "the Bishop," because after family, his vocation was the most important thing to him. But he was frequently away from home. As an itinerant clergy for the United Brethren Church, his vocation took him as far west as the Rocky Mountains and south to

Tennessee. Despite the physical distance, he remained involved in everything the family did, insisting on detailed letters.

He wrote of precarious train trips over new bridges spanning deep chasms and tunneling through mountains, and sent advice for our concerns, both great and small. In some ways, his words took on more importance this way, as we could read them over and over, with the meaning becoming clearer with time and introspection.

I helped with Pop's church duties and edited Orv's newspapers and sold advertising. We were safe and together, even as we bore the grief of slowly losing Mama a little more each day.

By late May I had to call Pop home, as I feared each day might be Mama's last. I wrote Reuch and Lorin, although I doubted they could leave their jobs out in Kansas.

In the wee hours of the Fourth of July, Pop called Orv, Katharine, and me from our beds to say goodbye to Mama. But she continued to breathe, slowly and steadily, although she barely responded to us.

Orv and I went to work, and all through the morning we heard scattered shots of what sounded like gunfire, but we realized were fireworks. We peered out the printshop's big window onto Third Street at a parade with fire wagons and bands, or jumbles of people setting off firecrackers and singing songs. But neither of us felt like celebrating. At lunchtime we closed up the shop as usual, but this time we hung a sign on the door that it would be closed until further notice.

We hurried home, instinct telling us there was little time left. We joined Katharine and Pop at Mama's bedside. Her skin had gone from pale to light gray, her lips darkening as we watched. Orv and I took turns saying goodbye. I think she heard and had been waiting for us, for she took her last breath shortly afterward.

Although we all knew it was coming and took a bit of comfort from knowing Mother's suffering had ended, Katharine seemed stunned. Just shy of fifteen years old, she normally raced about on bicycles with her friends, planted and weeded her garden, then made beautiful bouquets with the flowers or pushed us to eat the vegetables.

Our sassy, bossy, and busy sister had collapsed into a shell of sorrow. She curled into a corner rocking chair and the Bishop tried, in his firm but caring manner, to help her feel better.

"It's not helping, sitting around like that. Doing something useful will guide you through it," he said.

Katharine began to weep. At least it broke her silence.

The Bishop looked around at the many flower arrangements we had received. "Why don't you dry some of these?" He plucked a yellow rose and tried to hand it to her, then set it next to her when she didn't respond. "Well then." He stepped out of the room.

"It's not a bad idea, Sterchens." I extracted a few more blooms. "You love flowers. You could start a collection of your best ones. Maybe special ones, like from a beau."

This brought a giggle from her, a most welcome sound. She sat up and traced her finger on the petals of the rose.

"A beau is many years from now, of course," I added.

"I could make a scrapbook filled with happy memories. Things and people I don't want to forget."

❦

Over the next few months, we reorganized the household. I would need to find more ways to be useful, primarily in earning a steady salary. My older brother Lorin was both helpful and discouraging.

Upon returning to Dayton for Mama's funeral, he was in sad spirits, of course, but I knew there was something else afoot.

He was clean-shaven, like myself. Orv favored a mustache, I suspect to look different from his brothers. We all tended to wear sharply creased black or brown trousers and white shirts with suspenders, and had the same slightly receding hairline. But Lorin had something Orv and I lacked: a curiosity about people and why they committed crimes or did good deeds. He delighted in a big splashy newspaper headline proclaiming the latest scandal.

The ladies of our church had brought by platter after platter of sweets to show support for us in our grief. We gathered in the dining room, but only Lorin seemed to have an appetite as he piled an assortment of desserts on a plate. "The prairie is a fine place. There's sky for decades and adventurous characters of all sorts. But making a living turns out to be as hard as the baked earth. I miss home. I miss family."

Katharine poured from a flowery teapot. "But you have Reuch out there, and his family."

Lorin lowered his eyes. "Yes. But I'm always the odd man out. Reuch's wife has her own family about, and there doesn't seem to be room for Uncle Lorin. And Dayton is home. Don't you miss me?"

We all assured him that we did. But I wondered how we would manage another mouth to feed. I had been making inquiries, and there was not much work available.

Lorin was four years older than me, and I had planned to follow in his wake and move out west for more opportunity, just as he had followed Reuch. I could then send money home to help Katharine and the Bishop. "But you left home to seek your fortune. You said there wasn't enough in Dayton to make a decent living, but there is no limit out west."

"Sure, if you're born to one of the better families. If not, you can be a cowboy or an outlaw," he said, chuckling.

So Lorin returned to Dayton for good a few months later. I was grateful to have him at home, but the fact that he had failed in his quest to make a living haunted me. I had to figure out what to do with not quite a high school education and lots of experience as a "cook and chambermaid" as Lorin called it.

KATHARINE

Whoever invented the steam-powered fan had earned my eternal gratitude. Orv bought the contraption, sort of a propeller encased in a birdcage, not to cool us off, but to study how it moved air. Such is the nature of my peculiar family. Naturally, being a more practical sort, I was using it to survive a morning so muggy, I was already drenched with sweat before arising from bed.

A soft knock on my door reminded me of two things. One, it was well past time to cook the boys' breakfast, and two, it was Orv's and my birthdays—my eighteenth and Orv's twenty-first—and Will no doubt was eager to show us a surprise he had been hinting at for weeks.

I jumped out of bed, ran my fingers through my wild, wavy mane, used the ceramic pitcher of water and bowl to rinse, gargle, and spit, and then hollered "Come in."

Both Orv and Will, already dressed in sharp white shirts and brown trousers, quickly wrapped me in a three-way hug.

"Put your hair up. We're going on an adventure, birthday girl."

Will handed me my brush while Orv pulled an outfit from my wardrobe.

"Get out, you two. I'm not five anymore." I swiped a skirt from Orv's hands. "I can choose my clothes and dress myself, Little Brother." Even though Orv was older than me, he was younger and shorter than Will, so I rather impishly gave him that nickname.

"Oh, but you don't know the surprise. How would you know what to wear?" Orv had settled on a white shirtwaist and medium-full skirt for me. Even though we were far from the wealthiest family in town, Orv's clothes were always perfectly suited and neatly pressed. If he couldn't afford what he wanted, he would sew it himself by hand.

"See you downstairs. I made breakfast." Will kissed me on the forehead and the boys tumbled out of the room, saying something about the streetcar and rules to be broken.

Following a hot porridge breakfast that only added to the discomfort of the steamy morning, Will and Orv led me outside. Three brand-new bicycles were wedged in the narrow alley between our home and the neighbor's.

My hands flew to my mouth in surprise. The boys had been riding every day for years, on rather rickety contraptions they had put together themselves, but these were clearly several steps above.

"Do you remember how to ride?" Orville stood next to the smaller model, its frame bent low to account for a skirt.

"Of course. I had the best teachers. Is that one for me?"

"Yes, and that's not all." Will bent to pick up a package he had hidden. "This is for all of us." He handed it to Orv as I had already straddled my bicycle.

Orv opened the package and pulled out a set of binoculars. "Wow, how did you—"

"They're used, but in fine condition." Will beamed. "I've been saving my pennies for ages."

Soon we were off, heading downtown. I still didn't know where we were going, but Orv and Will were in high spirits, whistling and singing in harmony. Strange that Orv and I share a birthday, when it seems the two of them should have been twins.

After arguing their way onto the streetcar with the bikes, we rode to the line's furthest point south. Then the bemused streetcar driver helped us unload the bikes and off we went again. We had been riding for seven or so miles, and my legs ached. Mostly we followed old cart paths along canals, and then pedaled along the Miami River. Thankfully we took a break, and Will pulled canteens of water from his knapsack.

"Not too much further." Will hopped back on his bike before I had taken three swigs.

Various possible destinations ran through my head. We had left the city, and nothing but rolling fields dotted with farmhouses and outbuildings were to be seen. Maybe a flower nursery? The boys knew I wanted to add to our tiny garden. But it was far too late to be planting, except maybe fall bulbs. Or perhaps a horse stable? But none of us was particularly comfortable riding anything other than a bicycle.

We pedaled over a grass-covered hill and the river appeared again, with broad pebbly flats lining each side. The boys dismounted, grabbed their knapsacks, and ran toward the river. I followed, after shaking out my rather wobbly legs.

Hundreds of warblers, thrushes, and tanagers darted about, while clouds of swallows filled the air. Shorebirds such as egrets and tiny sandpipers skittered along the sand. We passed the binoculars between us, with Orv having to have them tugged away from him each time. Will jotted notes in a pocket-sized notebook, things like wing sizes and shapes and flap frequency. He and Orv timed how long a hawk soared with a pocket watch, and Will wrote it all down.

It was hard for me to see much through the field glasses, as my eyeglasses made the image jump around and my vision was blurry without them. I didn't let on though, as the boys were so excited with their new possession. Instead, I tried to identify as many birds as I could.

"Why are there so many?" I asked.

"They're migratory, fattening up on fish and insects for the fall trip to the south," Will answered.

❧

You would think after an entire morning and good part of an afternoon spent watching birds fly and analyzing exactly how they did it, my brothers would move on to something else. It was a Friday, after all, and a workday, so I expected they would go back to the printshop after our adventure at the river. I was between semesters at Oberlin Academy, so had little to do but cook and keep house, but the boys were supposed to be earning their keep.

After washing off the dust from our trip, I joined the boys, who were busy cutting up and folding stacks of newspapers on the dining room table.

"Too flimsy," Orv said, as he weighed a quarter of a page against the palm of his hand.

"Then double it," Will replied, his own stacks of papers neatly arranged.

"Have you got any of that school paste?" Orv looked at me, his big gray-blue eyes making him look like a little boy.

I sighed. "I'm in preparatory school now. Paste is for babies. But I'll see what I can find."

Orv smiled. "Good. And while you're at it, maybe a snack, too."

Off I went, shaking my head. I could not possibly love them more, but I was beginning to wonder when I could set out on a life of my own. Some of my school chums were already thinking about getting married. While that wasn't and couldn't be my goal just yet, there was a certain student with whom I longed to spend more time. Harry Haskell was my age, but so smart he was two years ahead of me. There had to be a way to both support my family and have some sort of romantic relationship.

When I came back with glue and some sandwiches, the boys were sailing paper gliders all over the room.

"While I'm grateful you took off to celebrate our birthdays, don't you think it's time to leave first grade and go back to work?"

Will stopped, his hand just about to release a particularly fancy glider, with turned-up wings and downturned nose. "Katie girl, we've got a bit of news." He exchanged a glance with Orv, who nodded his approval. "We're moving out of the printing business."

Startled, I dropped the plate of sandwiches onto the table with a clatter. There was no way I could stay in school on just the Bishop's salary. Money was tight with three of them working, but we could make do until I graduated and could help out. "And what do you propose to do instead?"

"We're good mechanics. Lots of people ask us to fix their bicycles. And the craze is growing bigger by the day," Orv said.

Will chimed in. "When we bought the birthday bikes, the shop owner was just beside himself, said he couldn't keep enough in stock to satisfy his customers."

"And then we bought three!" Orv chortled like a kid who had stolen candy.

"So you'll fix bicycles for a living?" I snatched a glider midair that was aiming for my head.

"That's right. Make them. Fix them. Sell them. Maybe take folks on guided tours like we went on today." Will refolded some newspaper.

Orv scrunched up his face. "Not guided tours. We don't actually like talking to people. Unless you'd like to do it, Sterchens? You'd be good at that."

Hearing the nickname wrapped me in both a warm blanket of love and a pang of pain, as it made me miss Mama.

I unfolded the paper in my hands and glanced at the newspaper article. It was about a man named Langley who worked at the Smithsonian Institute in Washington, DC. He believed powered, heavier-than-air aircraft were the future, and whoever won the race to build a successful flying machine would be a hero, and a rich one at that. The boys saved every newspaper and magazine article they could find on flying. Sometimes they found they had both obtained the same copy, and then they made paper aeroplanes from the extras.

"No," I said. The article, the day watching birds, the aeroplanes all came together in my mind. Orv and Will were trying to tell me something they didn't realize themselves. And maybe this could be the way I earned my own independence. Harry Haskell wasn't going to wait around forever. I refolded the paper as best I could. "I don't want to be a tour guide. And this…" I held up the slightly crumpled aeroplane. "This is what you were born to do. Fly." I set the thing sailing, but it dove directly to the ground. "Build real aeroplanes. With motors. Test them out. And keep building them until…"

Just then, Orv sent a folded paper clear across the room.

"Exactly," I continued. "You like working on bicycles, but your every waking thought is about flying. Everything you read. Every minute of your free time. There must be a reason God put you on this earth with that passion, with your mechanical talents, just when the world is needing them."

Will laughed. "That's just for fun. We still have to eat. Lorin tells us we can easily top the income of the printshop if we work hard enough fixing bicycles."

Lorin had finally found steady work as a bookkeeper, which was a good thing, because he now had a wife, Netta, to support. He had returned from the West thinking he'd make a career out of chasing down outlaws, but the idea of joining the Dayton police didn't have the same appeal.

"Then run your bicycle business in the front of the shop and build flying machines in the back. There won't be customers in there all day, will there? I'll help, and I'm sure Lorin will make sure it balances out."

The boys looked at each other and nodded. I could practically hear the wheels turning in their heads.

Will gave a military-style salute. "Yes, ma'am."

ORVILLE

Telling Katharine was the easy part. We still had to break the news to the Bishop. I imagined several different scenarios for his reaction. One, he applauded the idea, offered some seed money to get the new enterprise off the ground, and cheered on Katharine's idea as well. Two, he would insist we start the new venture while maintaining our responsibilities at the printshop, therefore increasing the family's income by thirty percent. Past experience with the Bishop made scenario number two far more likely.

In fact, there was a third option that we hadn't considered. We gathered in the dining room that evening, where Katharine had set the table with the Sunday china, even though it was Friday. She had climbed on a chair to light the candelabra over the table, even though that was Will's job. The Bishop had to know something was amiss.

He blessed the meal, and we had just spread our napkins on our laps when Will launched straight into our proposed plan. Katharine followed suit with a cheery review of the additional advantages: more time and space to work on our aeronautical studies.

The Bishop, who was serving himself his favored portion—a breast of chicken—quietly laid down his fork. I focused on the breeze making the lace curtains flutter in the window rather than look upon my siblings' no doubt concerned faces. I had been researching materials to build wings from. A light fabric like lace, but...

"Katharine," the Bishop commanded attention in his sternest tone, usually reserved for the pulpit. "Are you enjoying your studies at the academy?"

Bewildered, Will and I both swung our gazes toward our sister.

"Most certainly, of course." Katharine shot me a look, a question in her eyes. I shrugged.

"Oberlin is a preparatory academy, of course," he continued. "So what exactly are you preparing for?"

I relaxed a bit. Katharine would have this. He was starting a debate, which was one of his favorite family activities. We all had to learn how to argue both sides of whatever issue he presented. The most recent was a lively discussion of Darwin's theory of evolution. Katharine and I had won handily against the Bishop's and Will's defense of creationism.

"For a future of serving my Lord, my family, and my country."

"Yes, yes, but how? Are you going to continue your studies in order to provide a living income not only for yourself, but to support your brothers in this expensive undertaking?"

The Bishop fixed his intent glare at me. Was I supposed to argue the other side? As my mouth gaped open, Will came to the rescue.

"As a member of the fairer sex and entirely responsible for the running of the home, her duties will be well served in continuing that, if she so chooses."

"I'd like to continue my education and matriculate to Oberlin College," Katharine said.

Neither Will nor I had quite completed high school. But our sister was different. I swung my head back to see the Bishop's reaction.

"Your mother was a brilliant student. Gave up just shy of graduating college. I never quite understood why."

"I won't do that," Kate said. "Give up, that is. I want to be a teacher. I've got excellent marks in English and literature."

"Latin." The Bishop poured gravy on his potatoes. "Anyone can teach English, but Latin is the foundation for all the Romance languages. I presume you are in favor of your brothers' plan? This is your time to voice your objections."

Katharine scooped up two chicken thighs and some potatoes and plopped them onto her plate. "I am. No objections."

"Then it shall be so. We will forthwith work harder and longer hours in order to support Katharine's education. In return, she will return to us and teach Latin."

"Wait," Will said. "I have an objection."

I suppressed a smile. Of course he did, in true Wright fashion. The opposing viewpoint must be heard, even if the speaker disagreed with it.

"I will not have my sister enslaved to our goal. It is Orv's and my responsibility to earn, borrow, or do without." He helped himself to both drumsticks. I would be left with gizzards and liver.

All eyes landed on me as the platter of sorry chicken remains was passed. Time for the rebuttal. "Enslaved? That seems rather overstated. Perhaps a compromise is in order. Four years of support for a college education, followed by four years of partial support for our endeavors. Plus our undying gratitude, of course."

I snuck a peek at Katharine. She did seem relieved at my proposal.

"Very well," the Bishop said. "If there are no further objections… No? Then it is settled with Orville's stipulation."

The Bishop was always keenly interested in my businesses, from the time Ed, a buddy of mine, and I built a small printing press and sold our own newsletter to our classmates. I was fifteen and mischievous, planning to write a scandalous tale and attributing it to a teacher. The Bishop found out about it and forbade the plan.

But he didn't let our enterprise twist in the wind. He purchased a supply of used type and cleared space on a sturdy wooden table in the carriage barn for us to work on. Will and Lorin helped with the writing and distribution, and soon we had a fine little business, printing my friend Paul Laurence Dunbar's poems and advertising fliers. A grocery store once paid us in popcorn. Ed wanted to eat it, and I asked the Bishop what to do.

He advised me to accept the payment, and if Ed didn't like it, I should buy him out. So I used my share of the popcorn to do just that.

Likewise, the Bishop kept tabs on Katharine's marks in school, quizzing her nightly whenever he wasn't traveling. Somehow Wilbur avoided this scrutiny. Of course, he always had perfect marks and never got into trouble like I did, but it seemed he could float along, work or not, attend school or not, and it was all fine with the Bishop. I had a theory that might have explained this.

My parents lost a set of twins between Wilbur and my births. Otis and Ida were born too early and too small and lived a very short time. Mama and the Bishop never said much about them, except Mama once told me that Pop had taken the loss very hard. It was hard for me to imagine the strong and steady man as inconsolable, but that's how she described him. He wanted to have more children right away.

I've often thought that Katharine and I faced double expectations—all that we should accomplish for ourselves, as well as for Otis and Ida. I took up the challenge and never wavered from doing whatever I could to support the family, even if I was paid in popcorn.

KATHARINE

The next time we traveled by streetcar and bicycle to our bird-watching spot at the river, the boys were much more focused on the animals' mechanics of flight, specifically how they turned, as that had been a confounding problem for gliders and anything else humans had tried to fly. I was glad for the earthen berm that blocked the view of the river shore from the road, as the sight of the three of us, running about with arms spread, imitating birds would have made passersby think we were looney.

Orv studied a flock of starlings with binoculars as they dipped and swerved in a synchronous dance. "I think they pull in one wing in their turns, like this." He passed the binoculars to me, then held one arm out straight, and shortened the other by bending his elbow, then circled around, flapping both arms in a comical way.

I held the binoculars up to my eyeglasses, but with that awkwardness and the quick movements of the small birds, I couldn't see the difference in the wings. I focused instead on a red-tailed hawk that soared above them, no doubt eyeing an easy meal. As the bird swooped in a turn, his wings remained straight, but he seemed tilted.

I handed the binoculars to Will. "No, I think they turn like this."
I stretched out my arms and imitated the hawk in a wide circle, with
my body tilted toward the center of the circle. "Think of how you
turn on a bicycle. You barely turn the handlebars and lean into the
turn." Now I was riding an imaginary bicycle, once again glad we
were hidden from the view of others. "I'm not sure we even need
movable handlebars."

Will scanned the skies. "Well, I think you're both right. The bird
changes the tilt of its wing for wide turns, bends them and spreads
its feathers to make quick darting movements, just as you would turn
the handlebars for a sharper, quicker turn." Now it was Will's turn to
flap around, but he tucked his thumbs in his armpits, looking more
like a chicken.

"Do you think we could capture a few?" Orv had been chucking
pebbles into the river, but switched to pitching higher, toward the
birds.

"Stop that; you're frightening them." I sounded more and more
like Mama. "And I'm almost afraid to ask, but why do you want to
capture birds?"

Will nodded and smiled. "I bet I know why. To dissect them,
study the way the bones move, and how the muscles are attached.
Brilliant."

"We'd have to do it quick, before rigor mortis sets in." Orv was
taking aim with a stone, but an evil look from me stopped him.

"Or you could go to the library and look at some avian anatomy
textbooks," I said. The thought of them trapping and cutting open
harmless birds just to study their innards made my stomach turn.

"Okay, we'll do that," Will said. But I knew he said it with a wink
at Orville.

DAYTON

APRIL 1896

"Where are the boys?" The Bishop stuck his head through my open bedroom doorway without any further greeting. Sometimes it seemed I was less a daughter and more of a servant.

"Good morning. They're at the bicycle shop." I looked out the window to check the weather. The redbuds were shedding their deep-pink flowers, and the leaves were beginning to appear. It was my favorite time of year, when I could dig in my garden and plant fruits and vegetables. I had missed several months of classes, due to staying home to nurse Orville through a bad bout of typhoid fever. He was well on the mend now, and I would go back for the end-of-year exams and ceremonies.

The Bishop waved a newspaper. "Listen to this, and tell me if you think you need to go down there and let them know right away."

"I have to prepare for exams—"

"It says here that a fellow named Samuel Langley from the Smithsonian successfully flew an unmanned steam-powered fixed-wing model aircraft."

"Interesting. Why don't you go down there and tell them yourself?"

He stroked his long graying beard. "Well, indeed I shall."

That ushered in a new rhythm to our home life, and each morning the Bishop would appear with the day's news and ask if he should share it with the boys. Invariably I said yes and off he went. I was happy to see him take an interest in their work, without the usual questions regarding eventual profitability.

He was especially proud when a translation of a book he had ordered came in. It was by a German experimenter named Lilienthal.

He was known as the first man to fly, as he had invented a glider that he could hang from and control by shifting his weight. He held patents for many of his inventions, and like the boys, he studied birds to understand the mechanics of flight. His book *Birdflight as the Basis of Aviation* was full of formulas and sketches of birds, and the boys pored over it after dinner for weeks.

The adventures of Lilienthal weren't all that had captured the boys' imagination. They also followed everything written by or about Octave Chanute. The French-born engineer had been a bridge builder in Chicago before becoming obsessed with manned flight.

"Look here." The Bishop brought me the evening paper. Chanute had gathered a group of men to test gliders on the shores of Lake Michigan. "I'm afraid our boys will want to travel up there for this, and who will mind the store?"

"All you can do is share the news and let them figure it out."

I don't know what transpired in that conversation, but the boys didn't abandon the shop.

OBERLIN, OHIO
JUNE 1896

Although I adored my home life in Dayton, my days living in the charming college town of Oberlin were filled with exciting new experiences and people. I lived in a boardinghouse with several other girls. We bonded almost immediately and became lifelong friends. It was an interlude, not my real life, so I tried to spend every moment soaking up knowledge and skills to fulfill my promise to my family.

I never thought of myself as an outstanding writer, nothing on the order of Harry Haskell. So when I won the school's annual prize in history for an essay I wrote in my sophomore year, I was shocked. Everyone was sure the prize would be his.

That Sunday, as I stepped down the stone steps of our little chapel, I felt a tug at my elbow. It was Harry.

"May I walk you home?"

"Of course." I looked at him sideways. I knew that Isabel, a mutual friend of ours, was interested in him, and I suspected he wanted some hints about that. "Congratulations on winning almost every senior award. Isabel said you gave a charming speech."

"Oh, did you not think it was charming?" He fell in step next to me as I made my way back to my boardinghouse.

Heat rose in my face. I had been so flustered by winning an award myself, especially after missing so much of the school year, that I had failed to listen to his talk. "Oh, everyone thought so."

He chuckled. "I was watching you not paying a whit of attention, and I don't blame you. That was quite an honor they bestowed on you. I'm not sure the history prize has ever been awarded to a sophomore. Congratulations."

Glee spread through me like the prickle of a thousand tiny feathers. I had known Harry for years, and he was always ever so kind to me. But he was kind to everyone. We had reached my doorway, and I turned to tell him goodbye. "Tomorrow is your big day. I'll be somewhere in the crowd watching you get your diploma."

He surprised me by taking my hand in his. "I will find you."

❧

"A birthday present," Harry said, offering a small wrapped package.

We sat on a bench just after the graduation ceremony, his tasseled cap and honor graduate regalia in his lap.

"But my birthday isn't until August."

"I know, and I don't want you to open it until then."

I screwed up my face. It wasn't like Harry to play games. I handed the gift back to him. "You can come to Dayton and give it to me then."

We waved to the clumps of chattering graduates that were passing by and had been trying to entice us to join them in various celebrations.

"They're planning a little reception for me at home," he said. "Will you come to Kansas City to celebrate with us?"

The invitation startled me. That was a long way to go for a graduation party, and I wasn't even graduating. "Thank you for thinking of me. But I can't. I need to get back to Dayton. My brothers are probably eating grasshoppers by now. If I don't tend my garden soon, we'll all starve." I was only half kidding.

"Well, you see, that's just it. They're grown men, and you could just as easily plant vegetables in Kansas City."

Harry and I were friends, well more than that, as I had had a crush on him since he was my math tutor in prep school. But I had always kept an imaginary wall between us, knowing that he would return to Kansas City and I to Dayton. I wanted a relationship that could flourish, at least for now, through letters and occasional visits.

He slid closer to me on the bench. "It's more than just a party. I'm hoping you'll like Kansas City well enough to return when you graduate." He had an honest, open face, one I could always read. But not this time. "I'm more than speculating. I've talked with the schools. There's a great need for Latin teachers. One is retiring at a school very close..."

I shook my head. "Oh, Harry, that's kind of you. But I've promised my family. They paid for this"—I waved toward the expansive

campus with its castle-like stone buildings and fairy-tale grounds—
"and it will be my duty to repay them. I promised."

He tapped the gift, still in my outstretched hand. "In that box
is a ring. It is my promise to you. I want to marry you, but I know
you're not ready. But I will come see you for your birthday, and every
birthday after that, until you are."

A ring. I stared at the little box, wrapped in gold foil. Harry
was like no other man I had known, and I could easily imagine a
loving, interesting life with him. I looked at his kind eyes, then
looked away, it being too painful to see the hurt I was about to
cause. I remembered how ill Orv had been, and how thankful my
brothers and the Bishop were every time I returned home. I knew
where I belonged, at least for the next few years, and it wasn't
Kansas City.

"No, Harry. That isn't fair to you." I placed the gift firmly in
his lap. "You mustn't wait for me. You have to live your life and be
happy. I won't be the cause of even a moment of loneliness for you."

I stood up, tucking the printed graduation program under my
arm. "But I will write you."

And I did write, on and off. But I could sense his interest in me
waning, as I presumed it would. I told myself it was just as well this
way, since unless he decided to uproot himself and move to Dayton,
our worlds might as well have been the earth and the moon.

When I returned home, nothing had changed. I told no one of
Harry's proposal because I couldn't bear the inevitable discussion
and conclusion. The boys dedicated every spare moment to their
aviation quest, and the Bishop and I were sustaining them with food
and encouragement.

On a warm clear morning in August, I was looking forward to riding my bicycle to meet some friends downtown. As I packed a knapsack with lemon tea and crackers, the Bishop stepped into the kitchen, which was unusual in itself. His face was drawn, and he held out a folded newspaper.

"I think maybe it's your turn." He gave a nod and stepped out like Marley's ghost.

I looked at the folded paper in my hand. It had been turned to a page deep in the middle, so this was not a major headline. But it would be to the boys.

Otto Lilienthal Killed in Glider Crash

Oh no. The boys would be devastated. He was their hero, their inspiration, the patron saint of gliding. The back of the bicycle shop was their new favorite place, as they were building a box kite nearly large enough to ride on. It was to be in the fashion of Chanute, with modifications based on Lilienthal's writings. The Bishop was right. This was news I needed to deliver myself.

But when I got to the shop, the boys had already seen the newspaper and knew of the fatal accident. They had filled a chalkboard with drawings of glider wings, with arrows and numbers scrawled in every last inch of space. They had no need for me to console them; they had their own way of processing their grief.

SPRING 1898

As my graduation from Oberlin approached, I dithered on whether to invite Harry to come. As an alumnus, of course he could attend without any invitation from me, and I hoped he would do that. But then maybe that would be presumptuous of him, especially after I had spurned his offer of marriage.

My dithering gave way to utter inaction. At the ceremony, I scanned the crowd, hoping against hope to see Harry among them. But that was not to be.

After the ceremony I returned to my boardinghouse. "A package for you," my roommate Marilyn said cheerily. "From Kansas City."

She waggled her eyebrows suggestively, and my other roommate, Margaret, and she shoved each other to get closer to the opening of the brown paper-wrapped box.

It was a book of poems by Robert Louis Stevenson. I turned my back to my nosy roommates and opened the book to a marked page. There the poem "Requiem" appeared with some of the lines underlined:

> Here he lies where he longed to be;
> Home is the sailor from the sea,
> The hunter from the hill.

We both enjoyed the poet's work, but I wasn't sure why this particular stanza was meaningful to Harry, especially as it referred to a dead sailor. Nonetheless, I tucked away the book with my treasured things, to look back upon at different times in my life.

SPRING 1899

We had become entirely too comfortable. Seven years had gone by since the boys opened their shop. Sure, they had made quite a name for the Wright family, building, repairing, selling, and inventing new models of bicycles, but what had happened to the dream? Wilbur continued to follow every advancement in aviation from newspapers and magazines, while Orville built scale models of the more successful gliders, but their creativity ended there.

I chose the second Sunday in May for a special dinner I hoped would be a prelude to a thorough discussion of our next steps forward.

A large squab simmered in the Dutch oven, with onions and carrots and celery. I added salt and pepper and gave it a poke to test for tenderness. Another hour and it would be ready. Meanwhile, I gathered up Will's saved articles and clippings and made a display of the toy and scale-model flyers. I wanted the Bishop and the boys to know what was on the day's agenda.

For a bit of a surprise, I had obtained an article in a French magazine about a club for aviation pioneers. Using my knowledge of Latin and a French-English dictionary, I translated it for them. It seemed flight enthusiasts were steadily moving from lighter-than-air airships to winged gliders, which were both subject to the whims of the wind.

The smell of dinner on the stove drew in the always-hungry Orville, who reached for my oven mitt to lift the lid before I slapped his hand away.

"Let it be. If you want to help, set the table."

Orv stepped into the dining room, where the table was adorned with a dozen or so tiny wooden and cloth model aeroplanes. "Shall I clear it first?"

"No. We will be talking about what to do with all of that."

"Our models?" His face fell. "You can't mean you want to get rid of these." He picked up the Pénaud's helicopter and twirled the propeller. "We haven't outgrown our toys."

I shook my head. "And you never will."

After a quiet dinner, Will cleared the dishes as I explained my goal.

"I'm concerned that in our day-to-day routine, we've lost sight of our dream. You know I gave up my own, postponing any thoughts of marriage, because of your promise to work on your flying machine. What do you have to show for yourselves?"

"We aren't the slackers you seem to think," Orv said. "We've been saving money, haven't we, Will? How much now?"

Will paged through the articles I had gathered. "Oh, a thousand dollars at least by now. Enough to buy materials for our first glider. And we've been studying and reading everything we can find, but I'm afraid we've reached rather a dead end. Only the governments of France and the United States have more knowledge than us, I would say."

My mind perked up. "The U.S. government, you say? What is to prevent you from inquiring as to what they know?"

The boys looked at each other and shrugged.

Orville gave a little laugh. "I don't think that's how it works. If it is to be public information, it would be published somewhere."

"How do you know unless you ask? And where would such information be kept?" the Bishop asked.

Wilbur stacked the papers into a neat pile. "Samuel Langley has published a few things. I'm sure there's more, hidden away deep in a government vault."

The boys started teasing about the depth and breadth of some imagined clandestine space, and the Bishop excused himself from the proceedings. I rapped on the table for their attention.

"Boys, what I need from you is a decision. Is this still your dream, or are you happy with the direction your lives have taken? If it is the latter, I should focus on my own happiness."

Orville stopped fiddling with a rubber-band-powered propeller, a look of shock on his face. "Sterchens, have you been unhappy?"

"Of course not, for now. But if I am to be a spinster, I want more of a reason than keeping house for three quite capable men."

"It's still my dream. How about you, Will?" Orv said.

Will looked as if I had just proposed committing a major crime. "I'm sorry. It never occurred to me that you might want something else. Solving the challenges of manned flight has always been a dream for the three of us."

Orville nodded. "Then let's make a pact. We three will devote our time and energy from this day forward to each other and to our project, forsaking all others, no matter how long it takes." He slapped his hand flat on the table, followed by Wilbur, and they waited for mine to seal the deal.

I hesitated. This seemed silly and childish, but the boys looked at me with such sincerity that I could hardly refuse to join them. "Except for the Bishop. We can't forsake him."

On Decoration Day, the Bishop, Lorin, Orv, and I went to the military cemetery by the Soldiers' Home to pay our respects to our fallen veterans, then over to Woodland Cemetery to lay flowers at Mama's grave. Will did not come with us, insisting he had too much work to do. But when we returned home, he was sitting at my slant-top desk in the front parlor, surrounded by wads of crumpled papers and looking as if he had been in a snowball fight.

He nodded his welcome. "Sorry to miss visiting the cemetery with you, but I'm working on our pledge and writing to the Smithsonian Institute." He filled and blotted his pen and stared at a fresh sheet

KATHARINE, THE WRIGHT SISTER   41

of Wright Cycle Company stationery. So far, all he had written was *Dear Sirs*. "I have little hope for a response. What can I say to convince them that we're serious?"

I pulled up a chair next to him, then closed my eyes and conjured what I had learned in a course on rhetoric—identify yourself, state the problem, then state why you are best equipped to solve the problem. "Let's take it a step at a time. First, tell them how you came to be interested in the problem—human flight."

Wilbur wrote:

I have been interested in the problem of mechanical and human flight ever since as a boy I constructed a number of bats of various sizes after the style of Cayley's and Pénaud's machines. My observations since have only convinced me more firmly that human flight is possible and practicable.

"Good. Now tell them why you think it's possible. What exactly have you observed? For example, our days watching the migrating birds...what did we learn from them?"

"And bats. Percy Pilcher's bat glider flew seven hundred and fifty feet."

"Focus on your direct observations."

Wilbur nodded and added:

It is only a question of knowledge and skill just as in all acrobatic feats. Birds are the most perfectly trained gymnasts in the world and are specially well fitted for their work, and it may be that man will never equal them, but no one who has watched a bird chasing an insect or another bird can doubt that feats are performed which require three or four times the effort required in ordinary flight.

"What next?" Wilbur was such an eager and obedient student. If only my high school classes were filled with such pupils.

"Appeal to the emotions, or rational thought process. How do their goals align with yours?"

I believe that simple flight at least is possible to man, and that the experiments and investigations of a large number of independent workers will result in the accumulation of information and knowledge and skill, which will finally lead to accomplished flight.

"Excellent, now review your qualifications."

"Qualifications? I haven't any." Wilbur slumped. "Only my undying interest and self-study."

"This isn't like medicine or building a bridge. There isn't a vast body of knowledge. It's being developed, by people just like you. So admit that, and show you've done your homework."

The works on the subject to which I have had access are Marey's and Jamieson's works published by Appleton's and various magazines and cyclopedic articles. I am about to begin a systematic study of the subject in preparation for practical work to which I expect to devote what time I can apart from my regular business.

"All right. Now we come to the ask. What would you have them do, in order to accomplish this mutual goal?"

"That part is easy."

I wish to obtain such papers as the Smithsonian Institution has published on this subject, and if possible, a list of other works in print in the English language. I am an enthusiastic, but not a crank in the sense that I have some pet theories as to the proper construction of a flying machine. I wish to avail myself of all that is already known and then if possible add my mite to help on the future workers who attain final success.

I read over the letter. Something seemed missing. "Hmm, what is the final thing you must do to sell someone on your idea?"

"I know the answer to that one, after selling a few hundred bikes to people who didn't know how to ride. Overcome objections. Tell them how you will make it easy as pie for them."

I tried to place myself in the government official's shoes. "Objections—maybe it's a secret, not to be divulged to the public, or would be too much effort or cost for them?"

Wilbur twiddled his pen. "I don't want to get into secrecy. Why bring that up and force its consideration? And it might sound demeaning that he wouldn't have proper staff to handle such a request. But cost—that is worth addressing."

Wilbur wrote a final sentence in the two-page letter.

I do not know the terms on which you send out your publications but if you will inform me of the cost, I will remit the price.

"Shall we both sign our names?" Will offered. "You're as much a part of this as am I."

"With my obviously feminine name, I don't think that's wise. Put Little Brother's name on there if you please, but as it is in your hand, I don't see a need to raise a question in their minds."

"So be it."

Yours truly,
Wilbur Wright

WILBUR

As it turned out, the dissection of birds was unnecessary, much to Orv's disappointment. Our book by the Prussian pioneer Otto Lilienthal, *Birdflight as the Basis of Aviation*, featured detailed diagrams of the anatomy and movement of stork wings in flight. News of Lilienthal's death, while sad, did not discourage us in the least. It only reinforced our suspicions that flight required three-dimensional control before there could be any advancements.

Lorin was pleased with modest earnings on the profit and loss statement, but to me, the bicycle shop was a conundrum. At once our livelihood and space to work on our true calling, it was also a vexing interruption, usually just when progress was being made on an important aerodynamics problem.

I tinkered in the back of the shop late on a muggy July afternoon, studying Lilienthal and Chanute's work and puzzling over the double-decker box kite I had made from scraps of cloth and peeled sapling twigs. How could I alter its structure so it could change midflight like the wings of a bird? We had yet to solve the problem of how to create more lift on one side of the wing to aid in turning, as we had observed birds do by tilting their wings.

Orville had been fashioning a system of gears to rotate the right and left wings separately. This, we thought would enable the glider to roll in a turn as do birds. But the system would be too hard to control and far too heavy.

The jingle of the bells on the door alerted me that a customer had entered the shop. Orville had gone off on a camping trip, leaving me to man the store alone. I toyed with the notion of telling the customer we were closed for the day, but my inner conscience, whose voice sounded suspiciously like Katharine's, scolded me and I went to greet the customer instead.

It was a straightforward matter, a man in search of an inner tube for the bicycle he had purchased for his wife. I selected the proper size, removed the long straight tube from its box, and explained how to affix it to achieve the proper size and circular shape. But, confound it all, the man then wanted to peruse the shop for a gift for his son.

While he examined a small tricycle, I toyed with the cardboard box from the inner tube. It was long and narrow, and I estimated it to have about the same proportions as a double-winged glider that Chanute had developed. I imagined the top of the box to be the top wing, the bottom the lower wing, and the sides to be the struts that held it together.

I held opposite corners of the end of the box and squeezed, which slightly flattened the box and would create more air exposure to the top wing. This, I thought, would create more lift. Then, inspiration hit. I took one side of the box between my right thumb and forefinger, and the same on other side with my left hand and squeezed in opposite directions. This resulted in a warped or twisted shape. If

I chose the same corners on each side, the wing uniformly took on a diagonal shape, until the box flattened. I moved my fingers back to the opposing corners and squeezed. By holding opposite sides of the box in each hand, I could readily twist the "wings" and could imagine how the air would provide more lift on the side that—

"Mr. Wright? Um…hello there…Mr. Wright?" The customer rapped his knuckles on the top glass of the display case.

"Oh, pardon me, I was just…" But there was no sense in explaining why I was so interested in a box. I helped the man with his purchase, sent him out the door, and locked it behind him, my mind occupied with ways to somehow tilt the wing struts in opposite directions to warp the wings. It was so simple, so elegant. There would be no need to have separate rotating left and right wings or a complicated gear system. Some pulleys and cables could do it.

I had to talk to Orville.

KATHARINE

I t had been a disappointing day. After graduating from Oberlin the previous year, I thought I had a good chance at an open teaching position at Steele High School, just a quick streetcar ride away from home. But instead, while I could continue filling in as a substitute, they gave the open position to a man.

I busied myself with dinner preparations, enjoying the sizzle of bacon fat hitting the iron pan while imagining my colleague stuck at school with a towering pile of papers to grade. I lowered the flame and added sliced onions, stirring to give them an even brown. When the aroma told me they were nearly done, I sprinkled in some flour and stirred, stirred, stirred.

I checked my sourdough culture, making sure it was nice and bubbly for my biscuits. Mama had kept it alive for years, carefully feeding it a mixture of flour and water each week. Holding on to the tradition kept her close to my heart. Then, just as I was hauling my chicken stock out of the icebox, Wilbur burst into the kitchen. He didn't ask what was for dinner or give me his usual kiss on the cheek, but instead started talking a mile a minute.

Wilbur paced. I had to dance around him with my bowl of stock in the tiny kitchen.

"I think I've got it. Need to work on some things, but I've got the basic concept. I must talk to Orville. We should make a model. He'll know how to do it."

"It's just the two of us tonight. The Bishop won't be home until tomorrow and Little Brother is…"

"I know, I know. But I can hardly wait."

"What is this great discovery?" I poured the broth into the hot pan and set it to simmer, but I had the feeling I'd be dining alone.

"How to twist the wings to change the lift from one side to the other."

"In order to turn like a hawk?" Learning how to control turns was an incessant topic. Along with why Lilienthal's glider had crashed. *"We've got to somehow be able to adjust for the capricious wind,"* I had heard Wilbur say.

"Exactly. I'm thinking of attaching four ropes to a box kite. Oh, I wish Orville were here." He plopped onto the kitchen stool.

"Then go to him."

"I can't. He's out east, camping in the woods or some fool thing."

I pulled open a cupboard drawer. "Here's the address of the camp. Go now, before it gets dark. Stay the night, and I'll mind the shop tomorrow."

Wilbur's eyes widened. "Really? Maybe I should wait. I don't want to abandon you…"

I waved both hands at him. "Just go. Tomorrow is Saturday, and I have no plans that I can't change. You'll not eat or sleep a wink anyway, thinking up a million ideas, then Little Brother will just shoot them down. Together you'll solve it in no time."

He leaped to his feet, gave me a squeeze, and headed to his room to pack. "You're the best, Sterchens."

"Mm-hmm, I am." I mixed up some flour, baking powder, and salt, and cut bacon fat into it. My oven was nice and hot, so I quickly mixed in some buttermilk and my starter. No time for cut biscuits tonight, so I plopped small heaps of dough onto a baking stone and slid it into the oven.

As I filled a flask with hot onion soup for Will to take with him, I was torn by conflicting emotions. Part of me was thrilled with Wilbur's revelation and happy to be able to help by minding the shop. But somewhere deep inside me grew a big lump of hurt. It never crossed Will's mind to reveal much of his idea to me, or ask for my own thoughts about it. His first and only instinct was to get to Orv, and I supposed that was how it had to be. While I understood the basic principles they explained to me, I couldn't envision how to apply them. But I could make the biscuits to sustain them while they learned how to fly.

FALL 1899

None of us held out much hope that we would get an answer from the Smithsonian, but true to their promise, the boys continued with their research, following every aviation event across the globe. Without exception, each machine crashed within moments of launch, if they ever got off the ground at all. Newspapers poked fun at the efforts, calling them frivolous, or folly, or idle pastimes for the rich.

The Bishop was home from a monthlong assignment in Indiana, and we all gathered for our Sunday dinner at 7 Hawthorn Street, the home both Orv and I were born in. Although I sometimes groused about not having a life of my own, I couldn't imagine I'd be happy away from my three men.

The Bishop and the boys were outside sitting on rockers on the front porch they had built, while I sweated over a roast pork shoulder in the kitchen. Needing some rosemary from my garden, I went outside to fetch it. After I pinched off a few nice sprigs, their lively conversation floating down from the porch drew me in.

"Crash after crash after crash," Orv said. "We've got to figure out what they're all doing wrong. Unmanned kites can fly for hours. Manned gliders have flown a few miles with a perfect wind. But as soon as they add power…" Both Orv and Will pantomimed a crash.

I thought of how every paper flyer I created had quickly spiraled to the ground. "Is it the weight that's the problem? Not only the engine, but the sturdier materials of the plane itself in order to support it?"

Will studied a photograph of a glider with V-shaped wings. "These dihedral wings everyone is trying are not going to work. The hawk with flatter wings soars better than a vulture. The weight of a human and an engine must be factored in. That's simple mathematics and solvable by using stronger, lighter materials, or bigger wings, or—"

"Hasn't that already been tried?" Orv sketched an aeroplane with a pencil. He erased the wingtips and extended them. "All manner of shapes and sizes have been tried. We have a pretty good idea of the dimensions that seem to work, and the amount of camber in the wing that will allow it to fly."

"Camber of the wing?" It was a term I hadn't heard mentioned before. I held the rosemary sprigs up to my nose. The piney aroma was somehow both invigorating and relaxing, just like a good conversation.

Orv drew another figure, a half-moon shape, with the flat side down. "This is an exaggerated cross-section view of a wing. The air comes over the top from the leading edge to the trailing edge"—he drew an arrow—"and across the bottom"—another arrow under the wing—"at different speeds. Since the air going over the top has farther to go, it travels faster. This creates a difference in air density which produces lift. It's what holds the machine in the air."

Will continued. "There's an optimum curve, or camber. Too steep, and it produces too much air resistance, or drag, while if there is too little curve, there's not enough lift."

I closed my eyes and tried to picture a wing in flight, the air densities showing up in different colors in my mind. "But wouldn't the optimum curve be different at different speeds? And don't you need more lift when it's leaving the ground than when it's already up there?"

The Bishop held his hand out for the drawing. "I think she has a point."

The image of a wing ascending far into the clouds coursed through my mind. "And how do you control the lift? A hot-air balloon's movement up and down is controlled by raising or lowering the heat. You can't do that."

"Of course we've considered this." Orv's voice had a trace of testiness. "We're working on how to slightly modify or warp that shape to control the lift."

"And control it separately on each side," Will added.

I thought again of my paper aeroplanes that always seemed to nose-dive. "And how do you keep the nose up? Can that be controlled with the warping as well?"

Will leaned over to add to the sketch. "Chanute's theory is that two or more stacked wings are necessary to get enough lift. Otherwise the wingspan is much too wide to be practical. He was a bridge builder." Will drew two horizontal lines, then made Xs between them. "He connects the wings with struts and supports, much like a bridge. And his most successful glider had double-decker wings, but he was never able to steer it. There was no movement of the wings in relation to each other. To keep the nose up, he devised something like a rudder on a boat, but instead of moving left and right, it would move up and down. Like a whale's tail." He drew a rather comically large tail on his double-winged machine.

I slid the notepad toward me and added my own drawing. "Wouldn't that put a lot of weight on the back? What if you put it in the front to catch the wind, right where the machine first hits it?" I drew a horizontal line in the front of the wings and drew arrows for the wind. "The trailing edge would move up and down, and the pilot could see its position."

Orv added a shallow arc over my horizontal rudder. "Maybe, instead of flat, it's curved like the wing to add lift. And if it's up front, we could use the tail for another rudder to steer left and right."

Wilbur hovered over the marked-up drawing. "I think it's worth a try. But I don't think the tail rudder will be necessary. The warping of the wings will control turns by dipping and slowing one side or the other." He stepped away, holding his arms straight out to his sides, then dipping his left arm and tilting and turning to that side.

"I'm glad the three of you are working this out on paper first. Unlike the fools in the newspapers," the Bishop said.

"We need to build models and try them out. First operated with ropes like a kite, then eventually one big enough to ride on."

The image of my brothers riding a kite scared the starch out of me. But they were clearly excited, talking about going back to the place along the river where we had watched the birds. A fine place to fly a kite.

The back of the bicycle shop was not only a kite designing and building area. At the same time, the boys were tinkering with new bicycle designs, improving on the new "safety bicycle," which had two equal-sized tires and had overtaken the penny-farthing model with its large front wheel. The safety bicycle had encouraged legions of women to start riding. Since their feet could now touch the ground, and the pedals spun the rear tire with the assistance of a chain and sprocketed gears, women were using bicycles for transportation as well as leisure.

By some miracle, Langley himself responded to Wilbur's letter. He was in full support of our goals and promised to share the information the government had gathered. He also mentioned there were plans in place to build a prototype in the near future. I thought it was an obvious ploy to get the boys on board with his own project, which financially made much sense to me. But the boys wanted to keep their independence.

We decided to maintain an air of mystery around the flying experiments for several reasons. Now that my brothers had announced their intentions to the Smithsonian, a public entity, their experiments were subject to scrutiny. They needed to prevent the outright theft of their unique and hard-won designs until they could be protected by legal patents. Another was to keep out distracting curiosity seekers. Therefore, only family was allowed in the back of the shop.

We searched for a larger and more private space to house both the bicycle shop and the flight studies and found it at 1127 W. Third Street, just a few blocks away from home. The owner of the building, C. W. Webbert, was enthusiastic about the boys' "secret project" and offered whatever clandestine support he could give. He seemed more intrigued with the secrecy than with the project itself, but his help was welcome in any case.

It became my job, when I dropped by the shop after teaching or on Saturdays, to sell bicycles and take in ones needing repair. As the demand for my brothers' improved bicycle designs grew, customers came pouring in the door, and one Saturday when both boys were in the back building bikes, or more likely sawing up pine sticks for their kite, I had customers waiting for so long that some gave up and left. I noticed one man in particular roaming around, seemingly in no hurry, and when I finally had a free moment, I went to him.

"I'm so sorry, I don't mean to ignore you, but as you can see, it's been a busy morning."

"Quite all right, miss. I'm enjoying looking over your merchandise." He offered his hand. "Charley Tamus. I work as a mechanic just down the street."

Charley was about Orv's age, also the same average height and slender build, and also sported a slightly receding hairline. "Nice to meet you. May I help you with the purchase of a bicycle?"

"I can't say I'm any sort of rider. Work in a machine shop, with all sorts of metals. I can build anything and am always looking for new ideas. Hence my interest here."

My face must have shown some alarm, as he hurried to explain. "Oh dear, you probably think I'm a spy, here to steal your designs. I assure you, I'm just an admirer."

An idea formed in my head. We desperately needed some part-time help, and this gentleman seemed to have an interest and spare time. He should meet with Orv or Will, I decided. "Have you met my brothers? They own the shop. I'm just helping out."

"Oh, I'm sure you do more than that. You seem to have a good handle on running things. I'd love to meet your brothers as well." He leaned a little closer. "They're lucky to have you."

Feeling light as air from his compliments, I went to summon the boys. After a long conversation, it was decided. Charley would begin helping in the front of the shop after his shifts at his other job.

Charley knew his way around bicycles and could fix anything with a few simple tools, but we immediately butted heads in the shop. I was used to dealing with the customers and had systems and recordkeeping in place that had worked for us for years.

As I tried to explain our recordkeeping system to him, he waved me away like a pesky fly. "That's all well and good, but better leave that to me now."

"But you don't have any idea—"

"It isn't difficult, and I have my own way. Besides, you have another job and you're not here most of the time."

The same could be said about him, but I reluctantly gave him a chance. He managed to offend some regular customers, whom I had to placate with free tire tubes, but Charley quickly adapted and even developed a following of his own regular customers. Overall, his help left me some precious hours of free time.

We got along well when we weren't arguing over things like replacing our simple cash box, or whether customers could take a test ride unaccompanied. He wanted to take our cash box apart and rebuild it, while I wanted to support a local business and buy National Cash Register's latest model. It could keep track of our sales and reduce our need to handwrite everything.

While he thought it was fine to allow customers to head out the door to try a bicycle before purchase, I had to rely on my bossy nature to tell him absolutely not, at least not without a deposit of cash or their house keys.

"At least you're not asking for their firstborn child, because we don't need them running around here. How about instead of house keys, we ask for cookies? I like cookies." Charley joked.

Still, I longed for male company in something outside of work, and Charley did make me laugh. Despite our somewhat fractious beginning, I hoped he would see past my bossiness and perhaps ask me to dinner, but I was awkward in my efforts.

The opportunity arose when we were closing the store on a Saturday. I tucked a pencil over my ear, then opened the long green-covered book that was our sales ledger and prepared to sum up the day's tallies.

"What did you study in school?" I asked, hoping he would reciprocate my question, and that he might be impressed that I was soon to begin teaching Latin full time at Steele High School.

He stopped counting the cash from the box. "Pardon? Oh, schooling—mostly self-taught, and apprenticeship." After my rude interruption, he consolidated his piles of bills and started counting them over again.

So much for my efforts to develop a more personal relationship. I decided any movement in that direction should come from him.

❧

I missed my friends from Oberlin, the thrilling discussions of world events, of traveling and gossip and the latest fashions. So I invited my old roommates, Margaret and Marilyn, to visit me in Dayton, as it was difficult for me to travel out of town during the school year. I set out tea and little lemon tarts in the Sunday parlor.

My friends brought with them rather crushing, but not wholly unexpected news. Just moments after their arrival, they were gushing with the latest gossip.

"Harry and Isabel are engaged." Marilyn sat with her dress prettily splayed around her. With her big blue eyes and long dark-brown hair, she always looked too perfect to be real, a "living doll" we called her. But she was so sweet that none of us managed to hold that against her.

I sucked in my breath and tried to be nonchalant. "Well, isn't that lovely news. I wish the best for both of them." I lifted my teacup toward them in a weak effort to show my approval.

Tall and thin, Margaret contrasted with the two of us, who were more petite. Margaret lifted an eyebrow. "You can't fool us. We thought you and Harry would grow old together."

"I suspect there's another man taking his place?" Marilyn glanced around the room. "Hiding in plain sight here in Dayton? Perhaps a male teacher or principal?"

The girls laughed, entirely too loudly.

Marilyn must had seen the scowl on my face. She modestly covered her mouth. "Surely you don't want to reach thirty and still be alone."

"I'm barely twenty-five and hardly alone," I sniffed, although the thought crossed my mind nearly every day. No one needed to remind me that a woman unmarried by thirty was very likely to stay that way. I wanted nothing more at that moment than to go to my bedroom and have a good cry. I didn't blame Harry; he had to move on with his life without me, stuck as I was in the vortex of my family commitments.

I had potential suitors, both at school and at our church. But most of the male faculty seemed more interested in ensuring I didn't usurp the plum advanced courses rather than courting a competitor. As for the others, none held my interest in a conversation like Harry did. And none made me shiver at their touch, or desire to sneak off to a private space. There was also the matter of my pact with the boys. But surely that didn't entail saying no to romance forever.

Meanwhile, I could get my fill of family life with young children by minding those of Lorin and his wife, Netta. I adored my nephew and nieces, Milton, Ivonette, and Leontine. They lived just a few blocks away, so I could go snuggle with them anytime my heart desired.

Although nearly twelve years older than me and absent for many of my growing years, Lorin was becoming an important adviser. Now an established bookkeeper, he had forced Orv and Wilbur to be mindful of their spending on bicycle materials, and now on their flying hobby.

But for me, he acted almost in a paternal fashion, soothing my hurt feelings when the Bishop treated me like household help and the boys ignored my suggestions, being only a girl, after all. If I needed an evening out, I could send the boys and the Bishop to Lorin and Netta's house for dinner. I think that did them as much good as it did me.

With Charley manning the shop, Saturday became kite day at the river. Each week a new and bigger kite was tried out. The best one we tested had a double wing and a horizontal front rudder, much like we had drawn. Ropes and sticks connected to the wings, controlling their shape by shifting the top wing forward on either side to steer the kite.

But in many of the trials, there wasn't enough wind to get the kite to launch. We would trudge back by bicycle and streetcar, defeated.

One Saturday, the wind seemed ideal. We watched the early fall leaves flutter before gently drifting to the ground, and small clouds of dust rose up here and there along our route. This was going to be the day the kite soared.

I helped Will steady the thing, while Orv ran ahead, stretching out the ropes. Then we all ran at top speed, with me giving up first and Will holding the kite above his head. At last, it was airborne and Orv was able to stop running and manage the ropes. Will ran ahead to help him, there being four ropes, and together they were able to make the kite veer left and right several times. Then the kite caught a current and sailed straight up, then swiftly down. Orv took off running again, but the kite came down toward him like an eagle after its prey, then cartwheeled along the ground.

When we all gathered to inspect for damages, huffing to catch our breaths, I thought I should console the boys on the failure. But to my surprise, they slapped each other on the back, then grabbed me around the waist and lifted me off the ground.

"It flies!" Wilbur enthused.

"We need to start planning one big enough to ride." Orv wiggled the frame, checking for breakage.

"First, we need to find a place with more consistent wind."

"Indeed, we'll never make enough progress at this rate to beat Langley and the others."

Confused, I asked, "What? I didn't know we were in a competition. I thought this was a collaborative effort. Didn't Langley send you information?"

The boys broke the kite down into its main parts and divvied them up among the bikes.

"We're all scientists, doing experiments. We share scientific principles as a matter of course. But what we do with those principles, the inventions and designs, belong to ourselves."

"Otherwise who would be motivated? Aside from people with a government paycheck, that is," Will said.

"To the winner go the spoils," Orv added.

"I see. Well then, let's start looking for a windy place with lots of room." The idea rather appealed to me. I could use a change in scenery.

So the hunt began. First, we rode the streetcar as far out to the northwest as we could go, where there were large expanses of open fields. But the winds didn't seem any more reliable than they were at the river. Another trek west of town brought us to the same conclusion. Dayton, for all its wonderful mix of new technology and open spaces, didn't have what we needed.

Sunday dinners now focused on reports on our search. Me—Chicago and Cleveland. Will—Kentucky horse country. He also started a letter-writing campaign, and had a good response from their fellow aviation enthusiast Octave Chanute. Orv had insisted we needed a wide beach for soft landings, and Mr. Chanute agreed in his letter.

"Oh, you just want to put on a bathing costume and show off for the girls," I admonished.

"No, think about it." Orv said. "Lake Michigan has great wind, no doubt. But Chicago is teeming with people, and the undeveloped coast is too narrow or too rocky."

"And too flat," Will added. "We need some hills."

"Or sand dunes," I said. Mr. Chanute had mentioned the beaches of California and the Carolinas. I remembered some pictures of a wide beach somewhere in the Carolinas with tall dunes all the way to the water.

Orv nodded. "Precisely. Tall dunes for takeoff, soft sand for landings, reliable wind, and water for an emergency landing. And away from prying eyes. But where? An uninhabited island?"

"If it's uninhabited, there's a reason," I mused. "And how would you get there?"

We adjourned the meeting and ate my braised pork chops and applesauce. Our assignment for next the following week: find the perfect beach.

SPRING 1900

In a hurry to get to school, I took the streetcar rather than my bicycle, even though the late March sunshine promised to melt the last bits of snow. As the car approached the imposing brownstone building, its towers and turrets looming castle-like over the Miami River, I dug into my knapsack to find the keys. I was frequently the first to arrive and Principal James felt sorry for me having to wait in the cold, so I had my own set.

Mr. James had announced a new course in advanced Latin would be offered in the fall, and I aimed to write a lesson plan that would ensure I was chosen to teach it. Early morning was the only free time I had, so I bounded off the streetcar and headed to the arched entrance. As I climbed the steps, I saw a diminutive figure huddled in the doorway.

The pale young girl with a face sprinkled with freckles looked barely old enough to be a freshman. She wore a thin patched coat and no hat or gloves. "Sorry, I'll move out of your way," she softly whispered as she stepped aside.

I wasn't much over five feet tall, and nearly all the students towered over me. But this young lady came up to my eye level.

"What are you doing here so early, Miss…?"

"My name is Carrie. I, um, work for Mr. Riffle before class."

"The janitor?" I had many more questions, but it was cold and this poor girl was shivering. I opened the door and ushered her inside, where she promptly headed toward the basement.

Throughout the day I thought of the waif. She seemed barely in her teens, certainly too young to be doing janitorial work. Between classes, I hurried to speak to Mr. Riffle.

"Carrie has a tough home life. I give her some odd jobs to help out," he said.

After school I had a meeting scheduled with the principal. As I fidgeted, waiting in the hall outside his office, I thought more about Carrie than the advanced Latin class. How could I help her while respecting her privacy?

Mr. James wasn't aware of the unofficial school janitor, but assured me he would put a stop to her work, which made me feel worse for mentioning it.

"So." He moved on to the real purpose of our meeting. He looked down, tapped a finger on his cleared-off desk. "Regarding the advanced Latin class—"

Feeling the coveted assignment and accompanying raise in salary slipping away, I quickly pulled my lesson plan out of a folder. "I've been working hard on it. Here is a suggested syllabus…"

He waved away the papers. "There are men who support families who need the work more than you."

I pressed my lips into a straight line. Why did I work longer and harder than anyone else? Only to be passed over again and again.

"But what message does that send to students?" he continued. "They see, as do I, the effort you put into this job."

I opened my mouth to speak, but thought better of it. If not this time, maybe the next would be my turn, if I was gracious about it. I packed my papers away, the tension in my shoulders easing some.

"So, the new course is yours, if you still want it," he said.

I looked up, startled. "Really?" At his nod, I jumped up and thanked him heartily. "You won't be disappointed."

My next thought was to find Carrie and offer her an after-school job more suitable for a young girl, and in a safe place where I could keep an eye on her. With all the Wrights working, we could use help with housekeeping. My raise finally made it affordable, and if she didn't know how to so much as boil water, I could teach her.

WILBUR

Our shop wasn't wide enough for the wingspan of a glider designed to carry the weight of a pilot. Therefore we built it in sections that we could assemble once we got to the beach. We chose a site for our experiments by process of elimination and after a series of letters to Octave Chanute and the Weather Bureau.

"This one." Katharine stabbed her finger on a map of coastal North Carolina. "It's got the most consistent winds, wide beaches, and isolation."

Kitty Hawk was a rather desolate beach in North Carolina, accessible only by boat and occupied by a few friendly fishermen, perfect for our needs. I wrote to several of them, explaining our project and appealing to them for their support. A fellow named Bill Tate answered my queries, offering whatever assistance he could provide.

We planned to start out flying our machine like a kite, and when that was successful, we'd draw straws to see which of us would climb aboard and ride it like a glider. Katharine was out of the question for this, of course, it being far too reckless a thing to ask of a lady.

And besides, we needed her back home to keep the shop running and attend to the Bishop.

The three of us gathered in the dining room after supper. Orv and I studied maps of the North Carolina coast, planning provisions and a schedule while Katharine buzzed around us clearing the table.

"Earlier in summer is better, of course. Then I will have two full months to help Charley in the shop," Katharine said. I thought there was a bit of a glint in her eye.

I narrowed my gaze. Did she have some attraction to our helper? She was a vibrant single young woman after all. But I pushed all such thoughts out of my mind.

We all agreed to that plan, and Orv mentioned he and Charley had been looking for a lightweight engine. Those two words seemed a contradiction in terms.

"We may have to build one ourselves," Orv said.

I exhaled with a whistle. We were pretty good mechanics, but not of that sort. "That would take years. There's got to be something out there."

"Boys, I think you're getting ahead of yourselves." Katharine stopped cleaning long enough to look us both square in the eyes. "Remember all the crashed flying machines others have tried? Up and down, up and down. And why? Because they couldn't be controlled. You're barely controlling a kite with four ropes and sticks, and you're talking about riding on it? Powering it? What is the use of power if you can't precisely control the movement of the machine?"

"Valid point," Orville admitted.

She grabbed a model kite from the sideboard. "The thing that will set you apart from all the others is your control—when you want to go up, when to ease down." She nosed the model up and down in demonstration. "The roll"—she dipped the wings—"and left and right as you please, the yim and yaw or whatever you call it."

"Yaw." Orville said. "You're referring to the three-dimensional axes of control. We're well aware..."

"Right. When you can do that with ropes or levers or pedals for your feet, only then do you add power."

I shook my head. "We need power to get enough speed and lift for man and the machine."

Katharine threw her dish towel down on the table like a gauntlet. "You're not listening. Do you want your machine to wind up in splinters, and you as well? Or worse?"

"We always knew there was risk involved," Orv said gently.

"There's reasonable risk, and then there's foolish risk, like the others have done."

This brought Orv to his feet. "We aren't foolish. We know our glider and are not about to rush into anything. But we need power. That is the big divide. All else has been done, but we can't conquer the whims of the wind without it."

"Of course, you will have power when you are ready for it. But why did we just spend the last six months searching for a place with enough wind? To use its power before you are ready for your own. You need to learn how to fly. You need to do what the birds do, adjust your wings, adapt to gusts, make a turn into the wind like a sailboat."

"Control." Katharine was right, I admitted. "It's the key. We need to develop much more control, or we'll be the same laughingstocks as all the others."

KATHARINE

I made it clear right from the beginning that I would not be the seamstress of their wings. The design for the glider had yards and yards of fabric stretched over a wooden stick frame. Someone had to pull it tight around the frame and machine stitch it into place.

Just the sound of the treadle, the *chug*, *chug* of the needle head as it bobbed up and down, along with the smells of lubrication oil and cloth, caused a wave of nausea to rise in me.

My mother had taught me how to sew, or tried to at least, on the same machine Will had dragged down from the attic. Sick with consumption for most of the time I remembered her, she would pause to wipe her mouth after coughing fits, which somehow the sewing seemed to worsen. I would try to follow her direction, but inevitably a hornet's nest of thread would erupt from the machine, and she'd gently push me away as she pulled it all apart once again.

When she passed, with me not quite fifteen, I assumed her duties of cooking and cleaning and other household duties. But the Bishop carried the sewing machine up to the attic, where it had remained, shrouded in a drop cloth and all but forgotten.

Since I couldn't completely shirk my duty as a partner for this important piece of the project, I offered to research and obtain the fabric.

"We want it smooth, to reduce wind friction." Orv advised.

"Most importantly, it needs to be affordable. We'll need a lot of it." Wilbur added.

I showed them catalogs that featured the latest fashions made from several companies' fabrics. "This company has cotton, linen, and silk."

Orv whistled, pointing at an overly frilly dress with lace cuffs and flowery print.

"I don't care if it has red polka dots and big yellow daisies. It needs to be strong, smooth, cheap, and available in hundred-yard bolts," Will said.

While I rather liked the idea of polka-dotted wings, they wouldn't help our project to be taken seriously. I sent for catalogs and samples from every large fabric maker in the United States, France, and Germany. I considered the fine fabrics of Asia, but the shipping time was far too long and my language barrier too steep. With my knowledge of Greek, Latin, and some French, I could muddle through communications from Europe.

I settled on a white muslin with a sateen finish from France. It was surprisingly affordable, delightfully smooth, and passed my strength tests, which were mainly throwing rocks at it and rubbing it with sandpaper. The former test raised some amused glances from neighbors, as I took aim at what must have appeared to be bedsheets on my clothesline. Soon Orville joined me with a bucket of red paint and proceeded to draw a target and a few polka dots on the cloth. He then threw a few rocks.

"There. Now you don't look quite so crazy." Satisfied, he left me to my business.

⁂

I helped the boys stretch the fabric over the long wooden frame for the kite. After several failed attempts to keep the fabric tight, I remembered something my mother had taught me: to create some stretch and support in the bodice of a dress, one should sew it on the bias, that is, at a diagonal from the direction of the weave.

"Let's try this," I said, as I turned the fabric forty-five degrees.

Orv resisted. "That'll waste fabric. The box is a rectangle, the fabric…"

"Hush," I admonished. I pulled the fabric tight, and almost by magic it clung to the top of the frame and easily wrapped around the bottom for a perfect fit.

"Oh," Orv said rather sheepishly. "Thank you."

"No, thank Mama."

WILBUR

After much trial and error with kites and gliders, we were ready to build a glider large enough for one of us to ride. Two wings would be attached with vertical struts, and diagonal wire ropes would reinforce the connections. The plan called for the pilot to climb through an opening in the center of the lower of two wings, grasp the crossbars and run like the dickens while two other people would run alongside, pulling on opposite sides of the lower wing.

Once aloft, the pilot would lift his legs and lie on his stomach across the bottom wing to minimize drag. According to a formula used by Lilienthal and others, in a fifteen mile-per-hour wind, we needed wings of approximately eighteen by five feet to lift the glider and its pilot.

Having witnessed each kite's propensity to climb, controlled only by our strong pull on the guide ropes, Katharine was concerned. I had come into her room to borrow her trunk and valise for my trip to Kitty Hawk, but before she would turn her luggage over, she made me swear on Jesus's name that I would stay close to the ground.

"Not to worry, Sterchens. With my weight, the glider will hardly have the lift to clear the mounds of sand."

"I've heard you and Orv calculating. It all depends on wind speed."

"We'll thoroughly test the machine before I climb on it. And we'll measure the wind and have ropes attached to each wing."

Katharine picked up her valise, but instead of handing it over, she plopped on her bed with it in her lap. "I just wish I could go with you. I have an instinct about these things."

"And we have science and math." I sat down next to her. "We are not risk-takers, at least not in the physical safety sense. We would be doing no service to science and aviation if we were to injure ourselves—or worse. You must have faith."

KITTY HAWK, NORTH CAROLINA

Orv and I had corresponded with Bill Tate by mail soon after deciding to conduct our experiments at Kitty Hawk. He was enthusiastic and helpful, even arranged for a sailor to pick me up in Elizabeth City and transport me out to the island. After a harrowing overnight trip in a derelict boat, I was advised by deep-sea fishermen of a storm brewing. I spent my next two nights in a slightly sturdier wooden frame house with Tate and his family. He was a robust man, a fisherman, and also the local postmaster, grocer, weather forecaster, and, from what I could tell, mayor of those mostly uninhabited parts.

It was a cramped two days with Mr. and Mrs. Tate and their sweet little girls. The girls loved my card tricks, and I taught them how to play cat's cradle with a length of string. A pang of regret filtered through me as I realized the opportunity to have my own children was fading. It hadn't been a conscious decision, but my pact with my siblings and our single-minded goal had thus far precluded marriage.

Not wanting to overstay my welcome, once the storm abated, I asked Tate to help me carry and drag my gear to a sheltered spot near the beach. I respectfully declined the offer of his sailor friend to transport Orville when he arrived. Boatbuilding isn't my area of expertise, but after bailing with a bucket during the entire eleven-mile overnight trip, I believed even I could design something more seaworthy.

I hurriedly set up my small pup tent and dove inside it to help keep it in place. The howling wind had risen to a screech, and lying on the damp floor, I felt sand and rocks slipping under me. The tent was on the move, its canvas flapping violently in protest. The rain made its way through the fabric, rivulets running down the sides and water collecting in growing puddles.

If the still-crated glider and I survived the night, it would be just another step in our long journey toward the dream Katharine, Orv, and I would now no sooner give up than cut off our own arms. We needed to control the wind, the air. We would build a machine and use it to fly wherever humans wanted to go.

ORVILLE

Will had the glider parts spread from one dune to the next, with nary a thought to organizing them in order of assembly. I had arrived just in time. Assembly had always been my job.

"Where's the spruce for the wing spars?" I held up some pieces of wood that were clearly inferior and too short.

Will screwed his face into a frown. "Couldn't find any. Those are the longest I could get. We'll have to make the wings a bit shorter. I've already started resewing the fabric."

"Doggone it, Wilbur. We have to recalculate everything."

Will snatched the wood and set it back in place, while steam mounted in me. Weeks wasted. At least the white sateen cloth Katharine had ordered from France seemed just as sturdy as she had claimed after her rock-throwing experiments.

Wilbur did the oddest motion; it must have been something he read in a book. He made a fist with his right hand, chest high, and covered it with his left palm. He bowed slightly and said, "Your Highness arrived on the fairest of days and shouldn't complain about a little brain work. I nearly died getting here to set it all up."

There was no point arguing with Will. His little drama was his way of pulling rank. I would have done things differently, but he was the older brother and the boss. At least when Katharine wasn't around.

Will had constructed a tent in the dunes a few hundred yards from the water. We came here for the winds and Greek god Zephyr did not disappoint. I helped double and triple reinforce the tie-downs. Later, we'd build something sturdier, but this would serve for now. We had just enough space for our sleeping quarters, a small cooking area, and the rest of the space reserved for glider construction.

Once we had our supplies and a system in place, putting the glider together went swiftly. We had cut and presewn as much of the wings and forward rudder as possible, but they had to be hand-stitched in place once the struts were slid into their fabric pockets, and one end needed to be shortened on-site. Next came the wait for the perfect time to launch. Meanwhile, we trekked to the tiny fishing village to gather food and other supplies.

While there, we met a group of sturdy, bearded men who manned the lifesaving station, a small white clapboard building a few miles away. They were curious about us, and we explained our mission. Looking at their heft, it reminded me that our machines would grow bigger, heavier, and more difficult to move around as we progressed in our experiments. It would behoove us to remain in their good graces.

One of the men, John Daniels, told stories of rescuing crewmen from shipwrecks. "They call us surfmen," he said, "because we're always plucking sailors out of the surf."

With the aid of Daniels and Tate, we dragged the redesigned glider up a dune. Four ropes were attached to the four leading edges of the two stacked wings. We each took a rope and lifted the glider as high as we could above our heads. As the wings captured the wind, Will, on the opposite side from me, gave the order to start letting out some rope. Then he shouted, "Go!" and we all ran down the dune into the wind, each with both hands tight upon a rope. It was even more exhilarating than I expected. I could feel the glider straining to fly higher.

Will yelled for us to stop running, and we let out rope until we held the knot at the end. Now came the tricky part, which Will and I had rehearsed with box kites back in Dayton. He took the left two ropes, and I took the right, so that each of us had one rope connected to the top and one to the bottom wing. We took turns pulling one rope forward, which resulted in twisting the wing. We did every combination and watched as the glider reacted with swoops and swerves. When it crashed, we quickly repaired broken bits and repeated the launch. With each flight, we learned more about how much to warp the wings to tilt the craft before it came crashing down.

My heart pounded with the exertion and the utter joy of controlling flight. As the late afternoon sky bloomed with pink clouds, we took a break, collapsing on the warm sand like piles of spent seaweed.

The next day, we added the front rudder with its own rope to move it up and down. It proved more difficult to maneuver than the wings. I took it apart and refashioned its joints several times until it operated smoothly.

"It's like a marionette," Tate said. Where he had seen a string puppet show in this remote place escaped me, but he wasn't wrong in his comparison.

Our little group met at the lifesaving station at the end of each day. We swapped stories and laughed at the mishaps. The men swigged beer and teased Will and me about our weak Yankee coffee. I was at ease with them as I was with family. I wondered if that was how it was with other people; the "camaraderie" I had always heard about, had but left me puzzled.

When we felt confident that we had reasonable control of the glider, Wilbur slipped through the bottom wing and we prepared to launch with him aboard. We had six helpers that day, each holding a control rope to ensure the glider didn't rise dangerously high. We needn't have worried, as even with a fairly stiff wind, he lifted barely three feet off the ground, nothing like Lilienthal had accomplished four years prior.

After a short flight of twenty or so feet, he came down, not even having enough time to pull his legs up onto the wing. With Wilbur's added weight, the glider didn't smoothly skate across the sand as it had before, and the craft bumped and jostled like a bronco, with Will scrambling to stay upright.

"That was a pretty ugly start," I said.

"No argument there." Even so, Will was all smiles as he brushed sand off his tweed trousers and shook it out of his shoes. "We've got some recalculating to do. We're not getting the lift we predicted."

KATHARINE

Once Will left for North Carolina, it was hard not to fret, so I busied myself helping Orv record inventory in the bicycle shop. Then once home, I dried meat and fruit for him to bring with him when he left for Kitty Hawk. Not a word had come from Will, and I imagined him lost in a swamp or, worse, sitting atop his crate as it floated out to sea. I had pushed and prodded my brothers down this path. If anything happened to them, it would be my fault.

Orv left a few weeks after Wilbur, and with the Bishop also out of town, I could save hours usually spent cooking and cleaning. I wrote to my dear friends Harry and Isabel Haskell in Kansas City and updated them on our latest project.

Will had left a list of chores to keep me "busy and out of trouble," as if I might run out and rob a bank. He had contacted Mr. Chanute to inquire where he had obtained strong wire to support the two wings.

A fellow bridge builder, was his reply. *John Roebling, God rest his soul, invented wire rope. You'll find none better.*

I wrote to John A. Roebling and Sons in New Jersey to inquire as to the price and strength of their wire: *Would twenty-gauge wire be strong enough to hold together two wings at fifty miles per hour?* I promptly scratched it out. This would make no sense to them. I decided if their wire was strong enough to hold up the Brooklyn Bridge, it would be strong enough for our purposes, and knowing my brothers, they had specified the exact gauge they needed for strength without unnecessary weight.

Finally finished with all the tasks that kept my men functioning, I turned to my own project, campaigning for women's right to vote. Harry and other friends from my Oberlin College days were organizing rallies across the country ahead of state elections. It was time to have one in Dayton.

I did love a party, so I started a list of guests and refreshments. Wine, of course. What was the cocktail in fashion? I must run over to McKeever's pub to find out. The Bishop and the boys wouldn't touch the stuff, but I loved research. After all, organizing a rally needed not be a dull affair.

One last task: a letter to Will at Kitty Hawk, care of Mr. Tate. Once again, I begged Will to let me join him and Orv. His claims of it being no place for a woman, too harsh, or having possible snakes and other creatures seemed rather empty. What he really wanted was for me to stay back and keep the bicycle shop running. They needed the income while they poured heart, soul, and wallet into our flying passion.

I may not have had Orv's mechanical abilities, nor Will's knowledge of physics and math. But I was darn good at getting the supplies we needed and sweet-talking people into helping us. I chewed my pen in frustration, then crumpled the letter I couldn't finish. As much as it went against every fiber in my being, I had to abide by Will's decision; our little triumvirate required only one head.

Dayton was booming with new companies moving in by the day. Art shows and museums abounded, and the electric streetcar could whisk one away to all ends of a town rapidly becoming an important city. Our little house on the west side of the river was getting so encroached upon that I could stick my hand out a window and almost touch the house next door.

I decided to ride my bicycle to test a route for a rally for suffrage, down West Third Street to the Miami River, then followed along it. Development now crept further and further up and down the river, the once pure-green hills above it now studded with five-story buildings. Church steeples still dominated the view skyward, but hotels and office buildings climbed higher each year. At the foot of the Main Street Bridge, the towering stone facade of Steele High School presided over the river like a castle.

The city bustled with streetcars running down the wide streets, people hurrying to banks and shops and offices. I could feel the energy of progress and had plenty to keep me occupied between teaching at Steele, running the household, and keeping the bicycle shop afloat, but still, something was missing.

Or someone, as the case might be. At twenty-six years of age, my chances for a romantic relationship and marriage were rapidly fading. And as Orv and Wilbur had shown no interest in marriage, it seemed the three of us were destined to grow to be old coots together.

As I passed a street vendor with a cart laden with all sorts of colorful vegetables, I decided to try to change things. I didn't need to organize a rally just yet, but I could still host a grand party. The boys would soon be back from North Carolina and I'd invite some chums from Steele and Oberlin to welcome them. Orv seemed to be the crush of my friend Agnes, and I suspected he felt likewise but was too shy to do anything about it. I'd decorate with flowers and lots of candles, and perhaps have a violinist stroll about. Then my more practical self intervened, and I decided that some simple libations and party sandwiches would suffice. It would be a nice welcome home for the boys.

On a glorious day in late October, a dozen or so of my friends piled into our modest home on Hawthorn Street. They mostly sat on the floor, there not being enough room on the davenport and chairs. We laughed and played parlor games. Will told stories about his adventures bailing water out of a leaking boat on the way to Kitty Hawk, while the Bishop held court with tales from his trips out west. It lifted my heart when he added, "but none of that matters as much was what each of my children are doing. They are my most important flock, and my time is best served by encouraging their efforts."

I welcomed more guests and found them a group to join in the crowded rooms. Carrie buzzed about, serving food and drinks.

Orv offered to hang a coat for guests as they arrived, then promptly disappeared to a quiet corner. Frances, a fellow teacher at Steele, tried to engage him in conversation, but soon gave up. She and I liked to take long walks after school, and I knew her to be quite humorous and easy to talk to. One of her interests was in identifying trees, which Orv also liked. I tried to intervene in the awkward silence between them. "Frances can tell an oak from a maple from fifty feet away in the dead of winter. Can you do that, Orv?"

"Yes."

With that, I also gave up on Orv and Frances. But I had another trick up my sleeve. When Agnes arrived, I grabbed Orv by the elbow and steered him over to greet her. "Agnes, you remember my brother Orville, don't you?"

Golden curls surrounded her face, which lit up when she saw him. "Why yes, of course. We met when he visited you at Oberlin." She extended her hand to Orv. "So nice to see you again."

Orv's response, as he stared at his shoes as if expecting them transport him from his palpable misery, was something along the lines of "So...yes...that was...something." He scratched his ear. "It was...another time." Then he brightened; a concrete task had occurred to him. "Can I take your coat?"

I didn't need to look at him to know his neck would be flushing a bright pink. "Orv, why don't you show Agnes the kite out back?" He and Will had left the glider at Kitty Hawk, but kept a smaller model in the shed for quick experiments.

Orv looked up. "I wouldn't want to bore her with that."

I gave him a little shove toward Agnes, and she came to his rescue.

"Oh, but I'd love to see it. My dad used to take us kite flying in a park on Lake Erie."

With Orv and Agnes happily, if awkwardly, on their way, I turned to my other guests and refreshed their drinks. The group huddled around Will was teasing him that he had made up the stories he just told them.

Margaret challenged him, "I'll bet you can't even repeat the tall tale about putting up a tent in a typhoon."

"Oh, but I recorded our conversation on a phonograph," Will said. A tall tale indeed—we had no such capability. Will marched just out of view in the Sunday parlor, and pretended to play a recording. He imitated scratchy noises interspersed with indistinct dialogue. Clapping, cheers, and laughter served as response from his "recorded" audience, followed by the same from his real one.

I looked at my timepiece, hung from a ribbon about my neck. I had invited Charley, but he had not yet arrived. I decided to check on Agnes and Orv in the backyard, hoping against hope that Orv's utter shyness hadn't driven her away in tears of frustration.

But they were both still out there, walking around the six-foot-wide box kite, which was much like the Kitty Hawk glider but about one third the scale. Of course, I knew it was much more sophisticated than a box kite, with its maneuverable wings and specially designed rudder, but most people would see it as a mere child's toy.

A clean-shaven man in a newsboy cap had joined them. With a jolt, I realized it was Charley.

"Hello, Charley." I tried to keep the hurt out of my voice. "I didn't know you had arrived."

"Sorry, Sterchens. I came up the back way and got distracted."

His use of my family's pet name irritated me. He had not earned that right.

"Such a silly thing, but I prefer Katharine, or Kate, thank you."

Charley tipped his hat. "Sorry again, Kate. Won't you join us? Orville was just about to demonstrate his special wings."

Apparently Charley was far more interested in the kite than in me, and I had probably made matters worse, fussing over my name. "Oh, I have other guests undoubtedly searching the house for whiskey, so I should go see to them."

I scolded myself for being critical of Orv, who was too sweet and shy to attract a member of the opposite sex, while I was too nervy and blunt. Charley was pleasant and convenient, but that was all. Harry, the only man I had ever romantically loved, had been snapped up by someone else, which was completely my fault. And even if another perfect man came along, what would I have to offer him? I could never leave the Bishop or the boys. It was high time to forget about marriage and family of my own.

ORVILLE

Some people, like Katharine, are good at the social chitchat. And somehow knowing and, even more perplexing, caring about what others are thinking and feeling. I found all that small talk a tedious waste of time, but maybe that was because I was no good at it.

How to make conversation with people I didn't know, or barely knew, puzzled me. What if they were very aware of whatever I was telling them and I was boring them to tears or, worse yet, insulting them? When presented with a crowd of chatty people, how did one manage to angle in there and become part of the conversation without being rude?

My preference was to do something interesting to me. Any compatible sort of person would notice and ask questions or offer a helping hand. That seemed a more logical way for humans to interact. But I was also aware that I likely was missing some sense of these things that Katharine and others like her had, and Wilbur and I decidedly did not. Katharine seemed to think I needed a girlfriend, and I wouldn't have minded having one. I just didn't know how to make that happen, and it was all too exhausting to contemplate.

There was also the matter of my pact with Wilbur and Katharine. We had pledged to remain together, forsaking all others, and they were certainly holding up their end of the deal.

The pact had enabled me to do what I loved best, building flying machines. Ever since we got home from Kitty Hawk, Will and I had carefully planned our return, with a bigger and more maneuverable glider.

❧

Now that the time to return to Kitty Hawk had arrived, I checked my packing list at least three times. This time I would be traveling with Wilbur, so there would be no last-minute telegrams listing items forgotten or unplanned for. At least I wouldn't have to listen to his tales of hardship regarding his difficult trip. I knew how to build just about anything and was positive that if we had nothing but a vessel made of Swiss cheese and twine, I could get us back to the beach.

Katharine had left a few items in the humpback trunk she was lending me: notepaper for sending her "long detailed letters," enough dried meat, flour, and lard to last us to Christmas, and for some reason a length of pink ribbon. That was probably a mistake, but I kept it anyway.

Wilbur was packing his trunk in his room, which connected with mine, and we shouted our usual reminders and insults to each other. I was closing up the humpback trunk when the Bishop came in.

"You'll be off at first light, so I want to say our goodbyes now." He sounded solemn, not his usual enthusiastic self. His hair and beard were now quite flecked with gray. Having sons who insisted on such an erratic and dangerous occupation must have been difficult for him, a man whose most dangerous task had been riding a train through a snow-filled mountain pass. "I have these for you." He handed us each a pocket-sized journal with a brown leather cover.

"Thank you, Pop," Will and I said in unison.

"Read the first page, then see if you still wish to thank me."

I opened the journal, and there in his elegant script were the words, "I, Orville Wright, promise not to take unnecessary risks for myself or for my brother, and to use good judgment in all activities."

I looked at Will, and we exchanged a smile. His journal no doubt held the same promise.

Again in unison, we said, "Yes, Pop."

WILBUR

Our first Kitty Hawk glider was basically a box kite, much like the ones we flew on the Miami River in Dayton. But our new one featured sturdier wooden struts and fabric. The camber of the top and bottom wings was matched to the latest data from our friend Chanute at a twelve-to-one ratio. He had been most helpful in sharing his data, gained from both his own experiments and communicating with his colleagues in France. He even said he would meet us at our camp, although I thought such a visit premature.

The previous year, we had scouted out an area a few miles south of Kitty Hawk that had larger dunes and a wider beach. Known as Kill Devil Hills, it had the added advantage of being further from spying eyes, yet closer to the lifesaving station, but the disadvantage of having to carry our provisions and equipment that much further. Orv fashioned some carts with big tires that could negotiate the sand, which made the trek somewhat more bearable.

Soon after we arrived, we had a perfect morning to test out the new glider. With some helpers from the lifesaving station, we dragged it out closer to the water and found a suitable dune from which to launch. We then took turns holding it up and running forward, carrying the ropes.

When the wind caught it just right, the glider sailed along just beautifully. But with sudden gusts, which were frequent, its bearing quickly became uncontrollable.

"I've told you before." Orv inspected the frame after a crash from twenty feet above. "It needs some sort of a tail to balance it out, just like a kite does."

"I have to agree." My mind spun with how to construct and attach a tail with the supplies we had on hand.

Orv seemed to read my mind. "If we lengthen these struts in the middle, and extend the frame..."

"We'd have to somehow fashion the struts from several pieces of wood. These are the longest we have here. And I think we must reevaluate the aspect ratio."

"So do we take all the time-tested formulas and put them in the trash heap? Start all over again?" Orv looked like he was about to break a strut over his knee in frustration.

"No, we must consider them as a starting point. We've relied on the calculations of Lilienthal and Chanute, but they and others have hit a brick wall. We've got to figure out where they went wrong. For one thing, Chanute has never gone up in one of his machines himself. He admitted as much in his letter. That makes all the difference."

"Go up? We can barely keep the thing aloft without your weight on it."

"Let's try again when there's more wind. If it works, we'll load it with some sandbags to test for weight and go from there."

Over the next few days the winds picked up, and we got the kite up to a height of about twenty feet, then tried it with a hundred pounds of sandbags. It lifted a few feet, enough to convince us to try a ride.

It went without saying that I would be the one to ride. I was the faster runner and, as the older brother, considered myself in charge. There was no way I'd put Orv in that position. So we recruited young local boys to help and climbed an eighty-foot dune with the kite. I poked my upper body through a slit in the center of the bottom wing while Orv and the boys held ropes attached to both wings. We all took off running into a stiff wind, and before I reached the bottom of the dune, I was sailing above the sand. It occurred to me that the sharp struts were not the best landing surface, and I feared the craft would pitch itself into the sand, with me flying ahead headfirst.

But the wind let me down gently, and soon I was ready to try again. I quickly realized there was no point to leaving my legs dangling through the wing, as the little bit of extra speed we gained with my running on takeoff was offset by the drag they caused. Aloft again, with my legs already in place, I had more time to try to warp the wings with the bar at my feet. But the machine's nose reared up and down like a bronco. Just as in our experiments without weight, the forward elevator couldn't control the pitch.

I dragged myself up, and with Orv and the boys' help, we carried the machine back to our tent. Orv gave each of the boys a dime and a biscuit and sent them on their way.

ORVILLE

I could see Wilbur had no control. It was a miracle he landed as softly as he did that last time, with the kite going crossways to the wind. As it was, he had a few scrapes on his face and hands, so there would be some explaining to do when we went home. And we were going home, I was convinced.

Back in the tent, we went over each flight. Wind direction, height at start and finish, length, added weight, if any.

"Adding the tail seemed to help a bit, but warping the wings sometimes sent the glider opposite the direction it was supposed to go." Will poured the last of the coffee into his tin cup.

I rubbed my forehead. "That's not the only problem. I think the dimensions are off. We had better lift and control with last year's glider, before we used Chanute's numbers. It seems we've gotten what we came for. Unless you want to rebuild and start experiment-ing again?" I left all enthusiasm out of my voice. I was ready to go home.

Will closed the notebook in which he had faithfully recorded our failure. "Man is going to fly aeroplanes someday. But it might not be in our lifetime." He sounded even more dejected than I did. "What do you say we hike to the lifesaving station, chat with the boys there? Share a story, and tell them we'll be back next year, God willing."

We hadn't made nearly the progress we had hoped for on this trip. Talking to people about it was about the last thing I wanted to do. But I'd do it for my brother.

WILBUR

A letter for you, from Chanute." Katharine greeted me with a large envelope.

Just to tease her, I tucked it into my suit jacket pocket. "What's for dinner?"

With a glare that could melt an iceberg, Katharine stood her ground.

"Okay, okay, I'll open it."

A letter from a foremost expert in aeronautics was of course in itself reason for celebration. But this one was different.

"He wants me to speak to his aeronautical club."

Katharine's eyes widened. "You don't say!" She took the letter, read it for herself, then gave me an exuberant hug. "What an honor. You must do it, of course. What kinds of things would you speak about?"

"The results of our experiments, of course. Our analysis and theories, advancing current knowledge, my ideas of wing warping to cause differential drag. But I'm no speaker, especially to an audience of that magnitude. I will have to turn him down."

"Nonsense. You're an excellent presenter. I've witnessed that firsthand in all our parlor debates."

"Parlor debates are hardly a comparison."

"How so? You'll be presenting your information in a clear, convincing way. The only difference is the size of the audience. And how does that matter? You've gone on and on about your contributions to science. It seems you now have the opportunity, and I daresay the obligation, to share your discoveries, with some limitations, of course."

"I do owe a debt to Chanute and others. Science is a cooperative venture."

"The question becomes, how much should you share?"

We headed to the dining room, where the Bishop and Orville were already seated. Katharine filled them in on the development.

"Congratulations, Brother. And may I say better you than me," Orv said.

I pulled my datebook from my pocket. "The timeline is short. I would need to be in Chicago for the presentation next month. That gives us only a few weeks to prepare."

Orv helped himself to a spoonful of succotash. "I'll help. I can start tabulating numbers and writing out descriptions of the wing warping and our new formulas for lift and aspect ratios."

He passed the bowl of mixed corn, tinned tomatoes, and lima beans to me. I'm not sure why Katharine insisted on making it, other than it was "good for us." I avoided as many of the lima beans as I could. "That's going to be a delicate subject. I don't want to come out of the box refuting all that Chanute has taught us. It would embarrass him in front of his followers."

Katharine filled our water glasses. "It sounds like you've made up your mind to do the speech. We'll help you work out those details."

It occurred to me that she hardly sat down with us at meals, always fussing. I got up to pull out her chair for her. "Sit, Sterchens. Enough waiting on us."

The Bishop harrumphed. "Boys, you're putting the cart in front of the horse."

All eyes turned to him. Katharine asked, "How so?"

"You've made significant progress in the field, spent many months, years actually, and your own funds developing and testing theories. Now you must protect that investment."

"Everything we've done is in the spirit of science and cooperation. Now it's our turn to contribute. I don't see how we can refuse."

"There's a difference between people like Langley, a government employee, and Lilienthal, God rest his soul, who was a hobbyist, working together toward a goal. This is to be your livelihood, as I understand it."

Katharine bit her lips. I knew she would be smack in the middle of this. The debate moderator was a familiar role. "Quite so, Pop. We do have a financial agreement of sorts within the family. You are not independently financed or an employee, Will. We must consider how your work will be eventually compensated."

It was Orv's turn. "I've already been putting diagrams and descriptions together for a patent application. But we're still far from having the exact data we need."

"You need a minimum of a patent pending on any information you share with this group, no matter their intentions or credentials," the Bishop said.

Bile rose in my throat. I didn't like the idea of speaking in the first place, and now they were throttling my speech with things I couldn't say. "Well then, perhaps we put this off. By next year we should be able to give a much more interesting talk."

"No, you don't," Katharine said. "You don't turn down an invitation like this. It might not come again next year. These are the people with profound interest in what you're doing, and you may very well need their help in the future. Many others are trying to do the same thing, and they will simply find someone else to support."

"I think she's right," Orv said. "It may be a good thing that we need to dance around Chanute's numbers. We don't have to give away too much."

KATHARINE

With only weeks to prepare, working on Will's speech became the ritual each evening after dinner. Orv provided diagrams, Will explained them, and I put them into words that made sense to me, presuming they would also be understood by his audience.

We took turns reading the speech out aloud, so Will could listen and determine what needed to be emphasized or eliminated. I wasn't enamored of his title, "Some Aeronautical Experiments," but since the boys were happy with it, I didn't suggest something livelier.

Will remained less than enthused about it all. He, the Bishop, Orv, and I gathered in the front parlor one Sunday afternoon. Will stood and gave his presentation, sounding clear, concise, and knowledgeable. We clapped in an honest reaction, but Will groaned and shook his head.

I tried to raise his spirits. "That was outstanding. How do you think you'll do at the meeting?"

"Pathetic," was his response.

From the glowing letters that came later from Chanute and others in the audience, Will's presentation was very well received. I clipped several references to it from articles in magazines and newspapers and secured them in my ever-thickening scrapbook. My brothers were making the name Wright associated with more than bicycles. It was now mentioned with the likes of our heroes.

KATHARINE

I could hardly think of anything grayer than a January after-noon in Dayton. The sky was gray, the dirty snow a mixture of grayish-white to charcoal; the trees laced against the sky were yet another tone of the same dismal color. But Orv had come to my rescue.

Somehow sensing my doldrums, for I never would have openly complained, he was waiting outside my room at the top of the stairs when I arrived home from work that afternoon, a grin on his face and white spatters on his brown pants.

"What on earth are you up to, Little Brother?" I chided him, although his appearance and the smell of paste hinted at work on the walls.

He led me into to my room, where he announced, "I've been bringing the sunshine back in." He had taken upon himself to paper my bedroom in a happy light-yellow flower print, perhaps inspired by a quilt our mother had made that I had recently claimed from the attic. My heart melted at what he had done smack in the middle of the worst month of the year.

He was so proud of his work, explaining how he had carefully shielded the wooden doors and trim, and not a drop of paste had been spilled on my rug or furniture.

"You aren't planning to give me a 'rest cure,' are you?" I teased.

"A what?"

Apparently Orv didn't connect the yellow wallpaper with the short story by Charlotte Perkins Gilman we had read and discussed a few months back. It was a sad story and I decided not to expound on it. After all, Orv was doing precisely the opposite of the story's antagonist.

"Why then, when I would never ask this of you?" I asked.

"Precisely because you never would ask. And to celebrate your upcoming escape from bondage." He pulled a folded paper from his pocket.

I took the paper from his splattered hand. It was the simple contract we had all signed four years prior, when I agreed to work for the family for four years following college graduation. "Well, a deal is a deal."

Orv nodded solemnly, bit his lips. "But I'm afraid our need for your help has only grown."

"We have another deal, don't you remember?"

"Oh?"

"I think our three-way pact supersedes this." I held up the paper and made a show of tearing it in two.

"No matter how long it takes?" Orv's eyes glistened.

"No matter how long it takes, Little Brother."

"Well then, my time has not been wasted."

He lit the kerosene lamp and the room was bathed in warm golden light. Delicate white and yellow stripes flowed from the ceiling to the floor, each with an abundance of pale-yellow roses and white flowers to match. The walls seemed lit from within, and Mother's quilt was the centerpiece of the coziest space I could imagine. Yes, sometimes I longed for another life, with a husband and children and goals of my own. But for now, I was happy, loved, and needed.

ORVILLE

Will and I spread diagrams of the 1900 and 1901 kites across a big oak table in the second-floor office above the bicycle shop, comparing each variation. After the disappointing performance of last summer's machine, we needed to reexamine all the theories and equations we had been using.

"We've got to find a better way to control the wing warping. It works on paper, but I was never able to control it and the elevator at the same time," Will said.

I studied the drawing, imagining how each part looked on the glider. Which parts moved, which were stationary. "What if we changed the elevator control to a paddle over here, and we move the wing-warping control to your other hand?"

Will was a step ahead of me. "No, I don't think so." He slid the drawing back to himself and pointed to a big blob next to the stick figure representing the pilot. "Don't forget the engine. The pilot will need a hand to control engine speed, and whatever else. What if he gets a bug in his eye?"

"Then a foot pedal?"

"Something better. More like riding a bike."

"Slide your body? But Lilienthal tried that, and it wound up killing him. It's too hard to control precisely."

"Not forward and back like Lilienthal did, and we did when we were first balancing the glider." He stood up and swung his hips side to side as if doing an odd dance.

I laughed. "I saw hula girls doing that in a show once."

"Get your mind off the girls and think about it." He put his hands on his hips. "Some sort of cradle to rest your hips on, attached to wires that attach to the wing struts."

"I like it."

Will preferred his paper and diagrams, but I liked to work with objects. I gathered some wood and pulleys and wire and arranged them in several configurations, watching for stress points and estimating the materials I would need to build it.

My stomached rumbled, as we hadn't stopped for lunch. For many minutes the only other sound was the steady *tap tap tap* of the chalk as Will scrawled numbers and diagrams on our blackboard.

"Should we go back to the 1900 wing proportions, but add the tail and elevator?" he asked.

I grinned. "I have a surprise for you." I walked over to the corner, where my latest creation lay under a tarp. "While you were off giving speeches about grand successes, I was trying to figure out our failures." I pulled off the tarp to reveal a long wooden box up on four legs, which set it at the perfect waist height for comfortable experiments.

Will circled around the box, which was about six feet long and two feet high and across. "Well, it's too small to be a coffin, except for maybe a snake," he teased. Then he looked at the fan and its cone-shaped housing at one end, and the glass window on the top.

A crank I had purchased from a motorcar dealer worked through several gears to operate the fan, and Will gave it a spin. "This is a wind tunnel. Like the Russians made."

We both had read an article with a photograph of a similar machine.

I felt like a kid with a brand-new toy. "How else to determine if the accumulated data is accurate? We can test wing shapes, rudders, aspect ratios, you name it. Then we can better use our time at the beach with validated numbers."

Will cranked the handle and spun the fan as fast as it would go. "Only limited by our own endurance."

He wasn't as enthused as I thought he would be. "I've got an answer to that. We'll purchase a small engine, like the one running the belts downstairs." Long serpentine belts powered by a gasoline engine ran a table saw, lathe, and other equipment in the back of the shop. "Or maybe add a loop and run it off the engine we already have." I gave the handle a spin. Will was right. We would need to do hundreds of trials and our arms would soon tire. "Or maybe we'll get connected to the electric. Wouldn't that be something?"

"It would, but that's not something we can control."

Many parts of Dayton were already electrified. But convincing the Bishop to pay the fee when it reached us would be more of a challenge than convincing the power companies to cross the river.

Will clapped his hands, giving me a startle. "Well then, what are we waiting for? Let's make some models to fly in your little coffin."

KATHARINE

I arrived home from school to find Orville crouched on the sitting room floor, surrounded by an assortment of boxes, buckets, pieces of broken pottery, and clumps of twisted wire. I picked up a sharp-looking piece of metal and banged it against a crate for attention.

Orv looked up at me with a sheepish grin spread across his face. "Don't worry, I'll have all this cleaned up in a jiffy."

"What's wrong with the workspace we're renting?" If I didn't put limits on the boys, they would build flying machines in the Sunday parlor.

"Wilbur's working on a large bicycle order and the workshop is full. We need to find more space. In the meantime, you don't really mind, do you?"

He put on his most earnest face, knowing it was hard to for me to resist.

I rolled my eyes and huffed an exaggerated sigh. "Do I really have a choice?" I examined the shards of what was once a flowerpot that Orv had no doubt rescued from the trash bin. "So what are you building here?"

"Look at this." He handed me a journal article. "There's been progress made using wind tunnels. I don't know why we didn't think of it before. I've built a small one in the shop. Now I'm figuring out how to make things to test in it."

The article described recreating wind conditions in a box with a strong fan, then hanging models by strings inside the boxes to see how they moved.

"We're going to improve on the idea, of course. I'll be able to slowly raise and lower wind speed and have an anemometer to measure it, and a way to change its direction. And I'll be testing each part, not a whole model, because I'm looking at shapes and dimensions and ratios and such."

My mind muddled with confusion, trying to picture his contraption. "What's an anemometer?"

"Oh I wish I brought it home to show you. It's like a tiny windmill with a gauge that counts the rotations. It measures wind speed."

Now I had another contraption to envision. "Can I help with something?" Anything I could do to get this mess out of the house would have been lovely. How nice it would be to entertain guests or even have a quiet evening reading in the sitting room.

Orv brightened. "You can help me find the best materials to work with. I've got this lump of modeling clay. If you could work with it, soften it up, then mold it into these exact shapes and dimensions"—he flipped through some papers until he found one with labeled diagrams—"that will be most helpful."

I grabbed the clay, the diagrams, and a ruler and headed to the kitchen. "Fine, but I'm not sitting on the floor like a first grader."

The next day, true to his word, Orv had moved the wind tunnel model materials out of the sitting room by the time I returned from work. I set about making supper, but couldn't stop thinking of the experiment and how my little clay shapes were performing. I turned the heat low under my pot of chicken and dumplings, changed into a dress that wouldn't be ruined in the greasy workroom, and headed for the bicycle shop.

The shop itself had closed for the day, so I looked for Will and Orv in the back. I could hear them shouting at each other through the door to their upstairs office. Excited shouts, not angry ones. I ran up the steps to see what the fuss was about.

The wind tunnel was a large box, about the size of three milk crates end to end. It had a glass window on top, and they were taking turns peering through it.

"This one! This is it, Orv! Flies like an eagle." Will took his turn cranking a handle round and round, and the noise from a hidden fan grew louder. I joined Orv looking in the window on top of the box. A piece of metal sat on a hinge; as Will cranked faster, it began to lift from its perch, just like a bird. A piece of wire kept it from sailing backward. If the contraption had been one-fourth the size, it might have been an interesting child's toy. But I knew from their exuberance that this was much more. Gone were the scowls and moodiness they had brought home from Kitty Hawk, their demeanor as stinky and stiff as their salty, fishy clothes. Their excitement now was contagious, and I watched with a gladdened heart as they tried one model after another.

Orville, pencil in hand, made notes in a bound journal. "Are you sure? That's an aspect ratio of 6.7 rather than the 3.4 that Lilienthal and all the others suggest."

"The others are just blindly following along, just like we were. Those numbers are theoretical." Will tapped his temple. "And how do we know if his measurements were recorded and translated properly?"

Orv finally acknowledged my presence. "Sterchens, you're just in time for an exciting development." He held up several rectangles made of sheet metal.

I hid my disappointment that my clay creations weren't responsible for the discovery. "Wonderful. Now explain in plain English."

"Our friend Chanute, and pretty much all the experimenters, are using wings of this shape." Orv held up a piece of metal about a foot across and three or four inches wide. "But in the wind tunnel, we've found this to work better." He held up a longer, narrower piece. "The ratio of the length divided by the width is called the aspect ratio, and it's a critical factor in lift."

"Why is that? And how does that tiny model stand in for a real wing?"

Will answered, "Let's say we have a constant—an amount of weight we know we need to lift. That amount translates to a number of square feet of wing surface we must have at a given speed. Let's say our calculations tell us we need twelve square feet of fabric and frame. Should we make the frame twelve feet long and one foot wide? Six by two? Three by four?"

"My guess would be somewhere in the middle. Not too long, not too square." It was beginning to make sense to me.

"Right you are," Will said. "We experimented with different configurations, as everyone has suspected there's an optimal aspect ratio for lifting the most weight per square foot."

Orv jumped in. "And it's different from what Chanute and others have proposed. We trialed it at different scales, with different materials, from your little clay pieces to the biggest hunk of metal we could fit. And even at multiple wind speeds, the results are the same." Orv was fairly vibrating with excitement. "This explains why we didn't get the lift we expected from our last glider."

"Well, that is exciting." Their jovial faces lifted my heart, as did knowing my little art project had had some use after all.

"Tomorrow"—Will neatly arranged the test objects in a cabinet—"we'll test different cambers. I have a feeling the estimations were off for that as well."

I remembered that camber was the arc of the wing, with the top rounded and the bottom flattened. I foresaw another night of clay getting under my fingernails. Surprisingly, the thought of it didn't annoy me. It felt good to be of use.

Orv must have read my mind. "Don't worry, we'll use the clay models you've already made to bend metal to the proper shapes."

"Will you be taking the wind tunnel with you to Kitty Hawk next summer?" I flipped the pages on the wall calendar. "Because maybe making models is something I could work on. Right on the spot, when you want to change something, you don't have to risk your machine to test it. My school term ends—"

Will cut in. "Oh, no need to worry about that. We don't have time or space for that kind of testing there."

"Well, I'll do all the cooking and cleaning of course. But I'd also like to help with something a little more interesting."

Will and Orv exchanged awkward glances.

"What?" I had a sinking feeling. "What are you not telling me?"

Orv came up to me, gave me a demeaning pat on the shoulder. "You've been so much help already. We don't want to ask more. You deserve a summer off to do the things you want to do, not catering to your big brothers."

"Since when?" I was getting irrationally angry. His words were polite, considerate, but underneath them was a message I didn't want to hear. "We made a pact. We're in this together. I've already stayed back the last two summers."

Now it was Will's turn to soothe his little sister. "Sterchens, it's not that we don't want you there. But the conditions are not anywhere close to being fit for a lady. I barely survived that first summer, and this summer was only slightly better. The heat, the bugs, the rain, the constant wind. We sleep up in rafters, and there's no privacy. You would have to stay with a local, which is hardly better, or on the mainland, where you'd spend most of your time getting back and forth. It's just not possible."

"But this is the time. I know it. You'll finally create a controllable flying machine."

Orv flipped through the calendar, shook his head. "We're trying our hardest, but I don't think it will happen this summer." He looked over at Will. I could tell a compromise was in the making. "But how about this: if we are getting close, we'll send a telegram in time for you to come out."

Knowing I would lose this battle, I forced a smile. "Well, I guess it might be nice to have some peace and quiet around the house, have my friends over without climbing over the intimate parts of a flying machine." They were offering a compromise, but it still felt like I was being excluded. So much for our pact.

꒰ఎ

As if it would make up for not being invited to the beach, Orv came to me with a shopping list. He found me in the shed behind the house, where I was doing my most distasteful task: laundry. I filled the old wooden barrel with cistern water and strapped on the metal agitator that Mother and Orv had fashioned.

"Oh, I see you're busy." Nonetheless, Orv thrust a sheet of paper at me.

I blew a wisp of hair from my face. "Maybe while you're experimenting with shards of metal, you could invent a better clothes-washing machine."

Orv laughed.

"I'm not joking. Well, what is it?" I reached out a soapy hand for the note.

"A list of bits and pieces we need. Most importantly, the nice fabric you bought—from France? We need more. A lot more. We thought we had about thirty square yards left, but we're down to about ten."

I looked over the list—heavy linen rope, tacks, fasteners, most of which I could get at Hamburger's Hardware or Rike's downtown. I wouldn't mind the trip; it was always fun to look at the newest fashions. "When do you need it by?"

"Next week."

I raised my eyebrows. "It took three months to get the fabric the last time."

"Three months?" Orville scratched his forehead. "That just won't do. We need to cut the pattern, sew the strips together, sew the pockets for the ribs, punch the holes…all done by June. Are you sure you can't get us something by next week?"

"Not from France I can't. I'll have to order it locally."

"You're a saint," Orville said.

"In the meantime, why don't you start on the rudder with the material on hand?" I slopped a bedsheet into the rinse bucket.

His mission done, he turned back to the house, already focusing on his next task.

The next day I rode my bicycle to the boys' favorite hardware store, just a block away from the bike shop, to get the lines and fasteners. Then I pedaled over to Rike's Dry Goods on Fourth and Main, where I took my time sighing over the window display of Easter hats. I had never worn anything that fancy, but it was fun to imagine strolling down the street in a dress showing a bit of ankle, with feathers popping out from head to toe.

Upstairs in the fabric section, a store clerk with her hair in a tight silver bun came to assist me. I jingled the hardware in my day bag and said, "I'm going from bolts to bolts."

She cocked her head in confusion.

"Never mind." No sense explaining what all Wrights would find humorous.

The clerk led me toward the bolts of plain but sturdy fabrics, but just for fun, I ran my fingers over a sumptuous white silk with red polka dots. I had a mind to bring home a sample, just to horrify the boys with the price, if not the design.

The sales clerk showed me a table laden with unbleached cotton muslin, the "Pride of the West." It wasn't quite as smooth as the French sateen, but seemed every bit as strong, with just enough stretch along the bias. I bought a sample for testing and placed an order for the required yardage.

The shoe department was just across the aisle. Did I dare arrive home with a new pair to dance in? It would be a long summer indeed if I didn't find some amusement.

This wish was soon granted, when on my way home I witnessed something new. Wilbur was pedaling toward me, but not on an ordinary bicycle. This model had a horizontal third wheel spinning above the handlebars. He stopped to greet me and explain his invention.

"You see these flat pieces?" He indicated two pieces of metal sticking up from the spokes of the horizontal wheel. "I'm testing wing shapes. If the shape is such that it overcomes the drag, then the wheel won't spin."

"Naturally." I barely understood what he meant, but it was surely an amusing sight. "Well, enjoy your flying bicycle," I said in parting. "Maybe we can sell them in the shop." I laughed at the thought all the way home.

ORVILLE

KILL DEVIL HILLS

AUGUST 1902

K atharine hated the name of the place. "Can we please refer to it as Lucky Flyer Hills instead?" she proposed as she bid us goodbye at the train station. Prophetically named or not, Kill Devil Hills was even more isolated than Kitty Hawk, and all our gear had to be carted down the sandy shore. But the tall dunes and broader landing space made the trip worthwhile. In addition, the nearby lifesaving station, which resembled a tiny chapel, had become an important planning and gathering place. We reacquainted ourselves with a number of the men who worked at the station, along with several local boys. Bill Tate and John Daniels greeted us with enthusiasm and treats baked by their wives.

We arrived in late August, which is to say still hot as the dickens in North Carolina. I was thankful for the breeze off the ocean, which also helped keep the mosquitoes from attacking us. With the first breath of salt air, I felt at home. Even though we were far from Dayton, Kitty Hawk had become another part of me—the most fulfilling part. It seemed we worked all year in Ohio just for our few precious weeks on the sand dunes, building and testing, pushing the limits a little more each time. Trying and failing, adapting and making progress. Even as we picked up broken pieces of the machine and fought elements of nature, we were one with it. I couldn't imagine wanting to do anything else.

Our new glider wouldn't have looked much different to the untrained eye. But the men who gathered around as we assembled it could see otherwise. Bill Tate brought along his brother, Dan, who seemed every bit as strong, but not nearly as talkative.

"Look how skinny those wings are! They must be thirty feet wide," John Daniels said.

"And it's got a big tail." Tate added. "I told you it needed a bigger tail."

"Wings are now thirty-two by five feet," I said. "And the 'big tail' is a six-foot-tall vertical stabilizer."

Tate circled the glider. "She's gotta weigh over a hundred pounds. Sure she'll get airborne?"

John Daniels whistled his appreciation of the skids on the bottom, which would make for smoother landings. But of course smooth landings weren't his concern. "Good thing you added these things. Now we can just slide it up the dunes."

He had been a big helper the previous year, and I was happy to see him again. Not only was he fit and strong; he was observant. Several times he had found small cracks and other damage in need of repair that even sharp-eyed Will had missed. About thirty years old, he took time away from his wife and children to help us.

I wanted to give him something special to do as a reward. An idea came to me. I had brought a view camera to photograph our glider in flight. I could train John how to use it, which would enable me to concentrate on the flights.

In answer to the surfmen's observations, Will explained, "That's a change we hope will give us the best lift yet." He spread his arms across the chord, the front-to-back measurement of the wing. "We also decreased the curve from top to bottom."

Dan, the quiet one, asked, "Why do you think this is better?"

"I'm glad you asked. When we were back home, my brother here came up with a brilliant idea. We tested models against wind from a fan in an enclosed box."

They cheered and whistled with appreciation and my chest filled with pride. I wanted to demur and admit I hadn't invented the idea, but Will had led them to the front elevator to show them a few more changes.

Up until then, Wilbur had done all the flying. I knew he wanted to protect me, but I wanted my turn. So when we had set up camp and settled into our evening routine of cleaning and organizing the tools with cups of fresh coffee to sustain us, I brought up the subject. "How about tomorrow morning you give me some hands-on training on piloting? Of course, I know what all the controls do, but the specific things, like how much force to use, how fast things happen, whatever you can think of."

Will poured more coffee into our tin cups and I wrapped my hand around the cup, feeling its warmth. Coffee always tasted better in camp.

"I can do that, but I think we won't be ready to risk a new pilot for some weeks. I want to get full control, and we don't know how this glider is going to act."

"No, I think it's better if we take turns. There's quite a lot you can learn from watching from the ground, you know. Then we can put our heads together and come up with the right solution."

He jiggled his cup and stared at the ripples in his coffee.

I suspected he was thinking up excuses, so I pressed on: "I know there's some risk. And the farther and higher we go, the greater the risk. But we both must face that, and it's better I learn to fly, too, throughout the process."

"If anything should happen to you..." Will's voice faded to a whisper.

"If something should happen to *you*, then I'll be more prepared to carry on."

"I promised Katharine and the Bishop that I'd look out for you."

"And you are, and will be. This is not up for debate."

Will exhaled a long sigh of defeat. "I guess it's not fair for me to be having all the fun."

"Exactly." My face eased into a smile, even as the wind howled and pounded the tent canvas. "There's our friend Zephyr coming to call. Let's hope he doesn't let us down tomorrow."

With the machine built and a fine day for flying, we gathered the men and reviewed everyone's position and duties. I unboxed the camera, extended its bellows, and showed John the view plate and the shutter release. He had never used a camera before and took great care learning how to mount it on a tripod and adjust it.

We carried the glider to the top of a seventy-foot dune and laid a track in the sand for the skids to slide on. John prepared to take photographs, while Will and I checked every last wire and rib. Will climbed through the hole in the bottom wing, stretched out on his belly, fitted his hips into the cradle, and grabbed the control stick for the elevator.

At his signal, we released the restraining rope and ran down the dune. The machine began to lift before we even got halfway down the dune. Success! Will stayed up for over twenty seconds, long enough to briefly work the elevator to control the pitch both up and down.

We ran to greet him, and he was all smiles.

"Next, I want to test the wing warping. I'll try to get enough height to make a little turn toward the sea."

And so it went, each flight a little higher, a little longer.

August rolled into September; it was time to assert myself. After we dragged the machine from the shed back onto the dune, I climbed through the wing in the pilot's position. "Okay, Will, tell me everything you know."

WILBUR

It was inevitable the time would come that Orville would need to fly. In my mind, that time would be after we had control of turns with wing warping and pitch with the elevator. Not perfect control, of course, but enough that risk of crashes due to the design of these controllable elements was negligible.

But Orville wasn't having any of it, and I couldn't blame him. I could only play the boss in charge for so long. I poked through the slit in the bottom wing to join him as he lay flat on his stomach, his hips centered in the cradle. He worked the controls, with my hand guiding his. "Practice all you want, but it feels nothing like this when you're up there," I told him.

When, by the third week of September, we had established lift and a modicum of pitch and lateral control, I decided it was time to concede the pilot's position. We arrived at the beach on a Tuesday morning before any of our helpers. A straggly line of seaweed marked the last high tide and we had plenty of time and beach width available. The winds and waves were calm, a perfect opportunity for a piloting lesson. Orv was examining some seashells to add to our collection, but I picked up a slender piece of driftwood. I held it horizontally and called to Orv.

"Put your hands on this and pretend it's the control for the elevator."

Orv gave me a wary look.

"You wanted flight lessons, and this is important. You don't think I'm going to let you learn it all up there," I nodded toward the sky. "Now grab the middle of the stick and try to raise it, as if controlling the elevator. I'm going to provide resistance so you get used to how it feels."

He did as he was told and I varied the amount of resistance over several trials, even changing it during an up- or downswing. Perhaps I exaggerated a bit, but I wanted to do all I could to prepare him.

"Confound it, Will, you're not consistent."

"Precisely. You think the air is all the same, but it's not. You can't see them, but there are pockets of higher or lower density that will change how the elevator and the wings will react to the controls. You've got to quickly adapt if you want to stay aloft for more than ten seconds."

Next, I added two more sticks to represent the hip cradle. I made Orv sway back and forth while raising and lowering the piece of driftwood with his arms. We must have been quite the sight, luckily witnessed only by a few laughing seagulls.

"Okay, boss, am I ready to fly?" Orv said with a chuckle.

"No." He wasn't taking his lesson seriously enough. "Next, we'll do another dry run on the glider. I can't provide resistance on that, so some of this you'll just have to figure out yourself." The weight of responsibility hung around my neck like chains to an anchor. How could I explain the things I had learned that might just keep him alive? "There's no way to describe it, except that you must feel one with the machine." I took the driftwood from him. "You'll see what I'm talking about."

Our surfmen helpers arrived as Orv was lying on the glider, working the controls over and over upon my command. He was as ready as he ever would be, so we assumed positions and away we went, running down the dune. I let go of the wing as he lifted off, feeling both happy for him and concerned, as if he were my baby bird being pushed out of the nest. I had to accept both the bitter and the sweet; there was no going back from this moment.

He glided up to about twenty feet, his wings adjusting to keep him level. A perfect twenty-second flight. Then we alternated through the afternoon, each flight growing a little longer, or with a little more side-to-side movement. The beach was too narrow and our range too short to attempt more than slight turns, but Orv was pushing it more than I did.

The wind was dying down a bit, but we were still able to get enough lift for a straight flight. The prone position with my upper body lifted always caused strain in my neck and shoulders. This day the strain was more intense, but eased somewhat when I no longer had to watch Orv do his zigzags. A consistent problem was not being able to warp the wings enough to turn in a reliable manner. The few times I managed some directional change, it seemed to be a factor of the wind, rather than my steering.

By four o'clock, I was ready to quit for the day. The breezes tended to change direction as evening approached. But Orville insisted on one more flight. "You flew your last flight at nearly five yesterday," he argued.

We were all exhausted by that point, but knowing it was the last for the day, I got a surge of energy. So we all grabbed our assigned wing and trudged back up the dune, the glider's slide seeming to resist our efforts much more this time. We positioned her on the track, Orville climbed aboard, and we ran down the dune. But with the weaker wind and our tired legs, we were nearly to the bottom before Orville was able to lift the machine an inch. Though we kept running, the machine barely got off the track, then bumped along a little before nosing up. Too sharply, I thought.

I tried to yell to bring her down, but he was too far away. He rose, ten feet, twenty. No, he was pushing the elevator too far. His wings dangerously dipped to the right. "Level off!" I screamed.

But his correction sent the wings further in the wrong direction. Losing airspeed, the tail swung down and the machine tumbled, hitting the sand not in a graceful slide, but like a large branch falling from a tree.

The crack of the struts assaulted my ears as I ran to Orville. He was a bit cut up and limped when he tried to walk. But he was smiling, nonetheless. "I know what the problem is."

"I do too. You forced the elevator without enough airspeed."

He waved away my analysis. "Before that. We need the tail rudder to work in tandem with the wing warping. It's like the handlebars on the bicycle. It can't be stationary."

"Yes, we've talked about that before. But our hands are full with controlling the wing warping and the elevator. As Katharine says, 'A body can only do so much at a time.'"

Orv grinned. "And doesn't she also say that 'nothing can stop us when we put our heads together'?"

As we slid the machine back to the woodshed that served as a hangar, the tail rudder problem worked on my mind. When I thanked our helpers, I told them we wouldn't need them for a few days. Orv and I needed to do some redesigning.

ORVILLE

Wilbur sketched his ideas out on paper, while I tinkered with blocks of wood, metal, or anything else that was handy. I had a pile of toothpicks on our camp table and was building a model of a movable tail rudder, with a taped-together toothpick hinge and string to represent control wires.

"I think two smaller rudders rather than the one big one will be easier to control." Will was doing calculations in pencil, seeming to erase more than he wrote.

"Uh-huh." I was more concerned with where to control the thing. I thought of Will's observation that when you were flying, you were one with the machine, and how that was the same when bicycling; you used your whole body. And I thought of Katharine always saying she only had two hands when we asked for yet another thing while she was busy with something else.

"We have to control the elevator, the rudder, and two wings." I thought out loud. "And it's not a matter of having enough hands. We could use foot controls too."

Wilbur stopped his calculations. "A rudder with two pieces, but the same square footage of surface area. And yes, I presumed we would need to use a foot control. That's all we have left, unless you want to use your noggin."

"It's not only that. When I took my focus off the elevator to try to maximize the warping, even for the briefest of moments, I lost control of the pitch. The human mind can only do so many things at once, and there isn't time for corrections."

Will grabbed a long box and twisted it in the fashion that was now so familiar, representing the wing warping. "Control of the turn relies on two things: the direction of the warping and the angle of the rudder. What if we combine these two actions into one human action?"

"So when you increased the lift on one side, you would also be angling the rudder?" This was the revelation I needed. It was so obvious now. I arranged my toothpicks and the box to represent the wings and tail section controls, then stood a deck of cards on end to represent the rudder. "That's it, I think." Now we are down to two controls, quite manageable. "I'll add a cable from the rear rudder to the hip cradle."

Once my mind had the concept, it was an easy matter to devise a plan using the wood, metal, pulleys, and rope we had on hand to modify the glider. I couldn't wait to get started.

KATHARINE

DAYTON

SEPTEMBER 1902

The start of a new school year always brought with it a sense of growth and change. I looked forward to developing my new advanced writing course, and it was quieter without the sewing machine running at all hours. And without the boys around, I could entertain my Oberlin friends without stepping over mountains of muslin.

But I found myself rushing home to check the mail for news of their progress instead of developing my own life as I should. I sensed a breakthrough was imminent, and I stood ready in case I should be invited to travel out to see them. But that invitation never came. Oh, Charley got to go, and Mr. Chanute, and several of his worker bees. At one time the boys reported eight people sleeping in the rafters of their hangar. But not me.

Just as well, I scolded myself. While I moaned about the inconvenience of their experiments and the pressure on me and the Bishop to keep the bicycle shop running and the family solvent, I was intrigued by what they were trying to accomplish. I didn't need to see every little step with my own eyes.

Letters came nearly every day. Mostly from Orville, who liked to tease me about the hardships my students must be enduring from my tough lessons, but a few from Wilbur, who wrote more detail on the events of the day. I knew they had modified this year's glider to better control it in turns. Wilbur even thanked me for the idea of steering it like balancing on a bicycle.

There were a few days with no letters, and I grew worried. I put up gallons of fruit preserves and had pots of vegetables simmering each night, keeping myself distracted from imagining every awful thing that could be happening. I was just about to send a telegram inquiring as to their well-being when the Bishop presented me with the day's mail. He had already opened a letter from Will.

"Looks like a banner day for the Wright team! The new design is working. They've done hundreds of flights." He handed me the letter. "They wanted to stay a few more weeks, but it seems their best helpers have to go back to fishing." He laughed.

I read through the letter quickly. "They'll be home in no time!"

"That's right. On to the next challenge. Now that they've got control, they need power."

My excitement for their return was mixed with a sense of dread. The newspapers were full of stories of inventors all across the world who were trying to do the same thing my brothers were doing. And they were generally much better funded. If someone were to beat them to controlled powered flight, all the years of sacrifice and hard work would be wasted.

It was fine to have a goal, a dream. But what would be left for us if it didn't come about?

WILBUR

By late October we had done everything we had hoped to accomplish, and quite a bit more. The new steering mechanism was working well. Once we got used to using our bodies to lean into a turn, it came naturally. Orville had quickly caught up with me in flying skill and perhaps was an even more intuitive flyer. I tended to think my way through it: *left wing dipping three degrees, slide hips an inch to the right, climbing too fast in choppy winds, bring front rudder down five degrees,* and so forth. Whereas he seemed to anticipate the movements of the plane and correct things before they even happened.

We were taking apart the glider and packing the pieces into crates for the trip home, but our conversation was all about the miracle of flying and the sort of dance that existed between the pilot and the glider. "How do you know," I asked him, "when she's about to take a dip, for example?"

Orv was quiet for a moment. "After enough time up there, I have begun to sense changes in the air. Bumps that you can't see, but if you let your whole body become aware, it will tell you." He stepped away from the crates into the small open space. "Come and I'll show you." He held out his arms as if offering to dance. And that indeed was what he wanted to do.

I took his hand and he wrapped one arm across my back. I tried not to smirk at the silliness of it.

"You be the girl for a moment." He stepped forward and I stepped back. He swung me around, this way and that, faster and faster until I was quite dizzy and we both erupted in laughter.

"Okay, smart guy." I turned the dance into a wrestling match and quickly had him pinned on the ground.

"How do you know when I'm about to dip or turn?" he asked after I released him.

My mind went back to being on the glider. The slight feeling of weightlessness before a dip, a sense of heaviness on one side as a crosswind was developing. "I can feel the pressure of your hand on my back, just like the bump of wind."

"Right. Sometimes it's sharp, and you know something big is coming and you need to respond, or it might be gentle and you prepare a response, but mostly just ride it out," Orv said.

"You're a natural pilot." I resumed packing the crates. "I wish we had more time. A few more days, and I think I could work on that. We're going to need all the skills we can muster for next year when we add power."

Orv brushed my sentiments aside. "A body forgets those things by then anyway. We'll need to relearn it all next year. Aren't you eager to get working on the engine?"

With a start, I realized I hadn't much considered our power source, having no experience in such things. "I assumed we'd order up an engine with the power, size, and weight that we need."

"That might not be as easy as you think. I asked around before we left Dayton, and no one had the specifications we need."

"Well, we'll go to Chicago then. Or Cincinnati or Detroit. Someone will have one, or can build one."

Rain pattered on the tin roof of the hangar as we sealed up the last of the crates.

Orv marked them with some black paint. "We'll see." He shoved the crates in order. "The men are supposed to be here at first light to help us get these back to Kitty Hawk. I hope the rain doesn't make them change their minds."

He needn't have worried. Bill and Dan Tate, John Daniels, and a strong nine-year-old boy named David showed up at 7:00 a.m. in the midst of a terrific storm. Fishermen, most of them, they didn't seem to notice the pelting rain as we trudged through sand and seagrass the four miles to the boat awaiting us at Kitty Hawk. Not even the seagulls were around to see us off, as the waves crashed angrily against the shore. Nature was claiming back the territory we had borrowed.

But the miserable weather couldn't dampen my spirits. We had accomplished what no one else to date had, with data we had discovered ourselves. We could take off, make slight turns, and land smoothly, even with changing winds. We could fly fifty feet off the ground and, above all else, control all these actions with one hand and body movements, leaving a hand free to control the next and most critical step: adding power.

KATHARINE

When Charley returned from Kitty Hawk with the boys, I expected he'd want to move right back into managing the bicycle shop. Lorin and I had things running pretty smoothly, and we had hired a competent worker to man the front of the house. Not looking forward to the inevitable conflict, I was considering how we could work it out to all our advantages.

The answer came when I helped Will, Orv, and Charley organize the parts that had arrived for the next glider. The back of the shop was getting quite cramped between the powered equipment, belts and pulleys, and bicycle parts, and a whole other section with flyer parts. Orv had built a rack where drawers could be stacked all the way to the ceiling, but little space remained.

Charley stashed pulleys in the proper drawer. "Where're we going to put the big stuff like propellers and the engine?"

"There's still space upstairs," I offered. "And where is this engine? Shouldn't it have been delivered by now?"

Will had been paging through his notebook crammed with calculations and drawings of propellers. Material for them was expensive and hard to obtain, so they wanted to get the shape perfected before they carved the first piece of wood.

He slapped the notebook shut and groaned. "Not a single company has come up with an engine that will meet our specifications. We need at least eight horsepower and under two hundred pounds." He pulled a letter from his pocket. "This was our last hope, but it fails both. They keep trying to pass off what they already have, and our needs are unique." He passed the letter, which included a diagram of an engine, to me.

"Maybe right about here." Charley held out his arms in one of the few open spaces. "The engine will be about yay big, I figure."

I thought back on the first time I had met Charley. He was so proud of his ability as a mechanic. It was what made him come alive. Sure, he could run the store, was perhaps a bit too salty with the customers, but his real talent was more like Orv's—building things. I knew he had toyed with engines. He had rebuilt the one running the belts for the power equipment several times.

I looked at the engine diagram. The bulky main frame of it was labeled *engine block,* and there were smaller *cylinders* and *pistons* and *wires* attached to it. "Iron is so heavy. Isn't there another metal it could be crafted from?"

Orv joined me. "Aluminum is lighter. But no one makes engines out of aluminum, probably for good reason."

"Why is that?"

Orv shrugged. "Why do you think, Will? Too soft? Heat resistance? Manufacturing issues? Availability?"

Will climbed a stepladder to stow bolts of muslin above a cabinet. "It's only been in the last ten years they've figured out how to make aluminum commercially available. I suspect manufacturers haven't seen a need to switch over to something so untested."

I handed the last fabric bolt to Will. "Seems there's a need now. Wouldn't a manufacturer of engines be very interested in a whole new use for them?"

Will pushed the fabric into place then stepped down. "We could ask. But from the responses I've already gotten, there isn't an interest in building a unique engine. And building it out of aluminum is a whole other world of unique."

It amused me that my brothers would push themselves without limits, but surrendered easily when it came to involving others. "I have an idea. I'll bet we can get one of these companies to furnish just the engine block in something more lightweight like aluminum. Then Charley can build out the rest of it. We can clear out a workspace for him upstairs and he can work in peace without being interrupted by customers."

The prospect of getting Charley out of the shop might also have factored into my reasoning, but they didn't need to know that. They all cocked their heads, looking at me like I had grown a second one.

"I'll make all the phone calls and write the letters," I offered. "All you have to do is sign them."

"What do you think, Charley?" Will asked.

"When can I start?" was the response.

⁓

Some weeks later, I spoke to an engineer who was eager to mold an engine block out of aluminum. It seems he was searching for just the right project to try out the relatively untested material. Charley and I pored over catalogs and walked down every aisle of every hardware store, looking for the other parts he needed to build an engine.

In June when school let out, I started working more days in the shop. Customers were few on a particularly warm morning, and I was hearing strange chugging and banging sounds from upstairs, so I was pleased when Charley came down, wearing a grease-stained work apron over his white shirt, his sleeves rolled up to his elbows.

"Where are the boys?" he asked in his usual abrupt way.

"Good morning, Charley. It's a fine day, isn't it?"

He hung his head. "I'm sorry, ma'am. Good morning. And yes, it's a fine day, because I have something exciting to show your brothers."

"They're out running errands, but you can show me."

He pointed to the door that led to the stairwell. "After you."

A thick oak table had been set up in a corner of the cramped upstairs office. On it sat the engine, a big hunk of silvery-gray metal, with all manner of knobs and wires sticking out of it. My nose stung from the fumes in the air. I rushed to open the windows fully.

Charley poured water into a flask and tubing that connected to the engine from above. Then he poured gasoline into another flask and attached some wires. "Okay, cover your ears."

I did as he said as he bent over the machine. A small explosion burst from the thing, then several smaller ones. It banged like the gunpowder caps that we as children set off by hitting the tapes with rocks. The machine jiggled on the table and I feared the whole thing would come tumbling down. Blue smoke poured into the room, and we both coughed. After about ten seconds, mercifully the thing shut down.

"You did it!" I cried, amidst coughing.

"It runs! I've got much more to do and obviously need to fashion a way to exhaust the fumes, but it's going to work."

WILBUR

S etting up was almost routine now, on our fourth trip to the North Carolina coast. The fishy-smelling seaweed and salt air greeted me like old friends. We would have to repair the workshop and hangar for the damage caused by winter storms. The glider we had stored was in pieces. We could only salvage part of one wing.

We explored some areas in Kitty Hawk to see if the winter winds had formed smoother dunes with a good distance between them. With a much heavier machine, we would need a longer ramp and flatter area. But finding no suitable area, we headed south once again to Kill Devil Hills.

"Sheesh. Could they come up with a worse name for a place to launch a big old machine from?" Orv looked over the rounded hills, put out his hands to feel the wind. "We've got to consider how these random dunes might affect the steadiness of the wind."

"Could we go down one, then in between the next two?" I swooped my hand in an imaginary glide path. "We'd have some protection from crosswinds at critical takeoff time."

"Heck no. There wouldn't be enough airspeed for the precise control needed."

"How about just a little help with the lift?" I pointed to a flattened area with a gentle rise.

"That might work. If it's still like that tomorrow. These dunes change every day." Orv huddled in his jacket against the wind. "This machine is more than twice as heavy as last year's model, even before we add the propellers and engine. How many folks do we need to drag it down here?"

"Four more, if we can find them." I checked my pocket watch "It's almost five. We need to go to the lifesaving station. The boys should be gathering for change of shift."

The next morning, we had six big men and David to help us carry, roll, and drag the various parts of the partially dismantled machine to Kill Devil Hills. They wanted to help put it back together, but we nixed that idea. Orv led John Daniels to his camera. They moved it about several times, checking the view plate each time until satisfied they could capture the machine in flight. "Snap the shutter just as soon as it gets airborne, and if you have time to change the plates, take another one."

"No way he'll have time for that, Orv. We'll be lucky to be in air for a whole minute. Fumbling around like that just risks ruining the plate," I said. It seemed common sense to me, but sometimes Orv's enthusiasm got the best of him.

A minute might not have seemed like much, but a minute of controlled flight would be a record accomplishment. Each of our glider models had had several adjustments, but this was a whole new machine, and our excitement had been building for months. Orv and I would hardly speak of it, but we each knew this was a critical time. If we failed now, it would be hard to carry on.

The machine had double-decker wings like the previous versions, and a double front elevator to control pitch. We'd worked hard on the control for the rear rudder and wing warping, and were eager to test them out. Once we could make some slight turns and control the nose, we estimated we'd be ready to add power.

This presented a conundrum. We had promised Katharine she could come out when we made that momentous step. But it was quite clear we wouldn't be ready for months, and she had already started the school year. I had brought that up with Orv the night before, as we dug into some canned peas and beef jerky.

"Do we rush the engine test to, let's say, Thanksgiving, so Sterchens can be here?" I asked, knowing what his answer would be.

"It's a shock to hear those words come from your mouth, Mr. Everything in Due Time."

"We also might consider waiting until next summer. There's plenty of work to be done, repairing and refining from the current tests."

"And risk someone else beating us to the goal?" Orv collected our empty tin plates. "How about we present the options to Katharine? If we make the decision for her, there will be hell to pay."

"Because we both know what she will decide. She will hop on the first train and be out here. Then when the first attempts fail, as they inevitably will, she'll go back home disappointed and probably having risked her job. We can't have that." It pained me to think these things, but it was the most logical scenario.

"You're the boss. I leave it up to you to tell her," Orv said with a smirk.

"Coward."

ORVILLE

Will had successfully convinced Kate to wait until we were much closer to testing with an engine before coming to North Carolina. But as usual, I was at odds with both of them regarding the timing of things. The new glider was handling gloriously. Wilbur and I took turns piloting, and I felt my skills had caught up to his. After we had successfully added sandbags to represent the weight of the engine and propellers, I had an idea.

As we piled up the sandbags and readied the glider to be brought back to the hangar, I casually asked Will, "Tomorrow, why don't we go up together, instead of using sandbags, now that we know she can handle the weight? We could learn from each other better if we can watch firsthand."

Will pressed his lips together and ran his fingers through his thinning hair. I knew the answer would be *no*.

"You remember the promise the Bishop made us make back in '01?"

"Not taking undue risks, yeah, yeah," I said. "But this isn't an unnecessary risk, we will learn from it, and we've already tested..."

"There's something else that you don't know. The night before we left Dayton, he came to me in the middle of the night. I'm not sure if he was sleepwalking. Anyway, he made me promise that we wouldn't fly together."

"I understand his concern," I said. "One crash, and he could lose the both of us. But I maintain that with both of us aboard, we would be safer. You know how hard it is to control everything yourself. We could split the duties."

"But that wasn't his reasoning. I think he's long since come to terms with the danger of losing one or both of us. He said we couldn't take the chance because what we are doing is too important. Meaning that if one of us were to perish, the other could carry on."

"Oh." I had to dwell on that for a moment. It was both a kick in the ribs and a medicine ball of responsibility thrown at me. Of course Will would agree with Pop. An image of us flying together had flitted in my mind as long as I could remember. How else could we truly appreciate what we had accomplished? "I'll agree to that, on one condition."

Will moved the elevator to the down position. "This is not negotiable."

"There will come a time when we have full confidence in our machine and our place as inventors is secure. Promise you will fly with me then."

"There is nothing that would make me happier."

The machine ready, Will and I, along with several helpers, pushed it toward the hangar. It wouldn't be in this the one we'd fly together, but maybe the next one.

_____

My frustration mounted as Will insisted on trial after trial in every conceivable wind condition. We assembled the engine, drivetrain, and propellers, and ran them mounted on a stack of crates. Then we tried to mount the engine and propellers on the machine, only to have the propeller shafts break. We had to return to Dayton to make replacements, losing precious weeks of time.

In my mind, we were well past the testing needed on both the engine and the airframe by late October, and here it was already December. Waiting while we moved the sandbags forward or back an inch, adding this wire or that, was only going to put us behind Langley and his inferior machine. We were following him as closely as we could. His government backing not only gave him a huge economic advantage but also came with an aura of secrecy that protected him from the press. Even so, we were fairly certain that he was our main rival.

Our remoteness meant reporters didn't hound us. The lack of interest in what we were about to attempt to do was both fortunate and depressing. Fortunate because we didn't want the interference and delays that dealing with the press would bring, but depressing because it meant that all our hard work might be in vain. Someone else, likely Langley, might beat us to piloted powered flight. Even if we were first, if we failed to get the word out in time, it could spell defeat. And fussing with minor details was not helping.

Correspondence sometimes took over a week once the cold weather set in and the boat from the mainland became unreliable. A stack of letters arrived all at once: An encouraging note from Chanute; I reminded myself to write him an update. A chatty letter from Katharine, who was having a hard time managing her classes and the bicycle shop without Charley's help, as Charley had accompanied us in order to work on the engine. And most surprisingly, a letter from Langley at the Smithsonian.

Since the initial query Wilbur had sent back in '99, our requests

for information regarding the advances the government was making
were met with a form letter and a few pamphlets at best, and, more
often, stony silence. That was Langley's right, we supposed. But this
time, he requested to come see us fly at Kitty Hawk.

I nearly dropped the letter in my astonishment. This was quite an
honor and I ran to find Will.

Will was not enthused. "If his machine is as advanced as it should
be, given all the time and people's money spent on it, then he hardly
needs to see ours. Nothing good will come of a visit from him."

I knew from the report of the crash of the flying machine Langley
called an aerodrome into the Potomac River back in October that he
was far behind us, although he had claimed the crash was due to the
wing hitting the catapult at launch. A revelation washed over me like
the ocean waves we watched every day. We were Langley's equal, if not
his superior. We had progressed past our mentors, surpassed da Vinci
and Chanute and Lilienthal. At this moment, no person on earth knew
more about controlled flight than the Wright brothers did.

Curled in my pocket was a faded length of pink ribbon. Somehow
it showed up in my trunk no matter how carefully I packed.
Katharine had long kept it in a jar on her dresser. I suspected it was
important to her because she had felt badly for teasing me about it
belonging to a girlfriend so many years ago. But I was flummoxed;
the rest of that day had been nearly the worst of my life, after the day
we had lost our mother. Had she forgotten that? I certainly didn't
want to be reminded of it.

But as I thought about that day at the pond, it came to me that
I had done something most difficult for me in order to protect her.
We all had protected each other against a rotten bully. That's what
she meant with this ribbon.

I knew what I had to do. I had to decline the visit from Langley, and anyone else we couldn't trust. The Wright family had strived and sacrificed so much for this project. We must not let anyone steal our thunder.

❧

By the eighth of December, I was champing at the bit to take the next step. We had practiced with ever more sandbags to simulate the extra weight and drag of the engine. The glider took longer to get airborne, but its handling barely changed. The glider and the engine were as ready as they could be, and the weather would not hold out for long.

We were ready to put it all together, to give our glider power and make our first flyer.

I just had to convince Wilbur.

I found him at the lifesaving station, sitting in the circle of chairs with the men. They were passing around newspaper pages, shaking their heads and all talking at once.

"Orv! What 'til you hear this!" Tate bounded up to me, clapped a big arm around my shoulder. "We're not sure if it's good news or bad. I wanna go with good, but Wilbur here is undecided."

I pulled up a chair next to Will. "What's going on?"

He refolded a newspaper so I could see the big headline:

Aerodrome Crashes Again

"This is why we don't need press about," he said. "Can you imagine if they were around to report on every unsuccessful test?"

I looked at the photograph. It looked like the same machine Langley's team had launched in October, only to have it plunge directly into the Potomac. I wondered what modifications they had made. I knew they had a more powerful engine than we did, but I also knew their aspect ratio for the wings was off. And the cross-shaped tail defied logic.

"We believe there's no unsuccessful test, as long as there are no injuries, because we learn something each time." I looked around the circle of men, who were nodding in agreement. "And I think our competitors still have a lot to learn."

"Exactly. And I don't think this"—Will swatted at the offending paper—"amounts to a hill of beans as far as we're concerned. We need to stay focused on our own project."

"Yeah, where are we with that?" Tate said. "'Cause the missus wants to know when she should come out for the big event." There were echoes and cheers from the others.

"I'd like to be home for Christmas," I said. "What do you think, Wilbur?"

Will looked around at all the hopeful faces. "Let's send for Katharine. We fly next week, and successful or not, we'll be home for Christmas."

KATHARINE

The months dragged on without the boys to entertain and bother me. Of course my students kept my mind active, and I'd had several gatherings with friends and even a few evenings of dancing, but the Bishop was traveling five days out of seven and there were plenty of lonely times in between.

The boys were good about writing at least once a week, but I wondered what they were leaving out of their letters. How could nearly three months have gone by with so little progress?

Finally, on the eleventh of December, good news arrived. Orv wrote that I should get ready to come out, as they should have something exciting to see by next week. Next week! I paged through my school calendar. It would be finals week, the end of the semester and the last time I would see some of my seniors. How could I leave just then? I looked again at Orv's letter. What did "something exciting" mean? I needed to telegram them for clarification.

But the more I thought about it, the more I knew I couldn't go. If I were to leave at this critical time, I would surely lose my job. As it was, the male faculty had tried to push me out of the senior curriculum, and I had fought tooth and nail to teach advanced courses.

And I knew the boys didn't really want me out there. They had made it clear that I would be in the way, even though they claimed it was my own comfort they were concerned with. With sadness, I picked up a pen to write to Orville.

ORVILLE

Katharine wasn't coming. We had waited for days for her arrival, and I wanted to rip the letter with her sorry excuses to shreds. She had fussed and fussed at us, and now we were running out of days.

The daylight hours were few; it was dawn on December 14, nearly the shortest day of the year. By the sound of the wind howling outside the tent, today would not be the day for the flight. I poked my head out of my sleeping bag to see if Wilbur was stirring. He had already climbed down from his rafter and was filling the coffee percolator with water, which meant he had gathered more wood for the stove and braved the cold to get water at the pump. Somehow my brother could make me feel guilty before I even got out of bed.

"Make it double strong. Today's the day, even if it takes us 'til twilight," I shouted down at him.

"I think it's gonna snow," came his dejected response.

Pans clattered as he juggled one for another on our tiny camp stove. I climbed out of my warm bag and down off the rafter. Stiff and sore, I realized that at thirty-two years of age, I was getting too old for these spartan conditions. But Will was whistling and apparently in a good mood, so I did some calisthenics to warm myself up and try to match his good cheer.

Will stopped his motion, spatula in midair. "You hear that?"

I listened. "Nope, don't hear a thing."

"Precisely. The wind was at forty knots when I got up. Let's go check."

I grabbed the anemometer while Will unlatched the door. Out we went into the brisk air, still in our sleep shirts. The rising sun barely peeked through thick gray clouds, but the winds were steady at fifteen knots. Perfect for flying.

We raced back to the tent.

"I'll go get the boys!" I said, as I singed my fingers grabbing a sausage from the pan. Might be the only thing I had time to eat that day, if we were lucky.

With the addition of the propellers and engine, the machine, which we had dubbed the "flyer," now weighed in excess of six hundred pounds. It took all six of us the better part of the morning to set up the wooden rails on a flat-topped dune, then drag the flyer up the dune and set its skids on the rails.

I set up the camera on its tripod behind and to the right of the point where I expected the flyer to lift off. I checked the view screen, making sure the camera was as close as possible and still showing the whole machine, plus the air and sand under it, in the photograph. Then I slipped in the negative plate and called John Daniels over to man it. He knew the drill by now, but I reminded him anyway. "It's going to happen fast, so you've got to be ready."

John fumbled a bit with the camera. "Don't worry. I'm a little nervous, but I won't let you down."

That did not make me worry less. But there was no time to fuss about that, since we still had to go through all the checkpoints on Wilbur's list. We each had our favorite duties, but he insisted we switch them up so that we both knew every detail that had to be checked and rechecked.

Today he had the engine and propellers and I had the elevator, wings, and skids. As I checked every strut and wire, he started and stopped the engine several times. I could hear the timing was a little rough, but he soon had it adjusted just right. For my final inspection, I climbed aboard, lay in position on the lower wing, and tested the controls. One of the guys watched the parts of the flyer I couldn't see and gave me a thumbs-up. All looked well, except the front elevator control, which seemed a little sticky, so I worked it a few times. It probably needed to loosen up a bit, after a week of no use.

Just then, the wind picked up, and sand sprayed me in the face. I heard the shout of words the Bishop would not have approved of. I craned my neck to see Will holding his coat over the engine in an effort to keep out the sand. I climbed down, and Will motioned for all the men to climb the dune.

"Take a seat on the skids, boys. We don't want it flying off without us."

Indeed, the wings were lifting from their usual slight droop. Any more wind and we risked a disaster. We watched as sand swirled across the grassy dunes, hoping against hope it would die down.

By some divine interference, the wind settled back again. Maybe still a bit stronger than we would have liked, but considering the weight of the engine, that might not have been a bad thing.

Will popped up from the skid and took a wind measurement. With a broad smile, he asked, "Who goes up first?"

"You're the elder." I said. "It should be you. But if you're scared or something, let me go."

"No, we'll be fair." Will said. "John, do you have a coin?"

Will won the toss, and we all scurried around him, giving him playful punches and slaps on the back. I hugged him about the shoulders.

We all took our positions. Cameraman, starters, runners. I was a runner. Dan attached the batteries to the starter while Bill and I gave the propellers a shove, me on the right, clockwise, and Tate counterclockwise on the left.

The chug of the engine, the rattle of the drive chains, the whirring of the propellers, it all sounded perfect. I took one more trip around the plane. The smell of oil told me the lubrication system was working. All looked and sounded in order. We waited as Dan disconnected the heavy battery box, its job done. I stepped into position, my heart pounding with excitement. I raised my arm to signal "go" and Will adjusted the timing to increase the engine speed.

"Wait!" I shouted. I moved my hand down, but Will and the men took that as a sign to go, and the men pushed and the engine revved. The machine started to slide down the ramp. "Wait!" I shouted again but it was no use. I had forgotten to warn him about the sticky elevator control. It probably was all worked out, but I should have told him about it. Of course, he had tested it himself just moments before, but...

Down the ramp he went, all looked good, then just at the end of the ramp I looked at the pitch of the elevator. No, it was set too high. Sure enough, the machine climbed at an unsustainable pitch and promptly stalled. At least it was a pretty soft landing, the skids sliding through the sand with a loud hiss.

We all ran to check on Wilbur. He was completely unharmed. He blamed himself for the mishap. "Darn it all, I overcorrected for the engine weight. We haven't practiced with the sandbags enough. And I don't think the dune helps, because I lost speed at the bottom, just when I needed it most. Let's try it from even ground."

This resulted in whoops of relief from the men.

"You're up next, Little Brother." He playfully pulled my newsboy hat down over my eyes. "Do better than me."

I pinched my lips together. Should I tell him about the sticky control? That didn't actually seem to be the problem. And it would just make him mad that I didn't tell him initially. But if he found out somehow, like I talked in my sleep, then he might think I did it so I could have a chance at being first. No, I couldn't bear the thought of that. I decided to slice my dilemma down the middle.

"No, Will. You go again. Let's check all the controls, oil her up, then you go."

But Wilbur wouldn't hear of it. "Fair is fair. We need to check it over for damages, but you're next to fly."

But the wind picked up, and the light was fading, it being almost the shortest day of the year. There would be no more flying that day.

Three days later, December 17, the winds were favorable. Another round of inspection, lubricating, and engine tuning, and we were ready to go again. The more favorable wind speed made me happy, for if I was a success after my brother's failure, that alone could account for it.

My heart leaped in my chest as if it were ready to go up without me. I climbed aboard and lay in position, my hips secure in the cradle. My hands worked the controls like a practiced musician. The elevator was still slightly stiff, or was it my freezing fingers? I spread my fingers, then opened and fisted my hands to improve the circulation.

Will raised his arm and Dan started the engine with a battery on the ground that was connected by a wire. Once the engine rumbled to life, I disconnected the wire. Gasoline fumes stung my nose. Was there a leak? Hell, too late to do anything about that now. The propellers spun in opposite directions, balancing each other and not stealing the other's wind. Faster, faster. I gave a signal to release the tie-down. And in an instant, the machine and I were sliding down the ramp, picking up speed. The engine roared to my right, spewing hot oily air; the drivetrain clattered in my ears.

Go up! Go up! I commanded the flyer. I held tight to the stick in my hands, guiding the elevator just right. Not too high, just get her off the ground and keep her there for as long as possible. And then the hiss of the skids went quiet, and there was only the whine of the engine and swoosh of the propellers. I looked down—we were off the ground. It was just a few feet, but my heart soared as if I had reached the clouds. Steady, steady, I tilted the elevator.

"Keep the wings level," Will had said. "Just go straight down the beach until she wants to come down. Don't risk an updraft."

I adjusted my hips ever so slightly, warping the wings just enough to keep her level, just as one might balance on a bicycle.

We sailed along, the flyer and me, and each second stretched, capturing the magnificence of the moment. I imagined people gathering around a newspaper, the headline announcing, *Man Attains Powered Flight!* Then, just as I settled enough to enjoy the feeling of being aloft, the engine sputtered. I had a nice clear path of level sand ahead of me. I cut off the engine and guided her down, her skids sailing across the sand, her glide as smooth as the sateen of her wings.

WILBUR

Whether due to some mistake of my own making, God's plan, or fate intervening, I don't regret for a moment that Orville was the one to make history. I had my chance, but he was successful when I had failed. But it was just one step, a historic step of course, but just another interim goal accomplished. We had much more to do.

We took turns the rest of that afternoon, making three more flights, which grew in length and steadiness each time. Without the pressure to just stay airborne, we tried small adjustments to see how far we could push the machine and learn what to modify for the next attempt. We measured the length of each flight; the longest was 852 feet.

The seagulls had circled around us all day, screaming opinions of their human imitators. But as the winds calmed and dusk approached, they began to settle on the damp sand at the ocean's edge. It was quitting time for birds and men.

After recording it all in my journal, I rushed over to join Orv and John Daniels, who were huddled over the camera.

"Do you think you got a photograph?" I asked.

"All but the second flight, he thinks." Orv answered for him. "Thanks, John. We'll develop the plates as soon as we're back in Dayton, and I'll write and let you know."

⁓

While discussing whether to try again the next day or take our winnings and go home, a sudden gust of wind blew off my cap and I hunkered down to avoid being knocked off my feet. John Daniels was closest to the flyer, and he grabbed one of struts between the wings. But the wind lifted him and the machine off the ground.

The flyer somersaulted down the beach with Daniels trapped between the wings. It crashed nose first, the spruce struts splintering with a loud crack. There was nothing we could do but get out of the way. When the tumbling stopped, we rushed to help Daniels, who was entangled in wires but unharmed.

As I checked him over, he raised his arms and proclaimed, "First person to survive the crash of an aeroplane!"

Mother Nature had made our decision for us. This machine had seen her last flight.

But even that couldn't dampen our enthusiasm. We would salvage what we could and leave knowing we had made aviation history. I supervised packing up, while Orville rushed the four miles to the weather station to send a telegram. The first message would be to the Bishop and Katharine. How proud they would be! It saddened me that neither of them had been there to witness the event, but I vowed to include them in the even more momentous occasions to come.

When Orville returned, we gathered with our team to celebrate. The men didn't know it yet, but it would also be our farewell. We had accomplished our goal and had promised to be home for Christmas.

We gathered at the lifesaving station, shuffling in on the creaky wooden floors, worn from years of sandy shoes. The white clapboard building had become a lighthouse, a meeting place, a shelter in storms. The old wooden floors were as dear to me as those at home in Dayton.

I looked around at the now-familiar faces. They no longer sported beards; each was either clean-shaven or wore a mustache, just like Orv and me. They had given up their own time to help us in our mission and had asked nothing in return. When they could have been hunting or fishing to feed their families, or in their warm beds on a frosty morn, they were out in the dunes, dragging hundreds of pounds of equipment or sometimes just standing around, trying to keep warm while waiting patiently to be needed. A swell of gratefulness filled my heart as I bid them farewell.

"Gentlemen," I said. "It is with our sincere gratitude for all of your hard work and support over these past four years that I tell you we shall soon be on our way back to Ohio."

Rumbles of surprise filled the room.

"When are you coming back?" Bill Tate asked.

I exchanged a look with Orville. We had only briefly discussed this matter. We both thought it was time to move our experiments closer to home. We needed to prove we could fly without the strong and steady coastal winds, and we needed more time to build and design, not to mention maintain our livelihood, the bicycle shop.

At the same time, we realized that finding a suitable place near home might not be possible, and that our experiments might show we weren't ready to forgo the wind and soft sand for which we had come to Kitty Hawk.

Orville spoke up. "Well sirs, that is a question we have been asking ourselves. Rest assured, when we know the answer, you will be the first to hear of it."

KATHARINE

The wind whipped my skirt as I bicycled home from school. I had forgotten the strap Orv had fashioned to keep it in place, and I worried the fabric would get tangled in the chain. And mid-December was too cold to still be riding, Will would have counseled. I could take the streetcar, but with the walk to and from it, I hardly saved any time, and I rather enjoyed the bike ride, for it enabled me to clear my mind from the day. But it didn't stop me from missing my brothers.

I pulled up to 7 Hawthorn Street, and Carrie, who was now out of school and our full-time housekeeper, immediately popped out the front door. She must have been waiting for me, which made my heart sink. Did she have bad news to share? Indeed, she was waving a creamy yellow envelope—a Western Union telegram, no doubt. I set my bicycle against the porch railing and asked, "What is it? If it is bad, don't tell me yet."

"I haven't opened it, of course." She shoved the envelope at me and eyed me with deep interest. There would be no sulking off to a corner alone to learn of the telegram's contents.

Inside, I unburdened myself of my books and papers, took a deep breath, and opened the envelope. It was a telegram from the boys.

Success four flights Thursday morning against twenty one mile wind started from level with engine power alone average speed through air thirty one miles longest 57 seconds inform press home Christmas. Orevelle Wright

After letting the words sink in for a moment, I handed it to the expectant Carrie. "They did it!" We danced about like schoolgirls playing ring-around-the-rosy.

"And home for Christmas!" Carrie added.

A pang of wistfulness passed over me. I had chosen my job over seeing my brothers achieve our long-held dream. No matter. I pushed such thoughts away. They had done what they were born to do and would go on to do much more. I was just the sister, the bit of encouragement when needed, maker of hot meals and substitute businessperson who kept all things running for them. It was enough. It had to be.

~

After sharing the news with Lorin, who would contact the press, and with the Bishop, I went to my desk to write a letter to Reuchlin. With family notified, I next wrote to Harry and Isabel. I had visited them and Reuch in Kansas City that fall, and we had been trying to make plans to get together for the holidays. But with the boys coming home, it hardly seemed the time for that. Even though they liked Harry and Isabel well enough, there were bound to be dealings with the shop and with the press to occupy our time and minds.

In my letter I revealed the great news from Kitty Hawk and extended my best wishes for their healthy and happy holidays. Harry would no doubt understand the words not written as well as those on my crisp white paper. He had asked me once if I was living someone else's dream. No, I had answered back. I knew why God had put me on this earth, even if there were other things that I would rather do.

⤙

And a grand Christmas it was! Carrie and I cooked the turkey along with a ham, with sweet potatoes, bread stuffing, and corn and string beans we had put up that summer. Lorin and Reuch and their families joined us as well. Seated at the dinner table, we joined our hands as the Bishop asked us to bow our heads in prayer.

"Lord, bless this food and the hands that prepared it, and thank you for these many gifts you have bestowed on this family. We are grateful to your divine provenance in choosing our boys Wilbur and Orville to bring the miracle of flight to improve the lives of your people. In God's name we pray."

"Amen."

I glanced at Reuch and Lorin and their wives. Had they taken offense at being left out? I lifted my glass of wine with the wives, while the boys raised a glass of apple cider. "To all the Wright brothers and wives, may their successes match their efforts."

"Hear, hear," the others toasted.

Orville stood for his toast. "To the Wright sister. Our only girl, without whom all our efforts would be in vain."

By the cheers and smiles, it seemed no one had felt left out. So I smiled as well and let the warmth of the moment wash over me. The meal smelled heavenly, and I was exactly where I belonged.

WINTER 1904

"He's coming here, to Dayton!" Will said, rushing into the kitchen, a letter in his hand.

I was struggling mightily to pump some water into the kitchen sink, but that wasn't Wilbur's concern, of course. It was January, and no doubt the cistern was frozen. I'd have to brace myself against the cold and go outside to the well. "Who, pray tell?" I tried to keep some cheer in my voice.

"Octave Chanute. Look here." He ran his finger down the page. "'Congratulations on your success,' and so on… Here it is, 'I plan to train down from Chicago and meet in person to offer my sincerest praise and see your machine for myself.'"

"The machine? You mean the bits and pieces in the back of the shop, or the crates full of tattered remains?"

"Never mind about that. He's mostly coming to see us."

"When, exactly? I hope it's not next Wednesday, because I'm having my Oberlin friends over."

Wilbur turned the page over in his hand. "He doesn't say exactly, but I'm sure it will be Saturday or Sunday."

As luck would have it, Chanute telegrammed on Tuesday that he would arrive on Wednesday. "No matter, you can meet at the cycle shop," I told Will.

But he was having none of that. "Oh please, Sterchens, let him come to the house. He's a right friendly sort. I think your girls will get along with him splendidly. And it will take the pressure off Little Brother; you know he doesn't favor social visits."

"Okay, I'll have my friends help Carrie and me to prepare something special. He's French, so we can't have the sausage and tinned beans I had planned." It would be Chanute's second visit, as he had come shortly after the boys started their kite experiments at Kitty Hawk. But that had been almost three years prior, and I had little time with him, rushing to make a meal after my day teaching. I struggled to remember what we had served him back then so as not to do a repeat performance.

My friends Marilyn, Margaret, and Agnes arrived early in the afternoon, and we set about making the most impressive thing in my repertoire: roast duck with an apple and berry glaze made from my jarred and dried fruit. We added a leaf to the dining table and covered it with the last bit of the white French muslin, which Orv had cut to size and bound the edges. I scrunched up a smaller square of the newer but less shiny fabric to represent sand dunes. Topped with a model of the flyer and some candles, it formed the perfect centerpiece.

When Chanute arrived, all eight of us squeezed into the small dining room, but no one seemed to mind. Chanute was distinguished-looking, of perhaps slightly shorter than average height, with an impressive mane of white hair, a matching mustache, and a thin wisp of a goatee beard. His lovely accent and endearing manner made everything he said sound like a compliment.

I was a ball of nerves, but Mr. Chanute immediately put everyone at ease. "Well, if this isn't the most delightful gathering." He produced an expensive-looking bottle of French wine with a fancy label. The girls and I exchanged amused glances, for while the Bishop, Orv, and Will would only pretend to sip it to be polite, we would thoroughly enjoy it.

I stepped into the kitchen to check on the next course and find a corkscrew. Even in midwinter, the oven had heated the room too much, so I opened the back door for some fresh air.

Carrie handed me the platter with the entrée, then mopped her brow with her apron. "I'm afraid it's overdone."

"Nothing to do about that now. Can you please hunt down a corkscrew?"

When I stepped back into the dining room, the conversation had moved on to a rather unlikely topic.

Margaret caught my eye and said, "We were just talking about going to St. Louis for the World Exposition."

"St. Louis?" I blinked at the thought. "I can't just pick up and travel three hundred miles for a fair. How about the one up in Darke County? I've always wanted to go to that one. Horse racing, giant vegetables, what could be better? And I'm thinking of entering the jarred preserves competition."

Margaret helped me set the main course platter in front of the Bishop. I hoped no one looked at it too closely; the duck's skin looked shriveled instead of crispy. At least the caramelized apples and berries from my marmalade glaze smelled heavenly.

"It's going to be grand," Marilyn said. "They're calling it the 'fair of the new century.' It's still a few months away so we have plenty of time to make plans."

Orv surprised me by joining the conversation. He was usually so reticent around my friends. "Mr. Chanute's newest glider will be demonstrated, and he has suggested we enter a flying competition." All heads swiveled to him, seated next to me. "This is no jar of jelly. The prize is worth one hundred thousand dollars."

That caused some whoops and handclaps from the girls.

"My gracious." The Bishop had the honor of carving, but stared down on the bird, meat fork and knife held over it. I wasn't sure if he was perplexed with how to proceed or stunned by Orville's announcement.

Will waved away the idea. "We're nowhere near being able to do it. Fly ten miles in three hops? Impossible."

Carrie appeared with a corkscrew, and Chanute handed her the bottle of wine. I winced at her discomfort as she looked at me with pleading eyes. Just as I set down my napkin to go help her, Chanute sensed the problem.

"Allow me. These old corks can be tricky." He opened the bottle with a *pop*, then poured wine for everyone within his reach. "Ah, Wilbur, that's the point, you see. To stretch yourself, see what you can do. Why, just a year ago you were still flying a kite on the beach."

My brothers' faces both crumpled in consternation at his belittling words, but they held their tongues. Chanute's words hardly represented their accomplishment.

Again seeming to sense his affront, he quickly added, "If it isn't possible for you, at the forefront of aviation, why on earth would they set the bar so high?"

Will shook his head. "For publicity, of course. And if no one meets the parameters, they save themselves a hundred grand."

Although I enjoyed the lively discussion, something else struck me as Carrie came to the Bishop's aid, carving the duck, and I filled the remaining wineglasses. Mr. Chanute, Carrie, and hopefully I had a particularly valuable trait, one that many, including my brothers, seemed to lack. That was an ability to sense subtle clues of someone's true thoughts or emotions and to intervene when necessary without causing embarrassment. It seemed Chanute was my mentor as well as the boys'.

He continued to encourage them. "Certainly, but the prize is obtainable, given the perfect winds. Lighter-than-air ships can enter the contest, too."

I joined the collective groan of exasperation.

"Heavier-than-air craft have nowhere close to the range of a hot-air balloon in favorable winds." Will said.

"That's a ridiculous competition, but I still want to go to the fair," Margaret said.

"All right, then. Let's go." I said.

Margaret held up her wineglass. "Watch out, St. Louis."

That winter, a model of the flyer-in-the-making remained the centerpiece for our dinner table, and the favorite discussion topic was the search for a local place for testing the new machine. Ideally, it would be close to a streetcar stop, yet far enough removed to conduct flights away from prying eyes. Not that many took interest, even with the success at Kitty Hawk.

"Let all the focus be on Langley's aerodrome. The press has been vicious, but we will get the last laugh." Orv fiddled with the model's tailpiece as Carrie and I cleared the dishes. "How much takeoff room do you think we'll need?"

Will took out the pencil and small pad that were permanent residents of his chest pocket and made some calculations. "With our new estimate of the true formula for lift, I'd say we need about twice as long as in Kitty Hawk, allowing for a wind of at least seven knots."

One of the most important discoveries during their wind-tunnel experiments was that the formula for lift that had been accepted as gospel was wrong, leading experimenters to underestimate the square footage of wing they needed.

"What if you have no wind at all? Would it take off?" I asked.

"Of course. With enough power, anything will fly," Orville said. Both the boys chuckled.

"Just maybe not for long," Will added.

Their voices lowered and faces somber, they discussed the various fiascoes. Aside from Lilienthal, another that hit Will especially hard was Percy Pilcher. It was he who invented successful gliders he called "bat" and "beetle" and finally "hawk," the one in which he fatally crashed. And poor Pénaud had committed suicide after failing to find funding to build his invention. Other aviators had also perished, but I pushed those thoughts out of my mind.

The model flyer on the table didn't look significantly different to me than the previous model, which could only take off into a stiff wind. "Is it reasonable to find enough space, close enough to home to get there on the streetcar, with a place to store the machine?" I brought out a map of southwest Ohio I had been studying.

Carrie served shoo-fly pie on dessert plates arranged around the map. Rich with a molasses custard and topped with crumbs, the pie was a winter favorite.

"Nothing seems to fit those criteria. There's some nice flat, open space near Vandalia, but it's not on the streetcar line," I said.

Orv pointed to a spot on the map to the north and east of Dayton. "Our high school botany teacher took us on research trips out here, looking for some rare plants. I remember huge stretches of flat fields as far as we could see."

"Oh yes, I went there as well." I said. "Beautiful flowers and butterflies I'd seen nowhere else."

Will studied the map. "There's a banker named Huffman who goes to our church. He raises cattle and sheep on a ranch out there near Fairborn. Not far from a stop on the Columbus interurban line. I think he'd give us a fair price for renting his field."

"And here I thought you were at church to praise the Lord," Orv teased.

"Wouldn't hurt you to go. How about we check out Huffman's land next week?"

I decided to make a little adventure of it. Since we were to go on Sunday, our day of rest, I packed a box lunch and drinks. The intercity trolley was ever so much more pleasant than our ordinary windowless streetcar. It was akin to a luxury railcar, with polished wood paneling and rich green velvet seats. Light coming into the half-moon-shaped windows shimmered with a rainbow of colors due to the pretty stained glass.

The farm was only about ten miles outside of town, but it took nearly an hour to get there, and the boys had pilfered most of the food before we arrived. We were the only people in the trolley car for the last three stops, which we took as a good sign we wouldn't be bothered by press or bystanders. Orville especially had not grown accustomed to being recognized by complete strangers and looked at me pleadingly whenever he was asked a question out in public.

We needn't have worried. As we trekked from the stop down a dirt path, there was nothing but cows and a few pigs in vast green fields. The smell of their dung hit my nose in full force, but I didn't complain. I had to double step to keep up with the boys and their longer legs, but I also wouldn't complain about that. This was a Wright family adventure, and I meant to enjoy it.

After about fifteen minutes of walking, a faded red barn came into view, and Will pronounced, "That's Huffman's ranch."

The boys picked up their pace even more, and I lifted my skirts to aid my struggle through the long grasses.

Mr. Huffman was a pleasant fellow, and he walked us all around his fields, his pipe smoke creating a trail. The earth felt soft, almost marshy, and he explained the area had an unusual peaty soil that was good for flowers and animal forage, but not much else. The fields were surrounded by thick stands of tall trees, which I thought might pose a problem. The boys quizzed him on the length of each field and possible obstacles.

"Well now, you'll have to clear the cows before you do anything. And there's quite a few gophers out here. You might have to fill in some of their more elaborate accommodations. Of course they'll dig them right out again and you'll have to do it each time. Or I don't mind if you shoot the varmints. Fellow in Beavercreek will pay you a penny each for 'em."

I stifled a laugh. The Bishop knew how to shoot, but apart from wanting to gather birds for study, the boys had shown little interest. Orville liked to tell a story about shooting a mouse that had invaded their camp at Kitty Hawk, but he never made a believer of me.

"What do you think, Orv?" Will asked.

"We would need to cut back some of the tall grasses and level the gopher holes, but I think our biggest challenge will be the lack of steady winds that we had at Kitty Hawk. I think we'll need a much longer launch rail. Or perhaps some sort of device, like a catapult."

"A what?" I was only dimly aware of such a thing, remembering it to be something like a large slingshot. I wasn't sure if it was to cause the demise of a gopher or to launch the flying machine.

Will turned to Huffman. "Do you get much wind out here?"

Huffman palmed his whiskered chin. "Off and on, especially when a storm is brewing."

"From what direction, would you say?" Orv shaded his eyes with his hand as he looked toward the low winter sun.

"Generally I would say from the west. But we do get northerlies too. Heck, they can come from any which way."

Will shrugged. "The point of these trials will be to fly with no or little wind." He turned to me, ever the older brother instructing the little sister. "The catapult will add speed for takeoff. We'd build some sort of tower, put weights on one end of a rope, and carry it up the tower. The rope goes through several sets of pulleys, and the flyer is attached to the other end of the rope. When we're ready, we drop the weight from the top of the tower, and off we go."

He said it so casually, his hand sailing off in mock flight, but the very thought made my stomach twist into a knot. I looked at Orv to see if he was smiling at some joke. But he wasn't.

The boys discussed terms with the rancher, including allowing them to build a hangar to store the flyer. I heard Huffman say he wouldn't charge rent, which was good news, but the rest of the conversation was lost on me, as I imagined the wood and fabric flyer being yanked violently into the air, with one of my brothers barely hanging on.

In April the boys started making the trek out to the Huffman field every day except Sunday. Charley manned the bicycle shop and worked on a new engine, and I helped when I wasn't teaching. In the mornings before school, I helped them load up wagons full of flying machine parts to be taken on the trolley line out to the field.

ORVILLE

Huffman Prairie was a solid choice. If I wasn't a self-declared aviator and inventor, I'd have been a botanist. Whenever Wilbur allowed a break from scything the grasses, shoveling dirt around to clear gopher holes, or building a hangar, I would meander, identifying the wonderful abundance of flowers. Bees hummed in a quiet symphony, flitting from bloom to bloom with the ease of perfect aerodynamics. I imagined there must be a wonderful source of honey nearby, but never had time to find it.

We built the shed that was to serve as our hangar at the far side of the field from the trolley stop. Wilbur obsessed over people spying and taking photographs from the trolley, endangering our chances of a successful patent. This seemed rather odd to me, considering his speeches and publications, but it was not my place to argue. Though I did grumble about the need to carry the machine and shed parts across an entire field.

Once we got the hangar and flyer built, it was time for some test flights. As was our usual rule, Wilbur went first. He claimed it was because he was the better pilot, although I know the true reason was that he didn't want me to assume the risk of flying an untested machine.

Our first efforts were dismal failures. The engine and propellers started fine, and the machine slid nicely down the wooden track. But at the end it would simply slide across the grass before stopping, or sometimes bump along the ground a bit before giving up. We twiddled with the elevator and adjusted the tail rudder, but this helped little.

"We need more power, or more wind," I said.

"Perhaps we should try a longer track," Will replied. "Give her more time to gain the speed she needs."

So we built more track and tested again and again. We were at about two hundred feet of track and had gotten just a little bit more lift, but not enough speed to control the pitch. The soft ground helped cushion the small crashes, but we still spent more time repairing the flyer than trying to fly.

By May we were getting the machine a couple of feet off the ground, and Will was convinced it was time to garner some publicity to keep the public interested in flight. Our finances dictated that we would soon need investors and supporters to support a future in aviation.

We invited town leaders, reporters, and other influential people to witness the machine in action. On the appointed day, there were nice winds, but Will pronounced them too strong. As the crowd stood waiting, he walked among them, explaining what we were up to.

We kept them close to the trolley station, a good couple hundred feet from the flyer. We wanted them to witness flight, not to see and photograph our trade secrets.

The wind sock we had hung from a pole began to flutter instead of sailing straight out. I sprinted over to Will and dragged him away from the crowd. "It's time. We're losing wind and soon we won't get her up at all."

Will agreed and we hurried out to the flyer. Charley and I had built a small wooden cart that the bottom of the flyer's frame rested on. The cart was positioned at the end of the long rails, which were lined up to face the wind. The cart greatly reduced the friction of the skids and, like a train, helped keep the flyer from sliding off sideways.

Will engaged the starter and the engine sputtered to life. Charley and I gave the propellers a push, and they spun perfectly. Will climbed back onboard and worked the elevator stick and hip cradle. We were ready. I held up my arm to signal the release of the restraining wire.

Down the rail the machine went, smoothly at first, then bumping as Will pushed the elevator for lift. But the wind had died back and he didn't have enough speed to get off the ground. The flyer barely got off the rail before it skidded to an inglorious stop.

We decided to try again the next day, and Will strolled over to the crowd to explain what happened and invite them back, while a few helpers and I dragged the machine back into the shed.

But the next day, next to no one showed up. It was just as well, as our demonstration failed once again. Over the next few months, we fiddled with the engine, tried waxing and wetting the fabric of the wings, made longer and longer rails, but still could barely get off the ground, never mind exceeding our record flights at Kitty Hawk. It turned out it was a blessing that the press had taken little interest in our experiments, as what they might have printed could have made us seem fools.

"It's time to move on, I think," Will said after a particularly rough day, with both of us bearing the bumps and bruises of several rough landings.

"To what? A bigger engine? Larger wings? Another flying bicycle?" The last one was a joke, but Will wasn't laughing.

"You make fun, but that was a critical invention. But no, I'm thinking about your first idea when we were considering this site. A launching device, such as a catapult. Did you know that Chanute will be demonstrating such a device at the St. Louis exposition?"

"Yes, a motorized cart of some sort," I said. "Heck if we wanted to, we could tie the flyer up to a motorcar and get up to speed that way, but I don't think that serves our purpose."

"A motorcar would never get up to speed in these fields, and we can't risk the publicity of doing it on a smooth road." Will scratched the back of his neck, a sure sign an idea was hatching in his head. "I saw an old windmill not far from here. The vanes were mostly off it, obviously neglected. I'll bet we could take it off their hands for a pittance."

I waited for him to explain why he wanted an old windmill, especially one without vanes, but then it struck me: "The tower. We could use it for a tower to mount weights for a catapult."

"Exactly."

"I guess we've done crazier things. Well then, Don Quixote..." I raised my bruised and battered arm as if brandishing a lance. "Let's go tilt some windmills."

"'Who knows where madness lies, Sancho. To surrender dreams, this may be madness.'"

KATHARINE

ST. LOUIS

In June, I joined my friend Margaret at the World Exposition in St. Louis. Orv and Will had toyed with the idea of entering the aviation competition, but their failures at Huffman Prairie convinced them otherwise. Agnes and Marilyn couldn't get away, so it was just Margaret who met me at the train station.

I had written her that I'd be wearing an enormous yellow hat with purple feathers, which was a good thing or she would have never found me among the teeming crowd that tumbled out of the train.

"Katie!" I heard Margaret shout. She was about ten people away but I was being carried along like flotsam. Finally she caught up to me and we clung to each other like drowning swimmers.

"Oh, you're going to love the fair. I've already spent half a day. There's something for everyone. So much technology, transportation, machinery, all the things you Wrights adore."

"The other Wrights, rather. I'm more interested in the arts pavilion and the gardens."

We had a fine time. The massive stone buildings were nothing of what I had expected. I imagined fewer bricks and mortar and more giant cloth tents. But this was the celebration of the hundred years since the Louisiana Purchase, and it seemed they wanted to show off all that had happened in the world since then.

Strolling along the lakes and gardens was certainly a treat, but my favorite thing to do was sampling all the foods from around the world, much of which I hadn't tasted before. There was kuchen from Germany and many pastas from Italy. Little dumplings from eastern Europe called *pierogies* were served with a type of sausage they called hot dogs, although they didn't resemble dogs in the least. Margaret enjoyed the sweets, especially fairy floss, flavored sugar that had been spun into fine strands and piled like a cloud on a stick, while I enjoyed ice cream in a thin waffle rolled up in a cone shape.

Margaret was a big-city girl, coming from Chicago, but still her stomach wasn't used to all the new foods and fresh produce. When I mentioned trying yet another treat, she practically turned green and begged off. She wasn't better the next day, and in fact seemed so weak that I fetched a doctor to see her in our hotel room. After several days, she finally started to feel strong enough to go home, and we parted ways at the train station, with promises to get together again soon.

After two weeks, I was happy to be on a train heading for home. It was all quite grand, but I missed the rhythm of my every day, waking to the sunshine in my warm room, hearing the boys argue over breakfast about propellers and pulleys and who had made the softest landing.

DAYTON

Orville insisted on a hot breakfast, even in August. He stopped with his spoon of oatmeal halfway to his mouth. I had slipped some fresh biscuits into a basket, and he eagerly scooped one up.

"Remember those biscuits you tried to make on the kerosene stove?" Will's mind was once again at Kitty Hawk. It seemed the best time of his life.

"You weren't complaining, but they couldn't hold a candle to Katharine's." Orv slathered some strawberry jam on his biscuit. "By the way, Sterchens, isn't it about time you came to watch us fly?"

I had been back from St. Louis for over a month by that time, and hadn't heard much about the machine actually flying. "Of course I want to see that. Even if it's only a small hop, it would be nice to see you in action."

Shortly after that, on August 23, a day with a nice steady wind, I joined Orv and Will out at Huffman Prairie.

On the trolley car ride, Will tried to lower my expectations. "You understand, we can't promise we'll get off the ground."

"If you don't, then it will still be a great day, watching my brothers do what they love the most."

The walk out to the hangar wasn't as far as I remembered it being on the day we first came to explore the site. Flowers bloomed in the field, their happy heads waving in the breeze, much as they had during my visits with my botany class years before. Purple coneflowers mixed with white bergamot, along with blue violets, and a profusion of red and yellow flowers peeked between long swaying grasses. I freshened my lungs with deep breaths of nature's perfume as I strolled along the path, picking a few flowers along the way for my scrapbook.

The boys were much more interested in the speed and direction of the wind. Near the end of the path stood a metal pole. They attached a red fabric bag they called a wind sock to a rope and raised the bag up the pole like a flag.

A few steps away from the pole stood the hangar: a simple

wooden shed, perhaps longer than most and weathered to a drab gray from lack of paint. The boys opened the door that formed one entire end of it. Inside it was organized and swept clean, with tools hung in precise order along the walls and the flyer just barely jammed between them.

I had seen plenty of diagrams and a few photographs, all the bits and pieces and oceans of fabric and a small forest of wood. But I had not seen it all put together. The flyer was more elegant than I could have imagined, somehow strong and delicate at the same time. No wonder they referred to it as "she."

Some local men appeared and Orv and Will briefly introduced them; then they set straight to work. The flyer fit sideways in the shed, and they lifted her barely off the ground as they pulled her out and placed her on a long rail. Then more lifting as they fit a wagon underneath to help her roll down the rail. I checked the red wind sock, crossing my fingers that the wind would hold steady. The boys' trepidation would be greater with me watching them, despite my assurance that I could never be disappointed in them.

At last, all was ready. Orv filled the machine's fuel tank, and Will started the engine with the ignition box. The buzzing of the propellers astounded me, sounding like a million bumblebees, almost overpowering the chugging of the engine. Orville was to fly first, and he climbed aboard and lay on his belly across the middle of the lower wing.

Orv positioned his hips into what they called the *cradle*. It looked quite uncomfortable, but not as uncomfortable as the wood struts he had to lie across. He grasped a lever with his hands and moved the front elevator up and down. Will stationed himself at the end of one wing, and another man at the other. Suddenly the machine lurched forward, and down the track it went. It bumped once, twice, then lifted into the air, as easily as a butterfly.

My heart lifted right along with him as I watched the machine head away from us, straight between the bordering lines of trees. It wouldn't be long until they could rise above them, and then faster and farther. What would be the limit?

The flight didn't last long, probably less than a minute, but happiness bubbled up inside me, tears blurring my vision, as I realized one thing was now absolutely clear. My brothers were indeed flying.

WILBUR

Orv and I were consumed with building and repairing our flyer. We had tried in vain to match the height and length of our Kitty Hawk flights at the Huffman field, but barely got off the ground unless the winds were optimum. We did more testing in the wind tunnel, but it seemed our numbers were all valid. We just weren't getting enough airspeed to be able to lift past the cushion of air the wings created for a few feet up from the ground, and the wing and rudder controls didn't work without enough air flowing over and under them. Charley worked feverishly to build a more powerful engine, but that was still months away. It was time to build a catapult.

The farmer who owned the old windmill didn't care a lick about it and was only too happy for us to dismantle it, then move it to the field. Mr. Huffman was kind enough to let us build the system next to the hangar for the flyer. The construction created a bit of a sensation, and the curious started coming by to watch our efforts. One man drove his motorcar all the way across Ohio to see us. He was a bee specialist, of all things, so his interest made sense if you'd ever seen a bumblebee fly.

It took until early September to secure all the necessary parts and get the catapult built. The hardest piece of the puzzle to find were weights, but we found seven of them, two-hundred-pounds each. I calculated we would need about 1,600 pounds with no wind, so our 1,400 pounds should have been sufficient for takeoff into a light wind.

The beekeeper was a lovely fellow named Amos Root, from Cleveland. After meeting with him, it seemed he was a genuinely good person, not someone out to steal our ideas or otherwise harm us. He was actually quite helpful. As an owner of several patents for his beekeeping equipment, he gave us some guidance in obtaining our own.

"Something to think about," Amos said one day after we had given him a close-up tour of the flyer. "I can see your engine from two hundred feet away. And so can everyone else."

One had to be pretty observant to notice our aluminum block engine, but of course a competing inventor or his spy would.

"What can we do? Devise a cover?" Any material I could think of would either add weight, burn up, or starve the engine of air.

He just shrugged his shoulders. In return for his advice, I promised to let him know when something exciting was about to happen.

That day happened in early September, after our first few attempts at launching the flyer with the catapult were successful. I wrote to Amos and told him to drive out, for we were about to make a full circle in flight, something no one had ever done before.

On the planned day, the sun dawned in a clear bright sky, and we had a nice steady breeze from the northwest. Charley, Orv, and I rode the trolley, our lunch pails on our laps, suppressed smiles on our faces. I longed to go on about the winds and whether Amos would meet us, but there were other passengers aboard. Finally, we arrived at the Simms Station stop, and we fairly leaped off the trolley. We waited until it departed with its eerie electric buzz before we sprinted to the hangar.

Mr. Huffman was waiting with the team of horses we had requested. This made the work of lifting the weights much faster and easier. Orv scythed tall grasses from the launch path, then we repositioned the track into the wind. The four of us dragged the flyer out of the hangar and balanced her on the wheeled cart set upon the track.

We hooked the end of the rope to a tow bar on the bottom of the cart and anchored the flyer to a stake in the ground until we were ready to launch. The last step would be to attach the other end of the rope through pulleys to the weights, and have the horses pull the rope to lift the weights up the tower. We knew from previous launches that we would need all seven weights to gain enough speed, so they were piled up, tied, and ready for the horses.

With everything set to go, I called a meeting with Orv, Huffman, and Charley. I asked Orv if he was up to flying. He had been pretty sore from a rough landing a few weeks prior.

"It's up to you, Will. Maybe best I sit this one out."

I wondered if he wanted me to get credit for piloting that day, in case we made history again. But I didn't argue with him. We all knew our jobs; I was just killing time, hoping that Amos Root would show up. The fine weather had taken a turn and clouds had rolled in, but the winds remained steady. We couldn't wait any longer if we wanted to get several flights in. So we did the final connections and I climbed aboard.

I positioned my hips in the cradle, keeping my body stick straight. I raised my chest and rested on my forearms, then grasped the elevator controller in my left hand and the release handle with my right. Orv was in position, steadying one wing, Charley at the other. We all listened as the engine came up to speed. I glanced at the anemometer; winds were favorable at seven mph. The machine jostled like a horse pulling against its bit. At the peak of propeller speed, both Charley and Orv gave the go-ahead signal, and I released the rope attached to the ground stake.

First a jerk from the tow rope, then down the track, smooth as glass, lifting well before the end of it. Once clear of the ground by about six feet, I started a gentle turn to the south. My goal was to test the engine and control on this flight, not complete a circle, which was the ultimate goal for the day. I swerved right and left a few times, then pitched down slowly. As the ground approached, I cut the engine and glided, the skids hitting the soft grasses with a hiss. As she came to a stop in the middle of the field, I saw a slight figure of a man with a white beard and a derby hat approaching. It was Amos Root.

The men gathered about the machine as I climbed down. Charley went to check the engine, and Huffman shook my hand and said he needed to go back to work.

Orv asked, "Why did you stop? Looked like all was going perfectly."

Just then Amos caught up with us. I nodded toward him, and answered Orv quietly, "He's why." Orv would understand. So much of my attention had been caught up with patent issues. The government had issued nothing but denials and demands for more data, which weighed heavily on my mind. The same government that was funding our main competitor. Amos's experience represented an important path forward through that morass; besides, I enjoyed his company and enthusiasm for our work.

"Well done, sir." Amos said. "Sorry I was detained; it seems water for my steamer is not as easy to find across Ohio as you would think."

"Thank you for driving all that way. Not to worry, the best of today is yet to come."

ORVILLE

I could have flown that day. September 20 marked three weeks since my minor accident, and I was well-enough healed. But I sensed a change in Wilbur, a loss of will, ironically enough. He seemed haunted by the day-to-day worries of keeping Wright Cycle Company solvent and by months of failing to match our feats at Kitty Hawk. He needed a success to encourage him through more trial and error, for I feared the most difficult times were still ahead of us.

So I claimed lingering disability, although I think he saw through my ruse. I had made the first successful powered flight; he would make the first flight to land in the same place as the start. That might seem a small accomplishment, but indeed it was anything but. It showed complete control of the machine in its direction, no matter the wind, something that airships were unable to do. We both knew it was everything.

With Huffman gone back to his bank, Amos, as slight and elderly as he was, took his place and helped move the flyer back to its launching point near the catapult tower. After moving the track to adjust for a change in wind direction, we repeated all the steps we had taken earlier.

As Will climbed aboard, I was almost giddy with excitement. The engine revved and we all took our places. There was enough wind that it seemed the flyer would lift with less ground speed than before. I thought to warn Will to adjust the elevator accordingly, but just then I saw him do just that. Will fussed and fidgeted some more, but finally all was ready. He nodded at Charley, on the opposite wing. Then he turned to me. He broke out in a big grin and gave me a little salute. I knew he was saying *thank you*.

He released the rope; the weights fell and the flyer zoomed down the ramp and up into the air. I saw the wings warp ever so slightly into his first turn, the rear rudder moving in synchronization. It looked so smooth, so effortless, as if man had always been able to fly. Around he went, making another turn at treetop level, just before he left the field. Another turn, then another, making a near perfect circle. He started to descend, just as he came by us from the opposite direction he had taken off from. He was flying with the wind, not against it, the machine in complete control. A miracle.

He set it down just past us, and I had to take a moment to collect myself. Belatedly, I realized we hadn't asked Katharine to take the day off to witness this.

To assuage my guilt, I decided to surprise her with a night out at the Victoria Theater. After the show, Will and I took Katharine to a quiet little restaurant where we could relax and talk about the show. We were taken to the last table available, which unfortunately was next to the kitchen. Waiters in white jackets knocked their trays into Katharine's hat on their way in and out of the swinging doors.

Despite my plans to focus on our sister, our conversation soon turned to the events at the field that day. Will asked, "Does Amos Root have a point? Should we somehow disguise the engine?"

I frowned and nodded toward Katharine, who was straightening her big hat.

Will stood and motioned for him and Katharine to switch places. "I'm sorry, Sterchens, we should have invited you to come to the field."

But she didn't seem upset in the least. I could have saved myself three theater tickets.

Katharine settled into her new chair and waved aside Will's comment. "What does Mr. Root think is wrong with your engine?"

"We're trying to keep our methods and materials under wraps," I said. "We're using aluminum to cut weight. The vast difference in color is a clue to the material."

Will added, "And the silvery color stands out in photographs, making all the other parts more visible. So we need to hide or disguise the engine somehow, until we get our patent."

"I see." She fished around in her bag and brought out a fashion magazine of all things.

"Look here." She flipped through the magazine until she came upon an advertisement for dresses.

Will leaned forward, pretending to be interested, and I figured I'd play along. "I like the white one with the black belt. It would look fine on you."

She dismissed me with a wave. At least she was treating her brothers equally. "No, silly, look at the illustrations. You can barely see the detail on the black dress. The buttons and belt blend in, and there's no contrast from shadows in the folds to give you an idea of the fullness."

"Yes...?" Then it came to me. "The engine. If it were black, not only would it appear to be cast iron, but it would be harder to see or photograph the details."

Will grabbed the magazine and studied the pictures "So we cover it with black fabric? I'm afraid it would burn up."

"Why don't you just paint it black?" Katharine seemed quite pleased with herself. "Just find a paint that's not going to catch fire and give me something else to worry about."

I took out my pocket pad and wrote a note about finding paint, then held my pen at the ready as I acted like a brat. "Okay, smarty, how else can we improve the flyer?"

Katharine ignored my tone and answered thoughtfully. "Tell me, if you can turn a circle with perfect control, what is to prevent you from going anywhere you want?"

"We still rely on the catapult, for one thing. Those aren't exactly available every few miles. And our control is under steady wind conditions. We can't fly on unstable days."

Katharine signaled to the waiter. "But you had to face wind from all directions to fly in a circle."

I waited until the waiter came and left before answering. "We still have rough landings more often than not. There is still an element of control that we're missing."

Katharine sipped at the icy drink. I could not understand how she could enjoy those concoctions.

"Let's see. You told me that you need to control the movement of the flyer in three different axes." She held out her flattened hand, palm down, representing the flyer. "Nose up, nose down." She moved her fingertips up and down accordingly.

"Pitch. That's right," I said.

"And left and right, like this," She moved her hand back and forth in a horizontal motion.

"Yaw," Wilbur joined in.

"And this one I know is controlled with wing warping. Roll." She spread her fingers and tilted her hand, pinky down and thumb up, then the reverse.

Wilbur raised his eyebrows at me. This was all so elementary. I gave him a little shrug, encouraging him to be patient.

"That's right, Sterchens. And we control all of them. But not as exacting as we need. So we're working on that." I signaled the waiter for the check.

But Katharine was not done. She pointed to her glass, indicating to the waiter she wanted another. I added the cost of theater tickets, dinner, and drinks in my head. We'd have to skip lunch this week to stay on budget.

"The pitch is controlled with front elevator, which is connected to the bar in your hands. You control the rear rudder and the twist of the wings with your hips."

Will and I nodded.

"But there are three axes. It seems to me that you should have three separate controls."

"Ah, I see your concern." Will explained. "Both the rudder and the ailerons—the new term for adapting the lift of each wing separately—are used for making turns. Therefore it made sense to coordinate them. A pilot only has two hands and one mind, and it's best to simplify things when you can."

"I understand it's difficult, and you had to teach yourselves how to fly. But now, maybe it's time to review that decision." She set down her unfinished drink and dabbed her mouth with a napkin. "Shall we go?"

I tried not to calculate how much of the drink she had wasted, which only added to my irritation. She seemed to think nothing of the hours and hard work we'd have to put in to change the controls.

The whole way home I thought about her ideas. Will was quiet and I knew that he was thinking about them as well. I was itching to get back out to the field and test her theory regarding separating the steering mechanisms. We might have to learn how to fly all over again, but if it gave us the control we needed, it would be well worthwhile.

WILBUR

After huddling over pen and paper, making hundreds of calculations, I could see that Katharine was right. There was no way to get the precise control we needed without separating the ailerons from the rudder control. The only thing stunning about it was that we hadn't thought of it before.

The change made me also reconfigure the center of gravity, the airflow between the elevator and the wings, and the size and shape of all of it. In airspace, one small change affects many others. Finally, after several days of working on theories and testing them in the wind tunnel, I went to Orv to help me work out the mechanics of it.

But he was ahead of me. I found him in the back workshop, huddled over a pile of scrap wood, wires, pulleys, and screws. "I think if we disconnect it from the hip harness and run a lever, we can just squeeze in a paddle…"

"So you think Sterchens is right?"

"Of course she's right. The idea had crossed my mind a few times."

I held my tongue. No good would come from assigning blame for our lost time. We were still in a race to get our invention patented before others could steal our designs and claim them as their own.

"Let's see what you've got there. By the way, we also need to extend the supports for the elevator by a few feet so it's not stealing air from the wings."

"I think we've gotten everything we can out of the current machine. Guess we're on to Flyer III." Orv sounded rather delighted. There was nothing he liked better than building things.

KATHARINE

1905

As I left Steele High School on a bitter January day, I wanted nothing more than to go home and slip into a hot bath. I pictured emptying pot after pot of steaming water into the steel tub, then luxuriating in mountains of bubbles. But when I stepped into the kitchen, Orv was there, with stockpots on the cooker and open jars of colorful liquids everywhere. He was peering at a glass candy thermometer as he held it up to the light.

"Making rock candy?" I asked hopefully. It was one of Orv's hobbies from which I could enjoy the results. He would boil highly concentrated sugar water. Then as it cooled, he would dip strings into the solution to form crystals. But the stench in the kitchen was not of any flavoring I would want to eat. It smelled like turpentine.

"Nope. Paint."

I echoed Mother's voice screaming in horror in my mind. "You're making paint in my kitchen?"

He crouched to check the flame on the burner. "Your idea. The black paint at the hardware store didn't pass my tests."

"Hmph." I turned away from the stink and mess. At least he was fastidious about cleaning up after himself. As long as he didn't burn the house down, I wouldn't complain.

The next day on my way home from work, I dropped by the bicycle shop to make a telephone call. Already chilled from the ride in the open streetcar, I rushed the few blocks from the stop. The sun was low in the sky, and it would darken more before the streetlamps came on. At least the shop would have light and heat.

As I approached, it seemed the lamps inside had not yet been lit, and something was strange about the window display. We always showcased the latest-model bicycle in the window, along with a display of the various parts and accessories that we sold. But there was no bike, and just a few scattered boxes of tubes and chains. My heart beat against my chest. Had we been robbed?

The display window was intact, but the *Closed* sign hung on the door. It was only just after five, and the shop should still be open. I tried the doorknob; it was unlocked.

"Hello?" I asked tentatively as I kept one hand on the door. If there were a theft in progress, I would escape rather than confront.

A familiar voice answered from within. Lorin.

My words tumbled out in relief. "Oh goodness, you gave me a scare. What is going on? Why is the shop closed, and what has happened to our display? Have we been robbed? Are you all right?"

Lorin, dressed in his white work shirt, brown pants, and suspenders, greeted me. "Sorry for your fright. No, we haven't been robbed." His finger was tucked into the middle of a book, no doubt holding his place in a detective novel. "At least that would have been exciting." He nodded to the window, then pointed to the hooks on the walls that usually held new bicycles and wheels. "We're just very low on inventory."

"I see. But there is still the repair business. This is usually a busy time, as men stop in on their way home from work."

"We're also low on workers. Charley is at the field with the boys, and I can't run the shop and do the books all by myself."

I chose to ignore the "books" he had been doing. "What about the new hire?"

"Never showed up. And speaking of books, you need to take a look at them."

I knew we'd had a few bad months, with competition from other shops mounting right at the time when bicycles were falling out of favor. People wanted automobiles, not bicycles. And Orville and Wilbur were not only flying instead of manning the shop but also no longer coming out with the new and improved bicycle designs for which they had become known.

Lorin led me to the small office, which held the telephone I had been planning to use. But that was insignificant now. He stowed the novel, then opened the ledger and reviewed the numbers with me. Not only were we not making a profit; we had been in the red for the past three months, with each month worse than the previous.

Lorin quietly closed the ledger. "We can't sustain this. I can't spend more time here. I have my own business and family to support. Can you talk to Will and Orv?"

That was a conversation I really didn't want to have, and it didn't seem my place. "Isn't that your job?"

"I did speak to them, but it did no good. They said just hire someone else. It's just a short-term problem…"

I had received a modest raise at Steele, but it wouldn't cover this shortfall in our family's finances. Indeed, something was going to have to change.

ORVILLE

By now we were on our third generation, the Flyer III. To look at it, except for the black engine, you wouldn't think it was much different than the previous models. But with better controls and modified rudders, she was proving to be much more maneuverable. We were flying longer and under adverse conditions. Charley finally came up with an engine powerful enough to take off without a catapult on days with a slight wind.

But problems in the bicycle shop threatened to shut down our whole operation. Admittedly, Will and I were absent a good deal of the time, and Charley, Katharine, and Lorin were keeping it running and managing the books. Even so, sales kept declining; it seemed everyone who wanted a bicycle already had one.

❧

One Sunday afternoon, Katharine brought the long green book in which she recorded our sales into the dining room where we awaited lunch. This was not a good sign.

"Gentlemen, you've been too busy to attend our weekly sales

meeting, so I'm bringing it to you." She proceeded to read the sales numbers, along with the percent of decrease for each.

My stomach sank lower with each figure.

"We need to work on something new," Will said. "Better brakes or gears or something."

"You have something new," Katharine said with quite a bit of annoyance in her voice. "Your flying machine. Sell a few of those, and you can forget about building bicycles."

It was Wilbur's turn to be testy. "If it were ready, customers would be pounding at our door."

"Nonsense. Customers don't know of it, and your customers are not likely in Dayton, Ohio." Katharine closed the ledger.

"Do you have someone in mind?" I asked.

"Yes, it seems to me that your machine could be quite useful to the army. Think about how they could use it for communications and for spying on the enemy. Air balloons are too easy a target and too difficult to steer exactly where they want them."

Will looked at his pocket watch. "I have to pick up the Bishop at the station. I appreciate your ideas, but I'm afraid we're still trying to get it reliably off the ground."

"You don't need to have it perfect to sell it. Sell the idea of it, and let the government help you develop it to their needs. They're obviously interested. Look at all the money that was dumped into Langley's failures."

Wilbur nodded and excused himself. Seeing Katharine's disappointment, I offered an olive branch. "Sterchens, I think you've got something there. You know Will, never wants to take anything from anybody, thinks we can get there on our own. But it's not fair to you, who've been working so hard, to not try. I'll start writing some letters to the army. We'll see what happens."

She held her mouth in a thin line. "Humph. But in the meanwhile, between the lack of new inventory and paying for the unreliable help, the shop is about to go bankrupt. Either you two have to sell the shop for whatever you can get in a tight market, or we'll have to borrow against the house. And I don't need to tell you how the Bishop will feel about that."

It sent a dagger through my gut that she saw us as failures. "No."

"No what?"

"No to both of those options." My mind raced back to a conversation I'd had with Will concerning too many people learning of our doings out at Huffman Prairie. "Wait, just a second." I caught Will as he donned his hat, about to head out the door, and led him back into the dining room. I reviewed Katharine's proposals and my objections.

He peered into his bowler hat as if an answer would magically appear nestled in the black felt. "I agree, neither of those is a good option. So what do we do?"

"We were considering hiring a security guard to keep people away from the flyer..." I said.

"Yes, but that hardly seems feasible now."

"Because we don't have our final patents to protect us. Once we do, we'll market the heck out of it. We're at a point now that we just need a couple of days a week for final testing."

Will glanced from me to Katharine, squinting with suspicion. "What are you saying, Orv?"

"I say we get back to work at the bicycle shop. You, me, Charley. Build some inventory, get the business in shape to sell. Once Flyer III is tested, it's time to put her away until we have the patents."

Katharine's smile was all I needed to know I was doing the right thing.

KATHARINE

I was mindful of my promise to visit Margaret in Chicago, but between teaching school, managing the bicycle shop and home, there was barely time to write letters to her, never mind visit. Thus, I was distressed when I learned that she had fallen ill again, her stomach having never fully recovered from our trip to St. Louis. So I belatedly traveled to Chicago to see her.

She had grown too thin, much as my mother had before she died. I was not surprised when she told me that the doctors suspected consumption. Unlike my mother, the disease had invaded her digestive system, not her lungs.

We spent several days together, taking short walks around her fashionable neighborhood and chatting about our old times at Oberlin.

"I want you to promise me something," Margaret said.

"Anything."

"You have much to give, and someday you will have the time. Don't forget Oberlin and the students who could benefit from your wisdom."

"Of course." I wasn't sure exactly what I could do for Oberlin, but I could hardly say no to this request. "But this is something we can do together, once I can break away from my current responsibilities."

Margaret looked at me with a heartbreaking smile. "You know that won't happen. So I'm counting on you."

WILBUR

By October, we had Flyer III working flawlessly, although it still required a catapult on most days. It took all seven of the two-hundred-pound weights and still needed a headwind of five or so miles per hour, but we were able to take off, fly in circles for half an hour or so, then land in the same spot.

Meanwhile, we had written to the army and gotten a positive response from the Signal Corps, located at Fort Myer, Virginia. They were planning a list of specifications that would be necessary to achieve before they would consider purchasing. We also stayed in touch with Octave Chanute, but his claims to the newspapers that we were basically his workers, building from his designs and instructions, didn't sit right with us.

It had taken too long to get through our thick heads that we needed to protect our work with a patent. My first attempt failed utterly, being rejected out of hand. With Amos Root's help, Katharine had located an attorney with patent specialty, and we had refiled upon his advice.

Amos's ideas for specific diagrams, including ideas for construction and control that we had not yet attempted, would prove vital to our success. For example, we knew the concept of the aileron was key, and that there could be any number of ways to change the shape of the wing to accomplish a change in its lift. So we diagrammed or simply explained the most promising of them, in order to patent the concept rather than its specific execution.

KATHARINE

MAY 1906

The postman delivered a letter postmarked from Chicago. The return said simply *Meacham*, Margaret's married name, but it was not written in her hand. I didn't want to open it.

She was gone, my lovely, lovely friend, at not quite thirty years old. I had missed so many important times. I wasn't there for her when her preacher father died and the church had turned her and her mother out on the streets. The memory of that still angered me, even when the Bishop tried to explain the pressures on a congregation.

"You wouldn't have done it!" I had yelled back at him. Since then, I had become a rather irregular attendant at our own church downtown, even though it was not the same denomination. I could hold a grudge with the best of them.

I remembered my promise and started to stay in better touch with my other friends and read the newsletters sent to all Oberlin alumni. Someday I would try to make up for the church's wrongdoing in the way that Margaret had requested.

Her request that I support Oberlin's students challenged me. I lived too far away to be of much regular use to them, but perhaps a scholarship in Margaret's name would be the best way to honor her memory. My new goal was to somehow raise enough money to make an everlasting fund. Certainly my teacher's salary would not suffice.

My suggestion to the boys to market their invention had been mostly aimed at their well-being. But now I had another motivation to help that cause.

WILBUR

When Orv and I returned from the shop on a sunny day, Katharine and the Bishop were already seated at the dining table. But they weren't eating. Instead, they were focused on a single envelope propped against a vase of daisies.

"What's this?" I picked up the envelope. It was from the patent office in Washington, DC. "Oh, I see." I waited for Orv to join us, then offered it to him to open.

"Go ahead."

With all eyes eagerly upon me, I carefully slipped open the envelope. "We got it." I held up the letter. "We've won the patent for controlling the flying machine!"

As everyone cheered and Katharine produced a bottle of bubbling cider, I let myself relax. At last we could start marketing our invention.

KATHARINE

We followed the news of aviators across the world, all trying to repeat what the boys had done in North Carolina. Orville pointed out that one had flown seven hundred feet, nearly as far as Wilbur's record at Kitty Hawk.

We were gathered in the sitting room, as was our custom after dinner. Orville was tunelessly strumming his mandolin, and I was grateful when he stopped to return to their favorite topic, making a business of selling aeroplanes.

Will dismissed the story with a scowl. "Neither one of those pilots in Paris has any control, and without that, they have nothing. They are where we were back in 1902."

"But the French are going by droves to see them, while we can't get a customer to even look at us," Orv said.

"Some of that is by design. We have our patent, but it's still not clear exactly what it covers. Upon advice from our lawyer, until the courts decide, we can't seriously negotiate with anyone. Our discoveries will simply be stolen." Will folded his newspaper to display a particular article and handed it to Orv. "But you're right.

The French seem much more interested. We should write the French government, since our own has dismissed us as cranks."

In April, I discovered a major development that the boys had kept hidden from me. I had gone to the bicycle shop to make a telephone call. Orv and Will were arguing in the back room, shouting to be heard over the whine of the engine and serpentine belts that powered their equipment. Upon seeing me enter, Orv shut down the engine.

"I wonder if we should ask for a machine shop over there, or should we expect to ship crates full of parts?" Will asked Orv.

"Ship crates where?" I asked. Apparently the boys had been very busy in this back room; piles of wooden struts filled every corner, and metal baskets labeled *Pulleys* and *Wires* and *Screws* lined the walls. The air reeked of engine oil and exhaust, despite the exhaust pipes they had set up. Charley, his shop apron streaked with grease, had been tinkering with a large piece of metal but stopped when the system was shut down.

"Oh, Sterchens, we've had the greatest offer, but we wanted to work out the details before we surprised you with it," Orv said while glancing at Will, as if for permission.

Charley quietly filed out of the room. I bit my lips and braced myself for unwelcome news. Why else would they have waited to announce it?

"Go on," I said.

Will took my arm and guided me toward the shop-room door. "We've had a promising offer. Let's go to the office and we'll tell you all about it."

The three of us squeezed into the small office. Will sat at the desk, extracted a letter from a cubby, and handed it to me.

"Postmarked Paris." My spirits lifted a bit. Perhaps this was good news after all. I looked at the return address. "Who is Hart Berg?"

Orv's eyes danced with excitement. "He's an American businessman and engineer. We checked with our friend Chanute, and he's a well-respected fellow. Look here..." He pulled the letter from the envelope and rifled through the pages, then read, "'I have gathered a group of wealthy, influential men who were interested in aviation.'" His shy smile peeked from under his mustache. "We've been waiting for something just like this. We're taking the flyer to Europe!" He flipped some pages. "They've got a list of challenges. Nothing we can't do already."

Will swiveled toward us in the desk chair, his lanky frame filling it like a king on his throne. "We couldn't ask for a better international sponsor. We must be careful as we await clarification of the patents, but Berg and his investors have agreed to sponsor our transportation and lodging, with a promise to order flyers should the tests be successful."

"And they will be, of course." Orv said.

I wondered why this had been played close to their vests. "Of course. But what is the downside?"

Will tapped his tented fingers. "I will need to go to France very soon for negotiations. Orv will follow in a couple of months, certainly by July. You'll be off school by then..."

"I see." Questions swirled in my head. "But who will run the bicycle shop? What about your flyer at Huffman Prairie? And why go to France when you have yet to explore the market here?"

"I disagree. We have a stack of rejections. No one wants to take a chance this early in the game. Charley will stay back, and we'll hire more help. In fact, we'll be able to sell the bicycle shop entirely if this all works out."

I knew what this really meant, and why they were keeping it from me. I would be left behind once again, seeing to the Bishop's and his church's needs, managing Charley and the shop, while of course teaching full-time until late June.

What I really wanted was to be a part of this new adventure, and I couldn't imagine Orville doing much negotiating in English, never mind French. "Why don't I go to France with you? I speak some French and could help in many ways."

"In good time. But we need to you handle all the American business while we're both gone."

⁓

So they were off once again, and I took over their duties. With news of the boys working in France, Americans suddenly took notice: I was besieged with requests for more information on the aviation business. Businessmen showed up at our door with written offers of paltry sums in exchange for shares of my brothers' future endeavors. Even *Webster's Dictionary* wanted permission to feature a photograph of the flyer. Our country was belatedly waking up to the history made by two of their own.

I decided to take advantage of the relatively empty house and threw parties with friends from Steele High School and Oberlin. With Margaret gone, I vowed to stay in better touch. To my great sadness, I had another friend suffering from tuberculosis. Frances was also a Latin teacher who I had often chatted with but hadn't had time to be with lately. I needed to change that.

Frances and I resumed our long walks, which helped her lungs. I introduced her to my friend Marilyn, who was always a delight to be with and made me feel less guilty when I didn't have time to join them.

But all the exercise and fresh air was not enough to save poor Frances. On a drizzly gray morning, I stood next to a sobbing Marilyn as we tossed handfuls of earth upon our friend's coffin. I grieved for dear Frances. I grieved for the spark of a relationship with Orville that I had failed to nurture when I had the chance. I grieved for Marilyn, who I had thoughtlessly exposed to heartache and loss.

"What can I do to make up for these failures?" I asked the Bishop. He had accompanied me to the service, and as we clopped along in a horse-drawn cab, I explained how I had wronged sweet Marilyn and requested his sage advice.

He was gentle and kind, nodding quietly as I blubbered on about Frances and Margaret. I said it wasn't fair that we lost them, and Mother too, at such an early age. "Why?" I implored him. "They were good people." I wiped my drippy nose. "And what should I do about Marilyn? How could I have been so obtuse?"

"Oh, my dear child. It is not for us to understand the mysteries of the Lord. A life is not measured by its length in years, but in hearts that are touched. And your friends, and you, have touched many." He offered his handkerchief. "And it is not for you to decide or do anything for dear Marilyn. They are two souls that befriended each other briefly on this earth, and will find each other again in the next life."

I sniffed and nodded. If only I could believe it in my heart, and not just as a theory for my brain. "What then, can I do to make myself feel better? I need something tangible, something constructive."

"Of course. That is who you are. My opinion is you are already doing so much, you shouldn't feel a need to add more to your plate." He was quiet for a moment. "But in good time, the answer to your question will present itself. A challenge will come up, and you will need to rise to the occasion. Watch for this, and the Lord will show you the way."

His advice to wait and see wasn't what I wanted to hear right then. But I suspected he was right; it did seem that something was coming at me like a freight train. My intuition told me it would have to do with my brothers.

ORVILLE

Will thrilled the French, setting records by flying longer and higher than ever before. Katharine read a report in a French newspaper that Wilbur was "flying, while the Frenchmen were still fluttering about." Meanwhile I hadn't given up on the American government. While they were understandably gun-shy after the huge sums poured into Langley's failed machine, how could they deny our success and potential?

I wrote to every federal entity that could possibly have interest, from the Treasury to the Department of State. Finally, we had a glimmer of interest from the Army Signal Corps, as they had finally come up with a list of requirements. We quickly agreed to their demands for demonstration flights at their base in Fort Myer, Virginia.

It would all be at our own expense at first, but the understanding was if we completed the required flights, a contract would be in the offing. None of the requests were unreasonable; Wilbur had already exceeded most of the altitude, speed, and distance goals. But he flew in carefully chosen places, with plenty of takeoff and landing space.

They wanted us to do a cross-country trip as far as Alexandria, which we were sure we could accomplish.

A visit to Fort Myer revealed the space to be barely adequate. They offered a cleared field of about eight hundred by four hundred feet called the drill ground, used for ceremonies and parades. The field was encircled by trees and buildings, with Arlington National Cemetery just outside the gate and Washington, DC, across the Potomac River. Some of the test flights were to include a passenger, or *copilot* as the documents referred to him, further increasing the challenge.

By then, we had moved to a larger space for construction of our machines, and several were near completion. The current model had some modifications, based on Wilbur's recommendations. Good sense told me I should test the machine first in the familiar territory of Huffman Prairie, but the government had imposed a deadline that precluded that. So the machine was hurriedly finished and crated for transport to Virginia. I calmed my nerves by insisting that Charley come with me, knowing we would have time to thoroughly look over the machine once it was reconstructed, and the flights would not be open to the public.

As we worked night and day to prepare for the army trials, a family crisis loomed. Lorin's eldest son, Milton, came down with typhoid fever. The Bishop, Katharine, and I took turns each evening, visiting and keeping his spirits up to ease the strain on Lorin and Netta.

One evening, when I returned from my shift with Milton after working twelve hours at the shop, I collapsed on the davenport in the sitting room.

"Son, you need to leave these visits to your sister and me, before you're our next patient," the Bishop said.

Katharine joined in. "I agree. You can't let your preparations for Fort Myer slide. Papa and I will take turns."

I was too worn out to argue, except to say, "All right. But only after I make Milton a batch of caramel candy. He loves it."

⤝

Charley and I arrived in early September, which seemed to be still midsummer in Virginia, with temperatures in the eighties. I dispensed with my suit jacket as soon as I was out of sight of others.

Fort Myer was impressive, the clusters of redbrick buildings set against the greenest grass I had ever seen. They must have had a legion of gardeners trimming and mowing it to perfection. The scenic army base was set against the backdrop of a curve in the Potomac River. Before we even started unpacking the crates, I took the anemometer out for a stroll, taking measurements at many locations, and especially at an overlook above the river. I wasn't concerned with how high or low wind speeds were; I was interested in their consistency. Were there wind vortices between the multistory buildings, which would be much closer than they were at our previous sites? Did the numbers change at a bend in the river?

Satisfied that no unusual pattern showed itself, at least not on that day, I joined Charley in the work shed we had been assigned to. My mechanic had replaced his usual gray suit with a set of overalls. As I shook his hand in greeting, I gave the buckle on his shoulder a tug.

"Did you stop at a farm on the way?"

"Heck no, I found these on a hook." He waved to a thin wall on the opposite side of the shed. "There's another pair for you, if you like."

"Good idea. I should keep my suits in good condition for the demonstrations. Just have to hope no one comes nosing around while we're dressed like this."

I changed into the overalls as Charley extracted nails and opened the crates with a *crack*. Then together we lifted the various parts of the machine and set them up in our accustomed pattern. I unrolled a diagram Wilbur had sent with his recommended adjustments. It included modest changes to the skids for the longer landing space needed for the heavier, faster machine and some new wire reinforcements. I had done some calculations, but it didn't seem there would be a significant change to the weight or wind resistance.

"Orville, come take a look at these." Charley had opened the longest crate, which contained the propellers. One of the propeller blades was jammed into a corner of the crate. It took some finagling for us to wiggle it out of the space without damaging it. We both looked it over, but it didn't appear to be chipped.

"Wait, what's this?" Charley pointed to a thin dark line running from the tip of the blade halfway to the center of the propeller. "Is that just the grain of the wood, or is it a crack?"

I ran my fingers over the mark, but it felt uniformly smooth. This propeller was longer than previous ones to accommodate the increased weight and wingspan. Finding good-quality spruce to carve into eight-foot-long propellers had been a challenge.

"There isn't time to have another one made at this point. I think it's just a natural variation in the wood that we wouldn't even have noticed if it hadn't gotten a bit jammed up. Let's set up the engine and watch it spin."

So it went for every part that we unpacked and pieced together. Wilbur had drummed into my brain the importance of checking and rechecking every single part. Sometimes all his fussing did more harm than good, as we missed the best winds and light of day due to it.

In a few days' time, the machine was built and inspected. The army sent several soldiers to help move it into position on the field. They had also provided help building the catapult tower, and I trained some men on how to release the weight upon my signal. Horses already stabled right at the edge of the field would provide the power to lift the weights.

My first flight was to be a simple loop, up to the river, a gentle turn and return, landing as close as possible to the takeoff point. Quite routine, but my stomach roiled with queasiness for several reasons. Will wasn't there to obsessively check and recheck our work. The soldiers had never done a task like this before. I had never flown this machine before. I had never flown in this location before, there were now two seats on board, and I would now pilot sitting up instead of prone, both of which added drag. I took several deep breaths to steady my nerves, and climbed into the left seat. I started the engine and listened to its whine. Something was off. I killed the engine and climbed down again. Charley and a soldier came running up.

"Did someone change something?" I was wrist deep in the valves, which already were quite hot from their short run. I checked the narrow reservoir and line suspended from a strut to ensure they were full of water to cool the engine.

"I put in a little more oil," a soldier sheepishly admitted.

"Don't," I said.

I tightened the caps, and satisfied that all was in position, I climbed back into my seat, restarted the engine, and signaled for Charley and the soldier to give the propellers a push. My hand trembled as I reached for the rudder stick. The final thing I was worried about was the importance of this mission. If I were to fail, it would set back aviation in this country for an untold amount of time. I felt like I held not only the Wright family's future in my hands, but the nation's. As the engine came up to speed, I listened for the propellers' maximum whine and sensed the machine's force mounting against the restraining rope. I said a little prayer, unhooked the restraining line, then signaled for the catapult release.

I bowed my head in anticipation of the sudden jolt. The machine's skids slid down the boards as smooth as silk and the wings did their work, lifting the flyer and me, sitting up in a chair, gently off the ground. I straightened the rear rudder and set both wings for maximum lift as we gained speed. The engine chugged loudly, but in perfect synchrony, the drivetrain whirring as it should; the chains attached to the propellers behind me buzzed equally on both sides. Higher it climbed, and I let my muscles relax as the wind held me aloft in a space that was mine alone. A sudden downdraft sent the nose down a bit, but I easily corrected with the front elevator. Now to test the tilt controls. I increased the warp of the left wing and adjusted the paddle attached to the rear rudder ever so slightly. This caused the flyer to tilt and turn. To try to turn without tilting could send it into a spin. I slowly increased into the turn until we had made ninety degrees.

She was flying beautifully. Possibly better than any of the previous machines. After so much time away, my body once again came alive with the sensation of being aloft, and my heart filled with the excitement and wonder of it. I couldn't wait to write to the Bishop, Wilbur, and Katharine. We would get this contract. Our country would fly.

Having proved the aeroplane's airworthiness, I flew a string of passengers in the machine. Local politicians, wealthy influencers, army officers all took their turns, after my approval, of course. Each time I took someone up, I reveled in their excitement. I relived the thrill of my own first time by sharing theirs.

A polite but insistent lieutenant named Frank Lahm was eager to fly with me. He was the one who somehow convinced the army to let me do the demonstrations at Fort Myer. He had experience as a balloonist, and had won a race in France. He asked so many questions that I decided to take him up ahead of schedule just to save myself from so many explanations.

I was momentarily worried when I heard that President Theodore Roosevelt desired a ride. Not that I didn't admire the president, but if anything should happen, that would be the end of all of it. And as the president was a hefty man, I was afraid I wouldn't be able to compensate for our weight difference.

By the grace of God, someone talked the president out of it, but there did remain one passenger approved by the army that I didn't care for or trust: Lieutenant Thomas Selfridge, an army officer who had been involved with Alexander Graham Bell's competing experiments. We didn't allow photography at the test location, but he tried anyway. Charley also caught him sneaking around the machine, taking notes and undoubtedly mental pictures of what he saw.

Wilbur also distrusted the man and had warned me not to allow him anywhere near the machine, but I couldn't refuse the army's request.

The morning before our scheduled flight, we had a bit of time to chat as we did our inspection. I was curious about his army experience and how it led to an interest in flying.

"Oh, military service runs deep in my blood. My uncle and grandfather were rear admirals, and the same was expected of me. Just to be ornery, I went to West Point." He chuckled.

"Did you favor the army?" I asked.

"I wouldn't complain. Not fully what I expected. I helped out with rescue and cleanup after the quake in San Francisco, which was tough work but gratifying. When I heard about the new aeronautical division, I asked for a transfer, and here I am."

I already knew he had worked with Alexander Bell, but was curious about their progress. "The army has been most accommodating to us. Have they had you doing anything exciting lately?"

Selfridge paused as he looked over the engine as if he were taking a mental photograph. I wondered what our government-issued patents would be worth if the same government wanted to take them.

"You might have heard of the Red Wing, the aeronautical division's first powered aircraft? I designed it."

"Oh indeed, quite an accomplishment. And what became of it? Might I take a look at it while I'm in the area?" I was being deliberately obtuse; I knew exactly what had happened, as the lieutenant probably suspected.

"Unfortunately, it crashed and the airframe was destroyed. But we did learn much from the experience, and I successfully flew the White Wing shortly thereafter. I am the first of what will be many military pilots."

With his hands in his pockets and chest defiantly puffed out, he reminded me of the comic *The Katzenjammer Kids*.

"I'm real sorry about that. We've had our share of mishaps as well. A risky business we've gotten ourselves into."

As we circled the machine, I took note of the lieutenant's size. He was larger than my previous passengers, maybe thirty or forty pounds heavier than me. I wouldn't be setting any records with this flight. *Go up. Circle the area five or six times at one hundred and fifty feet and make a gradual descent for the spectators.*

"I'm sure you're an outstanding pilot, but I'm afraid I can't allow you to handle the controls on this trip." I tied my cap with a cord to keep it from flying off my head. "Ready?"

We climbed aboard. I sat at the controls on the left side and Selfridge took the seat on the right. I pointed to the strut for his handhold and the bar for his feet. He didn't say a word, just dutifully did as told.

It was a perfect takeoff and a gentle ascent. I did some especially long, graceful turns, showing off the maneuverability of the machine just a bit. Around the parade field and over buildings of the base we went, two, three, four times, each circle just a bit higher until we were at about one hundred and fifty feet. At that height we could see people waving from the fields and some buildings across the river in Washington, DC. It was a grand feeling to be flying, and I was even starting to enjoy the company of a man we had mistrusted. He had been nothing but respectful, aside from his surreptitious picture taking.

I pushed the engine to full throttle and continually adjusted for our slight imbalance in weight distribution as we entered our fifth circle. Just as I leveled the wings again there was a loud *CRACK*. I saw something fly off the right side, long and narrow, possibly a piece of propeller. Then the machine jerked violently and the nose headed down. I was able to push the elevators to the maximum and even us out a bit, and once we were in line with a clear landing path, I killed the engine. I looked over at Selfridge, but there was no time for words. I'm sure he understood my goal: glide her down as gradually as possible.

We dropped about seventy-five feet at a steep angle, the machine shaking violently as I used all my might to force the controls. Then there was another *snap* and a wire thrashed like a sword, slicing the struts between the wings. The controls were now useless, and the nose headed straight for the ground.

"Brace!" was all I had time to say.

"Oh! Oh!" Selfridge cried out.

The ground came at us at terrifying speed, and I was helpless to do anything but cover my face with my arms. We tumbled through blackness, then a searing pain ripped through my knee and chest. It felt as if my body was broken in two. *This is how I die*, I thought. I made peace with the Lord and prayed for the survival of my passenger.

I tried to shut my eyes and drift away, but the fire that seemed to be eating my leg wouldn't let me. My eyes fluttered open, but among the swirling mix of splintered wood, wires, and tattered fabric, I saw no flames. The air reeked of gasoline, and my lungs were burning, every breath a tremendous effort.

Just as I tried to surrender to the Lord's will, I heard men's voices. The world faded out of focus, but I heard Charley.

"He's over here!" Charley yelled. The voices were close. "Get two stretchers! We need a saw! Watch out, don't step there!"

I took a shallow breath. I was alive. It seemed God wasn't quite done with me yet. They were coming for me. What about the lieutenant? "Thomas?" I tried to shout, but my breath would not allow for it.

A hazy face I didn't recognize appeared inches from mine. "We've got you, Mr. Wright. Don't move. Just as soon as we can get you untangled, we'll have you out and patch you up."

"Am I...? Do I...?" I fluttered my hand toward my legs, hoping he'd understand my concern.

"You seem to be all in one piece, sir. Just sit tight."

To distract myself from the searing pain, I focused on the frantic efforts of my rescuers. Saws ground against wood, men groaned as they bent metal with their bare hands. Sounds of the fabric tearing and struts snapping meant they were getting ever closer. After what seemed like hours but was probably only a few minutes, they had me out and on a stretcher.

"My passenger…Selfridge…?" I kept asking.

Finally someone said, "He's alive. Out cold and took a nasty blow to the head. But they got him out and he's on the way to the hospital."

Waves of pain threatened to overtake me and I closed my eyes against it.

"This will help," someone close to me said. Then I felt something like a bee sting as medication was injected into my upper arm. Moments later, I still felt pain, but it was as if it was attached to another person.

I tried to order my thoughts. *Wilbur's going to be mad as hell. And if Selfridge doesn't make it…* I didn't want to finish the thought. The world seemed to close in on me. *This might be the end of all our work. We struggled and got this far. But it wasn't enough. And what would Katharine think? Dear, sweet Katharine. Oh, she'd fuss at me for not being careful enough. The propeller. Was Charley right about the propeller? Do I dare tell her about that? I think not. Oh, they're lifting me up into a bed.* I tried to raise my hand to tell them to cable Will and Katie, but I was drawn into a dream and I was flying, nearly touching the clouds.

KATHARINE

DAYTON

Carrie had the night off, and with Wilbur in France, Orville in Virginia, and the Bishop away at a church symposium, I was home alone one Thursday evening in mid-September. It was time to bring in the last of the tomatoes from the garden. I picked all of them, as well as the remaining bell peppers and onions, and piled them into my apron. From their lovely aroma, I knew they'd be full of flavor. With no need to cook for others, a fresh salad would be just fine for my dinner.

Heading back inside, I heard the squeak of the front gate as the Western Union messenger let himself in. Orville and Wilbur usually wrote letters. A feeling of cold dread passed through me but I forced myself to remain calm, assuring myself it was probably a message from the Bishop instructing me when to pick him up from the train station. I ran to the front yard to save the messenger a few steps.

"Just toss it right on top," I told the messenger, holding out my apron with its pile of vegetables. I carried it all inside and put aside the produce before tearing open the envelope with a dirty fingernail.

It wasn't a telegram from the Bishop. Orv had had a flying accident and was in the hospital at Fort Myer.

I braced myself against a wall, even as the same walls seemed to be closing in on me and taking away my ability to breathe. Orv. My Orv. I tamped down the panic that spread through my body like a wildfire until I could no longer think. I forced myself to read the message again.

He was alive. I would make sure he stayed that way. I had missed nearly a year of college while nursing him through typhoid. I could do this. But it felt like the freight train the Bishop had predicted was bearing down on me.

I took the stairs two at a time and hurried to my bedroom. I tore through my wardrobe to find my leather travel bag. It didn't see much use, and it was smashed into a corner under some worn-out boots. What to bring? No matter. I started stuffing whatever skirts and shirtwaists would fit into the bag. Some low shoes. A dress. No, a lighter one. How hot was Virginia in September? All the while, I pushed the images of my poor broken brother out of my mind. I dragged my packed bag downstairs and rooted through a drawer for the train schedule.

On my way to the station, I dropped off a note for my principal, then hurried to the Western Union office to send a cable to Fort Myer and to friends who lived in nearby Arlington. No time to wait for their response, so I could only hope they received it and would permit me to stay with them.

❧

In Washington, I was greeted at the train station by a tall, impeccably uniformed army officer. He introduced himself as Lieutenant

Lahm. He quickly escorted me across the river to Fort Myer in a drab green motorcar. The lieutenant told me that Orville was out of immediate danger but would have a long recovery ahead. His left leg was broken in two places, as were several ribs. Lieutenant Lahm also warned me that Orville's head was badly cut up and heavily bandaged.

The lieutenant tried to ease my nerves by chatting about his experiences flying with Orv and ballooning in France. I could hardly focus on anything other than my brother, but I did ask about Orville's passenger. The lieutenant pulled the motorcar to the side of the road, and we sat there a bit, the engine chugging along like a kettle on the boil.

"I'm afraid Lieutenant Selfridge did not survive his injuries." He stared straight ahead, with the stoic pose of a man trained to accept such things.

"I'm so sorry. That's devastating." I closed my eyes against the horror, which I knew was much worse for Orville. "Does my brother know? How did he take it?"

"He does, and as well as could be expected. We sent word to your father and to your brother in France as well." Lahm eased the car back onto the narrow road and we passed through a gate and on to Fort Myer. "We have our own train station here, and just over there is the drill ground, which is where the flying takes place." The congenial lieutenant acted as a tour guide as I watched a blur of two-story brick buildings go by, with immense trees guarding each of them. "We're smack up against Arlington Cemetery, final resting place of our most cherished warriors. I'm sure you've heard of it…"

A cemetery was the last thing I wanted to think about. Finally the lieutenant pulled up to a stately red brick building with two stories of white-balustraded balconies lining one side.

"You go on in, I'll fetch your bags." He nodded toward the building. A painted sign read: *Building 59 Hospital.*

Inside, a team of three doctors met with me. I was desperate to see Orv, but bit my tongue and tried to listen to their diagnoses.

"We're not so worried about the bones. They'll heal up well enough. Pain from the broken bones and a severely bruised spinal cord necessitates quite a lot of morphine, and that reduces his respiratory effort—his breathing, that is. Now with someone laid up in bed for a long time like he will be, pneumonia is a grave danger. What we're hoping…"

I had closed my eyes and was rocking a bit in my seat, taking it all in.

"Miss Wright, are you okay?"

"Yes, yes. Go on. It's a lot all at once."

"Of course. Well, we're hoping that you can stay with him during these critical first weeks while he will be in traction. Get him to talk, shout if he can, take deep breaths, cough, and exercise those parts that he can. This must be done every two hours at least, all the time he's awake. Our nurses do a fine job, of course, but we find sometimes a loved one can spend more time and give needed encouragement to our patients."

I was trying to follow all he was saying, but all I could think about was Orv still in danger. "Um, what is intraction?"

"Oh, sorry. Traction—your brother's leg is held in place by a system of ropes and pulleys, with his weight at one end and a set of weights at the other. It will make more sense once you see him." The doctor checked his timepiece. He no doubt had other patients waiting for him, and I felt ashamed for being so dense.

"No, I'm sorry for not understanding. This is all new to me. Traction sounds very uncomfortable."

"Quite understandable. And it isn't uncomfortable so much as it can get boring and frustrating, just waiting for time to heal things. Which is another good reason for you to stay."

"I will, just as long as I can." I didn't know how long I could be away without losing my job. But that was a worry for another time.

"Can I see my brother now?"

"Of course." The doctor led me down bright-white corridors and through a set of swinging doors with a sign above them that read *Orthopedic Ward*. It was an open room with a dozen beds lined up along the walls, about half of them occupied.

I soon saw what the doctor meant regarding traction. Some of the beds had ropes angling up from the patient's leg to a contraption bolted in a frame over the bed, then down, ending in a stack of weights at the foot of the bed.

"Mr. Wright is a very special guest, so he has a private room."

I was escorted to the back corner, where a door opened to a tiny room. I took some deep breaths and forced a smile so as not to frighten Orv with my reaction. But I need not have worried.

"Oh, here you are! Oh, Sterchens! I've never been so happy to see a living being in my life." Tears ran down Orv's face.

I went to him and bent down to hug him the best I could. Tears clouded my vision, but from what I could tell that, although the rest of his head was heavily bandaged, his face had barely a scratch. I pulled back. "Let me look at you. You do seem to be all in one piece, thank the Lord. Are you in much pain?"

"As far as they tell me, I have all my working parts. Haven't seen some of them myself, because they have me tied up for bad behavior. And no, the pain is not too bad now, because every four hours a sweet nurse comes in to give me a shot and make sure I haven't escaped on them." He laughed, which apparently hurt, as he braced his stomach with his arms.

Laughing should be good for him, I thought, remembering the doctor's warning about pneumonia. "Here." I grabbed an extra pillow from a chair. "Hold this against your stomach when you laugh." I remembered doing that when I fell from a horse and bruised a rib.

"Thanks, Sterchens. How's Milton?"

"Recovering nicely. Probably due to your caramels."

"Told you so." Orv's smile faded and his face darkened. "Have you heard about our casualty? My passenger, Lieutenant Selfridge?"

"Yes. I'm sorry, Orv."

He nodded, turned his face away. "Do the Bishop and Will know?"

"Yes. We're all very sorry. But there's no one to blame. We've always known this was a dangerous business and accepted the risks long ago."

"For ourselves, not others."

"Selfridge certainly knew and accepted the risks. I understand he was a pilot himself."

Orv nodded, then was quiet for some time. "I'm getting sleepy and I'm afraid I'll nod off on you. You won't leave, will you?"

His voice sounded like a little boy's, and that nearly broke my heart. I slipped my hand in his. "I'll be here as long as you need me."

WILBUR

S ome people would enjoy all the fussing and fawning, being treated like royalty. Although I admit I enjoyed having my own personal chef, it took three tries to find one who could make a simple, digestible meal, which was all I cared for.

The demonstration flights were going beautifully, and it seemed each day there were more and more hordes of people coming to watch. At first, it was just the well-to-do: ladies in flouncy dresses and parasols, men in morning suits, top hats, and shiny shoes. Then, everyone, or tout le monde, as the French would say: farmers in their overalls, fishermen and their wives, and families with children. Oh, so many children! I enjoyed talking to them when I had a chance, despite my lack of French.

Mr. Berg seemed to know every wealthy person in England, Spain, Italy, and France, and all of them trusted him implicitly. Orv and I had been hesitant to sign a contract with him to represent us as our agent overseas, but so far, his dealings and connections had been superb.

I traveled to Italy, where the events were much the same. A

different language and culture, but the enthusiasm was palpable in both places. It made me wonder why the Americans had been slow to embrace the future of transportation.

Back again at Camp D'Auvours, a few miles outside of Le Mans, I was just about to do my initial walk-around inspection for the day's demonstration when Hart Berg arrived in my shed. It was a perfect day for flying, with a steady breeze from the northeast and plenty of sunshine to keep the audience happy. I greeted Berg, but the look on his face did not match my positive mood.

"I've had a telegram from the U.S. Army." He handed me an envelope. "There's been an accident at Fort Myer."

The rest of his words faded from my hearing and breath was stolen from my lungs. The world blurred and spun as if I had been sucked into our wind tunnel. I tried to focus on the telegram in my shaking hand. My brother was hurt, perhaps severely. But he was alive.

The first thing I did was cancel the day's demonstrations. I needed to determine if I should go home.

What could have happened? Of course there were innumerable things that could go wrong, but by this time we had ironed out most of the trouble spots. Did the engine fail? Even so, the machine should glide to the ground. I tried to picture Fort Myer. Trees, a river. A number of buildings. Maybe Orv couldn't get to an open space. I had to find out more. I ran through the remaining commitments in Europe in my mind. I would cancel them all if need be.

KATHARINE

As Orv's breathing settled into a slow, deep rhythm, I quietly padded out of the room. I needed to contact my friends in Arlington and arrange for another place to stay if they couldn't accommodate me. Just outside Orv's door, the lieutenant who had greeted me at the station awaited me, giving me a startle.

"Oh, Lieutenant Lahm, I didn't expect you."

"I've been assigned as an aide, of sorts. Here to help with anything you need."

"How kind. I would like to freshen up and then see about my accommodations."

"Of course." He held out his arm to show the way.

⁓

The next weeks challenged us with one trial after another. Orv's pain was unbearable at times, but the medication interfered with his digestion and slowed his breathing, so they couldn't give him more.

He started running a fever, and we feared pneumonia was setting in. I tortured Orv with breathing exercises and turning him on each side as much as the traction apparatus would allow. I stayed with him throughout the day and late into the evening, leaving only to capture a few hours of sleep at the home of my friends.

While Orv slept, I wrote letters to the Bishop, to Will, who was still in France, and to my school principal, begging him to hold my job for me. On a clear day, I walked the neatly kept grounds, worrying about whether the accident would be the end of the family dream.

Just down the road was a lovely viewpoint where the high ground of Fort Myer gave way to a valley, with rows of white grave markers of the cemetery going all the way to the river. In the distance, the white obelisk of the Washington Monument shone in the sun. So stately, so everlasting, I saw it as a beacon of hope. This was just a setback, I told myself. One of many, not the first and certainly not the last. I would tell Wilbur to stay in France. *Keep doing what you're doing*, I'd tell him, because Orville would be joining him again soon.

As the weeks went by, Orv's temperature stabilized, and the doctors felt he was out of danger. Now came the challenge of keeping up his spirits. As Orv improved, he became frantic with worry over his promised demonstrations for the government. "We can't meet the terms of the contract. We'll have to start all over again," he lamented.

On a sunny afternoon in October, Lieutenant Lahm, who now insisted we call him by his first name, Frank, was trying to cheer up a despondent Orv. I had just returned to his room with a wheeled chair so that I could take him outside for much needed fresh air.

"It wouldn't surprise anyone if you have lost your nerve. I would have," Frank said.

"What do you mean?" Orv said.

"If you never want to fly again, the government won't hold it against you. Or you could ask for an extension of your contract."

"An extension?" A small smile peeked from under his mustache, the first time I had seen that since I arrived. Orv swung his braced leg over the side of the bed and twisted into the wheeled chair in one practiced motion. He nodded to a stack of letters on his bedside table. "Wilbur's over there setting world records. He brought a *lady* up with him. Ladies are flying! The only thing I'm worried about is how soon I can get back up there. I've got commitments to live up to."

A wave of relief washed over me as he propped up his leg and pushed his chair out of the room. This was the old Orv, back again.

Frank helped me solve a thorny problem. Orv insisted he would be well enough to continue the flights and meet the government's requirements by the middle of 1909. But the contracting officials weren't about to travel to a hospital room to work out the details, so Frank arranged for me to meet in their offices at Fort Myer and at the War Department in Washington.

Frank picked me up in a green motorcar that the army was testing. It seemed aeroplanes weren't the only new technology they were interested in. It was much like a small closed carriage with an oil lantern on each side, but minus the horse. He had asked me to be ready early so that we might take a drive around Arlington before heading to our meetings.

I was surprised by how hilly the area was. We bumped along dirt and gravel roads that wound up and down heavily forested hills. Here and there I spotted magnificent mansions, most constructed of red brick with impressive white columns and pretty windows. I imagined living in such a place someday. Wouldn't that be something!

Suddenly Frank stopped and fidgeted with the many sticks and pedals. "We'll have to back up this hill."

I held on to my hat as we jerked along, backward. "Why are we going in reverse?" I asked.

"I want to show you my favorite house, and it's at the top of the hill," he explained, without explaining at all.

The engine grumbled but grew steady as he navigated around a sharp turn. I couldn't imagine coordinating a steering wheel and all those controls, never mind backward.

Finally, we reached the top, Frank crunched the brake with his foot and set another one with his hand. "You see, the engine is gravity-fed with petrol. If we went up frontways, the engine would be starved and we would stall, and then we'd roll uncontrolled down the hill."

"Seems your motorcar is more dangerous than a flyer." I pictured the flyer's gas can, hung from the top wing. That engine was also gravity-fed. I tucked the information in the back of my mind, just in case it might be useful to my brothers.

"Look over there." Frank pointed to a long driveway lined with topiary shrubs. At the end of it was a beautiful Georgian-style mansion, painted a gleaming white. It was two stories high and featured a large portico in the center, reminding me of the White House.

"Oh, shall we knock on the door and invite ourselves in for tea?" I teased.

"I'm afraid this lowly lieutenant wouldn't be fit to fetch it for them." With that, he pushed some pedals and the hand throttle, and the steady tick-ticking of the engine grew louder and faster. It sounded quite a bit like the flyer's engine I had heard out on Huffman Prairie.

"You might qualify as their chauffeur, as you're an excellent driver," I said.

"That would be fun and would pay better than the army," he joked. "Someday, I hope the army will let me be a flyer."

"What do you like more, driving or flying?"

"There's nothing to compare to being up there." He nodded toward the sky. "The sense of freedom, seeing the world below looking surreal, like a painting. It's how I imagine heaven to be."

Orv and Will had said similar things, but mostly talked about the technical challenges. Frank was more in tune with his visceral reaction, which I found appealing. I glanced at him and found he had his eyes on me.

"Wouldn't that be a fun thing to do together?" He quickly returned his focus ahead. "We'll look down at these bumpy roads and laugh."

"Someday I will go up," I said. "But the thought of losing contact with the earth frightens me. And now with Orv so badly injured..."

"Give it some time. It will become safer and safer, at some point no more dangerous than crossing the street. But it seems you won't be the first; some other woman has beaten you to it."

I nodded, but my gut tightened with the thought. Rolling down the hill in this newfangled automobile that the brakes couldn't stop if the engine failed was already excitement enough for me. Not to mention the company of an interesting man.

The negotiations with the army officials went smoothly. In fact, they seemed rather surprised and pleased that we still wanted to continue the project. They gave the contract another whole year to be fulfilled.

After the meeting in the District, Frank took me to a famous saloon in the Ebbitt Hotel, just a few blocks away from the White House. A handsome building of six stories, the hotel had a tall mansard roof with pavilions on the corners and many large windows. An ornate clock hovering over the entrance showed the time to be one o'clock. We pushed through the door and entered the expansive lobby, paneled with carved dark wood. Loud conversation leaked from the twin saloons not far from the lobby.

Stepping through a huge mahogany door, I saw a room filled with gentlemen in dark suits. Not a woman among them.

"Just a moment." Frank excused himself, stepping aside to speak to the maître d'. "The women's salon is under construction, so we have a rare opportunity to dine together," he said with a big smile when he returned, as if sneaking in a woman due to a technicality were something to be proud of.

I was stunned by the dizzying array of art, taxidermy, candlelit tables, and enormous chandeliers. Hordes of men crowded around a long bar; a huge painting of a nude woman reclining in a lily pond dominated the wall. A series of lamps above it made the bar and painting glow, the patrons appearing in eerie shadows in front of it. It was almost surreal in nature, and I imagined the conversations of the journalists and political men that would frequent such a place.

A host led us to a small table. It was covered with a white table-cloth, topped by a crystal vase of orange and red mums.

"They're famous for their oysters, but you can have whatever you desire. Do you like beer? They have a stout that could serve as an entire meal."

"Why don't you order whatever you usually do? I've never had oysters, but they must be delicious, being the specialty of the place."

Frank picked up a small blue placard next to the flower vase and read it aloud: "'Many other famous statesmen, naval and military heroes, too numerous to mention here, have been guests of the house.'" He set the placard back on the table. "Teddy Roosevelt himself comes here quite often. They say those are his trophies up there." He waved his hand across the space high above, with a collection of bear heads, many stuffed birds, and animals I didn't even recognize.

"Really? And who else?"

"Ulysses Grant, McKinley, Grover Cleveland, just about all presidents going back to the 1850s. And you see those carved wooden bears? They're said to have belonged to Alexander Hamilton before his untimely duel."

Frank seemed to delight in sharing the history, and I soaked it all up. It wasn't my life at all, but it was certainly fun to peek in on others'.

"But this..." He tapped the blue placard. "This is why I brought you here."

That rather confused me. "Thank you, it's an honor to be in a place like this with so much history."

"That's not what I mean. I think that you and your brothers are the 'heroes too numerous to mention,' and someday, you will be recognized for it."

"Oh, my brothers maybe, but I'm hardly a hero." I blushed.

"Don't underestimate your contributions to their efforts. Orville has told me they couldn't have accomplished flight without what you have done. And will continue to do. He says he wouldn't be alive now if it weren't for you coming to torture him with breathing exercises."

Before I could respond, a waiter in a tuxedo coat delivered a platter of oysters puddled on open shells. The wet grayish blobs on each shell looked like the slugs I scraped off my tomato plants. I had no idea how to eat such a thing, so I said, "Please, after you."

While Frank squeezed a lemon, then some drops of a red sauce on his oyster, I considered his claim of our place in history. "Assuming Orv continues to recover, I imagine the boys will become known in certain circles. But I reserve the term *heroes* for people like Roosevelt or Hamilton."

He brought the half shell up to his mouth, leaned his head back, and slurped the concoction in all at once. "Whew, that's some spice." He wiped his eyes with his napkin. "You might want to go easy on the red sauce." He passed the small bottle to me. "You haven't been to France, have you?" He continued without waiting for an answer. "The people there are nuts for aviators. Wilbur is being treated like a king—well, a prince anyway—and all that glory is going to follow him home. You had better prepare for a different life."

"Oh, how so? We have no princes here. Wilbur may have to adjust back to being just another humble businessman." Although knowing Will, no adaptation would be necessary. He had always been nothing but humble. I assembled an oyster, just as Frank had, and slurped it down all at once. At first my tongue seemed to rebel at the texture, which could only be described as slimy. But then the sweet saltiness seeped in, tasting, I imagined, like the ocean I had never seen. The slime became velvety as I swallowed it whole, there being nothing to chew.

"Don't underestimate the lure of fame and fortune," Frank said.

"Ah, but you don't know the Wrights."

"I'd like to know them better." He gazed at me with a look that had nothing to do with the family business. "Especially this one."

I met his gaze with fresh eyes. He was quite the handsome fellow, clean-shaven with closely cropped dark-brown hair. He was at once cheerful, humorous, and completely serious about his favorite topic, flying. An awkward pause in the conversation followed, as I wrestled with admitting to my attraction to him. But it seemed too soon, too fragile, just a glimmer that if exposed might fade away.

I swirled the white wine in my glass before taking a sip. "Tell me about the balloon race. How do you control your speed to win a race in a balloon?"

He nodded, his eyes acknowledging what I hadn't said. "It was a distance competition, not speed. We started in the Tuileries Gardens in Paris and sailed over the English Channel at night."

"Oh my, did you navigate by the stars?"

"Yes, and the moon. It was full that night, and that's what I remember most. And the sight of the English coast in early-morning fog. It was welcoming and mysterious."

"Then you landed in the fog?" Scenes from the Brontë sisters' novels floated through my brain, dreamy and romantic.

"Oh no. We had to stay aloft as long as possible. We ascended and descended as needed to follow the prevailing winds to go as far as we could. We made it all the way to Yorkshire, over six hundred and forty kilometers from Paris."

"Winning the race. And making history. Plus the excitement of going to new places in a novel way."

"Not novel to me. I lived in Paris for several years, and my father was a balloonist. You could say I practically grew up in one. As a matter of fact, I flew that race for him because he wanted to go to my sister's wedding."

"Oh no, you missed your sister's wedding? And does this mean you speak French?"

"*Oui* and *oui*."

My attraction to him increased. A lifetime goal was to become fluent myself.

"I'm sure your sister forgave you. It was for a most important event, after all."

"Ah, but your brothers are about to put all balloonists out of business." He gave a rueful smile. Then he dropped his eyes, looking rather dejected. "Orv will be ready to go home in a matter of weeks."

"You say that like it's a bad thing."

"It's good for him, of course. And I'm sure you're eager to get on with your life, your teaching, if that's still what you want to do. The army contract and Wilbur's work in France are going to change your situation."

"Of course I'm going back to teaching. If they'll still have me."

He placed his warm hand over mine. "I'll miss you."

A wave of affection swelled within me, and a tear threatened to spill from my eye. "As I shall miss you. We must stay in touch." I yearned to protect this fragile new side of our relationship, but wasn't sure how. "Of course, thanks to your help, Orv will be back to finish the trials."

"Will you come with him?"

I wanted to promise him that I would. The boys had finally sold the bicycle shop, but I knew that between teaching and running the household, along with ever-increasing needs for the flying business, it was almost certain that I wouldn't. "I can try."

It was a weak answer and Frank took it with a nod and a hurt look in his eyes.

How I wished things could be different. Belatedly, I added, "Why don't you visit us in Dayton?"

"Sure. The army is good about things like that." He peeked at his pocket watch. "Well then, we should get back." Frank rose and held out his arm for me to precede him. Always a gentleman.

The goal was for Orv to make two complete circuits of the orthopedic ward, using two canes, and stand in place without canes for two minutes. We called it the 2-2-2 plan. We both longed to go home, perhaps he did even more than I, but until he could accomplish this feat, he wouldn't be able to make the trip. So I walked with him every day, a little longer each time, until he was finally ready.

On the last day of October, a small crowd of doctors, nurses, and army personnel that had come to know us gathered to send us off. Frank was there as well, and I was grateful for the others about so that I didn't have to face an awkward goodbye. A soldier drove us to the train station in a brand-new type of automobile, a Ford Model T, and Orv managed the stairs onto the train and short walks at the stations just fine. When he tired, he used the wheeled chair, but we both knew how important every step in his recovery was.

When we arrived in Dayton the next morning, the Bishop and Carrie greeted us at the station and we took a hired horse and buggy home. A small crowd had gathered on the street near our house, standing under the lines of tall hawthorn trees, which had given our street its name.

"Who are they?" I asked.

The Bishop scoffed. "Oh, just some sightseers. Apparently some newspaper declared us an attraction."

I sighed in frustration. Frank had tried to warn me.

"Wilbur will be staying in France, now that you've assured him we have things well in control," the Bishop said. "But when he comes

back, I'm sure all this"—he waved at the street lined with people—
"will get worse."

We slipped inside the house, but I peeked out through the
curtains. The crowd remained until a policeman came and cleared
them away. As the people climbed back into their carriages and a
few motorcars or simply walked away, a new thought jarred me. If
this disruption continued, or worsened, as the Bishop predicted, it
wouldn't be fair to our neighbors. It would take a lot of convincing
of my men, but I already knew—we would have to move house. I
thought of the lovely mansions I had seen in Arlington and imagined
having one built in the similar forested hills south of Dayton. If
ever we could afford such a place, it would be better for us and our
neighbors. We no longer belonged in this neighborhood.

I was exhausted from the trip, especially since I had carried both
Orv's and my hand luggage on and off trains and through stations.
Orv came into the sitting room and immediately headed toward the
stairs.

"Where are you going, Son?" the Bishop asked.

"To my room, of course. I'm tired from my ordeal."

I gently took his arm and tried to steer him to the front parlor.
"No need."

"No, no, I want to go to my room."

I had written ahead to the Bishop, requesting that he set up a bed
in the parlor for Orv. The thought of him climbing the steep stairs
to his own bedroom gave me nightmares of him tumbling down. But
I had neglected to warn Orv about the plan.

The Bishop and I won the argument that time, but within a week, we caught Orv climbing up the stairs, one hand on the railing and the other holding his cane.

"Now how are you going to get back down?" I asked.

"One step at a time," he answered, a smirk on his face.

My new routine became running up and down stairs through the day and night for Orv, while of course resuming the cooking and other household duties. I don't know how I would have survived without Carrie's help. And when I could get away during his long afternoon nap, I rode the streetcar to the outer city limits, looking for a new place to call home.

WILBUR

In Dayton I was an obscure experimenter, even thought a fool, but I never minded because our goals were clear to us. But in France, I transformed into a heralded man who held the very future in his hands, a challenge for a scientist and inventor, for whom the work alone should be the star.

Hart Berg and others had been quietly setting up a committee of supporters. They had the fat purses to spend on our flyers and the dreams to match. I tried to take it all in stride, but sometimes it seemed our dream was out of control. In addition to a large number of demonstration flights, I was to train new pilots. We would tour France and Italy, all the while attracting more attention and orders for our aeroplanes. I worried how all this was to be accomplished, especially with Orville still recuperating from his awful crash.

I had the finest accommodations, an apartment with a chef, a hangar, a crew to help with the construction and repairs, and a private car for transportation. Rows upon rows of seating surrounded the immense flying field at Le Mans. They must have expected half of France to attend.

The pressure was intense each time I took the flyer up at Le Mans. Another mishap after Orv's much-publicized crash would be devastating. But the new flyer took off beautifully and the catapult flawlessly accelerated us to proper airspeed. It was only a matter of time until we could build more efficient engines and wouldn't need the catapult at all.

It seemed the French were much in favor of celebration with banquets and award ceremonies in my honor. At an affair put on by the Aero Club of France, two hundred and fifty of the most influential people dined on the finest ham, pheasant, and pineapple glacé. My thorough training in humbleness was tested as I was welcomed with a slew of congratulatory speeches and lavish introductions. I heard words such as:

Mr. Wright is a man who has never been discouraged, even in the face of hesitation and suspicion.

The brothers Wright have written their names in human history as inventors of pronounced genius. They have achieved through straightforwardness, intelligence, and tenacity, one of the most beautiful inventions of the human genius.

The entire audience in the glittering room stood as a band played "The Star-Spangled Banner." At no time had such an event honored us in America. I am not given to emotion, but an errant tear threatened to fall from my eye.

But all I could think about, even as I signed my own name on several hundred menus as souvenirs, was that Orville and Katharine deserved this adulation even more than I. They would never seek it, as I hadn't, but my goal became to make their lives better, whatever I needed to do to accomplish that.

With this in mind, I decided to enter a new competition, sponsored by the Michelin tire company. The winner of the Michelin

Cup would be awarded a $4,000 cash prize. I would have to take off without the catapult according to the rules, but still, I felt no one could beat me.

So on New Year's Eve, a dreadfully cold day, I took off in rain that felt like needles of ice striking my skin. I flew longer and farther than anyone had before, setting a record of seventy-seven miles in two hours and twenty minutes. The Michelin Cup, and the fame that went with it, was ours.

But my victory felt hollow without my family there to celebrate with me. I needed to bring them over so they could reap the rewards of their hard work in a country that seemed to more fully understand and appreciate how high and far we were going.

KATHARINE

My principal at Steele had held my job for me, but finally had to give it away until Christmas to be fair to the students and the substitute teacher. I held out hope that I could return for the next term in January. But a letter from Will made me question that goal. I read it out loud to Orv and the Bishop.

Dear Orv and Sterchens,

I will be moving flying demonstrations to the south of France, to Pau, a city much beloved by the French for its mild climate and beauty. I would like very much if the two of you could join me there. I think an extended stay in such a place will do you a world of good. Katharine, I know you love "Old Steele," but I think you would love it still better if the briny deep separated it from you for a while. We will be needing a social manager and can pay enough salary to make the proposition attractive. So do not worry about the six dollars per day the school board gives you...

My heart beat fast in my chest. Virginia was the furthest I had ever been from home. I had studied the history of Europe, of course, and had always longed to visit. I had enjoyed the courses in French I had taken, but was by no means fluent. But could I really just pick up and travel overseas?

I set aside the letter. "It's impossible, of course. Orv is hardly ready for such a trip, and I'm hoping to go back to teaching after the New Year."

"Nonsense," the Bishop said. "Orv is getting around just fine, and the change will do him much good. And it seems your place is with them. Wilbur wouldn't ask such a thing if it wasn't critical. Social manager? I guess they do things differently in France."

"You'll come, won't you, Pop?" I asked, but my heart was not in the request. The Bishop was now eighty years old. Making the trip with Orv would be trying enough, but how would I care for them both?

"No, I can't join you. I'm far too busy, and a sea voyage might prove the end of me."

I turned to Orv. "You haven't said a thing. What do you think, Little Brother?"

"What's the sense in rattling around here, feeling useless, when I could put at least my mind and hands to work helping Will? Let's go."

❦

I requested an extension of my leave from teaching until the end of the school year and wrote to Will. We would set sail in early January. I didn't imagine it would be pleasant, crossing the Atlantic in the depths of winter, but I didn't care. I would be off on the adventure of a lifetime. Our housekeeper, Carrie, and her husband would move into our home to watch over the Bishop, and Lorin promised to keep a close eye on him too, so my worries about him were eased.

Most of the details of selling the bicycle shop had fallen to Lorin as well. I thought after so many years of pouring their time into it, the boys would be saddened by its loss. But they barely spoke of it, their hearts and minds having moved on.

Some new clothes were in order, and I went to my favorite dress shop. I could barely contain my excitement and told the shop clerk all about my traveling plans. Soon neighbors, friends, and interested strangers were dropping by the house, eager to chat with us about the upcoming trip. It was a new sensation, this interest, but I found it rather enjoyable. But Orv would promptly hobble out of sight whenever such a person dropped by.

KATHARINE

T he ocean voyage was as pleasant as could be, considering the season. Wilbur had insisted on buying first-class tickets, and Orv and I were treated like royalty. It was quite refreshing to being waited on, instead of serving others, and I became accustomed to it quite readily. After a seven-day journey, we landed in Cherbourg and boarded a train for Paris.

We emerged from the train car after midnight, weary and with our minds muddled from travel and the time change. Wilbur was there to greet us, along with Hart Berg and his wife, who presented me with a bouquet of roses and an American flag. They were ever so gracious and understanding, taking us immediately to our hotel near their flat on Champs-Élysées.

I tried mightily to keep my eyes open as we passed down street after street, all lit from tall gaslights and still buzzing with people even at the late hour. Restaurants seemed to spill right out onto the sidewalks, where patrons sat in wicker chairs at small round tables.

I gasped when we circled L'Arc de Triomphe, the most impressive monument I had ever seen. Spotlights bathed the ashlar stone, making it glow in the night. Many streets fanned out from it, like a giant horizontal Ferris wheel.

Once at the hotel, I thought poor Orv would want nothing but to head to a warm, comfy bed, but he surprised me by joining Will and me in our fancy sitting room, catching up until the wee hours of the morning.

The next day I went shopping with Edith Berg, the wife of Wilbur's friend and sponsor, while the boys went to a ceremony for the presentation of the Michelin Cup. Oh, to have to make such a decision—shopping in Paris, or watching my brothers receive that honor! But Edith was quite convincing. She had her own automobile, and she enticed me with all the places she would take me.

Edith was quite an attractive woman, with a confident and amusing air about her. I soon found out why.

"My former husband was also an actor," she said, assuming I already knew that she was as well. "We did hundreds of shows—New York, LA, and everywhere in between."

"You were married before Mr. Berg?"

"He's number three," Edith breezily announced. She was only a few years older than me and had managed to marry three times, while I seemed destined to be an old maid.

Intrigued and entertained by Mrs. Berg, I half-heartedly objected to her plan. "I probably should attend the ceremony."

"Oh, you'll have quite your fill of awards and speeches. Let's go have some fun lady-time now, for once you are discovered, you'll not have a moment's peace," Edith said.

So off we went, traipsing in and out of shops on the boulevard, and meeting with dressmakers, milliners, and jewelers. When Edith noticed the timepiece I kept on a chain around my neck, she insisted on purchasing me one on a bracelet instead. She said all fashionable women now wore wristwatches. It was all quite dreamlike to me. Having had a lifetime of budgeting and making do, this carefree, luxurious lifestyle was more foreign than the language to me.

We entered an elegant shop on the Avenue des Champs-Élysées that featured ornate ceilings and highly polished marble floors, but echoed with emptiness, appearing to have no goods to offer. Edith spoke in French to the stern-looking shop woman. They spoke rapidly, using words I hadn't learned in my school lessons. I did clearly understand *fourrure*, or fur. Oh my. I could not afford a fur, nor could I allow Mrs. Berg to purchase such an extravagance.

But the shop woman disappeared through a swinging door and returned with a brass cart loaded with coats and wraps of full-bodied minks attached head to tail. My objections were waved aside with some excuse like international goodwill. I chose a shoulder shrug created from an assortment of mink pelts, one that didn't feature any tiny heads, but its unusual, irregular shape appealed to me. I couldn't wait to see my brothers' faces when they saw me wearing it.

When we parted for the day, Edith asked if there was anything else I desired. I responded with my fondest wish: to improve my French. It was a lifelong dream, and I would be well ahead with my knowledge of Latin and Greek. Edith promised to set me up with her own tutor that very week, which made me happier than all the fine dresses she insisted on purchasing for me.

That night, I wrote several letters. I reported our safe arrival and excellent accommodations to the Bishop. At Wilbur's request, I added the news of his winning of the Michelin Cup, and that the payments from his supporters and other honorariums and prize money now amounted to $35,000, with much more in the works. For a man of the cloth, the Bishop had always been peculiarly interested regarding monetary reward.

Next, I wrote to a fellow teacher at Steele High School, and Harry and Isabel in Kansas City. After a long consideration, I wrote a breezy note to Frank Lahm, on the off chance that he might return to France. After all, he spoke fluent French and his position in the army centered on aviation, so it seemed to me a visit might be in order. But then I tore up the letter, fearing he would see right through it. I shouldn't be so forward; if he wanted to see me, he could arrange it easily enough.

⁂

Edith Berg, Orv, and I boarded a train to Pau to meet up with Wilbur, who had gone ahead of us. It was a lovely trip through the French countryside. Orv and I had lower berths in a sleeping car and were making our way through the paneled passageway toward them when the train suddenly lurched, throwing both of us off our feet. We landed in a heap, and the train continued to shake and roll and shudder. There was a scream of metal against metal, and objects came flying at us. My instinct was to protect my already injured brother, and I tried to shield him with my own body. Finally, the car lurched to a stop, and we were thrown in the opposite direction. It was clear the train had hit something huge.

Aside from aching knees and elbows, I was unscathed. Orv seemed bewildered; I was afraid he had hit his head. Soon a uniformed conductor came by to check on us, but seeing no obvious injury, hurried on his way. His canes lost in the confusion, Orv wrapped his arm around my shoulders, and we headed in the direction of voices.

We soon learned that we had collided with a freight train, and at least two people were killed. As the temperature steadily dropped, we were offered coffee and blankets as we awaited a new train.

Orville said little, and I pleaded with him to allow a doctor to examine him.

"I've been through worse, and there are many that have greater need."

I made him as comfortable as possible, then went to check on Edith Berg, who had already retired when the accident occurred.

We finally arrived in Pau, many hours late, but Will emerged from the crowd to greet us. An elegant carriage whisked us through the city. We passed a castle, which we were told was the birthplace of King Henry IV, who was born in 1553. How amazing that such things existed! In our own country, they were tearing down buildings that were mere decades old. We drove by another building that I took for a newer part of the castle, with a square turret rising from each corner. Built on a precipice, it soared over the valley. Our guide advised us that this would be where we would be staying, the Hôtel Gassion.

We disembarked from the carriage and stretched our legs on a promenade that wound along the edge of the precipice affording views of the Pyrenees.

Orv and I were shown to our adjoining rooms, which were charming but frigid. I immediately requested help in getting the woodstove properly fed, but with my limited French, it seemed the chambermaid thought it was working just fine.

"*C'est bon*," was her response to my pointing to the stove and crossing my arms in a shiver.

I unwrapped my mink wrap from its elegant box and delicate tissue paper and arranged it across my shoulders. Might as well make it useful. I thought it might accompany me to bed, but was pleased to find a mountain of pillowy goose-down featherbeds upon it. I had to use a small step stool to climb into it, but soon melted into the dreamy white clouds of bedding and fell fast asleep.

The next morning I awoke embarrassingly late, nearly noon. Immediately there was a soft knock at the door as if someone had been in the hallway listening for the moment of my arising. A maid in a black uniform and crisp white apron delivered a breakfast tray. She nodded her head, and departed saying, "*Merci beaucoup*," when it was I who should have been thanking her. I lifted a silver cloche to uncover a tray of the most sumptuous croissants, soft-boiled eggs, and coffee with fresh cream. I enjoyed every morsel, and tried a dab of all four of the luscious jams on my croissant, the apricot being my favorite.

Perky from the strong coffee and satisfied belly, I noticed a gilded desk in a corner of my light-filled room. Its top was buried under a vase of hothouse flowers and a huge stack of correspondence. I flipped through the envelopes, all of proper thick stationery, some with gold embossing or satiny trim. They were addressed to Will, often as *The Honorable Wilbur Wright*.

The return addresses mostly featured just a title, or a title and a name, for the senders needed no further identification. His Royal Highness, Edward VII. Alfonso XIII, King of Spain. Duke and Prince and Dowager and plenty of Marquis of this and that. To my embarrassment I wasn't sure what half the titles signified. And judging from the postmarks, answers to them were very tardy.

Social manager indeed; Will had not been overstating the work. I reflected on the contents of my trunk. I had brought two nice evening gowns and a number of smart suits and dresses from Dayton, and I had several lovely dresses purchased in Paris, but not enough hats to go with them. Perhaps I should have been more attentive to Edith Berg's shopping advice. But I was more excited than apprehensive. This was a dream come true, and I was not about to fret over titles and fashion.

Wilbur had taken Edith Berg up in his flyer, and she had gushed about the experience. "I'm sure you've enjoyed it as well," she said. "You lucky dog, you can go any time."

A wave of shame and embarrassment rolled over me. "I haven't yet had the opportunity." In fact, Wilbur had offered several times, but I kept thinking of Orv's terrible accident and all the smaller tumbles the boys had taken over the years. The idea of being up that high gave me the willies.

But pressure mounted on me from several angles. I trekked out to the flying field north of the city each morning to see Wilbur fly. No matter the hour or chill of the day, hundreds, if not thousands of spectators came. I gave interviews to the press, both in English and in my ever-improving French. Nearly the first question they all asked was *How did you enjoy flying with your brother?*

We were enjoying tea in our hotel suite one afternoon, and Orv and Wilbur were discussing strategies for increasing the public's confidence in flying.

"It seems to me the French are overly eager, if anything," I said.

Will shook his head. "You're only seeing a small percentage—the ones who come out to the demonstrations, the reporters who are fascinated by it. We need more—families, women, businessmen, politicians, everyone—to see this as the future."

Orv looked at me, his mouth twisted in a wry smile. He was aware of my misgivings. "You know what would go a long way toward that goal? A nice big photograph of our own sister flying. Now what could be more convincing of the joy and safety of flight than that?"

"He says, the moment his broken bones have healed," I said.

"Accidents do happen, I'm afraid," Will said. "Especially when you're pushed by the need to set records and satisfy demanding customers. But no such thing will be in play when you go up with me."

I squeezed more lemon into my tea, its aroma particularly soothing at that moment. "We did make a promise to each other. 'To support each other as long as necessary, no matter what it takes.'"

Will softened. "If you really don't want to do it, we won't hold it against you."

"We'll just be financially compromised, emotionally inconsolable, and set adrift," Orv added.

"Fine. Set it up. If I pass out from the fright, just hold up my head and smile."

On the appointed day, I tried to ignore the queasiness in my belly as I rode out to the flying field in a horse and buggy. For the better part of my life I'd been told of the wonders of flight, and how aeroplanes were faster and could go places horses couldn't, but it never seemed like something I would need to do. There wasn't anywhere I needed to go that a boat or ship or good old horse couldn't take me. But this was an important step, not only for me to get over my fear but also for the boys, to show that they could earn the trust of the fearful.

A gaggle of reporters had set up heavy cameras on tripods along one end of the field, which seemed to have been recently cut for hay, as round hay bales dotted the edges of the field. We passed a pen of oxen, displaced by the new purpose of the field, that seemed to be pining for their previous accommodations. Rows and rows of black automobiles and more colorful carriages filled the close end of the field, and throngs of people milled about.

The plan was for Wilbur to take a few runs to ensure the winds were perfect and the machine warmed up and ready to go. I inspected the ground before me, looking for a little flower to press into my scrapbook as remembrance of this day. The trampling of many feet had left little growing, but I found a hardy little clover leaf, which I slipped into my bodice.

Precisely at the appointed time, Wilbur finished his inspection of the flyer and approached me. He looked quite natty in his tweed suit and newsboy cap. I could feel my heart beating in my ears and my stomach rebelled, even as I smiled sweetly to the crowd.

Will slung his long arm across my shoulders and spoke in a low, comforting voice. "It's going to be grand; you'll enjoy the ride once you're up there, peering down on all this. It will be noisy, but don't worry, that just means all is working well. Toward the end, when we are on a glide path in, I'll shut down the engine, so don't be alarmed." He stopped and faced me, looking straight in my eyes. "Are you ready?"

I was not ready, never would be, but was not about to embarrass my brother. "I am. Let's go."

Orv caught up from a few steps behind us. He held up several lengths of thin rope. "Let me secure your hat and skirt." He proceeded to tie a loop, circling my hat and chin. Then Will helped me into the passenger seat before climbing into his own on my left. Orv tied another line, tightening my skirt to my lower legs, saying, "Just like the ladies of Paris."

"Rest your feet on the bar, and hold this strut with your right hand," Will said.

"What am I to do with my other hand?" I feared touching the wrong thing, even though I was fairly knowledgeable of all the parts.

"Wave to everyone," Will said with a smile. He worked the levers controlling the wings and rudders, looking around in all directions. Some men walked to the rear of the machine, ready to turn the propellers at the right moment. I clapped my hands to my ears when Will started the engine. Even though I'd been warned about the noise, the roar only a few feet from my ear surpassed what I had expected. The chains clanked, and the propellers behind us whirred like the fan in my room, times a thousand. The wind the propellers created threatened to blow off my hat, and we hadn't yet moved. Louder and louder the sounds grew, until the machine vibrated as it strained against the tie-downs, my seat feeling like I was in a carriage racing over cobblestones. Finally, Will pulled the release lever, and with a sudden lurch, we raced down the narrow track.

I gripped that strut with every ounce of strength I could muster. I pictured myself flying off the seat and surviving by holding on. But the wind was pushing me deep into the chair, not away from it. The sounds softened and I felt a strange feeling of pressure from above, like diving deep under water. But we were rising. We were suspended in the air!

The machine bounced a few times, but I remained calm. The boys had talked about "bumpy air" and now I understood what they meant—like bumps in a road jostling a carriage, except you couldn't see them. I looked down at the line of people, so strange from this angle. I waved, but wasn't sure if they could see me. As the wind blew in my face, and my body felt what birds must feel to be aloft, I forgot to be afraid. Softly, Wilbur tilted the flyer and we began to turn.

As we leveled out again in a new direction, Wilbur shouted over the engine and wind, "You okay?"

Now I knew what to do with my left hand. I made a fist with my thumb up, just like the ancient gladiators, for we were just as brave.

A photograph of my flying adventure graced the front page of all the newspapers, and I soon had my own stack of correspondence to rival Wilbur's. The kings of Spain and Italy wanted to meet me, and every socialite in Paris begged me to come to their affairs. Many came to Pau to watch the flight demonstrations, and I met with scores of them, taking orders for aeroplanes. I was thankful for having paid attention to my brothers' work over the years, as I was able to answer innumerable questions. Sometimes the technical bits were difficult in French, but an interpreter was nearby.

I was thrilled the language was coming to me so readily. The French people seemed so pleased to have me speak in their language, so I tried mightily to learn all I could. I continued my daily lessons and was told I had only a slight American accent. Of course, they were probably being courteous, but it pleased me nonetheless.

And it wasn't only the French who came. The king of Spain came to watch Wilbur fly, and I had a most pleasant conversation with him. He was absolutely delightful, telling me how he wished he could go up with Wilbur as I had, but his wife would not allow it. British royalty came to call, and I took lessons from a London friend of Edith Berg on how to curtsy. *Bend both knees, front leg just so...* But when the time came to perform the motion, I was so nervous I reverted to an American handshake. All was soon forgiven, and I had a most wonderful time chatting with them, gaining invitations to come *back home*, as they called it.

After a while, the daily meetings with businessmen, wealthy adventurers, and government officials became rather routine. Will said he needed to promote me from social manager to chief executive, but I assured him no such thing was necessary. Still, I felt a vital part of the team, perhaps for the first time. I remembered telling the boys back in their printshop days that flying was their destiny. It seemed I had found mine as well.

In two weeks' time, with Hart Berg's help, we had negotiated hundreds of thousands of dollars in purchases. We had developed a routine that was unlike anything we had done back in the States.

First, Mr. Berg communicated with his *prospects*, as he called them. As an engineer and expert in all manner of transportation from bicycles to submarines, he was well suited to understanding the prospects' needs and how they would be filled with the new flying technology. In addition to purchasers, we were engaging manufacturers of the various components.

Then the prospects were turned over to Wilbur, who answered specific questions concerning speed and weight and range limits. Next, they were sent to me, usually with a wife or female consort of some kind, and we would "close the deal." I had an enviable role because of course we took our customers and suppliers to the best places—the finest restaurants, the lovely gardens, riverboat rides, or a trip to the surrounding vineyards.

A favorite destination was the Ossau Valley, where we drove down the winding road between mountains, stopping at wineries and charming villages along the way.

The system worked, and orders flooded in. Surprisingly, they weren't government contracts for the most part. Landowners wanted

Wright flyers to observe and spray their crops. Manufacturers wanted them to speed up the time they spent traveling to their widespread factories. The family of the French prime minister, Georges Clemenceau, ordered dozens for themselves, which seemed to bode well for the future.

Orv and Will had worked out a price structure and offered pilot training as well. My mind whirled at the prospect of fulfilling all of these promises. But one of my first concerns was what to do with the bank checks that were flowing in. My friend Edith Berg once again came to the rescue.

"I'm sorry to be taking up so much of your time," I said as I climbed into the back of her open motorcar, a uniformed chauffeur in the seat in front of us.

"It is with my pleasure," she replied, her native English taking on a slight French accent.

I found the affectation quite humorous, but I would never let on.

"We must open an account with the Bank of France. They will give us the best exchange."

"Exchange?" I felt foolish for my lack of knowledge of international commerce.

"Exchange rate. You are being paid in francs, lire, pounds, or who knows what, and it needs to be exchanged for dollars to deposit back home. There is an official exchange rate, of course, but banks can be creative with their fee for the service."

Pau was a compact city, and the small downtown area was a short ride down cobblestone streets from the hotel. We pulled up in front of a sandstone block building with huge mahogany and brass doors. "*Banque de France, mesdames,*" the chauffeur announced.

A red-uniformed doorman showed us into the cavernous lobby, the blue-painted ceiling at least two stories above us. I turned toward the line of cashiers in their wooden booths, but Edith caught my arm. "Oh no, they're not for us."

A man elegantly dressed in a black suit and white shirt soon greeted us and ushered us to a private office, with two Louis XIV chairs set in front of a massive carved desk. He introduced himself as Monsieur Guidry, vice president. We were each offered a glass of champagne with a strawberry in it. I could adapt to such a life.

Edith and the banker engaged in a half-French, half-English conversation, but were using informal words and expressions I had yet to learn. Apparently something was quite humorous; they both broke out in laughter. When I looked askance at Edith, she apologized.

"Oh, that's terribly rude of us. Katharine probably hasn't heard of the hobble skirt."

Monsieur Guidry got up from behind his desk and took tiny steps over to a cabinet, as if his legs were tied together. Edith tried to explain, but was consumed by fits of laughter.

"You see, our Mrs. Berg is quite the fashion inspiration," Monsieur said. "All the women of Paris are wearing the new skirt shape which is so tight near the bottom they can hardly walk. Soon the women of Pau will be similarly afflicted."

"Oh? I have not seen Mrs. Berg in such a dress, but would enjoy a demonstration," I said.

"Do you have something...?" Edith looked around the room, then focused on the heavy velvet draperies, which were held back with gold cords. "Ah, may I?"

"*Bien sûr*," he replied.

Edith proceeded to remove a drapery tie back and tied it around her skirt below her knees. She hobbled around the room, laughing at the ridiculousness. Her gait reminded me of the women I had seen in a Chinese community in Cleveland who had bound feet. The Bishop had explained they broke the bones, then bound the feet of little girls so their feet wouldn't grow more than four inches. In their culture it was a sign of beauty, but the practice horrified me.

"You remember this, don't you, Katharine?"

I tore my mind away from the poor little Chinese girls. Just before my flight with Wilbur, Orville had secured my dress with a rope, much like Edith had done. He had mentioned something about the new Parisian fashion, but I thought he was just making fun to help calm my nerves.

"Some fashion designer witnessed my flight last October and created a sensation with his new design," Edith said.

"I think I will await his next inspiration." I didn't mention the resemblance the resultant hobble had to the abhorrent Chinese practice.

We all had more champagne and strawberries and told stories. Monsieur had only visited New York City and was curious about life in mid-America and California. Just as I checked my new wristwatch, fearing the bank would close before we ever got around to the business at hand, Monsieur Guidry presented me with some papers to sign.

"I'm sure you'll find the interest we pay and the exchange rate to be most favorable, as we are quite pleased to have such an esteemed and highly recommended customer."

My new bank account documents in hand, we bid farewell to Monsieur. My days in Pau were waning, which greatly saddened me. I had had a taste of a life of elegance in a beautiful place. I would have been happy to never leave.

In March 1909, my brothers and I accompanied the Bergs on a train to Italy, where we were to meet with even more businessmen and aviation enthusiasts. I was apprehensive that Orville would cancel on account of exhaustion and our recent train mishap. But he was the first one ready on the morning of our departure, joking and ebullient as ever. It dawned on me that Orv was most alive when he was with our big brother. When Will was absent, part of Orv was too.

In Italy, it seemed every deal took place over an immense midday meal. I thought nothing could surpass the delicious French cuisine, but I soon fell in love with the amazing freshness and heartiness of Italian cooking. Each meal would start with a light wine and usually some type of pasta—wide thick noodles, or long thin ones twirled into rounds like little birds' nests. A light sauce—lemon and capers, or perhaps tomato and cream, would accompany the pasta. Next, we would have a small serving of fish, always fresh and always simply dressed with peppercorns and lemon and the ever-present olive oil. By then I was usually satiated and could barely touch the main event—a braised pork shoulder, tiny lamb chops, or perhaps a collection of vegetables like eggplant and squash. It was only March, yet it seemed the season didn't matter; they imported whatever they wanted from Africa or the Middle East and put their own Italian twist on the dishes.

We toured Rome, and the ancient buildings and busy city both enthralled and intimidated me. Although the people were exceptionally friendly and the scenery and food wonderful, it was all just a bit too loud, too busy, and overwhelming. But the orders for aeroplanes kept pouring in, and every evening there was a celebration for the successes of the day.

Then we were off to Germany, where the food and scenery didn't disappoint. I brought along a German-English dictionary and studied it nightly, digging into the depths of my brain to remember the little bits my mother had taught me. We were met at every train station by a welcoming committee, complete with translators, but I found the Germans to be much pleased when I made my faulty attempts at speaking their language. Unlike the French, who often replied to my similar attempts in their much better English, the Germans would coach me on pronunciation or word use.

Instead of huge business dinners, we found our meetings in Germany to be in a great variety of places. We toured machine shops that were making engines and lumberyards where they were turning wood into propellers, and took riverboat cruises where we toured castles and old cities. I saw immense cathedrals that rivaled those in Italy, and traveled to cities with streets lined with half-timbered buildings and the more modern cities of the north with their huge factories. We went to Berlin and admired the ornate government buildings and expansive parks. The trolley system was much more advanced than ours in Dayton and perhaps even compared to New York City.

The Bergs hosted an event at a wine or beer hall in each city we visited. The Germans were very proud of their country and told me so over the immense beers they served. The empty glass mug itself was so heavy I needed two hands to lift it. Yet sturdy barmaids carried the mugs, overflowing with foaming beer, to the tables with a half dozen in each hand. We ate a hearty dinner of roast chicken or pork, red cabbage, and some sort of string beans that squeaked when you bit them. Every hall had at least one music ensemble playing rousing folk music, with accordions, trumpets, and tubas. The crowds sang along and danced, sometimes right on top of the tables.

In southern Germany, we were provided with festive clothing to wear: a dirndl for me, and leather knickers with embroidered suspenders—lederhosen—for the boys. I was entranced by the snowcapped mountains; the photographs I had seen hardly reflected their beauty.

In Munich, a waiter in a blue-and-white-checked shirt and lederhosen led us to a special table in the beer hall. *"Nur für Stammtisch."*

"He means this is a special table, reserved for regular customers and their close friends," Mr. Berg explained. "It's quite an honor."

After we settled ourselves on the long wooden benches, Orville surprised me by ordering in German. He requested the house specialty, *Schweinhaxe*—pig's knuckles. That didn't sound promising, so I ordered a safer dish, a breaded pork cutlet they called *Schnitzel*. But when Orv's towering piece of meat arrived, capped with a fatty crackling, I had to try it. The meat was moist and tender, by far the best pork I had ever had, and it sat in a small puddle of scrumptious brown gravy. We broke off pieces of the crackling and popped it into our mouths like fried chicken. Between the beer and the food, I felt as if I shouldn't eat again for several days.

All the while, our hosts peppered us with questions about American life. I happily told story after story, sprinkling in the bits of German I could speak. I said the closest thing we had to beer halls were events such as small county fairs or the bigger ones like the St. Louis Exhibition. I proudly told them of the progress in Dayton and our many inventors and scholars, and the beauty of the Great Lakes and our nation's capital. Wilbur could hold his own in all these discussions, although he didn't try speaking the language.

Orville needed some advice as soon as the conversation veered from the technical. One night, after witnessing several awkward pauses in his conversation with a German princess, we gathered in his hotel room for a lesson.

"First, try to do some advance research on whomever you'll be meeting. For example, today you met Princess Cecilie. If you had taken the time to learn something about her, it would have pleased her and made conversation much easier."

"And then what?" Orv looked perplexed.

"We are scheduled to sail back to New York on a ship named for her. You would make the connection and say something like, 'I'm excited to sail home on the *Kronprinzessin Cecilie*. I understand she's quite the beauty.' As you offer to refill her champagne glass, you might say, 'Were you at her christening?' Or something like that."

Orv looked defeated. "I didn't put that together." Then he brightened. "I get it. I could have mentioned all kinds of things if I had connected her with the ship. I've read all about it—she has two hundred and eighty-seven first-class, one hundred and nine second-class cabins, and seven compartments for steerage passengers, to accommodate a total of one thousand eight hundred and eighty-eight passengers, supported by a crew of six hundred and seventy-nine.

"She is seven hundred and six feet long by seventy-two feet abeam. Four reciprocating quadruple-expansion steam engines, two for each propeller. She sails at twenty-three knots…"

I slapped my hand to my forehead. "Stop. You can't just recite facts and figures, no matter how intriguing they seem to you."

"I don't understand. You said to do research, which to me means learn the facts."

"Yes, you should know important facts about someone you know you are going to meet. People like to know that you have taken some interest in them. But there's a line between subtle flattery and showing off."

"Well, how do I know where that line is? When customers know lots of details about aeroplanes, I'm not upset by that. I'm pleased."

"Because that is your obsession, and they know it. You need to pay attention to the signals people give."

"Oh boy." He sighed in exasperation. "Can we be done now?"

I was straying into difficult territory for him, but he could learn. "No, we're not done. But let's make it fun. Pretend that I am a customer. Say whatever you think the customer wants to hear. Then watch my face and mannerisms. Shut up when you determine I'm not interested, and go on when you sense I want you to go on."

We practiced several mock conversations. First, I gave obvious signals, like shaking my head, rolling my eyes, or twiddling my thumbs for negative reactions, and direct eye contact and leaning forward for positive. As he slowly sorted out the differences, I moved to more subtle clues. He soon grew weary of the game and was not improving. Finally, I came up with a solution he could always use.

"If you can't tell if someone is eagerly listening or bored to tears and just being polite, just—" I tapped his arm to help him focus, as he seemed to have accepted defeat. "Do this. Start a sentence, something you think is surely fascinating. Then feign an interruption—cough, swat an imaginary fly, whatever—and don't complete your sentence. If your listener is interested, he or she will ask you to go on. If not—well, then you have your answer."

"Or they will think I'm a scatterbrained nincompoop."

"No one will ever think that of you."

RETURN TO DAYTON
MAY 1909

The voyage back across the Atlantic was a blessing, giving us time to adjust from a fairy-tale life, living like royalty, to our perfectly comfortable but ordinary lives. The usual excited fans clamored for attention, wanting mostly Wilbur's autograph, but sometimes Orville's and even mine. We happily chatted with all the passengers and crew who were interested, and I did a short presentation of our trip in the theater so my brothers didn't have to keep answering the same questions over and over. I proudly wore my Ordre national de la Legion d'honneur during my talk. The French had seen fit to award this high honor to all three Wrights.

Orville came to my little stateroom the night before we were to land in New York, his face somber.

I had been writing letters, but I put down my pen. "What is it, Little Brother?"

He waved a creamy yellow sheet of paper, undoubtedly a telegram.

"How did you get that at sea?"

"Some kind of ship-to-shore magic." He tugged at his mustache and scratched at his ear as he scanned the message. "This outlines who will meet us in New York, where we'll be welcomed for a day of festivities. They expect thousands to greet us both there and in Dayton."

"Well, you deserve it." None of that would make him happy, but I hoped all the crowds in Europe had prepared him for it. I tried to temper his nervousness. "Only thousands? We had over two hundred thousand in France."

"How long, do you think? I mean how long will this craziness go on? It's going to interfere with our work."

"It won't go on forever. Is that what's bothering you? Missing work? Because there are things we can do, fences and gates and such."

He plopped on my tidy bunk, which was wrapped in blankets tight as a drum by a steward each day. I might miss the wonderful service of Europe and the ship, but then again it would be nice to return to a more normal life. Which is what Orville was really asking about. I had to be honest with him.

"Orv, I don't think our lives will be quite the same again. We won't have thousands greeting us every time we step off a ship, but you've done something far out of the ordinary, and you won't, and shouldn't, be forgotten."

He tugged at his collar and fidgeted. "Maybe we can rent a larger workshop, with space to live in too."

"You can't hide from the world. But don't worry, I'll be right next to you at every event. You don't ever have to make speeches; you can just nod and smile and let me do the talking."

His shoulders relaxed a little. "You did a fine job of that in Europe."

"Well then, we have a deal." I waved a hand at him. "Now go back to your cabin. I have work to do."

We landed in New York, and as Orv had told me to expect, there were crowds waiting. A caravan of shiny motor vehicles and carriages took us to our hotel, where we met with mayors and congressmen and all sorts of people who were probably equally as important. All along I kept an eye on Orville, who was holding his own. As long as he needn't talk to more than a person or two at a time, he seemed relaxed and engaged.

Dayton was a different story. We arrived at Union Station having spotted multitudes of people all along the last five miles of track. Policemen had to clear a route for us to a waiting parade of horse-drawn carriages. I spotted the Bishop and ran to embrace him. He fairly shook with joy and tried to say something, but the shouts of the organizers using megaphones drowned him out. We were guided to the carriages, very grand ones with gilt and carvings, each drawn by four white horses. I didn't get to sit next to the Bishop nor my brothers as I would have liked; the police wanted to stretch the family out over three carriages, better for crowd control, I supposed.

The throng followed us all the way to Hawthorn Street, which was so packed with people and carriages that it was nearly impass-able, taking us over an hour to travel the short distance. I winced, seeing our neighbors standing on their porches, hands on hips or arms folded. All this chaos was probably interfering with their own lives.

Flags waved up and down the entire street, and our house was bedecked with red, white, and blue bunting. Somewhere a brass band played Sousa's "Washington Post," and thousands waved *Welcome Home* signs. We climbed the few steps to our porch and waved to the crowd for another half hour. Wilbur was still smiling, but Orville winced in discomfort.

I took his arm in mine. "Come with me. I can't stand another moment," I said, guiding him inside.

Dayton's mayor awaited us in the Sunday parlor. I hid my disap-pointment at the interruption of my escape plan by pasting a smile on my face. "Your Honor. I thought we had left you back at the train station."

He laughed. "No, ma'am. I needed a quiet moment to go over the festivities we have planned."

I looked toward the window, from where the crowd could still be seen and heard.

Orville said, "You mean there's more?"

"Oh my, yes, didn't you get my letters?" He set a map on a tea table. "Here's the parade route. Downtown will be closed, except for shops offering rest and refreshments. We expect ten to twenty thousand people, with full police and fire squad support. You'll be up in the grandstand, able to see everything."

My mind whirled. The reception at the train station and home paled in comparison to this. I had been so focused on saying goodbye to all our new friends and business associates in Europe that I had hardly glanced at the welcome-home plans.

Orville blanched, wistfully eyeing the stairway up to the bedrooms. I needed to do something to reassure him. "Could we have a separate box for the family? And a way to get there with some privacy? I have an achy knee…" I lied.

"Of course. All will be arranged. I'll leave these plans for you."

WILBUR

Pomp and circumstance were far from our desires. We didn't request nor have need for any of it. As I watched the parade and the excited crowd, I thought about the newspapers who had refused to write about our accomplishments. Except for Amos Root, our beekeeper friend, the entire country had been left mostly in the dark. Seeing all this support now both gladdened my heart and worried me. How soon could we return to our work? We still had more to prove, a business to build. I did not want to leave my beloved city, but maybe Dayton now loved and depended on us a little too much.

Thankfully, little was asked of us on that grand day except to be there, nod and wave, and accept the praise and adulation. Katharine was so laden with bouquets of flowers at one point that I worried she would collapse. But she smiled and chatted with reporters and anyone else who managed to maneuver close enough. She hadn't requested any of this attention either, but she seemed much more suited to it.

In my briefcase were invitations to yet more grand events. We had been invited to the White House, where President Taft was to award Orville and me a medal. I thought we should accept only if Katharine were invited as well. After all, if it weren't for her, none of this would be happening.

Another invitation was to participate in a celebration of the three-hundred-year anniversary of the discovery of the Hudson River and the one-hundredth anniversary of Fulton's invention of the paddle-wheel steamboat. The mayor of New York City proposed that a flight up and down the Hudson, looping the Statue of Liberty, would honor the past while demonstrating the future.

I would have dismissed the idea out of hand, if not for the offer of $15,000. Even with our fattened bank account, that was too much to turn away.

On the carriage ride home, I slipped both invitations out of my briefcase and presented them to Orv and Katharine. Orv opened the one from the White House and said, "Okay. I'll go if you go," and handed it to Katharine. Then he opened the one from New York City and said, "Nope."

Katharine was squealing over the first invitation, but I shouted to Orv over her and the clatter of the carriage wheels as we went over a rough patch in the road. "Care to elaborate?"

"Same reason we decided not to attempt a crossing over the English Channel. What if the engine fails?"

"But we wouldn't be further than a few hundred feet from land at any time."

"When was the last time you were in New York City? There's water, and there's buildings."

The scenario ran through my mind. *The flyer buzzing along nicely at five hundred feet. The engine sputters a bit, smooths out, then stops altogether. I race to restart it as we begin gliding toward the water. After a few attempts, I must abandon the engine and attempt a landing. Down it goes, I level off inches above the water. But then the skids, built to slide along the ground, catch the water and dig in. The flyer noses into the water, and I am thrown into the support cables crisscrossing the wings. Soon I'm in the icy water, and the craft is sinking, pulling me with it as I fight to disentangle myself.*

I took a shaky breath. "We'd have to do some serious modifications. A backup engine would be too heavy, and there likely wouldn't be time to get it started."

Katharine tore herself away from the gold-trimmed ivory envelope and read the New York invitation. "You should do it. Fifteen grand is nothing to sneer at, and I'm sure you could make modifications for much less than that."

Orv shuddered. "It's the cables that worry me. When I crashed at Fort Myer, I thought they'd never cut me out of them. And there was no risk of drowning then."

I nodded. I had relived Orv's accident in my mind so many times it was as if it had happened to me. But it hadn't. One thing I had to ensure was that it was me, not Orv, who took this risk, should we decide to attempt it.

Kate returned the invitation to me. "What you need then is to attach something that would keep the flyer afloat long enough to be rescued, because help won't be far away in the middle of the Hudson. Perhaps a hydrogen balloon?"

"Not aerodynamic," Orv and I said at the same time, then chuckled at each other.

"Not to mention that's the old technology we're trying to replace," I added.

"Well, you'll figure it out." Katharine resumed waving to the crowds in the streets.

KATHARINE

After being feted in Europe by kings and queens, presidents and prime ministers, an invitation to the White House might seem to be expected. Strangely enough, it was no such thing, and the Wright family celebrated with a treat, a trip downtown to a fancy restaurant. I suspected my inclusion in the presidential invitation was the work of my brothers, but I didn't let on.

In June, we would have a reception in the East Room with a presentation of a special medal from the Aero Club of America by President Taft himself. A new dress was in order, and my dressmaker suggested the soft white lace I had brought back from France would be perfect for the occasion.

My mood was much more joyous as we returned to Washington, DC, by train. I tried not to think about the previous time I had arrived there, only nine short months ago, though it seemed much longer. Instead, I admired my brothers, who shared the private compartment with me. Orville had started flying again, and although he had a slight limp, he no longer required a cane unless he was very fatigued. Will looked rather gaunt from his long hours and travels, the natural vertical lines in his cheeks grown deeper over the years and his hairline steadily receding.

Members of the Aero Club, some of whom Orville and Wilbur had trained to be pilots, met us at the train station. They whisked us to the White House in a fancy steamer motorcar. Guards opened iron gates, and we drove along a long driveway to right underneath the north portico. Uniformed house staff greeted us, and we were escorted to plainly furnished rooms on the ground floor to freshen up and change our clothes.

We climbed a grand staircase to the State Floor, which was much more elaborate, with marble columns and Palladian windows. At the far end of the Grand Hall was the East Room, which rivaled the opulent rooms I'd seen in Europe, with floor-to-ceiling windows and enormous sparkling chandeliers. We were told a thousand people would be in attendance, but counting the number of rows and persons in each, my estimate was even more than that. A stage consumed one end of the room, fronting the rows upon rows of chairs for the audience. I had been asked if I desired to be on the stage with my brothers, but I demurred. This was their moment, plus I would have a better view from the audience.

After several introductions of important guests, the president was announced. The band played "Hail to the Chief," and the president and the First Lady strolled in, shaking hands all the way up to the stage. The room quieted as the president came to center stage. His large stature and bearing seemed to draw the air out of the room. One could hardly take their eyes off his spotlighted presence.

After a brief welcome, the president went right into his speech, seemingly from memory, although an assistant was flipping large cue cards.

"Mr. Wilbur and Mr. Orville Wright:

"I esteem it a great honor and an opportunity to present these medals to you as evidence of what you have done. I am glad—perhaps at a delayed hour—to show that in America it is not true that 'a prophet is not without honor save in his own country.' It is especially gratifying thus to note a great step in human discovery by paying honor to men who bear it so modestly. You made this discovery by a course that we of America like to feel is distinctively American—by keeping your nose right at the job until you accomplished what you had determined to do..."

I was pleased to hear him acknowledge Orville and Wilbur's tenacity and humbleness. So many seemed to think they simply put together the discoveries of others.

The president then spoke of Theodore Roosevelt and his deep interest in flight:

"No one had a more earnest interest, a more active interest, and a greater desire to see into the things that make for progress than my predecessor.

"There may be some reasons why some presidents have not figured in aeronautics. I see that these gentlemen who have flown in the air are constructed more on the plan of the birds than some of us." He pointedly turned to glance at Orv and Will, who were seated just behind him. The room erupted in laughter.

I smiled, remembered Orv telling me how relieved he was when each of these presidents couldn't make the time to fly with him.

"Mr. Justice Brown, in commenting on the law of patents, which is supposed to follow the proper rule in awarding merit to discovery, says that in the patent law it is the last step that counts—that is, the difference between failure and success, and that step you gentlemen have taken."

And then he said something that put in a few words something we always knew, but somehow had never talked about.

"I doubt not that whatever improvements are hereafter made for sailing the air in machines heavier than the air, the principles that you have discovered and applied and the method of their application will be the basis of all successful ones."

I tried to read my brothers' faces to see if this important point was striking them as it did me. But they were both staring nonchalantly ahead. Of course, this was no revelation to them.

The president continued on a topic that was a sensitive one for all us Wrights. "I decline to think that these instrumentalities that you have invented for human use are to be confined in their utility to war. I presume that they will have great value in war, and I suppose that all of us representatives of the various governments ought to look at this matter…from the standpoint of their utility in war, but I sincerely hope that these machines will be increased in usefulness to such a point that even those of us who now look at them as not for us may count on their ability to carry more than 'thin' passengers in times of peace.

"Many great discoveries have come by accident. Men working in one direction have happened on a truth that developed itself into a great discovery, but you gentlemen have illustrated the other, and on the whole much more commendable, method. You planned what you wished to find, and then you worked it out until you found it.

"I congratulate you on the result. I congratulate you on the recognition that you have received from all the crowned heads of Europe, and I congratulate you that in receiving it you maintained the modest and dignified demeanor worthy of American citizenship."

The crowd erupted in applause, and I was buoyed by the same sensation as the first time Will had taken me up in the flyer. These were all the things I knew in my heart, and to hear them come from the president's mouth was uplifting indeed.

⁓

While we were in Washington, Harry Haskell was also there on assignment, and we met for dinner and catching up. He told wonderful stories and made me laugh. I told him of being snuck into the all-men Ebbitt saloon by Frank Lahm. I'm afraid I wasn't such good company after that, feeling a desire to hide away and have a good cry over lost opportunities.

ORVILLE

T he most important part of all the folderol of being honored by the president was the conversation we had while gathering for photographs after the event. I knew the president to be a large man, but I wondered how Wilbur and I would look standing next to him in the photograph. Like half men, I thought, as Taft was easily the heft of both of us put together. I was quite amused to hear the president joke that he wouldn't be a pilot's first choice of passengers.

Katharine, who looked like a fresh flower amid all the dark-suited men, was completely at ease and chatted with all as if they were her fellow teachers in Dayton. I frequently envied her abilities and admit to taking full advantage of them to mask my own inadequacies.

As we assembled outside the White House for the photographer, the president raised the topic of the future of aviation, asking what he could do to ensure our country kept pace with the Europeans. In my mind, we had first to catch up, as they seemed to have infinite interest and financing and had pulled ahead while we struggled.

Katharine was prepared for the question and rattled off several foreign government agencies that we could emulate such as the French L'Etablissement Central de l'Aérostation Militaire and the German Aerodynamische Versuchsanstalt (Aerodynamic Laboratory). Taft seemed most impressed when Wilbur mentioned that the Russians had had such an agency since 1904—the Aerodynamic Institute of Koutchino.

Katharine added, "A photograph of their wind tunnel was the inspiration for my brothers to build one. I daresay our boys made better use of it, leading to the breakthrough calculations that enabled them to make their historic flights."

"You don't say." The president beamed at Katharine. "Well, we need to move quickly. We may have to light a fire under Congress. Maybe you could help with that." He was still looking squarely at Katharine, who waved off his proposition with a smile.

KATHARINE

DAYTON

I had pushed and pushed the boys to follow their dream and invent the powered flying machine. Now they had done it, and it seemed once again up to me to figure out the next step. One of the first things we did was to charter a new company, the Wright Company.

When the official documents came, the boys wanted to take the Bishop downtown for a celebratory dinner. But I had other ideas. I set up a stack of sandwiches and a platter of my pickled beets and cucumbers, and we gathered in our dining room instead.

I opened the discussion with a simple question for which we all knew the answer. "What is the purpose of your company?"

"To make aeroplanes, of course," Will replied.

"And work on new designs. Also make parts for the other companies who want to purchase rights to make their own machines," Orv added.

"And where is this to take place?" I looked around the room, big enough for the four of us and a few visitors.

"We do need to find a factory," Will said.

Orv: "Or build one."

"At Huffman Prairie?" The Bishop filled his plate.

Will: "What about the Moraine area?"

Orv: "I think closer to town, so the workers can ride the tram."

Ideas were flying fast and furious, which was my goal. By the end of the hour, they had munched a few sandwiches, and we had a solid plan.

"So, first thing tomorrow, we check out the farmland west of town," Will said, as if that had been his idea all along.

An intriguing name kept appearing in the newspapers. Mrs. Edward Deeds. I hated the tradition of usurping a married woman's given name, and in my mind, she was Edith Deeds, or Mrs. Edith Deeds, just as I was Miss Katharine Wright. I had met her casually at a church concert that the Bishop and I attended. I quickly sensed a kindred spirit, and soon learned that her husband was someone the boys should meet.

Edward Deeds was an engineer and inventor. His focus was on automobiles, but he was also in charge of National Cash Register and knew much about factories. I arranged for us all to meet in a cornfield of all places. Edith had promised that Edward would be very interested in hearing the plans for the aeroplane factory.

The men hit it off immediately. They all knew *of* each other; it had just taken some conniving by the women to get them together.

Soon the factory was under construction in that very cornfield, two long one-story buildings, where they could build many machines at the same time. One of the first spaces to be completed was a small office, which I claimed for myself. It had nothing but a desk with a typewriter, a file cabinet, and two chairs. But it pleased me to have an official workplace.

My first order of business was to place advertisements in the newspapers for assembly workers. To my chagrin, my ad for *Plane Sewer* became *Plain Sewer* and all the applicants wanted to sew straight lines, not the intricate work of fitting fabric to an airframe. By and large, they were men who had no demonstrable skill in the task, seeming to assume it was something any able-bodied man could accomplish.

So I was delighted when a diminutive woman in her late twenties peeked in the makeshift door to my office. "I'm here for the plain sewing job, if it's not taken."

"It's not. Come in." The boys had never hired a woman. Not for the print business, nor the bicycle shop, nor to help with the flyers. This was new territory. Once I studied the samples of the garments Miss Ida Holgreve had created, I was sure she was up to the job. My only concern was whether to ask permission from my new bosses to hire her.

No, I thought. That would send the wrong message. Did they trust me to make sound decisions or not?

I stood and offered her my hand. "Welcome to the Wright Company. You can begin straightaway." I showed her to the sewing room, where stacks of muslin awaited piecing together. We were laying out patterns when Orv and Will's raised voices could be heard over the steady din of the generators. "Excuse me." I went to find out what the fuss was about.

The smell of grease and gasoline fumes hit me as I left the confines of the sewing room. Orv and Wilbur were standing almost chest to chest.

Wilbur held a wooden knob about the size of a baseball under Orv's chin. "Well, I taught the pilots in France and Germany to use the stick, and I'm not about to go back there and tell them forget that, my brother has come up with something new," he shouted.

"It's too clumsy. Using one stick for the two actions isn't much better than having them synchronized like we did in the first place."

"Records set all over Europe by me and pilots I've trained would refute that." Will tossed the knob to Orville.

"Boys, what's this about?" I asked, though I was sure they were speaking of the hand controls for the rudder and wing warping. "You shouldn't be arguing in front of them." I nodded toward the long narrow room, where most work had stopped, workers in their tan jumpsuits idly staring at the three of us. I escorted my brothers back to my small office.

"Wilbur is standing in the way of progress. I've developed a better control, and he's too stubborn to learn something new."

"Why should I have to, when what we're making"—he waved toward the factory floor—"is well tested?"

"But I used the knob at Fort Myer this year. That's what the army is expecting. It's a contract, for God's sake." Orv juggled the wooden orb hand to hand.

"Give me that." I held out my hand for the knob. "So Will and the Europeans use a stick for two motions, back and forth and side to side. And Orv uses a stick and a knob. Why don't you offer both and let the customers choose?"

Will scowled. "It would be more costly to do both. Standardization is the key."

"You're just afraid they'll like mine better," Orv said.

I held the knob up to their faces. "As president of the board, I'm deciding. Make both. Charge more for the option."

They both started arguing their points again. Then they looked at each other and shrugged.

"All right," said Will.

Orv wasn't quite satisfied. "But which one is the option?"

"Flip a coin," I said. "Now let's get back to work."

WILBUR

The factories hummed along, producing the Model A, as the army had dubbed it. We liked to think that meant they planned on purchasing Models B through Z as well. Orv was off to Berlin for more demonstrations. He no doubt would be using his newfangled knob contraption, but I had to let go of that annoyance. I had a more pressing issue.

We had accepted the invitation from New York City to take part in their Hudson-Fulton celebration. This meant flying for either an hour or ten miles. Either of these was easily accomplished. The complication, of course, was flying over water.

Charley was now our lead mechanic of many, and I trusted his wisdom. We met in the factory after quitting time to figure out a way to keep the machine afloat, as Katharine had suggested, long enough for help to arrive in the event of a crash. He waved at a partially assembled flyer. "Should we take one out and dump it into a lake, see how long it floats?"

We walked over to a front elevator assembly. "If it hits the water, I'll be thrown forward and end up in a tangled mess of wire and fabric. It's not just about some part of the machine still afloat. We need more buoyancy altogether." We went round and round with different ideas, but none seemed practical, seaworthy, and flyable.

That night I pondered the question at dinner. The Bishop turned to Katharine. "You remember your art history book? It shows a painting of elephants crossing a bridge."

"The Brooklyn Bridge?"

"No, a floating bridge. In China, I believe."

Katharine's eyes lit up. She hurried to the library and returned with a tattered copy of a schoolbook. We never got rid of books.

She paged through it, then announced, "Here it is. It's a pontoon bridge."

We all looked at the photograph of a detailed painting. Sure enough, a group of elephants were crossing a bridge that rested on a series of small rowboats or canoes lashed together side to side.

"A pontoon. Of course." I thought out loud. "A canoe would have a perfect aerodynamic shape. If we find one light enough, it could fit within the skids."

<hr />

When Charley and I arrived in New York, our first order of business was to buy a canoe. I'm afraid we thoroughly confused the shopkeeper, a fellow with bright-yellow suspenders holding up trousers over an expansive belly. Wanting to be helpful, he pointed out the sturdy cane seats and beauty of the woodwork on various models. But Charley was measuring their length and width, and I was inquiring as to their weight.

"Ah, you're going to portage?" the shopkeeper asked.

"Portage?" I headed toward Charley, who was pointing to a canoe in the back of the shop.

The shopkeeper trailed behind me with a pronounced limp. "Yeah, portage. Carry it over bits of land between a chain of lakes, for example. So you want it to be sturdy, but light."

"Precisely. Something under seventy or so pounds, but can support the weight of three good-sized men."

Charley inspected a bright-red canoe. "She's sixteen feet. Perfect fit."

I had had qualms about how odd a canoe would look under the flyer. But I could imagine this bright-red beauty against the white wings and blue sky. She would represent our nation's flag in a whole new way.

The shopkeeper patted the canoe, resting on two sawhorses. "Ah, the Indian girl. Well-made of cedar, sixty-something pounds. What lake you heading to? I can have it delivered."

I paid the man and gave him an address on Governors Island. Then Charley and I made our escape before having to answer any more questions.

Orv had fashioned a series of straps and mounted anchors on the flyer's frame for securing the canoe. He included a note with specific instructions and these words of encouragement:

I wish I could be there with you. Godspeed, Brother.

We covered the top of the canoe with waxed canvas to make it waterproof, then secured her between the skids. I made an early-morning test flight with the canoe attached, and the flyer performed flawlessly. That afternoon, as I took off again into a light westerly wind toward Liberty Island, I wasn't thinking about the million onlookers, or even the symbolism of the famed statue. I was thinking about Orville, over in Germany, perhaps flying toward the setting sun. I thought of the Bishop, who remembered the Chinese painting and who had supported us in every way possible, and Katharine, who always knew how to piece together all our ideas to make something whole.

I felt I was the luckiest man alive, and I waggled my wings over the sparkling river for all of them.

ORVILLE

When we returned from Europe, Wilbur, Katharine, and I were the very same people who had lived in modest house on the west side, went to work regularly, to church not so regularly, and treated and were treated kindly by all. But somehow, Dayton had found itself to be known throughout the world, and our name was now inextricably attached to its fortune.

I felt immense pressure to succeed, now not just for the advancement of science and human progress, but for a small midwestern city that held huge parades for us. It was an uncomfortable position.

Nonetheless, we had patent battles to win, contracts to be agreed on, and needed all manner of support from the community. We had to stay in everyone's good graces, even as people like Glenn Curtiss ran our name through the newspaper mud of false and exaggerated claims. Curtiss was an expert on engines who had joined forces with Alexander Graham Bell to manufacture aeroplanes of their own invention. The problem was, they were using our patented designs.

So we planned for an exhibition at Huffman Prairie. We had yet to show our fellow Americans all our flyers could do in a public demonstration, something Curtiss had already done. We chose a spring day, in hopes of good weather, and invited the newly formed Aeroplane Club of Dayton and anyone else interested to watch an air show on May 25.

It turned out to be a fine day. A steady wind of ten miles an hour would make for smooth takeoffs and landings, and the white wings would glow in the bright sun. All the Wrights—the Bishop, Reuchlin and Lorin and their families, Katharine, Wilbur, and I—rode out in hired motorcars, which turned out to be wise, for the interurban trolley was full to capacity, with a crowd waiting for the next one. I wondered why, and my wonderment increased as we drew nearer to the fields and saw hundreds of people walking, or riding in buggies, or driving motorcars down the narrow road to the field.

Thousands of people had come to see us fly. Of course, this was normal back in France, but never had we seen such interest in our own country. My heart started to pound, not with nervousness, but with pride. We had turned a corner on a new life.

I was squeezed in the middle of the back seat of an open car, with Katharine and Wilbur on either side of me, smiling and waving to our fans.

"This is the day," I said.

"Indeed," replied Wilbur, grinning ear to ear.

"Today, we fly together. Not the first flight, let's get all the fancy turns and dips and soars out of the way, then we go up together, just as we agreed."

Wilbur was quiet a moment as he thought it over. "We have nothing left to prove. It's time."

Katharine took my hand. Of course, she had gone up with Will back in France, but I never had. "I will be watching and praying for your safety, my brothers." She smiled at each of us in turn. "It's time."

WILBUR

Orville and I did our final checks on the machine. We hadn't expected thousands of spectators, along with food and souvenir vendors, but were happy for it. We had agreed that Orville would do the "demonstration" part of the show, since he enjoyed pushing the limits much more than I did.

"You know the drill." I held his lapels to keep his attention, as I knew how much was running through his mind. "Circle, then figure eights, gain maximum altitude, steady dive, and one close-to-ground pass if the air is especially good."

He gave a quick salute. "Aye, aye, Captain."

The takeoff was swift, and he circled up, up, up. I stood between my siblings, all holding our hats against the wind. I tried to stop concentrating on the buzz of the engine, to stop analyzing the chop of the propellers and warp of the wingtips, and to just enjoy the moment. Orv did a lazy figure eight, using the whole of the field, as the crowd whooped with joy. Then he did tighter and tighter turns, until his wings seemed almost perpendicular to the earth. Just as I started to become alarmed, he pulled up and circled higher and higher, preparing for his steep dive. This was the riskiest part of the routine.

The crowd hushed as the flyer reached almost three thousand feet, her engine now muffled by distance. At that height, Orville could see all the way to Columbus, if the air was clear enough. No doubt he could see all of Dayton and the Miami River curling its way through it, while the field, encircled by the crowds, would be just a short glide away.

The low rumble of the engine changed; it grew louder and higher-pitched as Orv turned and was now coming toward us. Down he came in a dive that I knew made the wind beat at his face and pushed him hard against his seat. Running just past the field, he made a tight turn and circled back, again and again. The crowds, held back behind a fence, roared with each turn, and when he finally landed just a hundred feet away, they erupted in cheers and applause that was even louder than his engine and propellers.

I ran out to him, and climbed aboard before he could even hop off. "Congratulations, Brother. You have earned yourself a passenger. One more loop for the crowd?"

"No. For us. And Pop, Reuch, Lorin, and Katharine."

"For the Wrights, then." I waved toward Charley, who held a gas can. In a way, I was both thrilled with reaching this milestone and a little sad. We had reached this goal, and soon both of our attentions would be pulled in different directions—to the business of flying, rather than flying ourselves. Orv would probably continue, keeping his skills up and training others. But our livelihood depended on selling our invention, and already that took up more hours in a day then inventing ever had.

I slapped Orv's thigh. "As soon as you're ready to go up again, I'll be honored to be your passenger."

So up we went in the most bittersweet moment of my life. We spoke little. I knew Orv was feeling what I was, that we needed to savor every second, memorizing the thrill that surpassed being honored by the president and the heads of state of Europe. As the machine hummed and the wind blew, I tasted the sweetness of victory, the culmination of what we had set out to do ten years prior. We were soaring with the birds, flying together for the first and only time.

WILBUR

By June, between running the company, supervising the factory building airplanes, and fighting lawsuits, I no longer had time to fly. Orv gave the Bishop and all of our nieces and nephews a ride, but mostly flew to train pilots and pilot instructors. I was either riding a train to meetings in Chicago or New York, or writing angry letters to people such as our competitor Curtiss, or rather to his stable of lawyers.

The battle with Curtiss saddened me and took a toll on my health. Katharine fussed over my inability to eat properly, and I lay awake many nights, wondering if I hadn't thrown my family's fortunes to the wind with my foolish publications and speeches early on. For it was the very speech that they had warned me about in 1901 that Curtiss was using to get around our patent and build his own machines using our ideas. He claimed his machines used public knowledge and was put into action by him and his team. Curtiss tried to make me look like a selfish money-grubber, while he had offered the very engine we had desperately needed back in 1903.

His claim was partly true. He offered a fifty-horsepower engine, but since he was an associate of Alex Bell, I neither trusted Curtiss nor believed his engine would meet our needs.

I couldn't rest when I needed to fight this wrong and protect my family, especially Katharine, who had given up so much of her own life for this dream.

So I worked longer and harder, from meetings at our new head-quarters in New York, to a new manufacturing plant in New Jersey, to the pilot-training facilities in Virginia and in Dayton. We finally convinced the Bishop to retire, although he would still sneak to a church conference here or there. I knew Katharine had long yearned to get back to teaching, but she was now an officer in our company and there was nothing I could do to stop the continuing demands on her time. Instead, I worked on another of her requests, her ardent wish for a new home, more sheltered from the masses of people who still gathered at 7 Hawthorn Street, expecting to meet one of the illustrious Wrights.

I found a nice lot about two miles north of our home and was excited to show it to her. It was on the main streetcar line, and I thought she would be pleased with the easy access to town and enough space to build a privacy fence. But I knew something was amiss as soon as we alighted from the trolley.

"Tell me what you're thinking, Brother," she said in a tone that warned of disapproval.

"I know it doesn't look like much now, but you have to imagine it. We can build a grand home—five thousand, six thousand square feet—whatever your heart desires. And a fence all around to keep out the 'peepers.'"

Katharine looked up at me, her deep-blue eyes full of sincerity. "I appreciate your efforts. But perhaps your time is better spent on company business, and you should leave hearth and home to me."

KATHARINE

Will was so pleased with himself. He had found a plot of land of several acres, difficult to find so close to the city. And his plans for a grand home sounded just wonderful. There was just one problem, and that was Dayton itself.

We were proud of its history and the powerhouse it had become, with manufacturing, cultural venues, and a small but vibrant downtown. After lodging in drafty and overstuffed mansions and castles in Europe, I had come to realize I had no need for a grand house. I was perfectly happy with the one on Hawthorn Street, although indoor plumbing would have made our lives easier. But I now understood that we would need more space around us if we were ever to be able to enjoy a bit of peace and privacy. The crowds and supporters meant well, but I especially needed to protect the jangled nerves of Orville, who often had become a prisoner in his own home, unwilling to face people seeking an autograph or a chat.

And the north side of Dayton was not getting better with time, with an ever-growing number of low-wage workers and those seeking work, or seeking handouts from those who did work.

"I'm sorry, Wilbur. But we need to look at one of the quieter communities in the south or east."

"But you won't be able to ride the streetcar."

"Yes, but neither will the sightseers who invade our privacy and disturb our neighbors. Traffic would be limited to those with private transportation." He gazed at the expanse of the lot, and I could tell he wasn't convinced, probably because he knew how I treasured my independence.

"If you can fly an aeroplane, I can certainly learn to drive a motorcar." I thought wistfully of Frank Lahm. Perhaps I could travel to his posting at Fort Riley, Kansas, for some lessons.

Wilbur bit his lip; I sensed his disappointment. But he rallied quickly. "Well then, let's go buy an automobile, and we'll keep driving until we find the right place."

It turned out that the "right place" was in a lovely town just to the south of Dayton. Charming Oakwood boasted an abundance of redbud, oak, and maple trees, and large stylish homes spread out on spacious lots. The city planners had envisioned it as a "streetcar suburb" with a line going south down the valley that led to an area known as the Far Hills. But the experiment had failed; they couldn't get enough people interested in living that far away from all the amenities of the city.

But Oakwood seemed ideal to me, with roads snaking up and down the hills, giving it a sense of privacy and a slower pace of life. We found the perfect lot of seventeen acres, up on a hill and surrounded by so many trees there wasn't another home within sight. I could imagine a stately brick home with white columns like I had seen in Virginia, or maybe a half-timbered house as I had seen in Germany. Our new dream: a home with room to entertain if we wished, and the privacy we now needed.

ORVILLE

W e three piled into my motorcar to make one last walk of the Oakwood property before we put down our hard-earned cash. It consisted of a rounded hill, not the tallest around, but quite suitable for building. A considerable number of trees covered the lot, healthy and in full leaf, and I was happy to note that many of them were hawthorn trees, just like the ones that lined our current street. As we ascended to the highest point, the perfect name for our new home came to me.

"Hawthorn Hill." I said out loud. Katharine and Wilbur just nodded. As usual, we thought in unison.

Wilbur, who had been the least excited about the project, paced off a rectangle for the home site. "I think it should face this way, with the long axis here." He spread his arms, just as he had so many times in mimicking flight. "The sun will cross like this." He arced his arm left to right in front of us. "The front of the house will be bathed in sunlight all day, and the back porch shaded from the sun for summer entertaining."

"Yes, and I'd like a design like the Georgian mansions that grace the Potomac in Virginia," I added.

"With lots of windows to let the air flow through," Katharine said. She hated to be too warm.

My mind twisted and turned the plans for our new home, arranging windows in line with prevailing winds. Above all, I wanted Katharine to be happy. She deserved it.

But our agreement faltered when it came to the exterior materials.

"A home of natural stone that will blend in with its environment," mused Will.

Katharine shook her head. "I was thinking red brick, like the homes that Orv and I admired in Virginia."

We had walked the entire perimeter of our imagined home and stood in the middle, facing south. Neither of those ideas sounded right to me. Yes, the red brick homes were the model for the design, but it wasn't *us*.

"Katharine, do you remember teasing us about the fabric you wanted for the flyer's wings?" I asked.

"Red polka dots?"

"Correct. And we would have used whatever you chose. But you picked something better, perfect for us. Those cream-colored wings soaring against a blue sky are who we are."

Will scrunched his face. "So we'll paint it cream? A wooden house then, like Hawthorn Street?"

"Well, we can't paint stone." Katharine laughed. "But I do like the idea of the cream against the sky. With bright-white trim to represent the clouds."

"Neither," I argued. "Have you seen the new buildings that National Cash Register is putting up? Made from a blond brick.

Structurally sound, and maintenance free. No painting needed, no worry of rot."

Will put in a last effort. "I still see a grand home of natural stone, with exposed trusswork. That will last forever."

"How about a vote?" offered Katharine. "All those in favor of blond brick?" She and I raised our hands. "The bricks have it."

"Fine. I'm odd man out once again." But Will was smiling, as he no doubt was envisioning our dream being built on that very spot. Our castle in the clouds.

KATHARINE

Soon the land was ours, and Orv found an architect to draw up the plans. I felt sorry for the chosen firm before I even met them, knowing Orv would drive them batty with his special demands. A bathroom for every bedroom, a private space for his office. Electric doorbells and telephone wires and a vacuum cleaner that ran through the walls. I feared our home would resemble the aeroplane factory if he got everything he wanted.

Even though I kept saying I was happy at Hawthorn Street, I knew this was a long-overdue change. Orville would get the privacy he needed and electricity for all the experiments he wanted to conduct. Wilbur and the Bishop would have space for their books, and I could entertain to my heart's content without bothering any of them. And oh! The luxury of running water and a built-in bathtub, not to mention no more outhouse.

I even inquired as to whether the local schools would be in need of a teacher. "Of course," was the answer from several schools in Oakwood and in neighboring Van Buren Township. "We'll get back to you soon."

But "soon" didn't seem to happen.

Carrie was still our housekeeper and would be making the move with us. She sat at the dining table, polishing silver, while I flipped through the mail.

"Nothing from any of the schools I've applied to," I said dejectedly.

"Oh, Miss Wright, that time has come and gone."

"What do you mean? I may be a little rusty, but I'm sure I could get back to it with some review."

"Things have changed." She lowered her head, attending to a rusty spot like it was the devil himself. "How do you think the other teachers would feel? You've met with the president, and kings and queens. You've been in the newspapers and everyone in town knows who you are. No principal could tell you no to anything you wanted."

"Oh, that's not true. I haven't changed."

Carrie sighed. "I know that. But your circumstances have changed, and you can't be taking the job away from someone else who might need it, and who wouldn't be a distraction and treated special."

She was right, of course. Why I had failed to realize it wasn't such a mystery; it was something I didn't want to accept. My eyes welled up, but I refused to give in to tears. I had given up bigger things than my teaching career, after all.

~

Frank Lahm never made it to France, at least not while I was there. We wrote letters, first once a month or so, then more and more infrequently, as our fragile bond weakened due to busy lives. Was there not enough of an attraction to make us work harder to be together? My feelings for him were confused with the trauma of Orv's accident. Was he simply a bright light in a very dark time? I thought not.

The answer came in a letter. Frank was to be married that fall. I felt another opportunity, perhaps my last, slip through my fingers like the water from a well.

ORVILLE

Every day except Sunday I made the rounds between our businesses. The aeroplane manufacturing, the local office, my own research lab, and my favorite, the flying school out at Huffman Prairie. Along with trips out to New Jersey to check on the engine plant and New York City, where our company was headquartered, I was a very busy man. And every day I stuffed down the guilt I felt for leaving to Wilbur the tasks I didn't want to do—deal with all the legal and patent issues.

My brother was traveling even more than I and had a schedule that left him too little rest and without the comforts of home and good cooking. He had always been trim, but I could tell by the hollowness of his eyes that his body wasn't getting proper nutrition. I vowed that when he came back from his trip to Boston, we would discuss changes in our business. Hire more lawyers, sell off the company, whatever it took. I would get him flying again. It wasn't fair that I got to pilot once in a while and went up several times a week with my most promising students. I had a group of Canadian pilots who had me laughing so hard that tears ran down my cheeks.

Oh, how Wilbur would have loved that. But he was stuck on a train somewhere in Pennsylvania.

I tried to make up for my failure by giving Katharine everything she could possibly desire. We were planning the home of her dreams, a mansion worthy of a president, or at least a governor. We would break ground that summer, up on a hill surrounded by hawthorn trees, to build a home set in perfect solitude yet still just a short ride to the city.

In fact, it was the trees that convinced me that we had found the right place. Tree-lined Hawthorn Street had been our home for nearly all of our lives, and now Hawthorn Hill, as we had officially named it, beckoned. There we could welcome all the people who had assisted in our success, or whom we could help as they furthered the industry that we had started. It would be more than a gracious home; it would be a monument to our success and our vision for the future.

I would pave a long entrance, on which I'd teach my nephews to drive, install a trophy room for the magnificent sculpture given to Wilbur by the French, and fit a kitchen big enough for Katharine to put up hundreds of jars of fruits and vegetables, if that was something she still wanted to do. We would sit by the fireplace and read or tell stories by the hour. I imagined days of sitting on the porch with Will and Katharine, waving to children sledding down the hills in winter, picking wildflowers in the summer, and resting in the shade of the hawthorn trees.

WILBUR

All I really wanted was my own bedroom and a bathroom. After spending my entire life using an outhouse and having Orv trudge through my space getting to and from his own, how delightful it would be to have a room filled with sunlight to call my own.

So I looked at the blueprints and identified the southeast corner bedroom as my own. I pictured waking to the sunrise and having coffee on the porch overlooking the grounds. But the architect had wasted so much square footage on useless hallways and cubbies for this and that, that I had to get involved.

But how to get into each of the five bedrooms and bathrooms that circled the center stairway without many hallways? I thought of Hawthorn Street, with Katharine right at the top of the stairs, and Orv and me having connected bedrooms. Perhaps if we connected with adjoining bathrooms, we could each have our privacy, yet maintain the sweet secure feeling of closeness we had always enjoyed.

Meanwhile, while the home was being built, I would work through all the patent battles and get our companies running like well-oiled machines. I didn't think we would stray from our first love of aviation too much, but instead somehow return to our best times, the early times, when we were discovering new things each day, so proud of ourselves and each other. Maybe we should build a home on Kitty Hawk as well, where we could watch the seagulls soar and listen to the crashing of the waves. We could reminisce with the Tates and all the boys and eat fish fresh out of the sea. Those dreams were so close, I could just about taste them. I just had to get through these next tough months of arduous work.

KATHARINE

I was in the kitchen, stirring a pot of Will's favorite goulash, when I heard someone coming in the sitting room door. I rushed to see my brother, returning from an especially long trip.

"Ah, my favorite sister," Will said as he enveloped me in a bear hug. A skinny bear, that is.

"Oh my. It's a good thing I've got dinner almost ready. You look like you haven't eaten in a month."

"Next time you're going with me to teach those Boston people what real food tastes like."

At dinner, Will reviewed the struggles he had defending the patent. That old rascal Curtiss was still up to his old tricks and had the Smithsonian convinced it was Langley who should be credited with the invention of the aeroplane. Then we reviewed the plans for our home on Hawthorn Hill.

The Bishop was unusually quiet, spooning steadily into his goulash.

"What do you think, Pop? Do you agree with the changes that Will has suggested?" I asked.

"I'm quite happy here, but understand you want something bigger." He wiped his mouth with his napkin. "I worry somewhat how it looks for a man of the church to live in a place so grand."

A bubble of resentment rose in me. All the sacrifices the boys, and I as well, had made. Years of risks. The many mishaps and accidents. One nearly killing Orv and leaving him with constant back and hip pain even now, four years later. And our father was concerned with how a nice home would look to his flock, even after his retirement.

But of course, I couldn't voice my opinion on this. The dutiful daughter of the former leader of a church did not put herself first, second, or thirteenth. I swallowed my fury and pride, and passed a platter of bread.

The boys also didn't seem to know what to say, and the Bishop's comment hung there in the silence like the weight on the boys' catapult. Ready to launch at any moment, but with no plane to fly.

That May, the patent battles and our planned home took a back seat to another grave concern. In the week since Will returned from Boston, he had grown weaker and unable to eat. Then he began running a high temperature, and the doctor diagnosed him with typhoid fever.

This sent chills through my body. I remembered nursing Orville and Milton through it. It had caused Orv terrible stomach pains, and the weakness and fever had left him bedridden for weeks. He was lucky it never went to his heart, and his general good health and youth enabled him to recover fully.

But Will was forty-five years old and already in a weakened condition. I ordered him to bed and began round-the-clock checks on him, with as much bone broth and fruit juice forced upon him as he could stand. Our oldest brother, Reuchlin, traveled from Kansas City, we all took turns in the sickroom, and after a few days, Will rallied.

One morning he woke up cheerful and wanting to get out of bed. We helped him up, and he walked around a bit. I opened the window a crack to let in some fresh air and said a silent prayer for continued recovery.

But that was not to be. The next day he couldn't get up in the morning, his belly swollen and very painful. By late afternoon, his fever had risen to nearly 106, and we couldn't wake him at all. Again we called the doctor, but there was not much he could do.

"Try to give him sips of broth if he rouses enough, but otherwise, let him sleep. He's in God's hands now."

Orville came to my room that night. "What are we going to do?" I just shook my head.

"He must recover. He can't leave us. I can't go on without my brother." Then he laid his head on my lap, and I rubbed his shoulder. I could think of nothing to say except, "He's in God's hands, and we will make it through this together."

I checked Will several times through the night. He shook as if having chills, but he did not awaken. At about 2:00 a.m. I pulled up a chair and sat next to him for the rest of the night, in case he should wake and need me. He was flushed with a fever of 105, and I wiped him down with a cool rag, then held his frightfully warm hand.

I was just dozing off when I felt him squeeze my hand. "Yes, Brother?"

His eyes opened just a slit and his lips moved. I put a drop of water on his lips, but he was trying to talk.

"Sterchens."

"I'm here."

"I'm sorry."

I started to sob. "No. Nothing to be sorry about." He never said another thing. I was torn between running to wake Orv and staying with Will. I decided to stay. At three o'clock I knew from his rattling breath that the end was near. I woke the Bishop, Orv, Reuchlin, and Lorin so that we could all be with him as he drifted away from us, finally at peace.

The Bishop was crushed of course, but accepted it as he had accepted our mother's death and, I was told, the twins they lost before I was born, as God's will.

We buried dear Wilbur in Woodland Cemetery next to our mother. I followed the horses bearing the carriage on foot, up the steep and winding path. We stopped for a moment at the lookout point at the top of the hill. From here we could see the plains of the Miami River and the city of Dayton we all knew and loved so well.

I was numb with grief. It didn't seem possible that our vibrant, loving brother was lost to us. Orville acted as if a switch had turned off the light in him. He had always been a bit isolated in a shell of his own making, but now the mischievous and loving character that had existed within that shell shriveled and died with Wilbur. I didn't know if he would ever come back.

Ground was broken soon after for Hawthorn Hill, which seemed to represent our broken hearts. We were grieving too much to think of the future, let alone a new home without Will. Orv soon busied himself with the airplane company and the flyer school, but the emptiness in his eyes remained.

I couldn't make sense of it. How could my brilliant, good-to-the-core brother have been taken away? Why not me? I wasn't anywhere nearly as bright, and the world would not have missed me. I wandered about in a daze, alternately fuming at our Lord and trying to figure out why He had spared me.

A newspaper article gave me a clue. A new organization, the Women's Suffrage Party of Montgomery County, had reestablished the fight for an amendment to Ohio's constitution to allow women to vote. I had followed the movement off and on in other states, but this was the first I'd heard of a serious effort locally.

I noted the date and time of the next meeting. Even as I did so, it felt like a small part of the dark cloud that had enveloped me had lifted. This was something Wilbur would have wanted. Maybe with some luck I could interest the Bishop and Orv in the cause as well.

~~

I wasn't sure what to expect at the meeting. I had heard of protesters flinging rotten apples and eggs at the attendees, and meetings that erupted in so many arguments that nothing was ever decided. But the truth turned out to be quite different.

We met in the back room of a storefront on Main Street. The attendees included about thirty people, mostly women, but a few men in smart suits as well. I recognized the head of National Cash Register, John Patterson, and Orville's friend and fellow inventor Edward Deeds, along with his wife, Edith.

The meeting might have been a model for *Robert's Rules of Order*.

After a welcome and Pledge of Allegiance, the leader reviewed the agenda: to develop a campaign for the upcoming vote for an amendment. I took notes on things I thought the Wrights might help with—resources for printing of pamphlets and fliers, for example.

One of the stickiest problems was overcoming the resistance from the well-established beer and liquor purveyors. One speaker went on at length saying that they feared that if women gained the vote, they would vote for prohibition, which would destroy many businesses and only lead to crime and moonshining.

I had the urge to raise my hand and counter the argument, but I had no facts, no surveys, no hard evidence to back up my opinion that this was nonsense. And the more I thought about it, the more I suspected the speaker had a valid point.

Another speaker described several previous marches and expressed the desire to hold a much bigger one. I thought of the tremendous parade that had been held for Orville and Wilbur upon their return from France. The streets had been filled elbow to elbow for many blocks. Surely, with enough publicity, Dayton could play host to another magnificent event. We had many contacts in the community: the press, company presidents, religious organizations. They just needed the right hostess.

A stirring of excitement filled me, further lifting the dark cloud. I saw a place for myself in this important cause.

ORVILLE

O ne is never too old to dye Easter eggs. I liked to mix up a batch of beet juice and vinegar to make red ones to represent Christ's blood like the Greeks and Mesopotamians. But Lorin's kids liked all the new fancy colors, so on Good Friday I stunk up the kitchen with hard-boiled eggs, turmeric, and spinach. I had to raid Katharine's stash of jarred vegetables for the spinach.

But just as my kettle of water came to a boil, the wind outside picked up, enough that clothes hung out to dry had taken flight. I went out to fetch them and secure other possible projectiles. The sky was still clear, but the pains in my back and hip told me the barometric pressure was falling. The wind whistled through the trees; I didn't need an anemometer to tell me they were gusting over thirty miles per hour. The children would be disappointed, but I'd have to cancel our planned activity. Although only little Horace could still be called a child. The older three were nearly grown now, which made me even sadder. They wouldn't want to dye eggs with Uncle Orv much longer.

The winds were blustery all through Saturday and the skies darkened. This was no ordinary storm. I went to my laboratory as usual, but instead of working on my experiments, I spent the time securing anything that might be harmed in heavy wind and rain. I moved some boxes of important documents up high, just in case of some water getting in. The ground was already soaked from spring rains, so it wouldn't take much more to have standing water in the streets. There wasn't much I could do about the Kitty Hawk flyer, most of it still in crates in a shed out back.

Walking back home was an adventure, as I nearly toppled over every time I passed a building into a vortex of wind. The dark clouds and bluster made it seem like rain should be pouring down, yet only a few drops pelted me. Nature was building an angry storm, and it wasn't too late in the season for a blizzard. I decided I should gather some wood to keep us warm for a few days.

Katharine woke me early on Easter morning. "Orv, do you think we should put boards on the windows?"

The house was fairly vibrating with the wind. "Too late for that now. We'd become airborne ourselves trying to get them up. Let's do what we can on the inside."

We stuffed rags in the windowsills and moved the furniture to the center of the rooms. The rain had finally started, and we breathed a little sigh of relief that at least the ominous prelude was over. But it quickly built to a torrential downpour, coming down in sheets and obscuring the view out the windows.

There was nothing to do but read and play board games. We had to light the kerosene lamps at noon, and we were getting several inches of rain each hour. I worried about my lab and my records and the flyer. They were even closer to the river than our house. I cracked open the back door to see if water was standing in the yard.

We still had yards of muslin out in the shed; I wondered if I could make sandbags to protect the house. But a few hours of downpour on previously saturated ground left nothing but slimy mud to work with. The river had to be close to bursting its banks.

Katharine was worried about Hawthorn Hill, which was still in the early construction phase. "We should go over there, see what we can do."

"No," I said. "If the river levees fail, we will have to leave, but we can't go there. That hill will become an island and we could get stranded."

Pop, who had been quietly writing in his journal, took on a look of concern for the first time. "Do you think it's likely the levees will fail?"

"I'm no expert in civil engineering, but we've got five rivers that drain into the Greater Miami. It's flooded here before, which is why the levees were built, but they can only hold back so much."

When the wind and rain eased a bit late in the afternoon, I bundled up in a raincoat and fishing boots and headed to my office near our old bicycle shop. There I could make some phone calls to friends and ask for shelter if needed, as well as moving everything I could up to the second floor.

The rain was unrelenting for the next two days. Back at the house, Pop, Katharine, and I moved everything we could up to the second floor. The streets were under nearly a foot of water. Watching the ripples on its surface and feeling the continuing drop in air pressure in my bones, I knew it was going to get even worse.

My 1912 Franklin Roadster, one of my favorite possessions, was parked on the street. Franklin automobiles were setting records for both speed and fuel mileage efficiency, the two things that most intrigued me about the invention. I chastised myself for not starting her every day; the oil needed to circulate like blood to keep parts lubricated. Katharine always did this for me when I was out of town, but she probably had been too preoccupied.

By the time we had the household possessions moved, my lovely open roadster was quite soaked through. I could not get her started and she was now useless as means of an escape, which I increasingly thought would be necessary.

Lorin and I spent the day sloshing through the streets of downtown, climbing into houses wherever we heard people calling for help. We packed up and relocated the hardware from the first floor of our friend Hamburger's shop. He had always been so good to us, finding just what we needed when what we needed didn't seem to exist. The police had rowboats at the ready, and we rescued dozens who couldn't make their way to them.

The waters were getting more ominous by the moment. When we no longer heard shouts for help, I headed back for Katharine and Pop, worried that it might already be too late to get them out. Then I thought of Wilbur's red canoe sidled against the outhouse. "Pack your bags," I told them. "We're evacuating."

KATHARINE

I didn't argue with Orv when he said it was time to go. In fact, I already had a bag packed. Besides a change of clothes, I had two precious things: a photograph of our family and the sourdough starter that my mother had carefully fed for years and had made me promise to keep alive.

I went to check on the Bishop. He was in his room, just standing there scratching his beard. "Shall I help you pack?" I asked gently. I had to remind myself that he was now in his eighties, and nothing came quickly or easily to him anymore.

"Is leaving the right thing to do? Seems we are safer hunkering down than going out in this." He waved at the window, which clattered with the pelting of the rain as the house creaked with the strain of the wind.

"We don't need to go far. We have friends who live on a hill just a couple of miles away."

Lorin had a new home close by, but it was barely higher than ours and he already had a houseful of evacuees. Orville had a plan: We'd put on life jackets and take the canoe out of the immediate area. Then his friend would pick us up.

I grabbed some clothing and a few of the Bishop's most treasured belongings and tossed them into his travel bag. "Come on, we can't delay any longer."

I managed to get myself, the Bishop, and our bags down the steps.

Orville was at the door, donning his galoshes, then tying a rain hat on his head. "I'll be right back. I need to get something at the office."

Alarm spread through me. I held onto the Bishop's elbow as he tried to follow Orv. "No, you don't. We need to get Pop to safety right now."

"I can paddle fast when I'm by myself. It will only take me ten minutes."

"Not a chance." I had to stand my ground on this one. "Whatever is in your office can be replaced. Human lives cannot."

As if to emphasize my words, a gust of wind blew something off the house with a cracking sound. "Those levees could break at any moment. We might get very wet, but at least we won't drown in a canoe."

Orv peeked out the window, which was haphazardly blocked with plywood. "Someone's paddling up our walk."

It was a neighbor, in a rowboat. They had room for one more and were headed to their large house on higher ground. We decided it would be best for the Bishop to go with them, as they had more space to spare. The strapping son of the couple lifted the Bishop and carried him through the knee-deep water to the rowboat. We said a hurried goodbye as I tucked his bag next to his feet. I decided to keep his second bag, full of books, with me.

We did a last check of the house, piling pillows and blankets at each door and window and moving the most precious books upstairs.

Orville handed me my slicker. "All right, Sterchens. Let's go."

The water was barely high enough to float the canoe, but if we had to abandon it and walk, then we would. We settled the bags on the bottom, then Orv took the front and I climbed in the back. Steadily we paddled. We hadn't gone five blocks when my hands started burning. I should have thought to wear gloves; my skin wasn't accustomed to the chafe of the paddle.

Once we got into a steady rhythm, with Orv providing the power from the front and me behind, alternating sides to help steer, we made good time, especially since the water had a current taking us away from the river. As we crossed a creek that had become a river, we passed the floating body of a horse. I recognized a friend's chicken coop, tilted at an awful angle, with the squawking hens still inside. I shuddered as I thought of all the animals that would be lost. I prayed that at least the people would manage to get to safety.

We were still several blocks from our meetup point when the water got too shallow to paddle the canoe. Orville helped me step out of the rocking boat.

"Goodbye, old friend." I said to the red canoe as I reached for the bags.

"Leave those in there," Orv said.

"What? Why? I can carry them." Orv did have a rather massive bag of his own. But we couldn't double-cross the Bishop and leave his things.

"We'll carry the canoe with the bags in it."

"Surely you're joking. It must weigh a hundred pounds."

"Come on, old girl, you can do it. It isn't far, and we'll put it down every ten steps, or whenever you get tired."

Then I remembered. This was the same canoe that Wilbur had tied to his flyer when he flew around the Statue of Liberty for a special demonstration. Wilbur had fussed about the request, probably remembering how Langley's pilot nearly drowned in the Potomac. Twice.

"It's not the aerodrome you'll be flying, for heaven's sake," Orv had argued. But still, he had devised a way to attach a canoe to the flyer, just in case of a crash into water.

I suspected that in my brother's mind, abandoning the canoe now would be akin to leaving Wilbur behind. So, my hands already blistered from paddling, I took my place and grabbed a horizontal strut. "Let's go."

We were safe and comfortable in a cottage graciously loaned to us by a friend. I arranged an overstuffed chair, a lamp, and a pile of books, and settled in quite nicely. Orville was another story. Mostly he stationed himself at the front window, watching the wind and rain lash at the pane. It was hard to see five feet, so it seemed pointless to me.

"No news yet?" I asked. We were hoping to learn if our west-side home had survived, even as the rain continued to fall. We believed Hawthorn Hill to be safe from flooding, although certainly there would be some damage.

"Charley will come out just as soon as it is safe. I'm watching for the police to come by, and then I'll ask them what they know."

Finally the rains ended, but our worries were far from over. We were shoveling gritty muck away from the front door of the cottage when we saw Charley riding down the street on horseback. Orv rushed to him, but his first question wasn't about our homes.

Charley's face was grave. He took his time climbing off the horse and tethering it to a lamppost. "I'm afraid the worst has happened. The levees have broken, and the entire downtown is under six feet of water. I've spent the last two days helping to rescue people. I found this poor horse struggling in the current on Main Street."

He handed Orv a copy of a roughly printed newspaper and I looked on, gasping in horror at the photographs. The water reached halfway up the buildings. Many buildings had collapsed and were floating in pieces. Families were crowded into lifeboats, their eyes hollow with fear.

Orv flipped rapidly through the pages. "What about my office? The laboratory? How high did the water reach?"

Charley pressed his lips together. "I think you need to thank the Lord you escaped. Hundreds are dead. The NCR factory is sheltering the homeless."

Orv ignored this. "I moved the important documents up about eight feet. Do you think that's enough?"

"Maybe, but there's something else. With all the broken gas pipes and electrical shorts, a fire has erupted. It's working its way down Third Street right now."

Orv handed the paper to me. "I've got to get down there."

"I don't recommend that," Charley said. "It's all been evacuated, no one is allowed in, and you'd be foolish to try. They said it won't be safe for a week." Charley thumbed back toward the horse. "Everything I now own is in two saddlebags. Nothing will ever be the same, so you might as well accept that." He tipped his hat to me, then picked his way through the mud back to the horse.

Orv lifted his shovel off the ground and leaned it against the house. "I'm getting the canoe."

"Absolutely not," I said in a rather loud voice. Startled, Orv stepped back. "Absolutely not," I said again in a hushed voice. "You heard what Charley said; no one is allowed in. It's dangerous, loose electrical wires, fires everywhere..."

"I'll be careful. I have to rescue some stuff."

"Stuff? You're going to risk your life for stuff? Whatever it is, it can be replaced."

Orv paced. "No, it can't. It's irreplaceable. My life's work. Wilbur's entire life's work."

He knew that was my Achilles' heel, but I couldn't back down. "No, sir. I've already lost one brother, and I'm not losing another."

Orv wasn't giving up. "If the building is still there, I'll grab the most important things. There's nothing I can do about the flyer, for sure that's underwater. But the negative plates for the Kitty Hawk photos. Our documents with all the calculations. It's all we have to prove our case. That wretched Curtiss will refute everything we can't provide documentation for."

"Those photographs have appeared in newspapers worldwide. You have witnesses to everything you did, and patent applications submitted and approved. You won court case after court case. Breaking the law and endangering yourself will not bring your materials back if they're gone."

I was finally reaching Orv. He stopped his pacing and stared at his galoshes, like a sad little brother. Like he was losing Wilbur all over again. The "stuff," like the canoe, was all mixed up in his head with Wilbur. He looked like a little boy again, one who had tried to fight a bully and lost.

And now here I was, being a bully. A realization ran through me like icy rain. My brothers had often teased me about being hard on my students, and them. I did it out of love, I had believed. But what had all my pushing and prodding gotten us? Wilbur was gone. Orv was frantically trying to do the work of two men, and hardly having a moment to enjoy the results.

I had stopped Orv the first time he wanted to rescue his precious belongings, and now that it was even more dangerous, I worried he would sneak back when I wasn't looking. I sniffed back a tear, vowing to change my ways. As gently as possible, I said, "When we get the all clear, we'll go back. We'll put it all together, piece by piece. Until then, it is in the hands of the Lord."

ORVILLE

I t was two weeks before the devastated city allowed residents back. It was hard to keep my bearings as I walked along the shoveled paths snaking through the debris and river silt, the streets still impassable to motorcars. The acrid smell of wet rot mixed with smoke burned my nose, and I tied a rag around my head as a filter. As I passed burned buildings one after the other, my heart sank further.

But then a wave of relief washed over me. We had sold the bicycle shop back in 1908, but I was relieved to see the building was still standing. A few blocks away stood my lab and office without any fire damage, amid a block of razed homes and businesses.

From the gray-brown horizontal waterline running across the bricks just over my head, I could tell the waters had reached over six feet, but not eight. The door to my office was blocked with silt, so I grabbed a charred board to scrape it away. Then I kicked in the door, but found the inside of the structure intact, if wet and filthy. My important documents and photographic negatives were safe. Overwhelmed with relief and thankfulness, I lifted up a prayer straight from my heart, just as the Bishop had taught me.

I walked the few blocks to Hawthorn Street, passing no one on my way. I'd heard over four hundred people had died, with more unaccounted for. I kept an eye out for bodies, but saw none, no humans anywhere. Cats up in trees yowled for help, while dogs and a horse or two were massed into gutters.

A similar grayish-brown waterline wrapped around our home at just under six feet. I jiggled the door open and found the floor a filthy mess, and had to cover my nose and mouth once again due to the stench of rotten river water. It all could be cleaned and repaired or replaced. Katharine was right. The Lord had held us in his hands. I wasn't much for praying outside of church, but I had done ten years' worth in the last few days.

KATHARINE

1914

A year after the great flood, the city was booming once again. Orville and I attended rallies to raise funds to build an extensive dam system to prevent it ever happening again. Our friend Edward Deeds was managing the project. It seemed everything that man touched was a grand success.

Before the flood, he and Orville had started yet another company, the Dayton-Wright Company, and the two of them worked well together, so it seemed quite natural for us to be involved with the dam project. I found I enjoyed the rallies and being part of a cause, and seeing the mock-up of a giant thermometer tracking the progress of the donations.

But soon that excitement was over, and I needed a new cause. I had not forgotten my commitment to suffrage and it seemed time to get involved once again. The 1912 referendum to allow women to vote in Ohio had failed. I hadn't had time to organize a rally as I had wanted, so I set my sights on doing something extraordinary the next time. And there would be a next time. The newspapers announcing the defeat were barely in print before the Women's Suffrage Party was meeting in earnest once again.

The organization was successful in their push for the amendment to be on the statewide ballot for the November 1914 election. Since it was not a presidential election, the thought was that the media could pay more attention to the cause.

I started rounding up all my acquaintances from teaching, as well as the Bishop's and Orville's. They each handed over their address books and wished me good luck. Soon I had a stack of responses, with an overwhelming portion being in favor of the rally. I formed a steering committee of volunteers, opened a special bank account for donations, and we were on our way.

The date we chose was October 24, just ahead of the November 3 election. I wrote to every organization I could think of to gain support through donations, publicity, or attendance. Having learned a bit about how busy decision-makers are, I sneakily made things as easy and irresistible for them as possible. I sometimes would add suggested copy and was delighted to read it in print:

> Emancipate the Women of the World!
> The Republican Party Stands for Equal Rights!
> Vote for Human Progress!
> The Whole World Is Giving Freedom to Women. Don't Let Ohio Fail Them!

Orville and the Bishop marched right next to me, all of us dressed in smart suits. This was a bit in contrast to the sea of women in white dresses, but as an organizer I wanted the participants to find me easily, and unlike at every other grand parade, a gray suit stood out.

Although perhaps not the wild celebration that was held for my brothers, the parade was nonetheless spectacular, with thousands in attendance. Even better was the all-important press, for we needed to reach all voters across Ohio. The *Dayton Daily News* reported, *Hoboes and millionaires, society dowagers and humble domestic servants were represented in the parade, and they all carried themselves as though they realized that they were making history.*

Speeches, both for and against the amendment, were given at every street corner. Surprising remarks came from Katherine Talbott. She was from a wealthy family that had supported many good causes, and I had written to her for a financial donation. When none came, I hadn't thought another thing about it, but there she was, being interviewed by the press.

"We think the women have enough to do to attend to their household duties properly without mingling in outside affairs," she said.

I made a mental note to disinvite her from any further events and edged my way through the crowd so that I might offer a rebuttal.

But the leader of the organization, Jesse Davisson, beat me to it. "Isn't it about time to admit that most of the dirty work in the world is done by women? Are the washing of foul linen, the scrubbing of floors, the cleansing of dirty dishes, tasks which befit a creature too fine or too frail to go to the voting booth?"

I laughed. Her response was perfect. I sidestepped some *pommes de la rue* left by the horses that had led the parade. The notion that women couldn't possibly manage keeping house and casting a ballot was the weakest possible argument. The best one, in my mind, was the threat of prohibition. Certainly more women than men favored forbidding alcohol. Having enjoyed the best of wines in Europe,

I had to disagree. It seemed an outright crime to disallow it just because a few sought to abuse it. But I would never mention that reservation to anyone in public. That was an issue for another day.

Hawthorn Hill, our stately Georgian Revival mansion of cream-colored bricks, with columns surrounding the two-story portico, was completed at last. The meager furnishings from our old home could not possibly fill the much more expansive space, so Orville and I took the overnight train to Grand Rapids, Michigan, to order new furniture.

We were treated to a tour of a factory that had automated the manufacturing of wooden furniture. Instead of one craftsman pains-takingly carving each piece, the cutting implements were connected and many pieces were made at the same time. Orv was entranced by the process and was deep in conversation with a foreman, comparing it to Henry Ford's new assembly line. I had to lead him away so that we might see the finished product.

We hadn't even finished unpacking the crates of belongings from our former home when Orville started tinkering with the brand-new systems.

He didn't like the electronic doorbell and wanted it to ring into his library. So wires and contraptions of his invention snaked from the front door, through the receiving and living rooms, and into his office. He was enamored with all of Thomas Edison's inventions and thought he could improve on a few. For example, placing a disc on the phonograph for each song was too laborious. Instead he spent thousands of hours building a mechanism to automate the process. He never did get it to work.

He refused to add an air-cooling machine, thinking it was nonsense technology, but had a central vacuum system installed in the walls instead of using a simple broom and dustpan. I hated the darn thing, which frequently got plugged up and required many trips to the basement to get it going, plus the need to empty the canister should it ever actually fill. When Orville left the house, Carrie and I snuck out our brooms and swiftly cleaned the rooms the proper way.

We were still awaiting the new furniture we had purchased when guests started arriving to see Orv, now that he had an appropriate place to greet them. Mayors and governors and aviators and inventors all found their way to Hawthorn Hill. This schedule soon became unmanageable for everyday life and took a toll on Orville, who was easily exhausted by visitors. So I set up a system.

Guests were scheduled for an audience with Orville only three days per week. Carrie or I or other staff, depending on the importance of the visitor, would greet them in the front foyer and escort to them to the adjoining reception room.

Orville called it his Trophy Room, because here he displayed his most prized possession, the *Muse of Aviation*. Awarded to my brothers by the prestigious Aero Club of France, the bronze statue depicted angels hovering over the brothers and the flyer. Orv liked for his visitors to admire the piece, which was about two feet tall and set in its own gilded niche. Sometimes he liked it so much that he kept people waiting for hours. Hence, I started referring to the room as "Cold Storage." Occasionally his visitors gave up, despite Carrie and me bringing trays laden with tea and sandwiches.

Just like our home on Hawthorn Street, the bedrooms were on

the second floor. The Bishop, Orv, and I each had our own indoor bathrooms, and the lovely sunlight-filled corner room that was to be Wilbur's was now reserved for honored guests. A bedroom for Carrie and her husband was just down the hall from ours, but they insisted on commuting from their own home.

My bedroom was right at the top of the grand staircase and featured a small balcony perched over the front door, affording me a view of the vast lawn. The bedrooms were connected to each other through the bathrooms. This was Wilbur's idea, and although it was convenient to family and we were accustomed to the setup, it was rather disconcerting to the occasional overnight guest who suddenly found himself in my private bathroom. For the first time in my life, I found the need to lock a door.

Orville had stopped flying, instead falling in love with another form of transportation—motorcars. He delighted in driving as fast as the machine would go, flying down Far Hills Avenue and into the city. Police frequently stopped him for speeding and sometimes wrote a traffic ticket, but somehow it always got forgiven at City Hall.

ORVILLE

T he Smithsonian National Museum had twisted the history of our invention ever since its esteemed leader Professor Langley died in 1906. They showed utter disinterest in our offer to reassemble the 1903 flyer for an exhibit. Instead, the new chief, Charles Walcott, seemed obsessed with defending his predecessor's reputation as an aviation pioneer.

I found out about his latest shenanigans at a meeting with Pliny Williamson, the attorney I retained nearly full time. I traveled down to Lebanon to an old hotel and restaurant, the Golden Lamb. The place was a little too stuffy for my taste, but Katharine had said the food was excellent, and Pliny was buying. He wanted to share the latest of our court victories against the thieving Glenn Curtiss, who had ignored our warnings not to use our patented technology on his machines. We had no choice but to defend our rights.

We settled into the plush chairs, and the white-jacketed host handed us outsized menus that could have served as advertising posters. I had an urge to offer to run some electrical wires for more lighting. Dark wood covered all the walls, floor, and ceiling. My favorite feature was the only exception: a row of books on a high, narrow shelf encircling the room.

Pliny had become a highfalutin' New York lawyer, but before that he was a Dayton boy who knew Katharine at Oberlin and had been a friend ever since. I liked to tease him that he was Woodrow Wilson's illegitimate brother, because with his long face and rimless spectacles, he looked just like the president.

Pliny wasted no time getting to the point of the meeting, pulling a stack of documents from his briefcase. "Congratulations. Again."

"How many cases does that make won against Curtiss?" I said. "Seems you can retire now, on us." I was being a little facetious, but Pliny didn't smile.

"Orville, we've known each other a very long time. And while I'm happy to keep going down this path"—he patted the tower of paper between us—"it comes at a cost."

Feeling like I had taken a jab in the stomach, I retorted, "I've never complained. Paid your every last invoice on time..."

"No, I don't mean that, and I appreciate the revenue." He looked about at the other patrons and lowered his voice. "But there's another cost—to you, to the country."

"Oh? How so?"

"The Wright brothers were at the forefront of aviation. Hell, you practically invented an industry. But I'm concerned that by putting so much effort into protecting your claim, you're not moving forward. What research and development have you done? Where is the next breakthrough flyer that's going to put our country ahead again?"

Now that little jab in the stomach felt like a full-on punch. I didn't want to admit it, but he was right. Running the various businesses and pilot school, and the never-ending lawsuits, had usurped the time we used to spend inventing.

But I was not a quitter. I straightened up in my chair and leaned forward. "It does seem we're at a turning point. Wilbur liked to quote Shakespeare: 'One man in his time plays many parts.' I have to think about what's next for me." What was upmost in my mind was whether I wanted to travel the path Pliny suggested without Wilbur. "It might be best for others to take the reins."

He nodded, but something in his eyes seemed like he was sad, or disappointed, or didn't agree. I wished Katharine was there to interpret.

The waiter brought two huge salads, each enough for a family of four.

Pliny leaned aside so the waiter could pour salad dressing from a porcelain sauceboat. "Actually, I overhead a conversation that might interest you. It seems that fellow Walcott isn't giving up on the aerodrome."

Walcott had made claims that it was the aerodrome, not our flyer, to make history. I waved dismissively. Unfortunately, the waiter thought I was waving off the salad dressing, so I didn't get any. "I know, bunch of fools."

"Now you didn't hear it from me, but they've hired our favorite defendant to restore the blasted thing. Curtiss is going to fly Langley's machine in Hammondsport, New York, next week. Might be worth your while to check up on it."

"What do you mean? Spy on them?" I dug into an unadorned slice of carrot. "Might be worthwhile just to see him crash into Keuka Lake."

"You didn't hear it from me."

What those fools had in mind this time was a mystery, but if Pliny thought something was up, that was motivation enough for me. I drove straight from Lebanon to Lorin's house. He loved adventures like this. If he wasn't a bookkeeper and businessman, he would have made a fine detective.

Lorin was in favor, and the next week he borrowed my roadster and traveled up to Curtiss's hometown in the Finger Lakes. Upon hearing of his destination, Katharine and Lorin's wife, Netta, put in orders for some regional wine. When he returned a few days later, he brought a wooden crate full of bottles for the ladies and some distressing news for me.

"Pliny was right. They rebuilt that darn aerodrome. I'm not the expert you are, but it seems they stole your bracing system, put in a motor that was by no means in their 1903 model, and changed about every other detail to make it fly."

"And did it? Fly?" I lifted the crate of wine from my roadster.

"Yeah, it flew. Did some turns. Nothing that hasn't been done a thousand times by now." He leaned in close, sharing his detective work. "I heard folks claiming it proved Langley invented the aeroplane back in 1903."

"You get photographs?"

Lorin hung his head. "I did. Some real good ones from about fifty feet away. But I was recognized. They sent a three-hundred-pound bouncer to make me hand over my film."

"I can't really blame them for that." We had done as much in our early days. "Thanks, Lorin. Nothing to be done about it now, except hope they don't go public with this outrageous lie."

Several weeks later, Lorin brought me a newspaper a friend of his in DC had sent. "You're not going to like this." He read the headline out loud. "Successful flight of Langley's aerodrome at Hammondsport."

"Yeah, so?" I took the paper from him and read on. *Langley's machine proven to be the first capable of manned and powered flight.* Of course we knew the aerodrome had been heavily modified; the original couldn't fly any more than a sack of bricks, but that hadn't stopped them. "Well, I guess they can claim anything they want. It doesn't change the facts."

Lorin nodded at the paper in my hand. "There's more."

I scanned the article. The aerodrome was being prepared for a new exhibit in the National Museum, along with the false claim that it had preceded our historic flights by several months.

My head wanted to explode. "Those liars. But this can be refuted. There are photographs of the original that won't match this machine."

Lorin blew out some air, as if trying to prevent his own head from exploding. "Thing is, my friends tell me the Smithsonian plans to restore it back to its original specifications before displaying it."

What saddened me more than anything else is that Langley would have never done such a thing. In their attempt to honor him, they had done quite the opposite.

We held our tongues, not blabbing to the press with the injustice. Instead, we started another lawsuit to allow the courts decide, hoping to prevent the Smithsonian from making an embarrassing mistake.

My bond with Wilbur continued in the company we had formed together in 1909. But now, running that company, fighting the legal battles, and the constant travel to keep everything moving was draining my spirit. Pliny was right. Other manufacturers were making faster and more reliable machines. Even Curtiss had probably superseded our company as he charged ahead in development and we had moved first into pilot training, then into engines.

Never far from my mind was interest not only our military had shown, but that of Germany and Russia and France. In fact, all of Europe seemed to be in a race to add flying machines to their weaponry. I considered myself a patriotic American, but the idea of being a cog in that wheel left me cold. Surely others were more enthusiastic and better suited.

I talked it over with Katharine, who advised me to do what made me happy. But there was another voice I needed to hear to be sure I was doing the right thing. As I lay awake in bed one night, I asked the Lord to let me hear from Wilbur. And I heard his voice, clear as a bell.

"It's okay to let it go, Orv. You've done your part, and others will take it from here. Go have some fun. Give advice when asked, but there's a world of things to discover, and a family that needs you more than you know."

It was time. I would come up with a plan to sell our businesses in the morning.

SPRING 1917

On a day in early April, when the daffodils were blooming and the ground reawakened from its winter rest, I grew restless, consumed with the idea that our historic flyer remained neglected in a pile of flood-ravaged crates. Our businesses had been sold off or merged with others, leaving me in charge of nothing in particular for the first time since I was in my teens. We were about to go to war with Germany, and although I had stepped away from the business, I took some comfort in knowing our strong business ties with our allies had given them an important advantage.

"Let's go for a drive," I entreated Katharine and Pop. My purpose was to gain their support for a last effort to sway the Smithsonian toward correcting their falsehoods.

We soon sped off, but they surprised me. The Bishop waxed philosophical, and Katharine practical. Not that those qualities were surprising coming from them, but their blithe disinterest flummoxed me.

Katharine was riding in the front passenger seat, her hand outside the window, catching the breeze. She said, "Why are you obsessed with the National Museum? Donate the flyer to the French or Brits, who've been after it for years and will appreciate it much more. Sooner or later, people will wonder why the Smithsonian's version of the story is different from everyone else's."

Stunned, I took my attention off the road for a brief moment and nearly ran into the ditch.

"This is your legacy." The Bishop spoke softly from the back seat. "The truth will come out, and there is no use in presenting yourself as affronted, like a whining child. Be patient and prayerful, and the Lord will guide you."

We drove out to the flying field at Huffman Prairie. Our old hangar had been replaced with buildings from the flying school. The fields were full of early wildflowers, the grasses already nearly knee-high. I sucked in the scent of them, and closed my eyes and imagined Wilbur circling above, lying prone on Flyer III. A feeling of peace came upon me. This was something no one could take away.

"I think this is the last time," the Bishop said.

Katharine and I looked at each other, not sure what he meant. Lately he had been getting a little confused. Did he think we were going to fly? I wrapped an arm around each of them as we gazed at the blooming field, treasuring the moment.

The next morning, I got up early to make a special breakfast: fried eggs and porridge, and some of Katharine's jarred apples mixed with cinnamon and sugar. I set the percolator on the stovetop and adjusted the flame once I saw the coffee bubbling into the glass cap. The aroma usually brought Katharine downstairs, but I heard no one stirring.

I went to her room, knocked on the door, and announced breakfast was ready. Then I went down the hall to the Bishop's room. Oddly, he was still abed.

"Good morning, Pop." I drew open the curtains to let some sunshine in. But still he didn't stir. "Pop?"

I looked again; his color wasn't right. In fact, nothing was right.

He had slipped away in the night, without a complaint, without any fuss. I sat next to him, the wrenching feeling of sorrow and loss enveloping me as if I were being pulled under a deep, dark sea. He had told us it was the last time. And it was.

WINTER 1918

Katharine was always pushing me to go out more. Talk to people. When I reminded her that I had no need for such frivolity, she replied, "You have so much to give. Anyone could learn a life's worth of lessons by listening to your story. It's selfish to keep it all to yourself." And then the kick in the shins: "You know Wilbur would be doing it."

I knew Wilbur would have long since volunteered for the military, so I went downtown to sign up. But they said I was too old or too valuable or some such excuse. But after some more visits and stern letters, they said fine, I was a major in the army, but my duty was to stay home and advise. So I started meeting up with some men who were innovators and risk-takers: Edward Deeds, Charles Kettering, names that everyone in Dayton knew because they provided most of the progress we all enjoyed. We called ourselves "the Barn Gang," because we actually did meet in a barn.

After many a night of whiskey and cigar-fueled conversations, Colonel Deeds, a retired army officer, announced he wanted to form a real club, welcoming all the engineers, aviators, and inventors. My idea of calling it the Aviators' Club got outvoted, and it became the Engineers Club of Dayton.

We traded off being president and had a great time. Often we'd invite an outsider to join. After a few years, our membership grew enough that we needed a respectable home for our meetings and educational events. Naturally I suggested Schenck and Williams, the architects for Hawthorn Hill, and I soon found myself supervising another construction project.

The result was an impressive building at Monument Avenue and Jefferson Street, with dining rooms, private rooms, pool lounges, and of course plenty of liquor bars for those so inclined. Somehow the Barn Gang coerced me into making a speech at the building's opening ceremony.

It was early February and well below freezing outside, and I feared we hadn't fully tested the building's heating and hot-water systems before assembling a large crowd. I checked the water taps and the heating system, along with the electronic call system. Everything seemed well in order, and the banquet room thermometer showed sixty-six degrees. The room was paneled with dark wood and had a luxurious custom-made rug and rather ornate chandelier lighting. Wilbur had made many speeches in places like this, and I tried to carry his spirit within me, for I was no great orator.

Katharine wrote some remarks for me to make and assured me that I wouldn't melt under the spotlight. All I had to do was read out loud in front of a bunch of people. But the one person I really wanted to come had refused to on the grounds that she couldn't be a member.

"When those old men realize what they're missing by not allowing women, I'll be the first to join," Katharine said.

My name and vote weren't on the official charter, so I missed out on fighting that battle, for I would have pushed to allow the ladies. After all, I was proud to be first in line at Katharine's suffrage parade. Ohio was coming along slowly, allowing women to vote on school boards, and cities could decide for themselves who was allowed to vote in their own elections, but it pained me that our efforts had failed to make the change statewide.

Despite the men-only position of the club, Katharine helped me practice my speech. My main point was that the esteemed members, by virtue of their advanced education and position in society, had an obligation to further the advancement of others, both now and in the future. We shouldn't rest on our legacies; our accomplishments were most relevant if we pursued new discoveries.

That was the hardest part for me, and I argued with Katharine that I should take it out. After all, wasn't I resting on my laurels? Deeds had gone from developing motors and electrifying factories, to manufacturing automobile parts and even teaming up with me to build airplanes. He led the aviation effort for the war, probably in no small part the reason we were winning. I should have done more.

Katharine said I was being ridiculous, I was a hero, and so on. So the text of my speech remained as she wrote it. My footfalls were silent on the thick carpet as I walked up the aisle between rows of the audience of men in dark suits. About three hundred people were in attendance; even Ohio's Governor James Cox came to hear Dayton's favorite son speak. As I took the podium and arranged my notes, I fretted that no words would come out of my mouth. My stomach felt like it was on fire, and the flames rose and licked my face. I mopped my forehead and neck with my handkerchief. "Take deep breaths," Katie had told me. How easy for her to say; she spoke in front of crowds like she was sharing tea with a friend.

I pretended I was Wilbur. I put his smarter-than-everyone-else look on my face and got up there and delivered my talk. I had memorized the whole thing, but held on to my notes to give my hands something to do. The audience cheered at my short talk and even laughed at my little jokes, which I hadn't expected. Something else I didn't expect was to enjoy the undertaking. Maybe it was just relief at being done with it, but I did feel twenty pounds lighter when I stepped down from the podium.

After that, I spent many happy evenings dining alone at the club, while Katharine believed me to be out socializing. I figured I was meeting her expectation by at least fifty percent.

Feeling emboldened by the experience, I invited the Arctic explorer Vilhjalmur Stefansson to speak at the Engineers Club. I'd followed his adventures ever since I read his story of living with the Eskimos in *Scientific American.*

Especially intriguing were the controversies that developed when most of his party perished when an ice floe crushed their ship, causing it to sink. Stefansson was rescued by indigenous people, but most of his party perished. Knowing firsthand about the risks explorers take that escape the public's notice, and having survived a controversy or two myself, I wanted to meet him. I imagined I could scrape together enough of an audience to honor his achievements, and the Engineers Club's new building was a perfect venue. To my satisfaction, he agreed to come.

This fellow knew how to charm an audience. A little shy of forty years old, with a mop of thick hair and a ready smile, he had the room entranced with his tales of sledging across the Arctic, surviving on whale meat. He said he had charted the entire Arctic, survived shipwrecks and extreme temperatures, and claimed an island for the Brits. The room erupted in laughter when he admitted he had to cede it back to the Russians. All that, yet he'd "forever be known as the discoverer of blond Eskimos."

I invited him to stay with Katharine and me the next night, but that turned out to be a big mistake. They got along all right. Too well. The two of them chatted and laughed and drank until the wee hours. I finally had to give up and go to bed, only to wake up in the morning to find them sitting too close together on the living room sofa.

They looked up at me as if I were an intruder in my own home, but Katharine was quick to recover.

"Oh my goodness, we certainly lost track of time." She rose and rearranged her crumpled dress. "VJ, it's been such a pleasure getting to know you. You must visit again soon."

VJ? The nickname seemed too cozy for someone Katharine had just met. It seemed no harm had come to her, or to poor VJ's ears for having listened to her all night. I saw him out after inviting him to visit us at Lambert Island in Lake Huron the next month. "I own the whole island, and we go there each summer. There are several cabins, rather primitive, but that shouldn't bother you." I said something idiotic like he might enjoy it, being a Canadian after all. I could just about feel Katharine rolling her eyes behind me.

KATHARINE

VJ was a breath of fresh air. I was in my midforties, much too old for a suitor, but I saw no reason not to enjoy every minute of his company. He was a few years my junior, and quite dashing with his dark wavy hair and tall trim physique. Like Orville and me, he had been too caught up in his exploring and adventures to have a family. But he knew how to spin a tale and slip in a little kiss or a pat on the knee without so much as a howdy.

He had studied at Harvard Divinity School and at one time had wanted to become a minister.

"My father was a bishop in the United Brethren Church," I said. "He had a fulfilling life, but it seems you were a born explorer."

"Both careers suit me, as my devotion is truly exploring people more than places. In all my quests, discovering lands never before recorded, it was the people and their cultures that were the most fascinating. I braved the elements, risked my life and, I'm sorry to admit, the lives of others to bring knowledge of these peoples to the rest of the world."

Some of that disturbed me. I didn't want to insult my guest, but had to know. "I must ask, did the indigenous people want to be known to the rest of the world? And did the others in your party understand and accept the risks as you did?"

He paused for an awkward amount of time. I was just going to retract my question with an apology when he answered, "That's a very good question. We didn't coerce any information from the Eskimos, and they were nothing but enthusiastic. They wanted to know more of the outside world, and especially about what we had to offer in trade." He patted my knee. "Your second question amuses me, considering the risks your own brothers took. Did they not understand and accept them?"

"Points taken." To change the subject, I imagined living in the Great North. The straggly trees, the vast ocean of ice. I thought of the tickle in my nose when our temperature dropped well below freezing. "Is it hard to breathe at forty below zero?"

"Most importantly, you want to cover all your skin. Your nose does a fine job of warming the air before it gets to your lungs, but flesh can freeze in an instant. Then again, it's not always winter. The summers are delightful."

I imagined the people dressed in animal skins, weaving baskets with the long grasses. "What does the air smell like in summer?"

His arm wrapped around my shoulders was warm and comfortable. I thought I could sit and chat with him for days.

"There's a tree that grows throughout Alaska. Grows very tall, but its dark trunk and crooked branches don't make it attractive to look at. And its wood is too soft to be much use. But each spring, it puts out seeds that blow about in white tufts. It's everywhere, that cotton from the cottonwood tree."

"That doesn't seem very pleasant."

He shrugged. "No one minds. Because the buds on trees perfume the air with a sweet, fresh scent that can only be described as heavenly. In fact it's in the Bible, the balm of Gilead."

I closed my eyes and imagined this magical land. "I'd like to go there someday."

I wrote to and visited with VJ intermittently over the next few months. He brought me a few leaves and a fragrant bud from a cottonwood tree, which I dried and pasted into my scrapbook.

He came up to Lambert Island, and we had loads of fun hiking the trails. He shamed me into wading into the cold, clear water. When I objected that it gave me quite a chill, he went on about surviving a shipwreck in the Arctic Ocean. Just to prove a silly point, I handed him my eyeglasses, then dove off our dock, fully dressed in my light summer frock. His efforts to warm me up made it my plunge worth it; my skin tingled with delight as he rubbed me with a rough towel.

But our worlds were far apart, and it could never be much more than a special friendship. I felt VJ's absence when I returned to Dayton. He sent me signed copies of his latest books, and I sent him funny tales of life in mid-America. With the Bishop gone, it was just Orville, Carrie, and me rattling around Hawthorn Hill, and I realized how much I longed for romantic companionship.

All of this made Orville suspicious, although he wouldn't say a thing. The bratty little sister in me relished his discomfort almost as much as the relationship itself. And I started to wonder anew: Was it really too late for me to have a family of my own?

FALL 1919

To tell the truth, Orville was getting on my nerves. Oh, he sat on this board or that, followed the latest developments in aeroplanes and automobiles, and tinkered in his shop, usually inventing something absurd to add to our home, but still he seemed adrift.

Of course, *adrift* in his case meant motoring down Far Hills Avenue at the top speed attainable in the fancy Pierce-Arrow motorcar someone had lent to him. It seemed a good sort of advertisement to have the famous Orville Wright, waving madly at the scurrying pedestrians, demonstrate the superior speed and handling of their vehicles.

I scolded him every so often. "I put you back together after how many flyer crashes? I don't want to lose you to an automobile crash."

But he would just wave my ridiculous caution aside, so I decided to take matters into my own hands. I'd been following the work of the new federal commission on aviation.

President Taft had done all he could, appointing a national commission to study aeronautics in 1912, but Congress failed to pass the funding for it. Perhaps he had been serious about me taking up the cause for him when we met at the White House, but I had dismissed the idea out of hand. Regardless, when legislation was finally signed into law by President Wilson in 1915 creating the NACA—the National Advisory Committee for Aeronautics, I had seen an opportunity to make up for my previous failure to support the mission.

I had determined that Orville was a perfect candidate for the NACA committee and had told him so. Of course, I also had the rather selfish motive of getting Orv out of my hair.

"I'm too busy... It's unpaid labor...Why would I want to travel on my own dime to Washington, DC, to listen to a bunch of men tell me what I already know? No, thanks." He spouted every excuse, but I needled and pushed until the real reason slipped out. "I'll never forgive that bastard."

"Who?" I asked.

"Have you already forgotten who instigated all our patent wars? Who tried to steal our place in history?" Then he muttered, "Probably killed Wilbur."

Charles Walcott. I knew he had somehow convinced Congress to pass the legislation and was now on the committee but saw that as a positive thing. "I understand how you feel, but maybe there's a reason your paths are crossing again. It's time to move on, Orv."

It had taken four years, but eventually I had won, and Orv no longer objected to joining NACA. But he did little to make that happen. So I drafted several letters to President Wilson, our senators, and congressional representative, offering Orville's services. Once I was satisfied with them, I presented them to Orville for signature. He shrugged and signed, not believing anything would come of them.

And nothing did. A cursory response arrived from our members of Congress, but nothing from the White House. So I wrote to the president again, this time signing my own name. I added a plea for his support for the Nineteenth Amendment. Perhaps that was why it garnered a response not from the president, but from the First Lady.

Stunned, I read the letter over and over. She gushed over my brother and invited me to tea, to discuss and thank me for all my efforts. My second invitation to the White House!

On the appointed day, I arrived in plenty of time, having spent the night with my friends in the District. I took a hired car to the "Residence," as the handwritten invitation had referred to the White

House. As we passed through iron gates and up the circular driveway to the North Portico, my heart fluttered. Even though I wasn't to meet with the president himself, somehow I was even more thrilled this time.

An aide escorted me to a room on the ground floor that had been recently designated as the China Room. Instead of sitting in the offered chair while I waited, I examined the beautiful cases that displayed china collections going back a hundred years. They were intricate and beautiful, but none were as old as the ones I'd viewed in Europe, where I had witnessed displays going back several hundred years. But after all, we were relatively a new country.

"I'm so sorry to have kept you waiting." A voice startled me, and I turned to see a striking dark-haired woman, several inches taller than me and sporting a gracious smile. This was First Lady Edith Wilson.

She held out her hand to me as an aide announced, "Miss Katharine Wright."

I took her hand, hoping mine wasn't clammy. "I'm honored to meet you, Mrs. Wilson."

"The pleasure is mine," she replied in a soft Southern drawl. She nodded to the aide, who produced a silver tea service with porcelain teacups and saucers.

We made a little bit of small talk about the weather, and I tried to steer the conversation to my brother's request to serve on the NACA commission.

"Yes, yes, we'll talk about that," the First Lady said. "But first tell me more about yourself and your work."

My spirits lifted. Not since Europe had anyone given any thought to my contributions. I set down my cup with its unexpectedly sweetened tea.

"I want you to know how very important your illustrations were to the cause," she went on. "I have no doubt the food program's success stemmed from the publicity."

Food program? The gratification I had briefly felt turned to confusion. "Illustrations? I'm no artist."

She waved her napkin. "Don't be so modest. Of course you are. Just as much an artist as your brother, just different applications."

"He considers himself more a scientist than an artist. And I am more of a linguist, or communicator, I would say."

The first lady cocked her head. "Well of course, architecture is both an art and science."

Architecture. With a jolt I realized that she was referring to Frank Lloyd Wright, who, if memory served me, had a sister known for illustrating children's books and advertising posters.

"Oh dear, I think we have a misunderstanding. I'm Katharine Wright, sister of Orville and Wilbur Wright, the aviation pioneers."

Mrs. Wilson's eyes clouded in confusion. Perhaps she had been more attuned to the other issue I had mentioned in my letter. Orv had belatedly mentioned to me that the First Lady wasn't exactly the biggest supporter of women's right to vote.

I tried to avoid any embarrassment on her part. "I've also been active in the suffrage movement and was hoping to talk about supporting the Nineteenth Amendment. It's so close to passage..."

Her eyes widened, and I was afraid I'd be summarily be asked to leave. This was the wrong topic and I was the wrong person.

But she surprised me by laughing heartily. "Oh dear, I'm incredibly sorry for my mistake. As you can imagine, my schedule is quite full, and my visitors, many."

Heat rose in my face in my embarrassment. I rose from my chair and awkwardly tried to excuse myself.

"Nonsense. You sit right back down, drink your tea, and tell me all about yourself, and your brothers as well. There isn't much more we can do at the moment for suffrage, but the president and I are fascinated with the aeroplane."

Mrs. Wilson listened intently as I told her of the years of effort and harrowing accidents my brothers had faced, the loss of Wilbur, and some of my adventures in dealing with the business side of things.

She seemed most interested in my trips to Europe and told me of the horrible devastation she witnessed on her visit following the Great War. "You would hardly recognize France. Great forests reduced to charred graveyards. Miles of farmland pitted with bomb craters. We must thank the Lord that Paris was spared."

I left with a promise that Orville would soon be on the board of the NACA. Fait accompli.

ORVILLE

I was introduced at each meeting of the National Advisory Committee for Aeronautics as the "elder statesman" of aviation. At forty-nine years of age, I didn't consider myself elderly, nor was I a statesman, but I smiled and nodded anyway. Airplanes were growing more powerful by the day. Now they could hopscotch across the ocean with a few stops for fuel. I listened intently to all the new developments, but rarely offered an opinion.

Wilbur and I had pledged to provide the best life for the family for generations to come. Being Uncle Orv was one of my most important roles, but even my youngest nephew was in his twenties. I needed to determine what to do with the rest of my life.

Things that used to take much effort now came easily, such as obtaining hot water for a bath or lighting and heating the house, and I couldn't seem to adjust to the *easily* part. I invented improvements to the electric and plumbing systems, but the effort didn't seem to be appreciated by Katharine and Carrie, who preferred to do things the way the builder had set them up.

Wilbur always said that he hadn't time for both an aeroplane and a wife, while I said he was the eldest and it was up to him to marry first. Now both of those excuses were gone, and I was left with a steady supply of middle-aged women who wanted to live in Hawthorn Hill and bore me with their chatter of flappers and gin houses. I concluded that I had all I wanted, and shouldn't risk upsetting the apple cart for the purpose of having a respectable family life. Besides that, with two strongly opinioned women already in the house, adding a third could only cause the sort of upheaval I had endeavored a lifetime to avoid. This was Katharine's home, forever.

So I went to meetings and kept abreast of the latest innovations. Double-decker wings and pusher-type propellers were practically relics. More powerful engines enabled cross-country mail delivery along with any number of new businesses. The country was shrinking when you could order a part from Chicago at breakfast and have it delivered to Dayton by lunch.

At my laboratory I was working on a new invention, or rather a refinement of our previous invention—wing shaping via ailerons. With the increasing speed of airplanes came an increased need for maneuverability, especially ways to reduce speed even while descending. I built a mock-up of a split aileron in my lab, but had no wind tunnel in which to test it.

⁓

My hopes for testing rested with the NACA, which had approved the development of a facility to test aeronautical theories. They were an enjoyable group, a gathering of the most knowledgeable men in the business. Even that bastard Walcott was cordial toward me. I broadly hinted that the Smithsonian owed us a retraction and apology, and he seemed to be inching toward accepting that.

We met every six months in a government office building. Once in a while, we escaped to someplace more enjoyable, like the Army Navy Club, but on a day that was too hot to be stuck inside, the dozen or so of us crammed into a sweltering fifth-floor room. Even with the windows open and one underpowered fan, we had to dispense with our suit jackets and ties or risk melting into uselessness.

We argued about what to name the new aviation research laboratory in the Hampton Roads area of Virginia. The Army Air Service had dubbed it Langley after the adjacent airfield but thought the committee might like to rename it the Orville and Wilbur Wright Laboratory and Test Center.

"Thanks, but no need," I said. "We already have Wright Field in Dayton, and this new test center is in Virginia. It should be named after someone who was critical to the development of aviation, but lived right here."

Several men tapped their pens on the table or cleared their throats, but no one spoke at first. Finally, a young gentleman, one of the newest members, quietly said, "Langley."

Heads swiveled to me. My battle with the Smithsonian was legendary in this group and of course Walcott idolized his predecessor, its former leader.

"Exactly," I said to a room so quiet you could have heard a rivet drop. "He inspired the government to begin development of powered flight. He never gave up, despite failure after failure. His perseverance eventually led to the breakthroughs that we made at Kitty Hawk and Fort Myer." As I spoke, I heard the echo of Pliny's voice pounding against my ears. I willed the imaginary python he had warned me of to release the grip it had on me since 1906. I stared directly at Walcott. It was time to let go of the internal feud with him and Curtiss.

Heads nodded, a vote was taken, and keeping the Langley name was to be put forward as the committee's recommendation. Feeling inspired and magnanimous, I decided to put another idea forward.

"Gentlemen, now that the research center is well underway, we need to discuss what to request in this year's budget. I recommend we invest in the biggest, most powerful wind tunnels ever built. Ones that will take us through a century of developments."

This late in the afternoon, heads were drooping in the heat. But I pressed on. I explained my idea for the split aileron and the need to test it. I went to our big blackboard and drew diagrams to help them understand. Even as I drew the parts, with a few calculations and arrows denoting wind speeds, I grew more and more excited about my idea. I refined the shape, as I mentally accounted for likely airspeeds in a deep dive. The room was dead quiet, and I assumed my audience was rapt with fascination. I described vortices and drew little corkscrew shapes coming off my chalkboard aileron.

But then Katharine's voice niggled in my ear. "Listen to what people are *not* saying. You can't just recite facts and figures, no matter how intriguing they seem to you."

"And this represents a very important consideration…" I turned to my attentive audience, the group that I was sure was enthralled with my every word. Katharine had said that if listeners were interested, they would ask me to continue if interrupted. But no one did. A few actually yawned. I almost laughed, remembering Katharine's exaggerated antics.

"In conclusion," I said a little louder than necessary, "we need to buy giant wind tunnels." I set down my chalk and took my seat.

Applause erupted.

After the main decisions for the Langley laboratory were made, the subsequent meeting topics turned mostly to lessons from the Great War, and how to be more prepared for the next one. This deeply disturbed me, as I and many others believed we had suffered a war to end all wars. But it seemed we had only put out the main conflagration and left embers burning all over Europe.

We knew that when we sold the first airplane to the army, it would be used for wartime military purposes. But somehow, Wilbur and I envisioned scouting patrols and communications between the various units. We blocked from our minds—as effectively as any barricade might do—the horrible specter of carrying onboard munitions: mounted guns, even large bombs destined for remote targets unseen by the distant pilot.

My stomach roiled at the thought. What had we wrought upon the world, in a time before humans were ready to make peace among nations? If we had not invented the airplane, it would have happened anyway, but perhaps five or ten years later, after the world had settled back into peace.

But aviation superiority had tipped back and forth during the war. The final outcome went our way, because the allies had ultimately sustained the advantage from the air. My consolation was that as if not for our work, the Central Powers would likely have won the war.

So I put on a fine suit and wing-tipped shoes, went to meetings, and accepted awards without uttering a word, for there was nothing I should say, no defense I could mount. God and history would be our judges.

KATHARINE

SEPTEMBER 1923

I
f the airplane was Orville and Wilbur's best idea, then Hawthorn Hill was mine. Many visitors remarked how it reminded them of the White House, and the gleaming cream-colored mansion elevated my spirits every time I returned to it. Not that I did much returning, as I rarely had the desire or occasion to leave.

I accepted an offer to serve on the board of trustees at my alma mater, Oberlin College. Finally, a chance to honor my friend Margaret's wish. When my old friend and mentor Harry Haskell wrote to tell me he'd be passing through Dayton and would drop by Hawthorn Hill, I planned a nice luncheon to celebrate my new status, assuming his role as a fellow board member was the reason for his visit.

But his face was ashen, and he wasn't his usual amiable self as I led him to our dining room, where Orv was already seated.

They greeted each other warmly, and Orv invited Harry to come to Lambert Island on Lake Huron that summer. "Bring Isabel, of course. It's far from the excitement of Kansas City, but maybe she'll enjoy the sound of birds singing and crickets chirping for a change.

I can meet you in Detroit, we'll stop by and see my friend Henry Ford on the way..."

I cleared my throat to signal Orv to desist from his name-dropping. He thought nothing of mentioning the kings of industry or actual kings he knew, not seeming to understand how it might be considered crass by others.

Harry pressed his lips together and stared dolefully at his plate. "I'm afraid that will be out of the question. I have come to tell you some very sad news."

I put down my fork. Isabel had been ill for some time, but I thought she had rallied.

"My darling Isabel has cancer." He looked at me with glassy eyes. "I've come to ask if Katharine will come out to visit one last time."

A few days later, I took the train to Kansas City. When I arrived at their home, a charming one they had spent many years working toward, I could tell immediately that things had been much worse for much longer than Harry had let on, his letters having been infrequent in the past year or two. The Haskell home exuded a general lack of order and the heavy, oppressive feeling in the air that I was sadly familiar with.

Isabel was bedridden and apparently had been for quite a long time, judging from the accumulation of pill vials, disinfectant, and linens at her bedside. She slept peacefully, and I sat in the chair next to her bed and took her withered hand in mine.

Harry stood on her opposite side, his head hung low. "She's getting opium to help control her pain. But the doctor says she might still hear us."

I nodded and carefully considered what to say, knowing my words needed to be mostly a comfort for Harry. Having been the daughter of a bishop was useful in this situation. "I'd like to say a little prayer." I bowed my head. "Heavenly Father, as we prepare our hearts to give this gentle soul back to You, please be with her devoted husband. Our darling Isabel shall be in peace by Your side, but his human struggle will go on. Help me, Father, to be strong for Harry, and be a comfort to him in enduring love and friendship. Amen."

Knowing the end was near, Harry didn't accompany me to the train station, so we said a tearful goodbye on the street as I slipped into a taxicab.

"Thank you for coming." He squeezed my hand. "It means more to us than you'll ever know."

"Of course. Goodbye for now. I will write."

As I rode the winding streets of the well-tended neighborhood, I thought of how I had said the same thing to him many years ago. These could have been my streets; this could have been my life. I had turned it down to honor a commitment to my family. Harry and Isabel had had a happy life together, and now he had Henry, a handsome son now following in his father's footsteps. I fought off the pangs of self-pity. It was how it had to be.

AUGUST 1924

Fifty. I was fifty years old. It seemed remarkable to have achieved this landmark age. We had lost the Bishop, then Reuchlin four years back, and somehow I thought I should be next.

"Nonsense," Orv told me, when I lamented that our mother had died in her fifties and I feared I wouldn't make it out of the decade myself. "You're much more robust, like Pop. So start enjoying every moment, and go back to squeezing more into a day than will fit."

He was right; there was no reason to slow down. Dayton had become a prosperous place, the downtown lively with dance clubs and vibrant speakeasies that popped up everywhere. I had no problem finding a Singapore sling, mint julep, or gin fizz to sip on, and I adored having an abundance of friends. The city boasted an opera house and movie theaters, and even on an ordinary weeknight, people filled the streets, enjoying a new age of entertainment.

That was all fun and games, but it wasn't what I could see spending the rest of my life doing. I was no longer needed to lead rallies for the women's vote, and there were fewer visitors seeking Orville's advice, therefore less need for me to manage his time. Furthermore, he had finally hired an assistant to manage his calendar, but I found her more irritating than helpful. The last thing I needed was someone camped out in my home doing the things I had desperately needed help with twenty years before.

Orv asked little of me, spending much of his time consulting for aeronautical committees. He had sold off the manufacturing and pilot-training companies, so I no longer served as officer and adviser for them.

I was a society woman who craved a purpose, which was something that seemed to be outside of the norm. I needed to be needed. Maybe that was why my correspondence with Harry Haskell became something more than old friends catching up.

We had been writing regularly since he lost Isabel, and some of his letters were so dark with despair that I feared he had lost the will to live. I had responded by gently teasing him about all the widows who were vying for his attention. One of them, Arabella Hemingway, the aunt of a young writer he had helped find a newspaper job, had been particularly persistent. I had started to address my last note to him, *Dear Mr. Hemingway*, but stopped myself, not knowing if his sense of humor had returned.

Instead, I thought to express my deep understanding of what he had gone through. Of course, I hadn't lost a spouse, but I certainly had lost people very close to me and was intimately familiar with grief. Harry had just taken a trip to Italy and Greece, trying to forget. But forgetting isn't possible, and time and distractions can only soften the edges of the deep pain.

Now he would be returning to an empty house and the sense of loss would hit him all over again. How could I tell him there would be light again? I sat at my desk, took out a fresh sheet of stationery, and began writing.

Dearest Harry,

I know all about the things you found dark and forbidding when you got back to Kansas City. Imagination is the hardest part to endure. When you can finally walk up to the dreaded thing, it loses half its terror...

A week went by with no answer from Harry, and I began to fret that I had misjudged his state of mind and said the wrong thing. Despite what so many novels may suggest, a relationship wouldn't bloom to my satisfaction with letters alone. I went to Rike's Dry Goods to purchase a gift, arriving without a single idea and hoping to be inspired by the merchandise. I passed by the displays of hats and grooming tools, and skimmed past fragrances and bathing costumes and wireless radios in their beautiful wooden cabinets. Nothing seemed quite right. Finally I came to the stationery department, where a lovely assortment of fountain pens fanned across a display case. I found a very attractive black and gold pen I thought perfect for my writer friend.

Back home at my desk, I was twiddling my own pen, ready to try again to write something meaningful for Harry when Carrie placed a stack of letters on my desk. From their thickness and square shape I could tell they were birthday cards. Many more than the usual ten or fifteen, due to achieving a landmark age. Flipping through the envelopes, I spied one postmarked Kansas City, and my heart skipped a beat.

It was a lovely card, featuring an illustration of a bouquet of roses. Harry knew I loved roses, but they were hard to find in late summer when my birthday arrived. My scrapbook of collected flowers held a dusty yellow rose bloom, a gift Harry had preserved for me.

A slip of paper was tucked in the card, a note in Harry's precise script:

My deep wishes for your continued happiness and health. Thank you for all your kind thoughts and loving support. I think I am through the worst of it, and sunlight is now once again filtering into the dark crevices of my mind, and you are the one my mind sees with newly unburdened eyes.

The Kansas Star *has seen fit to send me on assignment for the tenth anniversary of the great Dayton flood. Only one year late! It seems the several dams that have been built have inspired a hydroelectric project here in Missouri.*

Not to bore you with all that, but would you see fit to joining me for dinner on the first of September? Hotel Gibbons, let's say 7 p.m.?

A sense of relief flowed through me; he sounded like his old self. I tried to tamp down the excitement that quickened my pulse. He was coming for business, after all. Seeing me was a pleasant interlude for him. I had grown to love Isabel and had long ago accepted that Harry and I would never be together. But still…

❦

Our brother Lorin and his children joined Orville and me for a lovely dinner party to celebrate our birthdays, plus our ten years at Hawthorn Hill. For days before the event, I found Orv intently carving tiny pieces of wood at his desk in the middle of his library, his favorite room in the house. Along with his own collection, it contained all of the Bishop's and Wilbur's books neatly arranged on the built-in shelves.

"Your new *Scientific American* magazine came. I thought you might be interested in this article, 'Dummy Airplanes as an Aid to Aeronautical Design.'"

"Good, put it on my chair, please." He nodded toward his reading chair in a sunny corner under a window. The chair had special holes drilled into the armrests so that he could mount a reading stand on either side, alternating due to the chronic pain he had suffered since his accident.

I added the magazine to the pile of untouched previous issues. With a pang, I realized how disinterested he had become in following the progress of aviation. It seemed that when I stopped pushing, he found other things that interested him more.

He had rigged an electrical cord to the chandelier to power the task lamp, so that no wires crossed on the floor to his desk, set squarely in the middle of the room. Glowing under the light of the lamp was a curious object.

"Orv, what on earth are you making? A baby bird?"

"You'll see." Orv used a handmade tool resembling an ice pick to scratch lines in his creation. His feet shuffled on the wooden floor, a sure sign that he had been sitting there too long and his back and hip were causing him pain.

Deciding not to address his carving, I said, "We need to put a rug under your desk; you're scratching up the floor with all that shuffling." I winced at how insensitive that sounded. Regretting my words, I expected and deserved a verbal lashing.

But he looked at me with his little-boy eyes, his mustache quivering. "I'm sorry, Sterchens. I'll try not to do that anymore."

I bit back my lips to keep tears from welling up. This was a man who invented the airplane. He had rewired the furnace and put in sensors that no one else seemed to understand. He installed a call system throughout the house so that no one was ever a step away from help, should he or she need it. Yet his answer to scratches on the floor due to his own severe pain was to suffer more for it.

"Oh, Little Brother, let me help you to your reading chair if your hips are bothering you." Even as my heart melted, I realized that it was time for me to move on. I had been his guide, his voice, his caretaker for too long. If I didn't leave, he'd never be pushed to do things he needed to do for himself. He'd always rely on me to cover for his weaknesses, and suffer silently rather than ask me for help when he needed it.

From that time on, I began to imagine a life outside of Hawthorn Hill. Maybe I would purchase a cottage on one of the lovely tree-lined streets of Oakwood. Close enough to check on Orv a few times a week, but out on my own for the first time in my life.

❧

The birthday party was a grand success. Carrie brought out an immense roasted turkey in a pomegranate and fig sauce, along with mashed potatoes laced with truffle oil I had ordered from France. Lorin and his wife and grown children joined us, along with some business associates of Orville's—Mr. Kettering and Mr. Deeds—all seated around the long dining table.

As Orv carved serving after serving of dark meat, the guests were all pleased to have their favored meat. Not that he ever complained, but Orv usually got the wings, or if he was lucky, slices of breast meat, as he always served himself last. Not this time.

I took a bite and was suspicious. It was delicious, but not turkey. "Orv, what did you do?"

He was tucking into a lovely rich piece of dark meat. He set down his fork, and with a grin turned the bird around for all to see. It had been mostly carved out, and de-boned roast duck had been stuffed into it. "Now everyone gets dark meat."

After dinner, when our guests were retiring around the fireplace in the sitting room, Orville dawdled at the table, talking to Lorin and our nieces and nephews. As I shepherded the other guests out of the room, I spotted a dark-brown inch-long bug creeping out from under my nephew Horace's plate. At the same time, Ivonette shrieked. The bug scuttled toward Orville, who was grinning ear to ear. Poor Horace was up out of his chair and about to dive under the table when Orv laughed and admitted to his practical joke.

Thus this solved the mystery of long hours at his desk. He had carved a perfect wooden replica of a cockroach and attached it to a white thread that matched the tablecloth. My old self would have chastised him for wasting time on this project when he could be designing airplane dummies for the NACA. Instead, I shook my head and followed our other guests, who were thankfully oblivious to the little prank.

He was just having fun, and I decided perhaps it was better to stay on at Hawthorn Hill. Who knew what crazy Uncle Orv would dream up if I wasn't there to temper his more outrageous pranks? But then there was the refrigerator incident.

Refrigerators were becoming more common in modern homes, and Carrie and I hinted, then outright insisted we buy one. In fact, the kitchen had been designed with a small adjacent space wired specifically for it. Instead, we had a large icebox in the space, which Orville refused to replace. Made of solid oak with a zinc-lined interior, it was admittedly nicer looking than the giant hunks of white metal that were the more modern way to chill food, but I was willing to sacrifice aesthetics for practicality.

One day, after the ice man had made his delivery, leaving a path of dirty footprints and melting ice chips across the kitchen floor from the back doorway to the icebox cubby, I forbid Carrie from cleaning up the mess. Instead I dragged Orv into the kitchen to witness the dirty floor.

"Oh, sorry. I'll get a mop," he offered, and tried to escape my grasp on his arm.

"Are you going to mop it every day?" I asked. "And drain the melted water from the icebox?"

"Don't exaggerate. It's not every day. We don't need a refrigerator and I don't trust the technology. Plus, it's wasteful."

Ah. I knew his weakness and preyed upon it. "Wastefulness? How about the food that spoils when the iceman can't make a delivery because we're not home? Not to mention letting a stranger have access to our house. What if they hire someone we can't trust?"

Orv twisted his mouth and nodded his head. At last I had won an argument. Or so I thought.

The next morning as I made my way down the stairway, I heard strange noises coming from the back side of the house. It sounded like gunfire or perhaps small fireworks. I looked out windows, but nothing seemed amiss. I thought about calling the police, but decided to investigate a little more on my own.

"Orv? Carrie?" I called. No one answered. I stepped through the living room and dining room, but all was quiet. Then I heard the sound again, muffled as if underwater, coming from the kitchen. I stepped through the narrow connecting passageway and could see Orv through the window of the back doorway. I raced to the door, fearing for his life, wishing I had had the presence of mind to fetch a handgun from Orville's safe.

But there was no one shooting. Orv swung a sledgehammer over his head and slammed it into the outside wall—the wall between the back entry and the icebox room.

I opened the door and yelled. "Stop! What do you think you're doing?"

There was already a hole three feet wide punched through the brick.

Orville stopped swinging and rested the sledgehammer on his shoulder, looking very proud of himself. "Making the entry we should have planned all along. We'll line up the icebox on the inside and install doors, so the ice man won't have to come through the kitchen to make his deliveries anymore. Problem solved." With that, he took another swing, and the stunning cream-colored bricks tumbled into the pile of rubble.

Our beautiful mansion. Orville's really, as it was Wilbur's and his hard work and genius that enabled them to build it. I was just the lucky sister of greatness. I stepped back into the kitchen to make some tea. I could sip it while I reflected on another reason I needed to find a new home.

⚜

On the appointed evening in September when I was to meet Harry, I chose my outfit carefully: a blue-sequined drop-waist dress I had purchased in New York. The obsequious shopkeeper had told me it was the latest fashion and perfectly matched my eyes. Would a long string of pearls be too much? Should I wear shoes fit to dance in? Would there be dancing?

Earlier in the day, Orv was in his favorite chair in his library reading the newspaper, when I told him of my plans. "Very nice. My regards to Isabel," was his response, without even lowering his paper.

How could he have forgotten? "Isabel has—" *Never mind*, I thought. No need to remind him that Harry might possibly be available to my aged self.

⚜

Orv had offered to drive me downtown in his latest motorcar, but taking a taxicab seemed a more prudent choice. Besides, part of the point of the evening was to give us a break from each other. I had casually mentioned he might have dinner with an old school chum of mine who'd been hinting at her fondness for him, but as usual, Orv ignored my suggestion.

I arrived downtown with enough time to stroll the bustling streets and calm myself so as not to overwhelm Harry with nervous chatter. Electric lamps now cast a warm glow, and the shops were lit from within, their wares displayed in large windows. I heard music coming from a shop and walked over to see if they had squeezed an orchestra into the tiny place. But there was no orchestra. Instead, the sound was coming from a wireless.

The papers had announced a radio station coming to Dayton, and now several stores' windows displayed the fancy wooden boxes, some with big brass horns that looked like giant petunias attached. Each would bring wireless communication right into the home. I could have stayed an hour listening to the enchanted music coming from thin air, but it was time to head to the hotel.

The Gibbons stood ten stories tall with arched stone carvings above each stack of windows. The gray-walled lower floors, topped by warm brown stone above, reminded me of the hotels I had seen in France.

Harry's follow-up letter requested I meet him on the rooftop of the hotel on the appointed evening. I thought that odd, but the liveried elevator operator brought everyone else in the gilded lift to the top as well.

The glare of the setting sun stymied my hunt for Harry. I walked around the perimeter, which was lined with boxes overflowing with greenery. Iron torchieres flickered on, lighting tables set with white linens and fresh floral centerpieces. The tables were spread across the rooftop, except for the center, where a string quartet played a sonata before a spacious wooden dance floor. Perhaps my shoes would take a spin after all. Chatty couples and huddles of women in flashy dresses and feathered hats were escorted to tables. Many of the men smoked pipes and cigars at the edge of the roof, admiring the view of the city.

"Is that you, Katharine?"

A familiar voice came from behind me. I swirled around, and

there was Harry. A little grayer, a little balder, but the same twinkly eyes and kind face. We engaged in the usual small talk as we settled at our table for two—*How was your trip out? By motorcar? Weather has been lovely this summer*—and all the while I could hardly take my eyes off him. We had champagne and little croquettes and red beets, which I barely tasted. A band started up, and couples flooded the dance floor. We moved our chairs next to each other to watch.

Fringy dresses swung, and dark-suited men swirled their dates, with not a hair on their pomaded heads falling out of place. They danced the latest fast dances—the Black Bottom, with arms and legs swinging wildly, and the Charleston. We laughed at the exaggerated moves of the tango. Then, after a pause for the dancers to catch their breaths, the strings played the first strands of the Viennese Waltz.

Harry said, "At last. Something my old bones can keep up with." He stood and held out his hand. "May I have this dance, young lady?"

"Oh, it's been some time, and my bones are as old as yours, but I graciously accept."

I slipped my hand into his warm palm and rested the other on his sturdy shoulder and we swirled away. As he led with his arm across my back, it seemed my body knew just which way to go. The dance floor had emptied considerably, so we had plenty of space for grand loops and spins. I laughed and stepped lively to keep up, as the stars above blinked awake in the darkening sky.

If this was the only night we had to be together, I'd still be happy and cherish the memory forever.

ORVILLE

I woke with a start and looked at the luminous dial on my bedside clock. It occurred to me that the same radium paint they used for the clock dial might be useful for anemometers and other gauges for flying in twilight. I should bring that up at the next NACA meeting. Of course, they'd probably already thought of it. I was not of much use to them anymore.

It was twelve midnight and I had not heard Katharine come in from her meeting with Harry Haskell. I wasn't worried about Harry particularly; he was a respectable sort and we had known him for years. But it was very unlike my sister not to be home and check in with me before 10:00 p.m.

There were some rough elements downtown, one of the reasons we had decided to move to Oakwood. Outlawing liquor seemed to have the opposite of its intended effect: drinking continued, but the quality and quantity of alcohol was much less controlled, and the distribution was now exclusively done by the gangsters who seemed to rule the city.

I got up to check if Katharine had slipped in unnoticed. She was not in her bed, but I heard a stirring downstairs. I rushed down to discover her just getting in the door. Her face was flushed and the remnants of her rouge and lip paint were smeared on her lovely face.

"Oh, you're up," she said. "I hope I didn't wake you."

"I was worried."

"Well, you needn't be. Good night." She started to head for the stairs, but I stood in her way.

"Wait a minute. I think some explanation is in order."

"Pardon? I'm fifty years old. I don't need to explain anything."

"It doesn't matter your age. It's common courtesy when you live with someone who might be worried about your well-being."

"Do I ask you where you've been? You go off to DC for days at a time. Do you check in with me each night?" Katharine had unclipped her hair and looked rather disheveled, not helping her position. Her blue sparkly dress looked cheap and out of place on a woman of her station. What had gotten into her?

"I will if you want me to." I kept my voice low and gentle. No sense adding to her unjustified wrath. "We have a telephone. Which you might have used."

"Sorry, I didn't know the rule. In the future, I shall confirm my whereabouts by 10:00 p.m. Should I include my company and activity of the moment? Because that's what we did at the boardinghouse in Oberlin."

"Now you're just being difficult. And yes, I wouldn't mind knowing whom you were with."

She sighed, closed her eyes, seeming to try to shut me out. What had I done wrong?

"You know I was with Harry Haskell. You know him well. And now, if you don't mind, I'm going to bed."

KATHARINE

Oh, how lovely it was to share a perfect evening with a
perfect gentleman. Harry insisted on seeing me home,
but declined to come in the house. We both knew why.
We had separate lives and a special friendship that relied on distance
and mutual respect.

But somehow his departure put me in a bad mood. It didn't help
that when I returned Orv acted like the father of a sixteen-year-old
on her first date. Why did it need to be this way? I wanted to slip
in quietly and just go to bed and sleep off too much fizzy fake gin
and aching feet. How could I be fifty years old and have the same
feelings as my twenty-year-old self?

Lulu, Reuchlin's widow, had told me that the women of Kansas City
had officially determined that Harry's time of mourning was over. A
veritable parade of women was lined up for him, and from what Lulu
could tell, he was enjoying the attention. No doubt I was just one of the
many women he was seeing, and that was how it should be. But it irked
me all the same. Still too wound up from the evening to go to bed, I
wrote a letter to Harry, meant to arrive before he returned from his trip.

I thanked him for the wonderful evening and acknowledged that he undoubtedly enjoyed many similar moments with his admirers in Kansas City. But I couldn't help cautioning him, *"Just watch your loneliness and make sure that you really want what you are drifting into."*

We started corresponding as fast as the mail would allow, which amounted to about once or twice a week. We circled around our feelings for each other. Instead, Harry updated me on one of his latest journalistic investigations—to expose a plot to undermine Orville and Wilbur's biggest achievement.

ORVILLE

S ome men had no honor. I didn't blame Langley for the Smithsonian's travesty, as he was long gone. It was his successor, the bilious Charles Walcott, who set the seeds for the intentional misleading of the public. Thanks to Lorin's sleuthing, we knew it was he who had hired Glenn Curtiss to modify and fly Langley's failed aerodrome, using our patented ideas and inventions.

Despite court battles and my many letters explaining how I knew they falsified their claims, the Smithsonian continued to claim that Langley was rightfully the inventor of the airplane. Of course, a gaggle of expensive lawyers had proven him wrong in court, but the public remained confused. I had pledged to let go of the resentment toward Curtiss and Walcott, but I couldn't allow history to be rewritten.

I sat in the armchair in my library, fuming over the rumors that the Smithsonian had a new exhibit—Langley's aerodrome. Carrie stepped in with the newspaper I had requested. I had to pull twice to remove it from her grip.

"It's not good news," she said.

There was indeed an exhibit of the aerodrome. The same

unmodified one that had plunged into the Potomac. The same one that I had determined from the fuzzy photograph back in 1908 would never fly. The splashy article stated the exhibit was of the first powered airplane capable of flight. Capable, my derriere.

This could not stand. The steady burn that had been building in my stomach ignited into a conflagration. The bulk of the remains of our 1903 Flyer, the real first real airplane, languished in storage downtown, with some salvaged parts still in the shed behind our old home. I had been meaning to dig them out, but that also meant digging up thousands of memories of working with Will. I hadn't been able to face that pain in thirteen years. But now it was time.

Katharine had sold our Hawthorn Street home to a former employee, but it was a simple matter to arrange access to the shed. I drove over in a Ford I had converted into an open-bed truck. The house looked much the same, but so much smaller than it had seemed in my youth.

My heart sank to see that the towering trees that once shaded the street were mostly gone, victims of the flood, or perhaps chopped down to make room for automobiles. Without them the street had lost the very reason for its name, and a sense of life changing with the seasons.

I let myself in through the small gate in the fence to the back-yard. Patchy grass struggled in the back corner of the yard, where Katharine had once grown the most delicious tomatoes and bell pep-pers. I pictured her giving them a squeeze to test for ripeness, then slipping them into the apron she had cupped into a makeshift basket.

The shed sagged onto its foundation. If I had time, I should bring some wood and tools and shore it up. A rusted padlock on an even rustier hinge secured the door. I whacked it with a hammer and it dropped into my hand like a dead fish. The doors resisted my efforts to open them, clearly for the first time in years. I got a crowbar out of the Ford and pried them open. The smell of dead rats and rotten wood made me retch.

I gingerly picked my way past a few rusted bicycles in various states of disrepair, past cracked flowerpots and a laundry tub, to the crates that held the flyer parts. Stacked in the back corner, they were right where Will and I had left them just before Christmas in 1903. A dark-gray line encircling the entire shed reminded me of the 1913 flood. Another thing I wanted to forget. I closed my eyes and felt the house shaking from the pounding rain, saw the Bishop and Katharine stuffing rags onto the windowsills, not that they did any good. I pictured paddling Will's canoe in brown water past the floating remains of disrupted lives.

Turning my attention back to the crates, I moved the items blocking them and loaded them one by one into the Ford. Will was in my head with each box I lifted, and I asked him what I should do, once I got the flyer outfitted.

She should never fly again, Will said. *Fix her up so that she could, but her job is done. The new contraptions in the air would make her silly by comparison, and I couldn't bear that.*

I drove the few blocks to the storage building downtown, near where our old printshop had been, where the bulk of the flyer had been stored. I glanced up at the big window on the second floor of what used to be our printshop. From there, Will and I had witnessed so many changes—from horse and carriages, to electrified trams, to the early automobiles. Some strong-looking boys were hanging about, so I paid them some coins to help me load the crates onto my truck.

I took the disassembled flyer to my laboratory and worked on her bit by bit. The brown and tattered fabric of her once gleaming white wings was useless for my restoration, so I folded up some of the better pieces to give away as souvenirs, and replaced all the muslin. A few of the wood and metal pieces were also beyond saving, so I recreated them.

Will was with me the whole time. We argued about what was worth saving and what was too far gone. He wanted it to look pristine, as it had in Kitty Hawk, and I wanted to keep as much of the original as possible. It was both an enjoyable time of memories and companionship, and also finally time to say goodbye.

When it was nearly finished, I drove up to Woodland Cemetery on paved roadways, where there were once only dirt and gravel paths. The engine groaned and the gears ground as I went up the steep hills. Up, higher than our flights in 1903. When did we fly that high? Surely by 1905.

The family plot was near the top of the hilly cemetery. I got out and walked the rest of the way, huffing a bit from the exertion. Some might think the place of honor would be right at the crest, not just below it. But it soothed my heart to see the Bishop, Mother, and Wilbur together for eternity in that special spot. Just as in life, they were as high as they could go, yet leaving room for others to come.

KATHARINE

SPRING

Harry and I made plans for him to visit Hawthorn Hill. Orville had invited all manner of businessmen, politicians, actors, and the like to stay with us, so a visit from an old friend didn't seem so out of the ordinary.

What was out of the ordinary was that Harry offered no business excuse for coming to town. He had won a prize for his piece on the sham that Curtiss was perpetuating, but that was done and dusted. I told Orv that Harry was coming to see me, risking the same wrath he showed after our date, but Orv offered no objections.

Harry and I visited a different venue each day. We saw a live show at the Victory Theatre, attended a lecture at the Dayton Museum of Arts, and snuck into a few speakeasies, which were so noisy and crowded that we were standing chest to chest and still had to yell to hear each other speak. We went to a ballroom and danced the Charleston, from the hit play *Runnin' Wild*, which Harry had seen on Broadway. It was oh so grand. As we swished our feet, first in front, then in back, Harry shouted he must take me to see the musical.

"Just say when," I shouted over the music.

This could be my life, I thought, as the fringe of my dress swung with the driving rhythm. I no longer needed to worry about financially supporting my family. *Step front, step back. Grab Harry's hand and twirl.* There was only Orv to take care of. *Step front, arms high.* He seemed quite content with his NACA and other board positions. *Step back, arms low.* My hair was graying, my breath coming harder. It seemed finally time to live my own life, while I could still dance.

On the ride back home in a taxicab, I mused about my time with VJ on Lambert Island. The island was still quite rustic, with several small cabins with no running water or electricity. But it was far from the buzz of daily life. I thought it would be perfect for Harry and me to get away and truly explore where our relationship was headed.

In early July, Orv and I drove up to Canada. Along the way, as we chatted about the projects he wanted to get done and buying a speedier boat, I casually mentioned inviting Harry Haskell up for a couple of weeks.

"He's good company for both of us," I said, with only a small pang of guilt.

"Good idea. Why don't we use the telephone in the general store to call him when we stop for supplies?"

While Orv shopped, I called Harry. Of course, he already knew of my plan and the call was just to confirm that Orv was on board.

"See you soon, then, if you're sure I won't be imposing."

Hearing Harry's voice always soothed my soul, even with the simplest of statements. "I can't wait."

We drove the roundabout route necessary because of the lakes, until we could go no further by car. Then a hired boat motored us the short distance to the island. I liked to stay in the main cabin, perched on a bluff overlooking the sparkling water and the emerald-green puffs of the nearby islands.

Orville preferred a smaller cabin down by the dock, where he had a fast motorboat and one of his most prized possessions—a canoe. The same canoe that Wilbur had tied to a flyer to fly around the Statue of Liberty, and in which we had escaped the great flood. *I might just have to bury Orv in that canoe.*

Soon we were settled into the rhythm of our island days. I tended the rosebushes in my small garden. The yellow ones I had tried to transplant from Dayton didn't survive the winter, but the pink ones were happily climbing a trellis on the south wall of my cottage. I foraged for mushrooms and berries while Orv went fishing. On a clear crisp morning in late July, I watched from my little porch as Orv paddled the faded red canoe away from the dock, always the first thing he did each day.

Harry was due to arrive the next day, and we needed to arrange for his accommodations. I saw no reason he couldn't stay in the small extra room in the main cabin with me. But fearing this would upset Orv, I made up one of the other cabins, one that Orv didn't have in some state of rebuilding, up on the ridge only a hundred feet from me.

When Harry arrived, Orv helped him from the small hired motorboat onto the rickety dock. The dock also in a state of rebuilding, I cringed as poor Harry stepped awkwardly over a pile of lumber. Soon, Orv and I took him on a tour of the island, showing him all the latest improvements—for example, an outboard motor running a pulley and cart system that ferried supplies up to the cabins.

One of the most useful contraptions was a cooling system, a kerosene-powered fan that waved over a tub of ice; and a machine to wash clothes that consisted of a drum that circled on a bent post, fed by a stream of water sucked out of the lake by yet another outboard motor. I believe Orv was happiest tinkering on this island, inventing conveniences, and didn't miss the modern niceties such as the indoor plumbing and electricity we had at Hawthorn Hill.

Several pleading looks from Harry convinced me I needed to find a way to spend some time alone with him.

"Why don't you take Harry fishing?" I asked, knowing Orv could hardly resist. "I'd love to have some fresh walleye for dinner."

Harry understood the plan and announced, "Splendid. I'd love some fish from these pristine waters. But I'm afraid I'm too weary from my trip to be of much help."

So the two of us took our leave and wandered in a roundabout way to my cabin. There we lit the fireplace and settled into the comfy divan. It wasn't long before we were in each other's arms. Oh, the joy of human touch. Of the warm welcoming of another being, a compassionate being, who wants nothing else but to be with you. Half of my mind was determined to enjoy the pleasure of the moment, while the other half worried that it would inevitably be over too soon.

I spent a fitful night sleeping alone in my cabin. I was tempted to pull on my robe and slippers and sneak over to Harry's cabin. But it was so dark, and I was afraid taking a lantern might serve as a signal to Orv. Instead I spent the time lamenting my frustrating position. In the morning, I needed to have an important discussion with both Harry and Orville.

⁓

The smell of burnt toast greeted me the next morning. That could mean only one thing: Orv was in the kitchen, experimenting with another contraption to make his favorite breakfast treat. He had already devised a special cutting board so that each slice of bread would be precisely cut to his preferred thickness. Back at Hawthorn Hill he had wired some electric plates to toast the bread, sometimes with flaming results. I had thought the Lambert Island kitchen was safe, as it lacked electricity, but the cloud of smoke emanating from it proved otherwise.

"Good morning, Sterchens!" Orv said in a voice too cheery for the hour. "I thought our guest might enjoy 'toad-in-a-hole.'"

"Not likely that one." I sniffed at the hard-cooked egg in the center of a charred piece of bread.

Orv regarded his iron skillet and shrugged. "Don't worry, I'll eat this one."

What worried me more was that Orv would likely monopolize all of Harry's time if I didn't intervene. He would keep him busy working on his never-ending projects, or out boating and fishing and all the other things men like to do when away from women. I had to come up with an activity that Orv wouldn't favor, so as not to hurt his feelings by not inviting him.

"I saw some blueberries ripening out past the flagpole," I said, slathering some jam on the least-burnt slice of toast I could find. "How about we gather some, and I'll make a pie for dessert tonight?" A little guilt pricked my conscience. I knew full well the rocky area was too difficult for him to navigate with his bad hip.

Orv buttered the skillet for another try at toad-in-a-hole. "Could you manage without me? I'd like to get some work done on the dock. Maybe Harry would like to join you."

I had to bite my lip to suppress a smile. "Mmm, maybe. Why don't I go call him to breakfast and ask?"

Harry and I had the most wonderful morning exploring the island, talking about everything and anything while we plucked fat, juicy blueberries by the bucketful. He had read most of the books I had, had similar taste in music, and like me, longed to visit Italy and Greece.

"I adored Rome," I told him, and he let me go on and on about my European adventures. There weren't many people in my life with whom I could talk about these things. If they hadn't traveled, they couldn't understand or were simply envious of my adventures. And I was loath to show off all the amazing things I had done and people I had met.

But Harry was different. He was very comfortable with himself and accomplished in his career. His writing had won important prizes, and his investigative reporting had exposed wrongdoing and put things to right. Of course, I was most grateful for his work on the Walcott-Curtiss affair.

After dropping off our blueberries, we hiked the perimeter of the island along the thin ribbon of sandy shore.

"I'm not sure we appropriately thanked you for the series you wrote on the patent disputes. They seemed to be the final push Orv needed to finally let go and move on to other things."

"No need to thank me; it's my job. And the best part is when I can right a wrong done to people I care for."

I rested against the scaly trunk of a tamarack tree. "You're a kindred spirit, Harry. Easy to talk to about so many things. Not to mention the sense of comfort I have being with you."

He leaned close and kissed me. "I feel the same about you."

Harry and I had two glorious weeks together, and as the time came nearer for his departure, I grew restless, needing to know when I would see him again. After Orv had departed for the evening, I curled up next to Harry in our favorite spot in front of the fire. I listened to the hoot of the owls that resided in the neighboring trees and felt the warmth of the fire on my face as I puzzled how to broach the subject. But Harry seemed to read my mind and, as usual, came right to the point.

"May I assume I've been good company for you?" he asked.

"Of course. The best." I snuggled closer.

"Well then, when will I have the pleasure of seeing you again?"

"I was wondering the same thing."

"Must I keep making excuses of business trips to Dayton?" He nuzzled my neck, sending a shiver down my spine. "Because I do have another proposition in mind."

"Oh?" I pulled back, wanting to see his face. Was he teasing me? But his expression was sincere, his eyes hopeful, and maybe a little sad. "What is that?"

"I love you, and I believe you love me too, although you haven't said as much." He paused until I nodded in agreement. "I understand your family commitments, and possibly nothing has changed since I first proposed to you all those years ago. But I'm hoping that now, finally, we are both in a happenstance that we can be together at last."

"I love you. I always have."

His eyes crinkled in his still serious face. "Well then?"

I cocked my head. "What exactly are you proposing?"

At last a grin spread across his face. "I love you and you love me, and there is no longer anything or anyone to keep us apart. I propose we marry, just as soon as we can make arrangements."

My first response was glee. This was something I'd wanted, waited for, for three decades of my life. But before I could let myself feel that joy, I had to think it through. I thought of the wonderful home I shared with Orville, which I had assumed would be my home for the rest of my life. I would have to move away, of course. I wouldn't ask Harry to move to Dayton. He would probably do it if I asked, and that was the problem.

I pictured the look on Orv's face when I told him I wanted to marry. Although he was no longer dependent on me to be his "social manager," he would feel abandoned. Or would he? Maybe he didn't want to live with his sister for the rest of his life. There certainly was a steady stream of interested women that he had always held at a distance. Was that because of me?

Harry pulled away, took a sip of his brandy. "I don't want to push you, my beloved. But we are, if not *in* our twilight years, able to see them from here." His chuckle seemed to get stuck in his throat.

"I do wish to marry you," I said. "I'd like to run away and spend the rest of my days as we have the past two weeks."

"But—?"

"I have no reservations regarding marrying you. But we can't run off and do it just yet. There's a lot to think about and I need to talk to Orville first."

That was how we left it. I waved goodbye to them as Orville motored out of the lagoon with Harry onboard. I considered what would be the best time to tell him of our plans. Not up at the lake, I decided. It would be a very awkward drive back to Ohio if Orv was less than pleased, and I had every reason to believe he would be.

Back at Hawthorn Hill, we busied ourselves opening things back up and attending to neglected business. The optimum moment hadn't appeared for several weeks, so I kept putting off telling Orv about Harry's proposal. When letters arrived from Harry, I let them sit on my desk unopened for a day or two, knowing he deserved an answer I couldn't yet provide.

Weeks went by, then months. I tried to find a quiet moment when Orv was relaxed and in a good mood. But there were family visits, and dinners with friends, and the never-ending parade of dignitaries that loved to come chat with the great Orville Wright. I sensed from his letters that Harry was growing impatient, even as he insisted I had to do what I felt was best for all of us.

I went to Lorin and Netta's house to find comfort with my nieces and nephews and told all of them about my engagement. They were ecstatic, practically knocking me over with enthusiasm.

"Now, you mustn't mention it to Orville quite yet," I warned. "He might not take it well, and I need to find the perfect moment."

ORVILLE

W hat had come over Katharine? Maybe she was going through the change. Her formerly considerable powers of attention seemed to have drifted away like the clouds she was always staring at. I wanted to help, but I couldn't even bring myself to ask, fearing I'd make her feel worse.

Everything I tried to do was wrong. Admittedly, knocking a hole in the kitchen wall was perhaps not my wisest decision, and we could have easily afforded a refrigeration machine. But since then, I'd kept my home improvements to a minimum and only tinkered with things like my record changer in the basement.

It was that Haskell fellow. Ever since he lost his wife, he'd started sniffing around, looking for a suitable substitute. I liked him well enough, and when he came up to the lake, he was a good sport about fishing for our dinner and having no plumbing or electricity. But now that Katharine finally had all she wanted and needed, he came and turned her head.

They thought I didn't know what was going on in the cabin once I went back to mine. I knew, and didn't care; they were adults, after all. But a little tryst can turn into the complete upheaval of one's life if one isn't careful. And after all these years of Katharine looking after me, feeding me, sheltering me from the crowds, and speaking my heart when I couldn't find my own voice, it was time for me to protect her.

KATHARINE

Finally, an opportune moment arrived. Orville had summoned me to his office, where he had a spotting glass set up at the window.

"Come look, Sterchens. The geese are taking flight. A sure sign of fall."

It was the opening I needed. "Oh, they're off to warmer climes. Seasons change. Birds and people do too." I peered through the scope. My eyeglasses got in the way, but I didn't let on. "It's a good thing to welcome change, don't you think?"

"Remember watching them along the river with Will? That was the start of it all, you, me, Wilbur." He repositioned the scope for his height. "I can still see him, running about, flapping his arms." His eyes watered as he chuckled with the memory.

Orv's mind was in a different place. It wasn't the right moment after all.

"Speaking of traveling, you'll go with me to meet President Coolidge, won't you?" he asked.

With my mind occupied with a marriage and move halfway across the country, I had nearly forgotten the trip to New York City and Washington, DC, that Orville had planned long ago. Maybe that would offer the perfect opportunity to tell him of Harry and my plans. Away from this home that we had shared for so many years. In a new light, we could both see that change was a good thing.

But New York was too intense, and we were both exhausted at the end of each day. On the train down to Washington, I considered how I would present my position. Perhaps just before meeting with the president of the United States was not the best time.

Our meeting with Calvin Coolidge reminded me of one of the reasons I did need to marry and move out. The president had the same reticence as Orv. The discussion wasn't so much as a discussion as it was me asking a host of questions, answered with single-syllable responses. I was reminded of the story of a dinner guest who once bet the president that she could make him say three words. "You lose," was his reply.

I had been speaking for Orville since we were schoolchildren. Since the day Will got clobbered by the punk at the skating pond. It was high time I stepped away, and he would manage without me and even grow a bit.

⁂

But even once we were home, I never seemed to get up the nerve to tell Orville. Finally, I wrote to Harry, telling him that he would need to tell Orv himself. Sort of like the custom of the groom asking the bride's father for permission to marry.

Harry agreed and planned to come by during a business trip.

"You need to tell him without me in the room," I explained to Harry. "I know I'll just cry, and that will mess up everything."

ORVILLE

I drove out to Union Station in my old Franklin Roadster. Harry didn't seem to be much of an automobile aficionado, but who could resist a splendid ride in an open coupe?

I was a few minutes late, and I spotted him outside under the clock tower that crowned the station. He was all business aboard the roadster and failed to appreciate the smooth ignition from inside the vehicle, thanks to my friend Charles Kettering who invented the starter and gave me one as a gift. But Katharine had told me to stop dropping names like that, so how was he to know? As we headed down busy Ludlow Street, he clutched the door with white knuckles, which rather amused me. I'd flown airplanes made of cloth and stick at faster speeds.

It was a quick ride home. Had he been a more enthusiastic passenger, I would have taken him over a few bumpy roads where with enough speed we could become airborne for a second or two, but I would save that for another day. Or night... It was certainly fun at night.

Katharine, who had been out of sorts for several months, suddenly lit up at the sight of Harry. There had been something going on between them for a year or two, but I didn't pry into their private affairs. And an affair was what it was now; I was sure of it from the way they looked at each other too much.

Katharine had made a nice dinner, strangely enough pot roast—one of my favorites. Was it Harry's too? Katharine always catered to guests, and I remembered his favorite to be fish.

After dinner, Katharine shooed Harry and me into the living room while she helped Carrie clear the dishes. We settled into the wingback chairs flanking the fireplace. It was May, and too warm for a fire, but this was our place for important discussions outside of family. And I hoped one was forthcoming.

We made some small talk as I waited for whatever it was that Harry needed. He had won an important prize for his series on our patent fights, and I expected he'd ask for an exclusive interview for the twenty-fifth anniversary of our Kitty Hawk flight. I offered him a cigar, which he refused, then settled back for his sales pitch.

But he fumbled around, pulling at his shirtsleeves and the tie about his neck.

I helped him along. "So you wanted a private meeting with me?"

He cleared his throat and finally started to get to his point. "As you are no doubt aware, Katharine and I have known each other for many, many years. It seems that over the past year or so, we've now developed deeper feelings for each other."

"Yes, yes. That's nice." I shifted my weight, as my lower back muscles were spasming. I was anxious for him to get to the point of the meeting so I could go sit in my more comfortable library chair.

"So, we've decided to, ah, um…" The man who lived for words seemed to not have any of the right ones handy. "Spend the rest of our days—whatever number the Lord sees fit to bless us with—together."

"How's that?" My head felt whiplashed, as if I'd just made a hard landing.

"I'm not asking your permission, of course, but we would like your blessing."

Harry stared at me, I guess awaiting some sort of response, but I still wasn't sure what he was talking about. "Blessing?"

"We want to get married. Not someday, as if we were still starry-eyed twenty-year-olds. But soon, and right here, if you'll have it."

The room darkened around me as if I were on a train entering a tunnel. The hall clock ticked, telling me I needed to say something. But all I could think of was *What could this man be thinking?*

"Orv? I–I hope this means you're happy, for Katharine certainly is."

My lips quivered, but no sound would come out. Here, I thought he was a friend. A professional as well, here for a new joint endeavor. Well, he wanted a joint endeavor all right. Just not one I wanted to be part of. I finally thought of something to say: "You should go now."

I stepped away and through the trophy room, which now seemed too dark with the heavy brocade walls, and into the foyer. I grabbed Harry's hat from the coat-tree, brought it back to the living room, and handed it to him in a gentlemanly manner.

Footsteps against the wood, then a soft padding on the rug told me Katharine had entered the room. I turned to look at her face, the one face I could read, which would tell me immediately her feelings about this nonsense. Her face was uplifted, a smile crinkling her eyes... That is, until she looked at me. Her face then drooped immediately, telling me everything. She was wholly engulfed in this man's treacherous web. She had to be, to even consider leaving me and the fine life we had built together.

The offending man accepted his hat, then stood there fingering its brim. I brushed by him and took my worn-out bones to my office. Where nothing was allowed to change unless I said so.

KATHARINE

Carrie and I stacked the dinner dishes into the kitchen sink.
"Your man didn't eat much," she observed.
"My man? What makes you think he's my man?"
"I have eyes. I have a heart." She ran the water into the sink.

"You're right. We wish to be married. You'll stay with Orv, won't you?" I kept my voice low, while I strained to hear any conversation from the living room. I was hoping for some excited congratulations, but would have settled for a pleasant hum of chatter. But there was nothing but silence.

"Of course." She jutted her jaw toward the doorway. "You better go in there."

Apparently I wasn't the only one who sensed a dark cloud in the next room. I tucked back an errant wisp of hair and fixed a smile on my face, then walked through the dining room, from where I still could hear no conversation. I took a deep breath and stepped through the entry to the living room. The two men were standing, with Harry facing me and Orv turned toward the fireplace. Harry worked the brim of his hat, a nervous habit I had not noticed before.

Then, upon seeing me, a small smile crossed his face and I had hope. He stepped over to me, kissed my cheek, and whispered, "My part is done. He's all yours now."

Orv's eyes brimmed with the same look of hurt and pain as they had when Wilbur died, the worst moment in both of our lives. I knew from that moment that he would never accept Harry as my husband and never wish us well in our new life, no matter how much we promised to visit.

"I... We..." I stammered. How could I possibly explain my desire to follow my own heart for the first time in my life? Anything I said would not make that hurt go away. I wasn't a grown woman with needs and desires, I was his center, his partner in life, the one he had built everything for.

Orv didn't say a word. He didn't have to. Instead he went to his library and closed the door.

The next day, I telephoned my brother Lorin and his wife, Netta, and updated them regarding Orv's reaction.

"He'll come around," Lorin said. "And if he doesn't, I'll give him a good talking-to. He can't justify this emotional blackmail. You deserve better."

"I may take you up on that." I chuckled, but there was no mirth in my heart.

Life returned to more or less normal at Hawthorn Hill. Orv acted as if nothing had happened, perhaps spending a bit more time fiddling in the basement or at his downtown lab, but he never mentioned my leaving.

I wrote lots of letters to Harry, who of course was anxious for everything to be settled so that we could make plans. In a particularly black moment, I wrote him, *I have done an awful thing.* His response was simple and only served to make me love him more.

Long ago, I told you I wanted to help you find what was in your heart. I haven't changed since, and I couldn't possibly ask you to do what you thought you shouldn't. I love you, forever and always, no matter what happens. He was so kind, so patient, so understanding. Why couldn't Orville be that way? Of course I loved my brother deeply, and one loves someone with all their faults and shortcomings.

I wanted to get married in the living room at Hawthorn Hill, just as my nieces had. A simple family affair, with just a few close friends. Reuchlin's widow, Lulu, could play the organ and my niece Ivonette would sing. We'd collect roses from the garden and have hors d'oeuvres on the porch if the weather was nice. But we couldn't do that without Orville's blessing and permission. It was his house, after all.

After a few weeks, it seemed that Orv was coming around. He fixed a few things around the house that I had been nagging him about, as if, in his own way he seemed to be accepting the change that was coming about. So I thought it might be time for an important discussion.

He was on a step stool in the trophy room, polishing his prized possession: the statue given to Wilbur in France. He never let anyone else touch it. He dusted inside the scalloped niche created just for it. He shouldn't be climbing on stools with his bad hip, but I refrained from admonishing him.

Once he climbed down, I said, "That is the perfect spot, isn't it?"

Orv nodded toward the wall. "I'm thinking of taking down the brocade fabric. It's dark and steals attention from the sculpture."

I admired the walls, with the intricate raised pattern of the fabric. More elegant than the flowers and stripes he had decorated my old room with, but nothing could replace the warmth that wallpaper had brought. "I do like the cozy feeling the brocade brings, but then again, walls painted a creamy white might better focus attention, as you say, and be a fresher, cooler look."

He nodded. "Then I'll put it up in the fall and take it down each spring."

"Little Brother, you don't need to do that for me."

He gave me a little smile and a wink, just about melting my heart.

"Although there is something you could do that would make me very happy."

"What's that?" He gathered his cleaning supplies into their tote.

"Wouldn't this be the perfect place for everyone to gather before the wedding?" I said. "It would feel like Wilbur and the Bishop are with us."

"What?" Orville stopped folding the step stool. He looked at me, his face crumpling once again with that hurt look, which put a ball of lead in my stomach, making me want to immediately back down from my request. I'd swear he knew exactly what that look did to me.

"I thought you gave up on that outrageous idea." He must have seen the shock on my face, because he quickly backtracked. "Have him visit whenever he likes, I don't mind. And go see him out there in Kansas if you like. Fly on one of those new airlines. We can afford it."

"Orv, you don't seem to understand. We are in love and want to be married. To spend the rest of our lives together." But his blank stare told me I was getting nowhere. It was time to play the last card in my hand.

❧

Lorin, Netta, and I planned a family dinner at their home, but I had second thoughts and telephoned Netta. "I fear Orv will suspect that we're ganging up on him."

"Well, we are," Netta replied. "This show is moving on, as it must. But I want you to remember one thing. Orv may never come around. If that's his choice, there's nothing you can do about it. You have to decide based on what is right for you and Harry. Promise?"

I so promised, and on the date of the dinner, I took a bubble bath to settle my nerves and was ready to go promptly at 6:00 p.m. When Orv failed to appear at our agreed departure time, I sought him out. He was in the basement, in a dress shirt and tie, tinkering with the stupid vacuum cleaning system.

"Little Brother, it's time to go."

"I think I've finally got this"—he twisted a screw that held a clamp—"off." The bucket that held the dirt fell to the floor, raising a cloud of dust.

I set my teeth. I had pledged to reduce my bossiness, but sometimes there was no alternative. "Please go upstairs, wash up, and change your dirty shirt. We're leaving in ten minutes."

❧

The dinner was about as pleasant as the predinner episode, despite a valiant attempt by Netta and Lorin. After stilted conversation, unusual for Orv who generally loved to involve family in a lively debate, Lorin and he retired to the smoking parlor.

Netta, Ivonette, and I chatted about wedding plans, skirting the topic of where exactly the nuptials would take place.

"The church, right here, back in Kansas—wherever you choose, it will be lovely," Netta said.

Soon, Orville and Lorin reappeared. Lorin slightly shook his head to Netta's inquiring look.

Orv had his suit coat slung over his arm. "Thank you, Netta. Ready to go, Katharine?"

I hugged everyone goodbye and joined Orv as he quick-walked toward his roadster. It had started raining, and the car was open. Perfect.

He tried to start her up from a switch he had wired to the dashboard, but she liked being rained on even less than I did. He climbed out and opened the hood and clanged around while I got wetter and more fretful. The engine started up, and Orv slammed down the hood and climbed back into the driver's seat. We sat there an awkward moment while the engine warmed up—something about the oil circulating like blood.

He stared straight ahead in the idling car, gripping the steering wheel like it might fly away at any moment. "Let me make this clear," he said. "I have told you how I feel about this nonsense of marrying at your age, but I cannot tell you what to do with your life."

A wave of relief passed through me. I could live with his passive acceptance.

He ground the car into gear, and we lurched forward, the rain speckling my eyeglasses and the windscreen.

"But if you choose to marry anyway, I will have nothing to do with it. You won't be married at Hawthorn Hill, and you will cease to exist for me."

My breath caught in my throat. He couldn't really mean this. I glanced at his profile as he drove, his features fixed, his eyes deadened. An awful weight gathered in the pit of my stomach and I feared I would lose my dinner. "Oh, Little Brother. No."

ORVILLE

Sometimes it is absolute hell being the only one in the room with any sense. When it was just Will and me, he always came around to my way of thinking, as he was good at looking at a problem from three hundred and sixty degrees. Not so with my emotion-driven sister and her new cohorts: my corruptible brother Lorin and his wife.

I could clearly see what they apparently could not. That Haskell fellow was after a replacement for his wife. He saw a woman of means who could elevate his standing in that awful city. Lorin had spent time there and he left for good reason. Okay, maybe that wasn't Kansas City's fault so much as that Lorin had missed home. As Katharine no doubt would, but by then it would be too late. I wanted no part of it and said so. If they thought I would change my mind, or "come around" as Lorin said, they didn't know me very well, even though I haven't changed in all these years.

If I was selfish and hard-hearted, then the Lord would punish me. But I was acting as a protective older brother, not out of self-interest.

After all, I wouldn't choose to shun the one person in the world I treasured most. I believed the Lord would see it my way.

A few nights after the disaster at Lorin and Netta's, Katharine came down to the basement, where I had set up some strings of lights to get some vegetables started. Here it was well into May and I hadn't gotten the tomatoes planted.

"At the rate you're going," Katharine said, "you won't have them in the ground by Decoration Day."

"So you're still speaking to me?" It was hard for me to judge her mood when she avoided me.

"I'm not the one who threatened to sever our relationship."

Testy. Her mood was definitely testy.

"I'm only looking out for you. Sometimes it's hard to see what's the best path when you're too close to the situation."

"And you're the expert on romantic relationships?" She practically sneered, which was not helping her case.

"I'm the expert on you." I sprayed the tomato foliage with liquid fertilizer. They would thank me when the warm sun sped their growth.

"No. You're not. I'm giving you another chance to think this through. But I am going to marry the man I love."

"I don't have to think it through. But in the interest of family peace, let's say I will. Go about your planning, I won't interfere. Just don't plan to have the wedding here."

KATHARINE

FALL

Harry and I planned the bulk of our wedding by letter. He proposed to have it in Kansas City, since Hawthorn Hill was not an option and picking somewhere else in Dayton just saddened me. We finally settled on Oberlin, where we had first met and still had several mutual friends.

This way it was neither his home nor mine, a new beginning for both of us, at the same time a link to our past. A small gathering at a friend's house suited us perfectly. We decided on November due to his schedule and to give me few months to sort out my new life. I was excited at the prospect of living in a new city, meeting new people. I felt like I knew everyone in Dayton, and everyone knew me, and there were no new challenges.

All the while I shopped for my trousseau and packed my household belongings, I prayed for a change in Orville's heart. Surely he would come to understand I needed to finally do something for myself. He couldn't hold a grudge forever.

I invited Carrie and her husband to the wedding and begged her to convince Orv to accompany her. Perhaps he wouldn't say no to that, as neither Carrie nor her husband had any experience traveling.

It was a sweet, simple ceremony in our friend's home. I wore a cream-colored silk dress Orv had purchased for me in France. November isn't the best time for fresh flowers, but dried and silk arrangements were just as festive. As we awaited the minister and chatted with guests, I snuck glances out the window, hoping Orv was just running late. He hadn't answered my telephone calls, but surely he wouldn't miss this important day. But as the minutes ticked away and no motorcar came screaming down the street, my heart grew heavy as my hopes faded.

"You look lovely." Harry softly took my elbow and steered me away from the window. "Everyone is here. It's time."

We exchanged vows in front of a fireplace, the warmth of the flames chasing away the bitter chill of Orv's absence. I needed to focus on Harry now. My brother would come around when he was ready.

But the grudge held. I wrote letter after unanswered letter, inviting him to come visit us in Kansas City, telling him how happy Harry made me. There was nothing but silence in response.

Harry tried to soothe my wounded soul. He came home from the newspaper one evening with a stack of travel brochures. "Let's plan some trips." He fanned out some delectable choices: Italy, Greece, the Caribbean.

My spirits lifted, but my thoughts turned once again to my brother. "I wonder," I thought out loud, "if Orv would consent to join us. Maybe if we're in neutral territory, and he sees how happy we are…"

Harry's smile drooped a bit. "Of course, whatever you want."

"You don't seem enthused with the idea."

"It's not that I wouldn't love to have him along. I don't want you to be upset again. I'm pretty sure he'll refuse your offer, and you'll be hurt anew."

I dreamed of a wonderful vacation. Maybe sail to Europe. There'd be plenty of space on the ship for us all to do our own activities, and then splendid dinners where we could talk things out. I could just see it—the white tablecloths, the beautiful crystal chandeliers, the walks along the ship's promenade. We'd be reliving the glory days of 1909, but with all the worries of that time far behind us.

The answer to my invitation was worse than a no. I got no answer at all. After several weeks, I telephoned Carrie to see if Orv had gotten the letter.

"Yes, I handed it to him myself. I knew it was important, and I told him I would stand there hanging over him until he read it."

I pictured Orv at his desk in the center of his library, surrounded by his precious books, the rewired lamp shedding light on the offending letter. He would wait a bit, until Carrie stepped away, then he'd toss it in the green and gold metal trash can. But I could not give up, would not give up.

Never one to sit idle, I set about making a comfortable home for Harry and me. When I first arrived, Harry had sheepishly taken me through the rooms, apologizing and picking up old journals and boots and empty whiskey glasses. The yellowed wallpaper was peeling in places, and it seemed dust upholstered every article of furniture except his favorite reading chair.

"I meant to have it in better order, but..."

"This explains your desire to marry an old coot like me," I teased. "A housekeeper and a cook would have been less expensive."

He looked at me, his head cocked with uncertainly. We were in uncharted territory in our relationship.

"I'm teasing you. But seriously, how do you feel about changing things? Does it bring you comfort to have things as they've always been?"

His lips curved up. He looked around at the dark and sad-looking room. "Why no, not at all. I'd love to have a fresh start for us. Change whatever you please, with my blessing."

A wave of relief passed through me. I could have managed with things the way they were, but I was used to being the mistress of the house, and sooner or later it would become an issue between us.

I set about changing all the wallpaper, draperies, and much of the furniture. I had brought very little with me from Dayton aside from my clothing and personal items. As the home took shape, it pleased me thoroughly. I hadn't realized how much I would enjoy free rein to decorate, without Orville's idiosyncrasies.

SPRING 1927

Even as my new life blossomed, I missed the old. I wrote to my friend Agnes in Dayton often.

I hadn't supposed anyone could be so good to me as Harry has been. He is so concerned over having brought me away from all my family and friends. It is very pleasant here, in every way. The house is pretty and comfortable and we have pretty much made it over inside.

I begged her to write me with all the gossip from Dayton. But when she did, it felt like a punch in the gut. I wrote back:

Your letter made me homesick. In my imagination I walk through that house, looking for Little Brother, and at all the dear familiar things that made my home. But I never find Little Brother and I have lost my old home forever, I fear.

In May, Charles Lindbergh became the American darling of aviation by flying solo from New York to Paris. I was absolutely stewing with frustration that I couldn't talk to Orville about it. How did he feel? In desperation, I imagined a conversation with him, which went something like this:

Me: "Are you upset that Lindbergh is getting so much attention, when hardly anyone noticed your achievements at Kitty Hawk, not to mention the dangers you and Will faced for years?"

Orv: "Why would I be upset? He's doing what we worked so hard for. I don't need to go globe-trotting around to prove my worth, and I'm rather insulted that you would insinuate that."

Okay, maybe I didn't need the conversation with him to know how he felt. But darn it all, we should have been sharing the moment together, with me raising a glass of wine and him raising some bubbling apple cider.

My mood did not lighten when I read a letter from Carrie, telling me in the gentlest terms that Orv had hosted Charles Lindbergh at Hawthorn Hill. She wrote:

I wouldn't say anything because I know it would be hurtful to you to miss such an event, but I also knew you'd likely find out anyway. It's been in all the newspapers, and all that anyone has talked about. There was a great crowd gathered on the property, we had to have the police come. Poor Mr. Wright was fearful they would storm the house with their chants of "We want to see Lucky Lindy!" I suggested they go out on the front balcony (your room—I'm sorry!) so that they could wave to the crowd from the safety of the second floor. That seemed to do the trick and all ended well…

Ugly thoughts ran through my brain, such as Orv purposely planning the event to get my goat. My anger grew and I needed to do something physical to tamp it back down into place. Bread. I would make bread. So out came the flour, my precious sourdough starter, and some salt. I mixed and folded and pounded and kneaded until my hands and arms ached and my heart found a way to forgive.

Harry came into the kitchen and stood silently, taking in the piles of dough and flour dusting every surface, including me. "So…doing some baking?" He gave me a tentative kiss on my powdered cheek.

"Baking helps me sort things on my mind." I told him about missing out on hosting Charles Lindbergh.

"Well, I have some news that might soothe your ruffled feathers. The owner of the *Kansas City Star* has passed away."

I raised an eyebrow. "That's not soothing."

"No, he was a good fellow whose time had come and will be missed. But it's always been my dream that the paper would be owned by the employees. I thought it would help us attract the very best reporters, the best staff. I mentioned that to him on more than one occasion, urged him to sell the bulk of the shares and enjoy life with the proceeds. He dismissed the idea. Or so I thought."

"And now?" I was still far from being soothed.

"He willed his stock to be portioned off to the employees, by order of tenure. And guess who's the most senior?"

The light finally came on. "You? So you own a big chunk?"

"That's right. And I'll be promoted to editor in chief. It will be a sizable increase in salary."

I dusted off my hands and gave him a belated hug. "Congratulations, dear. You deserve it." But my mind reeled with the consequences. What would happen to our plans for traveling the world? I remembered how Orville and Wilbur's success had changed everything about our lives, some for the better, but brought about much sorrow and probably poor Wilbur's death. I felt the floor slipping out from under me and leaned heavily on Harry. I didn't want him to see the tears welling in my eyes.

KANSAS CITY
JANUARY 1929

After two years of marriage, Harry and I had found a nice balance. He had new responsibilities at the newspaper, but he also had a large staff to help him with details. He still traveled, frequently to Baltimore to see his son, Henry, but also to Chicago and occasionally Dayton as well. We planned a holiday in Italy and Greece in March.

I was very excited by the prospect of returning to Italy and couldn't wait to show Harry all the places I had visited with my brothers. Were the flying fields where Will flew for the king of Italy still recognizable? If they were, I hoped that staring at empty fields wouldn't bore Harry to tears, even though he would never complain.

I resisted going with him on the Dayton trips. Orville still refused to talk to me or answer my letters. I wrote anyway, doing everything short of apologizing for marrying the man I loved. I think he was waiting for my marriage to fall apart and for me to come crawling back. But that was not going to happen. When stubborn meets more stubborn, it creates an impasse only an act of God can dismantle.

In February, Harry was scheduled for surgery up in Minnesota. I thought it would be a good time to get away from the city and see a true winter wonderland. We took extra days for him to recover, and we enjoyed a lively time in Minneapolis, seeing shows and watching ice skaters on the many lakes.

"You've been awfully quiet," Harry said.

We were huddled under woolen blankets, drinking cocoa while watching some college boys play ice hockey. Listening to the clacking of the sticks against the puck and the scrape of the skates gave me a chill that had nothing to do with the weather.

"Sorry. I was thinking of something that happened long ago. It started everything."

He raised his eyebrows in question. "Do tell."

I had sometimes pondered that a childhood brawl had led to inventing the airplane, and I wasn't sure how to explain that. "Back in Dayton, there was a pond that froze in winter, where the boys and I used to skate." I related the story, minus the bit about Wilbur losing his will to live for two years. "That bully went on to kill his own family and was executed." I sighed, letting go of the whole fiasco, possibly for the first time. "But if that fight had never happened, if Orv hadn't tried to save me, and then Wilbur got so badly hurt defending both of us, then the chain of events might never have happened."

"I think they still would have done something great. Some things are destiny."

"Maybe so, but I believe Robert Frost was right."

"'The Road Not Taken.' One decision leads to the next, and you never come to that crossroads again." Harry wrapped a warm arm around me. "Frost might be my new favorite poet."

"But Robert Louis Stevenson will always be ours." I cuddled closer, so happy to have a wonderful man who understood poems and life and consequences, and me. Stevenson's words sounded to the beat of my heart:

Home is the sailor from the sea,
The hunter from the hill.

Alas, all that sitting around icy ponds, speaking of Frost, and breathing frosty air had its own consequences. I returned home with a nasty cold and took to bed for the first time in ages. Harry, bless his heart, brought me a steady stream of chicken soup and tea, and after a few days, I started to feel a little better. But then I woke up feeling very chilled, my body shaking with fever. I immediately thought of Wilbur, and my nephew Milton, and Orv before him, shaking with chills from typhoid. But I had not suffered any stomach distress. It was just a bad cold, or perhaps bronchitis, I thought.

Harry fetched a doctor despite my objections.

"I'm fine. It's just a cold," I said to the doctor, who hushed me as he pressed a stethoscope to my chest.

After listening intently across my entire chest and upper back while making me take deep breaths, he finally pulled the instrument out of his ears. "I'm afraid you have pneumonia." He fished around in his bag for a bottle of cough syrup and some other potion. "Take this as needed, not more than four times a day. Bed rest and lots of fluids."

My mind whirled in its fevered state. I had recently lost two friends to pneumonia and one from an infection after surgery. I became more worried about Harry. "Can you check him too, please? He just had surgery..." To my great relief, Harry was hale and hearty.

I behaved myself for once, staying in bed while Harry brought hot soup, even as I begged for hot toddies instead, they being better for congestion. My voice left me, and I had to write notes for what I wanted, but soon that became too much of a bother.

I knew I was in real trouble when Harry came to take my temperature and try to goad me into eating something. Not from the number he said as he shook down the thermometer, but by the look on his face. His eyes had the same pained look as when we lost Isabel.

"I better call Lorin," was all that he said.

ORVILLE

Someone was pounding on the front door. "Use the bell, for God's sake," I shouted as I pushed away the bedcovers and got up. My bedside clock reported 6:00 a.m. *Sheesh, who comes around at 6:00 a.m.?* I wrapped my robe around my pajamas and hurried my creaky bones down the stairs.

It was Lorin. "Oh, did I wake you?" he asked. "Thought you were usually up by this time." A cold wind accompanied him as he barged in.

I hated February, but at least it was short. I ran my fingers through my ever-receding hair. I checked out Lorin's hairline when he took off his hat. His was an inch or two ahead of mine.

"What's up?" I asked. "Did I forget a breakfast date? Or did you decide the crack of dawn was the best time to return my tools you've had for eight and half months?"

But Lorin just squinted as if in pain. He never had much of a sense of humor. "No, uh, I just had a telephone call from Harry."

"Harry who?" I knew who he was talking about; I was just being difficult.

"Sterchens's Harry. He says our sister's taken a turn for the worse, and that we need to get out there. I'm booking a flight for us to Kansas City. It'll be faster than the train."

"Who are you telling that a plane is faster than a train?" I snapped. Now I was being worse than difficult.

"Orv. Stop it right now. Get your butt dressed, and we're going."

A cold shudder ran through me, and it wasn't just the chill air Lorin had brought in with him. "You think she might..." I couldn't say it. "Is this another useless attempt at forcing a reconciliation? You know I told her..."

Lorin looked at me with watery eyes. I wasn't adept at reading faces except for Katharine's, but I thought I saw anger mixed with sadness. "Harry said we need to come, and that's enough for me."

I wasn't convinced. "Tell you what. You fly on out there and call me as soon as you know what's what. Then if need be, I'll come out, bringing a doctor or whatever it is she wants. Can't trust those cow pasture docs."

"It's Kansas City, for God's sake." He slammed his hat back on his head. "Fine. But you are on your word."

That day I went about my business. Time in my lab, a few business meetings, writing letters to the Aviation Board. Katharine was in the back of my mind, but I didn't pack a bag, sure that Lorin would find her under the weather but more crotchety than usual and mad that Harry was making such a fuss. Still, as soon as I got home, I asked Carrie if Lorin had called long distance.

"No, Mr. Wright. And I've stayed near the telephone all day. It isn't like Miss Katharine to not call or write for a week. I'm real worried."

I ate a solitary dinner, all alone at a table big enough for fourteen. Katharine should have been there with six friends that dropped in, at least four of whom I'd never seen before.

"Mr. Wright! The telephone is ringing!" Carrie called.

I hurried to my office and answered it, "Lorin?"

"This is the long-distance operator. Will you accept a call from Mr. Lorin Wright?"

"Yes, yes. Put him through."

Lorin came on. "I'm here."

He sounded quite calm. Relieved, I slipped into my desk chair. "She's okay?" I was thinking I should at least answer one of her letters. I ran my finger down the stack that had collected on my desk. "Tell her I'm writing her back right now."

"Orv. Listen to me." The telephone buzzed with static, but I made out these words: "You need to get on a plane, a train, whatever will get you here the quickest. There isn't much time."

I felt the blood drain from my face and it was suddenly hard to breathe. "I'm sorry, did you say, 'There isn't much time?' Should I bring a doctor?"

"If you want to see our sister, do not waste a minute."

My mind reeled. I shook my head, trying to make sense of it. Katharine had never been sick. She had nursed us through typhoid and broken bodies and broken dreams. She was stronger than anyone I knew.

"Orv? Are you there?"

"I'm here." Then I knew. I had to be *there*. "Tell her I'm coming."

KATHARINE

A familiar voice filters into my dream. Lorin. Harry must have called him. I'm grateful, but now I know I haven't got much longer. It's not so bad, really. I had a wonderful life. I feel bad to leave Harry—he deserved more than two years after all he put up with to marry me. And I'll never see Greece. I see it now, in my imagination, holding hands with my beloved on a white boat in sparkling blue water. The sun is shining warm on my face and I'm happy.

The weight on my chest is growing heavier by the moment. I can just give in now and sleep. I will see Momma and the Bishop and Wilbur and Reuchlin. Oh, how I've missed them.

Harry is holding my hand, asking me if I can hear him. He tells me Lorin has arrived. I give his hand a squeeze. I try to open my eyes.

Now I feel Lorin's hand taking mine. It's cold, so cold. "He's coming, Kate. Orv's coming."

When? I want to ask, but my lips barely move. It is too late. He shouldn't come. I don't want him to see me like this. He should remember me bossing him around and making his biscuits. I allow my body to let go. I will watch him from heaven.

ORVILLE

I don't bother to pack a bag. I tell Carrie I'm leaving, grab my hat, and drive to the station. I decided to take the train, because by the time I figured out which flying service and all the routes and stops and discussing it all with some stranger to book it all, I could be halfway to Kansas City.

All the way there, I pray. It occupies my mind and stops the voice in my head that chastises me for my selfishness. My stupidity. *Dear God*, I fume. *Why didn't you tell me?* I thought she'd outlive me by twenty years. She was going to come around. She would come back. Even if she dragged that conniving Harry with her, I would have welcomed them.

The blur of automobiles, trains and stations, taxicabs and walking make me wish I flew. My back and hips scream for a rest, but I know now, deep in my soul that there is no time.

Finally I am at the house. I check the number against my address book. I don't knock; I just burst through the front door. Lorin is sitting in the front room, his head in his hands.

My heart thumps. "Am I—am I too late?" I need to tell her I'm sorry. She doesn't have to forgive me, but I need to tell her.

Lorin gets up and gives me a hug. "She's waiting for you."

He takes me upstairs to her room. *Harry's and her room,* I correct myself. Harry is by her side, pouring water into a glass. He nods at me and leans down. "Katharine. Orv is here. Do you want to see him?"

I don't blame him; she shouldn't welcome me.

He leans his ear close as she whispers to him, and my heart collapses. She looks so small, cuddled under a heap of quilts. How can she breathe under all of them? I want to throw half of them off; she hates to be too warm. I want to make a machine to help her breathe. To give her life. Harry moves aside, and I go to her, sit on the little chair at her bedside. "I've missed you, Sterchens."

Her pale lips move. I think she's saying she's missed me too.

"I was wrong, Sterchens. So wrong. You probably shouldn't forgive me, but I'm sorry. The only thing I want right now is to change places with you." Then my throat chokes and I can't speak anymore, barely holding back from melting into a blubbering pile of sorrow.

She whispers something. I think she is saying, "I love you." She turns her head toward her nightstand.

Harry nods an unspoken agreement between them, and lifts a small blue velvet-covered box. I know what it is before he even opens it, as I have one too.

He pulls off the lid to reveal her French Legion d'honneur medal. "She wanted you to have this."

She knew I would come. She's been holding on, waiting for me. Her raspy breathing becomes quiet. The clock ticks, and her hand grows cold in mine. I kiss her goodbye, then give Harry his place next to Katharine.

I stumble downstairs to be with Lorin. After a while Harry comes down and we three men sit in silence. For some reason, my mind drifts to something I read about Teddy Roosevelt. After losing his wife and mother on the same day, he wrote in his diary: *The light has gone out of my life.*

If I were good at those things, those are the words I would say.

❧

Lorin has returned home to his family, leaving me to sort through Katharine's belongings. Harry is inspecting his bookcase, of all things. I guess we tend to go to the most comforting places in times like these. What are mine? Hawthorn Hill. Kitty Hawk. Huffman Prairie. But thinking of them just makes me miss Katharine and Wilbur, bringing on another mountain of grief.

"Here it is." Harry pulls a wide book from a shelf. I recognize it from the yellow color, once bright, now faded. Katharine's collection of dried flowers and other mementos.

"I want you to have it."

The book creaks when I open it, releasing a musty and slightly sweet scent. On the first page is a piece of pink ribbon, now aged to golden on the edges. It matches the piece I had kept in my pocket for years. The day that started it all. When I finally asked her why it kept showing up in my trunk, she said if that terrible day hadn't happened, neither would have the chain of events that led to our invention. And that it tied the three of us in a bond that could never be broken.

Next are the dried and flattened remnants of past loves and events. Some wildflowers from Huffman Prairie. A packet of waxed paper with a collection from "the boys." A pink rose from Lambert Island, along with tree buds bursting with cottony tufts. I can just make out two initials: *VJ*. A yellow rose from Harry. Some blue petals from Frank. Baby's breath from her wedding bouquet.

I swallow hard, but the ball of pain in my throat won't go away. Did my possessiveness prevent my sweet sister from a happier life of her own choosing?

It is much to ask of Harry, but I do so anyway. "Will you allow me to bring her back to Dayton? So she can be with our mother, the Bishop, and Wilbur? She will be at peace there, and when, some day—far in the future—you can join her...and us."

Harry wipes his spectacles with his handkerchief. His eyes are red-rimmed. "I only had her for two years, not nearly enough." He forces a weak smile. "But thank you for finally allowing me to join the family. I just need to die to break down that wall."

I have already placed the knife in my chest, and he is twisting it. "She visited the family plot in Woodland many times," I say. "I heard her tell them she would join them someday."

He nods. "Forgive me; I'm not myself. I'll make the arrangements. I want whatever Kate would have wanted."

I am bringing her home. I try to assuage my guilt by telling myself that I gave poor Harry two years without interfering. Time was the most precious thing she had to give to him, and my sacrifice gave him more.

Following the hearse up the winding hilly trail, I shake with grief. For Mother and Pop of course, but one expects to lose their parents, and at least the Bishop led a long and happy life. But, oh, how I miss Wilbur, who shared everything with me, knew my thoughts before I did, and was the reason I made anything of myself. I thought there could be nothing worse than losing him. Katharine, as always, has proven me wrong.

I'm rebuilding the Kitty Hawk flyer, I tell her. *Going to send it to the London museum, just as you suggested. Tell Wilbur and Pop. I'm sure that will make them happy.*

I almost expect to hear Katharine agree with me. But my listener is horribly silent, neither responding nor asking me to elaborate. I don't know how I can go on.

The rumble of distant engines grows louder as they draw nearer. Slowly, my spirits begin to lift. I had arranged for the army to fly four planes in a formation over Katharine's resting place. One for love and the family to whom she had dedicated her life. One to ask for forgiveness for my selfishness. One for peace and the country she had served, largely unnoticed. And the last one for Katharine herself, her spirit and devotion that soared above all of us.

I imagine her flying above, her soul happy, her life on earth complete. I am left alone to try to live a good life. She would want that.

Goodbye, my beloved Sterchens.

AFTERWORD

It might be said that with worldwide efforts to produce controllable powered flight, the Wright brothers' discoveries were perhaps just a few months ahead of others and didn't significantly impact the industry. But a review of the timeline reveals that other experimenters were years behind, and even they benefited from the knowledge gained through the hard work of Orville and Wilbur Wright.

It is interesting to wonder, *What if?* If it weren't for a playground bully, the mystery of ascending in the opposite direction from his downward spiral—the puzzle of flight—might not have been solved for another generation.

If the brothers had not succeeded in developing the first machine capable of manned powered flight and selling it to the British, French, and U.S. militaries, would World War I have had a different outcome? And the central question addressed by this book: If Katharine Wright had not been the powerful force behind them, using her voice, her enthusiasm, her powers of persuasion, what would have happened?

But we can't know the road not taken. We can't know the ultimate effects of our own actions or inactions. We can only do our best and strive to make a better world.

AUTHOR'S NOTES

The character Charley Tamus is a combination of two real-life people who functioned in similar positions and were both named Charley: Charlie Taylor and Charley Furnas. They have been combined in this story for simplicity's sake. Charlie Taylor began working for the Wrights in June 1901, a bit later than represented in the story.

Another minor character, Mr. Harrison the druggist, is fictional but takes his name from two sources: from my eldest grandson, as I frequently name characters for beloved people in my own life, and from the 1914 Harrison Narcotics Act, which proclaimed cocaine and other drugs to be controlled substances.

I purposely left out Katharine's engagement to Arthur Cunningham during her college years, as they broke up before her graduation for unknown reasons. Although Harry's first marriage proposal in the story is undocumented, Harry and Katharine were known to be very close at that time.

The telegram sent from Kitty Hawk in December 1903 appears as it was received, with at least two errors that occurred in the transmission process. The longest flight time on that day was fifty-nine seconds, not fifty-seven, and Orville's name was misspelled.

READING GROUP GUIDE

1. This book is written from three points of view: Katharine's, Orville's, and Wilbur's. What do you think the three perspectives add to the story? Why do you think the author included them all?

2. Along with Katharine, the Wright family also included two *more* brothers: Reuchlin and Lorin. Did you know about them prior to reading this book? Were you surprised to learn about the other siblings in the Wright family?

3. Katharine's mother has a long hard illness, eventually leading to her premature death. What effect does her death have on the Wright family and on Katharine in particular?

4. Orville and Wilbur study birds to learn more about the mechanics of flight. What other things have we or could we learn from studying nature?

5. Katharine, Orville, and Wilbur dream of flight from a very young age, and they persevere in their adulthood until they achieve it. What keeps someone invested in a dream for so long? What might cause someone to give up on a dream?

6. Katharine is worried she will grow old as a spinster, as she is unlikely to marry after age thirty. What does this tell you about the time period she was living in? What do you make of a statement like this in the modern era?

7. It is clear from this book that Orville, Wilbur, and Katharine needed to work together as a team to succeed in their dream of flight. What is the power of working as a team versus working individually? What do you gain from opposing opinions and diverse ideas? What are the difficulties of working with teammates?

8. Katharine believes that the soundest argument against the women's suffrage movement is the idea that they will vote for prohibition. What do you make of this argument? What other arguments were there against the movement?

9. When Orville reflects on his family's accomplishments, he thinks about the consequences of selling his and his brother's invention to the military. He ultimately decides that he cannot judge, but what do you think? How responsible are you for your inventions? If your intended purpose was not to harm, yet the creation was used for harm nonetheless, are you still responsible?

10. Katharine, finally taking steps to become independent, chooses to marry Harry for love and leave Orville. What do you make of Orville's reaction? Do you think Katharine should have (or could have) moved away from her family sooner?

11.   What have airplanes done for our world? Think in terms of convenience, travel, connection, military use, etc. What do you think the world—and history—would be like without them?

12.   In the afterword, author Tracey Enerson Wood speaks of the what-ifs of Katharine and the Wright brothers' story and how so much could have changed if things had gone slightly differently. Are there what-ifs in your life, paths you could have taken? What do you imagine your life would be like if you'd taken a different path?

A CONVERSATION WITH THE AUTHOR

What drew you to Katharine's story?

My passion is finding women in history who had significant, even world-changing impact, yet are relatively unknown. Katharine fits squarely within that description. I was immediately entranced by her indomitable and lovable spirit. Add to that how very famous her brothers became and the fascinating history and many failures of the invention of the airplane, and I was further intrigued. The setting of Dayton, Ohio, has special significance to me as it's my husband's hometown and the site of many of our family's most precious memories. But it was when I discovered the tightly knit siblings' relationship along with the bittersweet love story that I was completely hooked.

Katharine is often forgotten in the stories of the Wright brothers' marvelous inventions. Why do you believe it is important to tell stories like hers and like those of other forgotten or invisible women in history?

I think it's important to understand much more about history than the outcome of events, dates, major players, and so forth. What were the issues of the day? How did the morals, values, knowledge differ from today? Frequently, we can learn these things from studying the characters behind the scenes, often women who provided critical guidance and support.

It's also important to honor these stories, as they may provide encouragement and meaning to the lives of the multitudes of people today who quietly toil behind the scenes. Their work is no less valuable than the big names who get all the credit.

This is Katharine's story, yet we have three perspective characters: Katharine, Orville, and Wilbur. Why did you choose to use three perspectives? Was it difficult to weave their storylines together into one book?

This was a challenging decision and a departure from my previous books' single point of view. There were two main reasons.

First, there were important scenes in which historically, Katharine was not present, as she was busy working to keep them financially solvent. I could have related the scenes in dialogue or other devices but felt readers would lose the full impact as this technique would create an emotional distance.

Second, I wanted to view Katharine's contributions from her brothers' perspectives. I sense she was quite humble in real life, so it seems more natural for her brothers to sing her praises.

I did not find weaving their storylines difficult; indeed their interdependence and common goals helped move the story forward using the voice of the most-impacted character at that moment.

What do you hope readers take away from Katharine's story?

I hope they get to step outside of their own busy lives for a moment and steep themselves in a different era. I'd love if they gain an appreciation of the many, many years of sacrifice, hard work, and risk it took to create the field of aviation, so important to our everyday lives.

Or perhaps they achieve a sense of the importance of the roles of all the supporting players throughout time and in our own lives.

I hope they are entertained while learning and perhaps intrigued to learn more. I hope they laugh and cry along with Katharine and feel a part of her journey.

And finally, I hope this story stimulates discussion on the complexity of family relationships, how even good intentions can ultimately hurt the ones we love the most.

What are you currently working on?

I have several stories in various stages of development, each fighting for my full attention. One is the story of a woman who immigrates to the U.S. from Africa, falls into the world of the rich and powerful, and ultimately becomes a philanthropist in her own right. Loosely based on a real person.

Another is sort of *The Time Traveler's Wife* meets *American Wife*. Except I promise it will not have *Wife* in the title!

Yet one more, with the working title *Shattered*, a darker story of a family facing a devastating battle—a legal kidnapping—and how they become whole again. A mother-daughter story set in Alaska, it is also loosely based on a true story.

All of them have a personal significance, which may be why I'm having such a tough time choosing!

ACKNOWLEDGMENTS

Thank you to the wonderful staff at the Henry Ford Museum of Innovation and Greenfield Village, which has a full-scale model of the Wright Flyer and many other informative exhibits. Special thanks to Earl Wilkerson, guide at the Wright Cycle shop, and Pamela Anderson, guide at the original Wright home. Both these buildings were moved from Dayton, Ohio, to Greenfield Village in Dearborn, Michigan, by Henry Ford in 1938.

The Dayton History organization has wonderful exhibits, including the 1905 Flyer, and offers tours of the Wright family mansion, Hawthorn Hill. My deep thanks to tour guide Chris Marks and the Carillon Historical Park for a wealth of information not only on the Wright family and their homes but of their home city and its colorful history.

My deep appreciation to Wright State University, Wright -Brothers.org, the Engineers Club of Dayton, the National Museum of the U.S. Air Force, Joint Base Myer/Henderson Hall—especially the military police who guided me to the buildings and locations I needed to see—and to Alex Heckman, vice president of Dayton History Museum Operations, and the Woodland Cemetery for answers to questions I could find nowhere else. I can't wait to revisit, as they peel back the layers of history to discover even more!

This story came to my attention through the sharp eye of my son-in-law, Scott Riffle. When he learned of Katharine's story, he immediately knew she would be a great heroine for me to write about. He also came up with the perfect title. Thanks, Scott, for the inspiration and for being a wonderful son-in-law and father to my grandchildren.

Once again, I pledge my eternal gratitude to Anne Lipton, my friend, muse, and early reader. Thank you for all your suggestions and corrections; I am a better writer for knowing you.

My literary agent, Lucy Cleland of Calligraph, has been an unfailing supporter and guide. Thank you for all your hard work behind the scenes that brings my books to life.

And to the wonderful team at Sourcebooks, especially my longtime editor, Anna Michels; sharp-eyed copy editors Jessica Thelander and Diane Dannenfeldt; cover maestro James Iacobelli; and publicists Cristina Arreola and Anna Venckus.

Kathie Bennett of MagicTime Literary calls herself the "author killer" due to the extensive in-person book tours she arranges. Well, I've lived through several now and am grateful for all the amazing authors, readers, booksellers, event coordinators, and others I have met. How wonderful to share my love of books with them! Thank you, Kathie and Roy, for all you do for me and all your other lucky authors.

And as always, my love and gratitude to my husband, Dave, whose patience and support enable me to research and write the stories that capture my heart.

ABOUT THE AUTHOR

© Katie Beyer Photography

Tracey Enerson Wood loves discovering amazing women whose stories have been lost to history and bringing them to life for today's readers.

Her debut novel, *The Engineer's Wife*, the story of the woman who saw to the completion of the Brooklyn Bridge, is an international and *USA Today* bestseller. Her sophomore novel, *The War Nurse*, tells the unforgettable tale of Julia Stimson and her nurses in WWI France. Both novels are published by Sourcebooks.

Her coauthored anthology/cookbook, *Homefront Cooking: Recipes, Wit, and Wisdom from American Veterans and Their Loved Ones*, was released by Skyhorse Publishing, and all authors' profits are donated to organizations that support veterans. *Life Hacks for Military Spouses* is her latest nonfiction release, also an anthology from Skyhorse.

Tracey has always had a writing bug. While working as a registered nurse, starting her own interior design company, raising two children, and bouncing around the world as a military wife, she indulged in her passion as a playwright, screenwriter, and novelist. She has authored magazine columns and other pieces of nonfiction, and written and directed plays of all lengths, including *Grits*, *Fleas and Carrots*, *Rocks and Other Hard Places*, *Alone*, and *Fog*. Her screenplays include *Strike Three* and *Roebling's Bridge*.

Other passions include food and cooking and honoring military heroes.

A New Jersey native, she now lives with her family in Florida.